by
invitation
only

a novel

Dorothea Benton Frank

wm

WILLIAM MORROW
An Imprint of HarperCollins*Publishers*

BY INVITATION ONLY. Copyright © 2018 by Dorothea Benton Frank. All rights reserved. Printed in the United States of America. No part of this book may be used or reproduced in any manner whatsoever without written permission except in the case of brief quotations embodied in critical articles and reviews. For information, address HarperCollins Publishers, 195 Broadway, New York, NY 10007.

HarperCollins books may be purchased for educational, business, or sales promotional use. For information, please email the Special Markets Department at SPsales@harpercollins.com.

FIRST EDITION

Designed by Bonni Leon-Berman
Exclusive edition illustrations courtesy Shutterstock

Library of Congress Cataloging-in-Publication Data has been applied for.

ISBN 978-0-06-239082-0 (hardcover)
ISBN 978-0-06-287352-1 (BAM exclusive edition)
ISBN 978-0-06-287351-4 (B&N exclusive edition)
ISBN 978-0-06-287350-7 (Target exclusive edition)

18 19 20 21 22   LSC   10 9 8 7 6 5 4 3 2 1

In memory of my sweet brother,
Theodore Anthony Benton

Remember, anyone can love you when the sun is shining.
In the storms
Is where you learn who truly cares for you.

UNKNOWN

contents

*"I can give a party if I feel like it. Who says it's not the correct
etiquette? What if I don't want to go to Chicago?
He's my only grandson."*

—Virnell Bruce English

CHAPTER 1

meet diane
english stiftel

august 2016

MOUNT PLEASANT, SOUTH CAROLINA

My mother stood at the kitchen sink, scrubbing the ancient cast-iron pot as though it was encrusted with the residue of mortal sins, sins somehow fused into the metal. In fact, it was coated with scorched beef stew, tonight's dinner gone forgotten. She looked out the window and sighed so hard, I would've sworn it was her frustration with herself and not the late-afternoon breeze that moved the Spanish moss in the trees all across the yard. Eighty was creeping up on her, snatching bits of her memory and stamina, and it infuriated her. No woman really wanted to be eighty and still working full-time unless she was ninety and still working full-time. As for me, well, I was too old for leggings. Let's leave it at that.

The window over the kitchen sink was propped up by a wooden spoon, held in a slightly lopsided position. As the heat of the day had broken, every window in the old house was raised, held open with a book or a Coke bottle or another household object. When the cool air of the afternoon wafted in, the house itself sighed in relief, or so it seemed. In any case, opening the windows was a ritual we performed at the same time every day all summer long, year after year. You'd think someone would go to the hardware store and buy those little swinging hooks used for this very purpose, but no. Just like you'd think someone would've checked the stew before it burned.

Still, even with all the open windows, you could have cut the humidity and the silence with a knife.

"It was just beef stew," I said. "We have hamburgers in the freezer. I'm happy with a burger."

"You know I hate waste," she said.

"So do I. But what's really the matter? Something else is bugging you," I said, not particularly eager for the answer.

After a long silence she said, "That diamond is a bad-luck stone."

"There's no such thing," I said. "Diamonds are diamonds."

"My own flesh and blood doesn't have the brains to know when to be superstitious," she said. "Law! Where did I go wrong?"

"Oh, Mom."

The diamond in question was given to me by my ex-husband when we became engaged over thirty years ago. It had been his mother's. *That* woman. Agatha was truly the most awful woman I have ever known, and I thanked the good Lord every day for erasing her from my life. Still, my sweet mother honestly believed that poor single carat was tainted with the DNA of my ex-mother-in-law's black heart. In the Lowcountry we believed such things, or at least considered them. Maybe it was cursed. Anyway, Agatha sure enough ruined my marriage with all her meddling and second-guessing, that much was certain. But she didn't ruin my life; I was made of stronger stuff than she could ever imagine. I tied a bow around Duggan's big fat head and sent him right back up the highway, home to her apron strings in Raleigh, North Carolina. Due to his family's lack of interest, I raised our son, Fred, here on the farm in my parent's house. It wasn't the worst thing for him or for me. I never heard a word from Duggan again. Or his mother. When Fred went to college at Clemson, so did I. He became a CPA and I earned a degree in agribusiness. Fred's now a young man, ready to propose marriage to the love of his life, Shelby Cambria. He would seal the deal with that diamond. His family's heirloom. What's my future daughter-in-law like? Let's just say I had more reservations about her than I did about the diamond.

Shelby was a city girl, as poised and polished as one might imagine an urban young woman could be. She was sophisticated. But I feared she was too exacting, which made me nervous. She had to go for a run every day or she said she couldn't function. Really? She used only soy milk in her decaf latte. Ick. She saw the dentist four times a year. Seemed excessive unless she had a situation with her gums or something. She never cursed, at least not in front of me. Okay, but truly? She never had a credit card balance. Admirable, sort of. She used a fountain pen only when writing thank-you notes. Prissy. Sorry, but it is. Her car had never run out of gas. Anal. To my mind these were the characteristics of a perfectionist, which could lead to becoming small-minded and judgmental, unforgiving, and ultimately a cold wife. But I was keeping my mouth shut and zipped. As long as she loved my boy, I loved her. If she broke his heart, I'd kill her with my bare hands. This seemed reasonable to me.

But still, I worried. The combination of her polish and my suspicions about what was beneath it made it difficult for me to see her blending well with my family. I just couldn't see it. Here's why.

Let's just start with my younger brother, Floyd. He lived in his rusted-out trailer and had a tire garden past the barns on our farm. He kept dubious company and odd opinions about the federal government, global warming, and the real possibility of alien abductions. Never mind his wardrobe choices (camo), his very old pickup truck, and the pack of howling dogs that followed him wherever he went through the years. Thankfully, now he was down to just one, Moses. He brought three girls into the world with two wives. His daughters never came to visit and had expressed no interest in living here. At least he believed in love. His current live-in fling was called Betty Jean, BJ for short, an unfortunate nickname given the parlance of the day. She was a grammar school teacher, bless her heart. At least she was age appropriate, forty-five to his fifty.

We were a family of, well . . . I guess the nicest way to describe us might be to call us a little eccentric and nonconformist. When you didn't live in a strict corporate world, you didn't have to worry about fitting in and being politically correct all the time. You could afford the luxuries of self-expression. We took advantage of self-expression in spades.

I don't know how Fred came out of this environment like he did, but he did. I had mysteriously given birth to a wholesome Midwesterner. Shelby and Fred were as buttoned up as two young people could be. They met in college and now worked for the same large accounting firm in Chicago, where they lived. My greatest fear was that after they were married she would keep him away from us, from me. Every woman with a son worries about that. And although she was very polite, behind her personal restraint I knew she thought we were a tribe of hillbillies. We weren't hillbillies.

So there we were, doing the lunch dishes in my mother Virnell's kitchen. We didn't have air conditioning, and it was a mighty paltry bit of air the afternoon was meting out. Pop was the reason we didn't have central air. He thought almost every invention of the twentieth century was unhealthy. He was probably right.

To be completely honest, most of our farmhouse stood in the shade of sprawling live oak trees that had to be hundreds of years old, so generally the temperature wasn't completely intolerable. And most of the rooms now had ceiling fans, a concession my father made four years ago after my mother fainted dead on the floor while six huge steaming pots boiled away on the stove as she sealed Ball jars filled with her famous peach jam. But these were the dog days of August, thusly named for a dang good reason. There were moments so miserable you'd have been happier in a hole under the front porch with the dogs. On days like this a freshly dug hole was no doubt the coolest spot in the entire Lowcountry of South Carolina.

Mother washed; I dried. I watched as perspiration trickled down the back of her neck. I didn't like it. It didn't seem right that a woman of her age should have to sweat from work. And it bothered me that my parents would never be able to retire and travel and maybe own a condo overlooking the ocean somewhere. But then, neither would I. That's what farm ownership was – never-ending work. We didn't have so many acres that we had to hire huge crews to harvest, but we produced enough to keep three generations of us alive at the same time. There was considerable pride to be had in surviving by your own grit.

It wasn't a glamorous life – up at dawn every morning. By the end of the day, I can tell you, we were almost always bone tired. I'm really not complaining, because the outside world held little interest for me and there was a deep satisfaction that came with knowing our produce, especially our peaches, was highly anticipated each year. I had everything I wanted. Well, almost. I'll admit that there were days when I wished for a reprieve – maybe a trip somewhere I've never been. I had my dreams, to be sure, but now it was time for my son's dreams. Mine could wait.

I glanced at my mother's hands, gnarled with the ravages of arthritis and spotted with age. How much longer would she even be able to do the work she did? And ever since Pop's last heart attack, all he seemed to be able to do was sit on the front porch or in his La-Z-Boy recliner down at the farm stand and whittle the day away. He made whistles and toys that we sold there. Figurines of deer and turtles and coyotes. Little soldiers. Children loved them. And him. Sometimes he'd tell children stories about the Catawba and Sewee Indians that held them rapt while their mothers filled their bags with corn or butter beans. My parents were dearly loved by all our customers. But their mortality was becoming a concern. What was going to happen to the farm and to me? There was no next generation.

My brother, Floyd, with his succession of women, would be happy to make his contribution and then to sing "Polly Wolly Doodle" all the day. Ah, Floyd. Well, he was a pretty great brother, but I didn't think he had the wherewithal to take over the family enterprise. Not all on his own. It was too much for one person. He tried hard to pick up the slack for Pop.

I slipped an armload of dried plates into the dishwasher. The dishwasher was a surprise gift to Momma from Floyd three years ago when he won some money with the lottery. It stood alone like a piece of sculpture and untried, as my mother didn't trust it either. She still sterilized the jars we used to put up jam in the same huge pots of boiling water that sealed the jars when they were filled. So we used the dishwasher as a cupboard, a good solution for the scant storage we had.

"All those darn things do is waste water, run up your electric bill, and fade out the pretty flowers on my plates. Who needs that?"

If Virnell was anything, she was old-fashioned and practical to a fault. But it was her feistiness that held Pop's heart. She tickled him to death.

Our kitchen was the pulsating epicenter of the sagging, sway-in-the-wind, 160-year-old farmhouse where I grew up with Floyd. The pale blue appliances and knotty pine cabinets were so old that they had come back into style. Needless to say, the bathroom fixtures were dated curiosities. Family mythology says that even in its youth, the house was so unappealing that Sherman's troops let it stand. The officers said it wasn't worth the flick of the flint it would've taken to torch it, and the Yankees had slept in the barn by choice. I heard somewhere that the real reason they took to the barn was that my great-great-great-great-great-great-grandmother was especially frisky, but I'd never repeat that. I'd always hoped that my mother's version of the story was the true one — that her great-grandmother of six generations long gone had charmed General Sherman's men with peach delicacies and declined their offers of romance. While wearing a hoop skirt, corset, and lacy pantaloons? Doubtful. Our family tree didn't grow femmes fatales. We grew peaches. Acres upon delicious, fragrant acres of them, as far as the eye could see. And smaller amounts of strawberries, plums, figs, watermelons, canta-

loupes, tomatoes, string beans, butter beans, asparagus, pecans, and corn. And no doubt, her great-grandfather of that
day had drained his supply of peach brandy to keep the ras-
cals at bay.

"Did you say something?" I said.

"Daydreaming again? I *said,* how is our Fred planning on
proposing?"

"Oh, he's got a very elaborate scheme cooked up. As soon
as the ring is finished . . ."

Mother dried her hands on her apron and turned around
to face me, putting her hands on her hips. "What do you
mean, finished? It didn't fit, or what?"

Virnell was easily provoked in the heat.

"Just what I said, finished. You know, she wanted something more modern, so they had a jeweler mount it in a halo
of little bitty diamonds . . ."

"A what?"

"A halo. You know, like a little circle. It probably makes
the diamond look bigger."

Mother looked up at the ceiling, then down again, and
cocked her head to one side, squinting her eyes. "So, one carat
isn't big enough for her? And she already knows what her engagement ring looks like? Good gravy."

"I guess so. Anyway, as soon as he has the ring, he's going
to take her down to the shore of Lake Michigan. He's hired
two musicians from the Chicago Symphony to suddenly appear and play some Vivaldi or something. A friend of his is
setting up a champagne bucket with glasses and all that, and
another friend is going to film it with a drone."

"A drone." Mother's jaw dropped. She shook her head in disbelief. "What next? A daggum parade with a marching band and the Goodyear Blimp?"

"Oh, come on, Mother! I know it's a bit over the top, but I think it's very sweet! I didn't even know Fred had this kind of poetry and romance in him!" I refolded my dish towel and took a stack of bowls to the cabinet.

"Romance is for fools," she said. "Grown men popping up out of nowhere with violins? Public consumption of alcohol? He'll be lucky if he doesn't get arrested."

"Probably. But if he manages to stay out of jail, it's incumbent on us to give them an engagement party."

"No, it isn't. It's the bride's family responsibility. This is not how *we* do things in *this* family!"

"Well, Mom, a lot has changed since I married Duggan. These days, when the bride is from far away, both sides might throw a little something to honor the happy couple."

"So now we have to give a party for the family and friends of Miss Fancy Pants?"

"Looks like it."

"On second thought, you're right. Why shouldn't we celebrate with our family and friends right here? Maybe they won't want to go to Chicago."

"My point exactly!"

"Besides, Fred is the only grandchild you gave me. Let's throw him a party no one will ever forget!"

"Who in the world uses boxed, handwritten invitations for an occasion like this? How will I explain this to my friends?"

—Susan Kennedy Cambria

CHAPTER 2

meet susan kennedy cambria

CHICAGO, ILLINOIS

O h, dear," I said to Shelby as I read the invitation. "It appears your father and I will be making a trip to South Carolina for an engagement party."

"You sort of have to, Mom," Shelby said. "You're the MOB. I gave Frederick the list of people to invite. It wouldn't look good if you and Dad didn't come."

"You did what?"

"Well, I had to. It was a question of timing."

I could feel my blood pressure rising. Did my daughter,

my only child, think she was going to take control of her wedding, without me?

"Well, do you think I might trouble you for a copy of that list?" What was she thinking? "Is this party by invitation only, or is just anyone allowed to come?"

"Mom, I didn't invite the entire world. And there's still time for you to ask whoever you want. I've got twenty-five extra invitations at my apartment because I knew you'd flip out."

"I am not flipping out. And we are planning to have our own party for you and Frederick."

"Okay, whatever. You know I love you, Mom. I've got to go. I'm meeting Frederick at Tiffany's to pick out china and silver and do the registry thing, which he thinks is stupid, but of course I insisted. I don't want to wind up with stuff I hate or forty salad bowls."

I looked at her and wondered how she had become so grown-up. When I thought of her in my mind's eye I saw a little girl with a long ponytail and skinned-up knees. When did she become old enough to get engaged and think about things like china patterns and silver? That realization almost took my breath away. And she obviously didn't want my opinion either. My God. My little girl was gone forever.

Shelby blew me a kiss and hurried to the foyer.

"I'll drop the invitations off with the doorman, okay? What's the matter? You look upset."

"Oh, no! I'm fine! Just wondering what to wear, that's all. And where we should stay. You know, logistics, that's all."

I sank into a chair and stared at the invitation again. It

was a simple lightweight card of no particular significance with a cheesy champagne bottle and two flutes in the margin. *Please join us to celebrate the engagement of Frederick Stiftel to Shelby Cambria* ... just like that. Here came the mail with an invitation announcing that my daughter was going to marry into a family of strangers from far away, written on flimsy card stock with no imagination. Good grief. We'd probably be drinking from jelly jars and eating something on picnic tables. Alejandro was going to hate this party. I was already dreading it. And worse, how was I going to stop our friends, most especially Judy, from attending? I had a lot of phone calls to make. Judy Cunio Quigley (aka Judy CQ, and she called me Susan KC), my nemesis/bestie, wouldn't miss this for the world. The relished details would roll from her lips behind my back for months. Ever since I agreed to cochair the Lyric wine auction with her, she was in my life, one-upping me, every day.

That night my husband and I discussed our day over cocktails at our club. Alejandro and I had been members of the Union League Club for more years than I could count. It was nice to have a place to go where you knew everyone. The membership was made up of successful financiers, attorneys, and other professionals who enjoyed the clubs around town. We were waiting for a potential client of his to arrive and I was swirling my olive around in my vodka with a tiny bamboo skewer.

"What's the matter, *amorcita*?" he said.

"You know me too well," I said. That was Alejandro's pet name for me.

He glanced at his watch. "He's already ten minutes late. You know how much I hate it when people are late."

"It's rush hour, Alejandro. He's probably stuck in traffic."

"But we're on time, aren't we?"

I nodded. There was no reason to belabor the point. Never mind that we both worked within walking distance of this divine spot. Punctuality was my husband's particular pet peeve.

"Don't scowl, darling. It makes you look ancient." He immediately changed his expression to something more civil. Neither of us liked looking one day older than we were. "So, here's what has my knickers in a twist."

"Tell me."

"It seems we are obliged to make an appearance in South Carolina, where Frederick's mother is throwing an engagement party."

"Well, that's pretty standard, isn't it? What's the problem?"

"I think it's our prerogative to decide who gives the engagement party."

"Oh, come on now, darling. It's 2016! They can have a party and we can have one too."

"Shelby has already invited half of Chicago to go to this shindig in South Carolina."

"So, invite the same people to a party here and let them decide which one they want to attend, or both!"

"You don't understand—you're going to be miserable the whole time," I said.

"And what makes you think that?"

"Because I suspect they are very unlike us."

"Meaning what? They have taxidermy and a gun safe in every room in the house?"

"Dear God! I hadn't even thought about that! Do you think they keep guns?"

"Let's calm ourselves, shall we? If they have firearms I'm sure they have a good reason. I spoke to Frederick's mother when we called her. She sounded normal enough to me."

"Oh, I agree. It's just that I think we'll have a hard time finding common ground with them. They are very rural."

"They're farmers. *Of course* they're rural."

"It's just that . . . oh, I don't know. I feel uneasy."

On the way to the powder room, I glanced up at the Monet hanging in the grand stairwell, bought for a song in 1895. I stopped and really looked at it, even though I'd seen it a thousand times. *Apple Trees in Blossom.* All the white flowers were so beautiful against the rustic ground. I thought so, anyway. I felt so lucky then to be a member of a club that appreciated how the world looked through the eyes of a great artist. I could come here and see this remarkable painting any time I wanted to, as though I sort of owned it. It was a rare privilege and one for which I was grateful. I wondered then if Frederick's family had ever even heard of the Impressionists. Surely not. Oh, dear. Well, what could I do?

Picnic tables and southern food. We would fulfill this obligation with a smile on our faces if not with a song in our hearts.

"Alden is not my boyfriend," Diane said.

"Well, he ought to be," Virnell said.

CHAPTER 3

diane's southern soiree

september

The screen door slammed with a loud thwack. It was just after six A.M. Suddenly my brother Floyd was in our kitchen, where I was putting breakfast together.

"Morning, Floyd. People are still sleeping, you know."

"Mom and Pop are as deaf as doornails, and your boy ought to be up anyhow. BJ is pig sitting."

"Good. You want something to eat?"

"Nah, but thanks. Anytime I leave a roasting pig unattended, I worry about a grease fire."

"As you should."

The first barbecue pit Floyd built was too close to a stand of azaleas. There was a strong wind, a flare-up, and whoosh! The azaleas became a part of our family lore and we became acquainted with the Mount Pleasant Fire Department.

"These folks had better be grateful. Irma was my favorite sow," Floyd said. "Such a high-spirited old girl."

"It was her time," I said, smiling to myself. "Besides, this is a noble cause."

Floyd had Irma in the smoker and had been tending to her all night. He needed a shower and some strong coffee. His well-worn overalls were splotched with grease, and the stench of woodsmoke and beer traveled with him. I filled a mug and handed it to him.

"Fred really still sleeping?"

"Oh, yeah. Poor baby didn't get in until midnight. His flight was late."

Floyd grunted. "Ain't no baby if he's old enough to marry." Floyd felt every able-bodied man ought to be up and working when day breaks. "When's the princess coming?"

"With her folks, this afternoon."

"Are they staying out here with us?"

"Oh, heavens, no! They're at Zero George."

"Zero George? That's way too highfalutin for my blood. So they're fancy city people."

"Big-time," I said, feeling my heart quicken a little from insecurity.

"La-di-da. Wait till they get out here and smell this air! They're gonna fall in love." Floyd smiled at me, trying to show support. "How many heads we aiming to feed?"

"The count's coming up to the better part of a hundred," I said.

"Well, just one of Irma's haunches will feed that many. No problem. What else are we cooking?"

"Alden has a whole Lowcountry menu going. We figured they can't get authentic Lowcountry food in Chicago."

Alden Corrigan was my sometime boyfriend without benefits. I'd known his family all my life. My mother always said that his mother had the cleanest house in South Carolina, which was a peculiar claim to fame, if you ask me. But for as much as I loved to cook, I couldn't handle a crowd as large as the one we were expecting without some serious help. Besides that, the night was too important for me to be hanging over a stove or a barbecue pit, coming away smelling like my sweet brother. This is the first time we ever had a catered party here. I wanted to impress Shelby's parents by showing them their daughter was marrying into a nice family. I hoped I wouldn't have to muzzle my brother.

Alden was a retired naval commander and his catering business was his retirement job. He liked nothing better than telling people what to do when and how to do it. I'd known his ex-wife. She was perfect, and if it was perfection that got his motor going, I definitely was not the girl for him. It was probably his very exacting management style that took an intimate encounter with him off the table, so to speak. But he ran events without a single hiccup, and given the stress and anxiety I was feeling, I was grateful to have him in my corner. And honey? He was one gorgeous man. Floyd was plain jealous. And Alden made me a little nervous.

"He should be here by ten to oversee setup," I said.

"Aw, Gawd. *Alden!*" He called out his name in a falsetto voice. "That sumbitch ain't coming over here and telling me how to cook my pig, is he?"

"He wouldn't dare," I said. "Everybody knows you're the pit master, even him."

Floyd harrumphed, shrugged his shoulders, and refilled his mug. "So, you didn't answer me. What's Pretty Boy serving? Itty-bitty finger foods in dainty pastry cups with a little lacy napkin?"

Pretty Boy. Lace napkins. In Floyd's opinion, despite Alden's military history, he still wasn't manly enough. My brother had a nickname for everyone. I just shook my head and picked up the ten-page contract from Alden's catering company and read it to him.

"The usual Lowcountry stuff. A mountain of boiled peanuts next to a huge presentation of shrimp and grits. Then he's roasting May River oysters if he can get them. Coleslaw and potato salad. Deviled eggs. Bluefish spread on toast points. Deviled crab cakes. Corn muffins. Biscuits. And of course, Mom's peach cake with homemade vanilla ice cream."

Floyd harrumphed again. "That ought to make 'em happy," he said. "And if it doesn't, they can all go home and scratch their mad place."

"Amen."

No one ever really defined what one's *mad place* might be, but it was assumed to be in the area of one's personal Lowcountry.

"Well, I don't want you worrying about tonight. I've got

clean camo pants and a new T-shirt from the Dollar Store. Me and BJ gon' charm the manure out of everyone."

Manure. I just looked at him and he could see the horror on my face.

"Just fooling with you, Lady Di. I got brand-spanking-new khakis and I'm gone douse myself good with a bottle of swell smell I got for Christmas. BJ's got not one but three new dresses and an appointment at the beauty parlor. And I spit-shined my Weejuns. Don't worry, sister. We're gonna do you proud!"

"I wasn't worried for one second, Floyd." And the Academy Award for Best Liar goes to . . . From the moment I started to plan this party, I'd had recurring nightmares about what he might do. "Not for one second."

He put his mug in the sink and turned back to face me.

"It's gonna be a wonderful night, sister. Irma is as tasty as she was beautiful."

"Only you, Floyd. There's only one like you."

"Later!"

Needless to say, he slammed the screen door nearly off its hinges on the way out of the house as well.

I pulled out the old cast-iron skillet and filled it with strips of cold bacon. Pipes rattled and toilets flushed, signaling the start of the day for my parents and for Fred. As soon as the bacon began to sizzle they'd flock to the kitchen, beckoned by the irresistible smells of maple and brown sugar. I slid the double griddle pan across two burners, brushed it with butter, and, as soon as water drops bounced, ladled batter onto its surface.

"G'morning!" It was Pop. He came into the kitchen, neatly dressed, freshly shaven, and smelling like Old Spice. "Pancakes?"

I flipped three onto a plate and drizzled syrup over them. No one ever saw my dad in his pajamas unless he had the flu.

"Can I tempt you with this?" I said. "Coffee?"

"I'll pour my own. You know I'm watching my waistline, but why don't you set that plate on the table right there and let's see what happens." He winked at me and said thanks.

I turned the bacon over onto paper towels and refilled the skillet. Next came Fred.

He appeared wearing freshly pressed linen Bermuda shorts, a knit shirt tucked in, and his alligator belt with the monogrammed gold buckle. His short hair was neatly combed and his breath smelled like toothpaste. Here was my boy, a man now, about to be married. He was capable, affable, and self-sufficient. Self-sufficient. It gave me pause to realize this, and I almost choked up. Was I really ready to release him? *Was* I releasing him, or had I been deluding myself all along that he was ever mine to release? Was I gaining a daughter? There wasn't much positive evidence on that last one. Why didn't anyone tell me how emotional this would be? Suddenly the business of my only child getting married felt like a kind of death.

"How's the greatest mom in the world?" Fred said and kissed my cheek. "Pancakes! Oh, wow! Hey, Pop! How are you?"

A tiny smile crept across my father's craggy face and his eyes—lined with red, faded to a pale shade of nickel, and sagging from the harrows of age—twinkled with affection for my son.

"Every day above ground is a victory, I reckon. You?"

"Ha-ha! That's a good one! We got any juice?" Fred said.

His head was inside the refrigerator when my mother walked into the room.

"Here's my baby doll!" Pop said and raised himself from his chair.

"Don't get up, sweetheart," she said and kissed his cheek.

She was wearing a floral-print dress with pockets and sensible shoes that could traverse the yard to the farm stand without her feet suffering the roots and rocks that pockmarked the distance. She was still pretty spry for her age, but lately I'd noticed her using handrails to pull herself up a flight of stairs and struggling with lifting things more and more often. I hated every single hint that my parents were aging.

"On the door, second shelf," I said. "G'morning, Mom!"

"Good morning, everyone! Come give me a hug, Mr. Grown-up, soon to be a married man, grandson of mine!"

"You bet!"

Fred hugged my mother like a caveman and lifted her off the ground.

"Put me down, you young whippersnapper!"

She was laughing, pretending to be offended, when we all knew she loved every second of attention that he gave her. When he finally put her feet back on the floor he planted noisy smooches on her cheeks.

"Oh, you!" she said. "Oh, my! I'm a little dizzy!"

"Better check your pressure," Pop said.

"Check your own pressure," she said. "Mine's fine!"

Fred held her chair for her and she sat down at the table.

"All right now. Here's coffee," I said and placed the mug on her right.

"Thank you, sweetheart. Now just tell me how I can help you get ready for tonight."

"I'll know more after Alden gets here. We're going to do a walk-through. Why don't you come?" I liked to include my mother whenever I could.

"I'd like that," she said. "You might have overlooked an important detail."

"Like the outhouse they delivered yesterday," Dad said. "It might be stinky. I'd check it out."

"Outdoor toilets?" Fred said and laughed, raising his eyebrows.

I knew immediately that he was wondering how his future in-laws would take to the idea. Admittedly, portable johns would hardly enhance our reputation as country squires. But we had too many guests for our meager indoor plumbing to accommodate. Surely Shelby's parents had attended an outdoor concert at some point in their life and had used one.

"Hmmm. They're from Royal Restrooms," I said. "I'll have y'all know it's actually considered a luxury restroom trailer. Three thrones and a vanity with two sinks. Frankly, the one in the yard is more up-to-date than the ones in this house. Which reminds me, I need to put some flowers in there on the vanity and a basket of things people might need."

"Like what?" Fred said. "Bug spray?"

"Oh, dear! I hadn't even considered the bugs."

We cleaned up the kitchen, and when everything was put away, I wandered outside with my mother to find Alden. She made a beeline for Floyd's pit and I searched the small army of workers for Alden. He was in the side yard, a wide and deep space in front of the barns, talking to the supervisor from Snyder Rental who was overseeing the final details for the evening. Strings of lights crisscrossed the yard and the tent. They were the old-fashioned kind, clear and round, the size of golf balls. Farm tables and folding chairs surrounded the dance floor. Bales of hay decorated with buckets of wildflowers and greenery, pots of chrysanthemums, late-season watermelons, early pumpkins and gourds, flanked the walkway and bars. Tall buckets of wildflowers with trailing tendrils of ivy decorated the buffet tables anchored with large lanterns that held fat columns of candles. The inescapable and delicious perfume of Irma was everywhere. I dared Shelby's parents not to fall under her spell.

"Alden!" I called out. "Good morning!"

He turned when he heard my voice, and I saw his face brighten. "Good morning, Diane! It's a beautiful day for a party, isn't it?"

"I think you're right," I said.

He walked toward me and I thought anybody could see the love in his eyes. It was a shame that I wouldn't let myself feel it for him. He was such a great guy. The truth was, I hadn't had any heat for anyone in decades, having decided the orange of romance simply wasn't worth the squeeze. Or maybe I was just too tired all the time to give it a try.

"I was just talking to the guy from Snyder and I told him they had to move the generators. Too noisy."

"Good catch! I probably would've realized that tonight in the middle of everything when it's too late to do anything about it."

"Well, that's why you depend on me, isn't it? You don't do this every day. I do."

A sudden breeze came from nowhere and pushed a loose section of my hair into my eyes. He reached across the space between us and moved it away. For a moment, there was something. I heard his sigh and knew not acknowledging his feelings was the safest way to handle them.

"So, you're coming tonight, aren't you?"

"Wild horses couldn't keep me away," he said, smiling.

"Didn't the Stones record that back in the day?"

"Yes, ma'am. I can sing a few bars if you'd like. Hmmm?"

"Save it for another time, I think." I winced.

He pretended to be hurt and insulted. "Ma'am, your words cut me to the quick."

I smiled and shook my head, and he laughed.

"Oh, Alden! What about mosquitoes and no-see-ums? Just tell me the party's going to be flawless."

"I've already sprayed the bushes. It will be perfect. You may depend on it."

"Okay, then. I'll see you later."

I was dressing later on that afternoon, busying myself with thoughts of gratitude that the weather had held and that we weren't besieged by afternoon thundershowers. I sure didn't want a muddy driveway. Then I had a thought about what Shelby's parents were wearing, their shoes in particular. What if they assumed that the outdoor tent would have flooring? Of course we had not rented flooring because the expenses for the night were already in the stratosphere.

By five o'clock my parents and I were in the front parlor, pacing, waiting for Fred to arrive with Shelby and her parents. We had invited them to come early so we could share a glass of iced tea or coffee if they cared for that. I just wanted to give them the lay of the land and show them who we were if time allowed. I hoped maybe a tour of the packing sheds, the barns, and the farm stand would quell any reservations they might have. I would try to bypass Floyd's trailer, saving that architectural wonder for another time. Besides, that crazy-looking, highly territorial dog might terrify them. Moses sure terrified me, especially after dark.

I said to my mother, "Don't you look nice?"

To which she replied, "Thank you. Why are we all so nervous?"

"It's normal given the circumstances," I said.

"Now, what are the circumstances?" she said. "Party jitters?"

"Meeting Shelby's parents," I said and thought, Is she kidding? But then again, I thought, lots of older people get a little confused when they're under pressure.

"Oh, shoot. That's nothing."

"They're here," my dad said. He was standing by the windows, peeking through the curtains.

"Get away from the windows like a Peeping Tom!" Mom said. "You want them to think we're a bunch of weirdos?"

There will be plenty of time for that, I thought.

"They seem awfully nice, but I don't know how they live like that," Susan Kennedy Cambria said.

CHAPTER 4

really? pig pickin'?

I had just stepped out of the black car that delivered us from our hotel to the home of my daughter's future in-laws. At first glance I had to say that the landscape was pretty breathtaking. There was a chalkboard in the parking lot of the farm stand that said, STOP THE CAR — YOU NEED PIE! How utterly charming! I took off my sunglasses and squinted. Gorgeous oaks with long tears of Spanish moss were everywhere. And I could see the peach orchard in the distance. It was larger than I had envisioned. There were planters of flowers on the front steps of their house. Pretty, I thought. But If I had to live in a battered old house like this, I'd weep day and night. Thank God I'd had the presence of mind to get my invitations for our party out early and that my gossip girl Judy CQ canceled her trip here at the last minute. She was invited to another friend's ranch in Montana to fly-fish for the weekend and felt she couldn't decline because our other friend was recently separated from her husband, who was of course screwing his secretary. (And they were flying private, Judy's drug of choice.) This was news? Really? Men screwed their secretaries? Please.

"Alejandro?" I said his name quietly.

"Yes?" He was trying to make a call on his cell. "I can't get enough bars."

"They're staring at us from behind the curtains."

He looked up briefly and then his attention returned to his phone, madly punching in the numbers again.

"Who cares? I have to be on a conference call with our bank in Geneva now! Damn it! Do you think someone here might have a landline?"

"Darling, this is very bad timing. Conference calls on a Saturday night?" It seemed odd. I smoothed the wrinkles on the skirt of my black linen dress and swatted a huge mosquito on my arm. There was blood. I reached into my bag for a tissue to remove its carcass. "Nasty!"

The kitten heel of my sandal was sinking into the pea gravel walkway. I had a bad feeling about the evening, but it was my duty to be polite and congenial. For the sake of Shelby and because we cared so much for Frederick, I was determined to be the perfect candidate for an in-law if it killed me. Alejandro could spend the entire night on the phone if he wished. I'd seen him do it before.

As I began my way toward their house, which hadn't seen

a paintbrush since we'd put a man on the moon, the line from the old song began running through my mind on an obnoxious endless loop: *Be it ever so humble, there's no place like home.* When I reached the steps the front door opened, and out came Diane, Frederick's mother. She seemed genuinely happy to see me.

"Oh! I'm so glad you're here!" she exclaimed. "Please come in! Come in! Is that your husband?"

I turned to see Alejandro walking across the yard with his cell phone held to his ear and his other hand on his hip and then gesturing.

"Yes, that's Alejandro. Please forgive him. He's on a conference call. He'll be along in a few minutes."

"Oh, it's no problem! Come meet the family!"

She stood there in the late-afternoon light, hair uncolored, pulled back into a simple clamp. Her face was bare, except for a swipe of pale pink lipstick that I knew on instinct she seldom wore. And her unpretentious beige linen shift matched her beige flat sandals. *Mother of the groom. Wear beige and shut up.* I was her polar opposite in every single way. I wondered then if I should sneak into a bathroom and wash my face. And my next thought was that it must be liberating in some *Little House on the Prairie* way to dress so plainly and to be so unadorned. I wouldn't go to my yoga class without a full face of makeup.

"Thank you. I'm so glad to meet you at last!" I said this, thinking she really was a handsome woman, although her face had clearly had never enjoyed a committed relationship with a good moisturizer or an aesthetician. Nonetheless, natural good looks were rare and to be treasured. Maybe at some point down the road, she'd come to Chicago and I'd take her to Mireille's and let Mimi work her magic. I just loved the name *Mimi*.

I stepped across the threshold and was immediately accosted by a very large cat, who hurried to my side and began to walk between and around my legs.

"Shoo, kitty!" I said. I was not a cat person.

"Oh, don't pay Gus no mind!" an older woman who had to be Diane's mother said. "He's an old pain in the neck." She came over, leaned down, and scooped him up with one arm where he hung from her hip like a rag doll. "I'm Virnell, the GMO the G."

I smiled, delighted to discover some wit in the family. I shook her hand and scratched the nice kitty gingerly behind the ears.

"Then that makes me Susan, the MO the B!"

"Well, that's just fine! And that's Floyd Sr., but we all call him Pop."

The older man in the recliner gave me a nod and a little wave.

"Hi, there!" I said and gave him a little wave in return.

Virnell said, "Come on in and let's get you something to wet your whistle!"

I had stepped back in time. Who said "wet your whistle"? My head swirled and the years slipped away. I was on Walden Pond.

"I'm sorry?" I had missed whatever it was Diane was saying.

"I said, would you like a glass of iced tea? It's sweetened with our own peach syrup."

No vodka? Not even wine?

"That sounds wonderful!" I said, climbing on the sobriety train.

She handed me the frosty glass and I took a sip. It was absolutely delicious.

"This is so refreshing!" I said and quickly drained the glass. "May I?"

Virnell said, "Law, Diane, quick, get Susan a refill! The poor thing's parched like a cactus garden!"

"Thanks," I said and handed the glass back to Diane.

Cactus garden? Wasn't that sort of a contradiction in terms? But what did I know? There were lace doilies under every lamp and a large hooked rug on the floor. There was no artwork on the walls, only a large photograph of Frederick as a boy in his scout uniform. The tabletops held a collection of family snapshots from different occasions, all in unmatched frames. And there was an ashtray and a candy jar filled with peppermints. I had entered a time warp. Maybe it was me, but in Chicago, we hid our ashtrays and no one offered refined sugar anymore.

And then a tall, handsome, muscular, and, may God forgive me, super sexy man entered the room. When we locked eyes, I must've turned every shade of red in the spectrum.

"Hey, I'm Floyd, Fred's uncle."

"Floyd helped me raise Fred along with his daughters. Who's watching Irma?" Diane said.

"Irma is done," he said.

"Who's Irma?" I asked.

"My favorite sow. You'll love her."

A sow? He looked at me like, I don't know, in a very personal way. Certainly, Alejandro had never looked at me like that. Uncle Floyd was not smiling. He was assessing.

"Well, I'm Susan, Shelby's mother."

"I figured that," he said.

He took my hand in his, and I swear, his hand all but swallowed mine. Stop it this minute, I thought, chastising myself thoroughly for wondering what it would be like to sleep with him. And it seemed like he lingered a second too long before he released my hand, and I felt my temperature rise again. Then she appeared.

"This is my current friend, Betty Jean, but we all call her BJ."

"How nice to meet you," I said, thinking, I'll bet they call her that for a specific reason, but I didn't raise one hair of an eyebrow, thanks to the wonders of Botox. And what did he mean *current friend*? This was just the kind of thing I worried about, that perhaps Shelby was marrying into a family of people who had little regard for the sanctity of marriage. On a side note, BJ was not into fashion, but she did have notable cleavage.

"It's nice to meet you," she said with a faint smile. "Floyd? Would you like a glass of tea?"

"Sure. Thanks. Hey, sis!" Floyd said. "Look at you, all gussied up."

Gussied up? If Diane was gussied up, I must've looked like I was ready for Halloween.

The door opened again and Alejandro entered.

"Finally!" I said.

"Alejandro," Diane said, hurrying toward him, "we are so happy to have y'all with us tonight! We just love Shelby so dearly!"

"Yes," he said. "Thank you. Do you have a landline I might use for a few moments? I need to call Geneva back right away. I'm afraid it's rather urgent and it's already midnight there."

"In Geneva, Alabama?" Floyd said.

Alejandro looked at Floyd like he was a total idiot and said, "No. Switzerland."

"Switzerland!" Floyd said quietly and narrowed his eyebrows suspiciously, as though he could not conceive of the necessity of talking to someone in a place so far away, especially if it was midnight.

"Well, you can give it a try," Virnell said. "There's a phone out there at the end of the hall on the hall table."

They still had a landline? And probably a telephone table, one of those odd little painted tables attached to a small painted chair that had a special spot for the phone book. My grandmother had owned one of those. I remembered that I used to chip off the black paint with my thumbnail when I was upset with my mother, which was frequently. I followed Alejandro down the hallway to see, and sure enough, there it was. Not every piece of midcentury furniture was museum worthy.

Well, Alejandro began dialing and getting all sorts of recordings and becoming very frustrated. I hated his dark moods. Finally he put the phone down and looked at me.

"I've got a hundred euros that says they don't have an international plan."

"I'm sure you're right," I said. "Why would they? Would you like something to drink? Diane is pouring iced tea."

He looked at his watch. It was six thirty. Martini time.

"Iced tea? You're kidding, aren't you?"

"No. I'm quite serious."

"I'm going back outside to see if I can get a signal. Please apologize for me. I won't be long."

"Why don't you ask Siri? I'll bet she knows a way to do it."

"Siri's an idiot," he said in disgust and left the house.

I went back to the living room and immediately their lively chatter became dead silence. I hated when that happened. So I did what all battle-ready urbanites do — I took it in stride, ignored it, and brought up a new topic.

"So! Has anyone heard from Frederick and Shelby? Hmmm?"

"They should be here any minute," Diane said. "Fred wanted to show her where he went to high school."

"Susan," Virnell said, "Pop and I were just wondering about what y'all do for a living."

"Well, Alejandro owns a private equity firm. It's small, but he's been very lucky. Before we were married, I did public relations for a large firm in Chicago. Once Shelby arrived, I began doing volunteer fund-raising for different arts and cultural institutions. Keeps me busy and out of trouble."

Pop said, "What's private equity?"

"Well, basically a select group of people give my husband money and he invests it on their behalf. It's a very personal business built on trust. But Alejandro is practically clairvoyant when it comes to what to invest in next." I said this to them and it was clear to me they had no idea what I was talking about. "Let's say you open a savings account at the bank, right? That money doesn't sit there. The bank uses it to invest for you and for the institution. Alejandro is sort of a one-man bank." We lived in a very different world.

Virnell said, "Well, every time the banks around here open a new branch, I set up a little account."

"Because she gets a free toaster oven!" Pop said and slapped his knee with a laugh.

"Or a blender! What's the matter with that?" Virnell said defensively.

"Nothing!" I said. "Not a thing in the world!"

Virnell was a pip. She reminded me of an aunt I used to have. Spunky and spry.

"Here's another thing I wanted to know," Diane said.

All eyes were on me.

"Isn't Chicago really, really, terribly, unbearably cold in the winter?" she said. "How do you stand it?"

I laughed out loud then. "You're right! Sometimes it's so cold you could scream! But you get used to it. Let's be honest. It's no colder there than it is hot and humid here."

"Touché on that one," Floyd said.

"Well, the caterer has taken over our kitchen and I can hear the band, so I guess we'd better make our way to the party," Diane said. "We have so many nice friends who are very excited to meet you and your husband."

Virnell said, "And to welcome Shelby to the Lowcountry! She's not the first Yankee we adopted!"

"I'm originally from Vermont," BJ said.

"Midwesterner, Mom. Shelby is from the Midwest." Then Diane whispered to me, "She means well."

"'She' is the cat's mother!" Virnell said.

I had no clue what that meant, but I guessed it meant Diane shouldn't refer to Virnell as *she*.

"Vermont is a really beautiful state," I said as we stepped outside.

BJ smiled nervously at me. Why was she nervous? I could see Alejandro about a hundred yards in the distance; his fist was dug into his hip and he was holding his cell phone tightly to his ear.

"Thank you," she said. "One of Floyd's daughters lives there."

"Oh, really?"

"Stephanie is about twenty-three. She's lives in a commune and makes cheese."

"I see," I said and thought, She's probably a stoner, a term I learned from Shelby.

BJ sighed. "I miss the Canadian maples when they change color in the fall."

"I'd miss that too!" I said.

I smiled back at her. I got the feeling then that she didn't have many friends. But then, if I was being honest, neither did I. Not real ones anyway.

"Ain't nobody got your feet nailed to the Lowcountry floor," Floyd said. "I'm going on ahead to check on Irma."

BJ gasped a little. "I don't know why he says things like that," she said to me. "He promised to behave himself tonight."

"Oh, don't worry. Usually men say things like that so you'll reassure them there's nowhere else you'd rather be."

"Or because they don't care if you stay or go," she said.

Oh, boy, I thought. Here's the first crack in the wall. "Or because all men are babies sometimes? What do you think?"

She paused for a moment before she spoke. "I think you're a smart cookie," she said.

We made our way along the gravel driveway, following the others who were hurrying toward the tent. I looked over to a field of sorts where arriving guests were parking, directed by young men wearing matching T-shirts with a company logo. Shelby and Frederick drove past us, parked by the barn and got out of their car. I waved to them.

"I'll wait for them," I said to BJ.

BJ stopped, looked at my face, looked away and then back at me again. "You know what?" she said.

I waited and then she said, "Men are stupid. That's the real problem here."

"I don't know if they're *all* stupid, but I can attest to the fact that the little boy in them never completely grows up. I'll see you in a few minutes!"

The poor thing. She walked away.

My beautiful daughter, poised and graceful, moved across the distance between us on Frederick's arm. Alejandro was still on the phone. I turned to the tent. There were beer kegs. And a pig splayed across a large table with an apple in its mouth. Floyd caught my eye. He was staring at me. He slapped the pig on its butt and grinned at me. What was I to infer from that?

"Alden did such a great job!" Diane said.

"You ought to reward him with a kiss!" Virnell said.

"Mom!" Diane said

CHAPTER 5

irma is served

As we meandered down the driveway toward the tent, I started getting excited. We didn't throw parties, so a barbecue of this magnitude was a very big deal, and more special because of the occasion. Our bluegrass band was in full swing, and there was a great vibe. We stopped along the way, saying hello to arriving friends and introducing Susan to everyone. People had already begun to eat, as was the custom. When the pig was done, people lined up.

"Come on, Momma," I said to Virnell. "Let's get you and Pop a seat and I'll fix y'all a plate."

"That would be very nice," she said, "although we're not exactly infirm yet." She smiled at Susan and Susan smiled back.

I just shook my head and led my parents to a table. Everyone was talking about the food, but especially about how moist and delicious the pork was. Most of our friends already had a little grease on their chins and they were literally licking their fingers. Irma was working her voodoo.

"Make sure you try a piece of the crackling," I said to Susan, pointing to the pile of crispy skin all stacked up inside the rib cage while I wondered if her eyelashes were ones that she grew.

"Believe it or not, I went to a pig pull once, years ago. As I recall, the skin can be very difficult to chew," she said.

"Not the way Floyd roasts it. He has a special technique. Ask him; he'll tell you. He loves to talk about barbecue."

"These peanuts are wet," she said.

"They're boiled, not roasted. Try one."

She carefully popped one open and looked at the little peanuts floating in brine with more consternation than was called for.

"Just pick these out?"

"Oh, for heaven's sake. Like this." I took one from the pile, snapped it open and slurped the peanut and brine together. "Delicious!"

She then put the shell to her lips and did the same. "Wow! That's really good!"

"Another convert!" I said and we laughed.

We were in the buffet line together. Her husband was

still on the phone. Shelby and Fred were dancing closely, doing the walk-around waltz despite the lively music that was playing. I had hardly spoken to them. They were oblivious to everyone. I wondered what it was like to be so deeply in love. Love required a dangerous amount of surrender, something that held no interest for me. And then there was the issue of trust. Another huge problem. And time spent to keep the flame going. I had no time to spare.

"Maybe I'll try a small piece of skin," she said, as though I'd suggested a lung donation might be fun.

"Oh, come on, honey, step out of your box!" I said, picking up the tongs. I put a lovely thin piece of crackling on her plate. "Give it a whirl."

"Did you just call me *honey*?" she said, picking it up with her fingers and biting off a small piece. She was smiling.

"Down here everyone's *honey*," I said. "So how do you like Irma's crackling?"

"It's better than sex," she said and laughed. She accepted a small portion of shrimp and grits and a scoop of the tomato cucumber salad from the server.

I was surprised she would make such a familiar remark, so I laughed with her and said, "I'm afraid I wouldn't know about sex, but I do love the skin." She sniffed at the corn bread and the biscuits and declined them. Should I have reminded her that grits have carbs?

"Well now, that's *truly* a shame!"

"I don't have the time for all that nonsense. And at my age? I mean, do you see a line of eligible men lining up at my front door?" I said. I shook my head and smiled. "It's always been slim pickings around here to start with."

"Honey, there's slim pickings all over the world, and yes, I called you honey. When in Rome, you know? You're too young to feel that way."

She returned to the buffet table and took another large piece of crackling and a handful of boiled peanuts. I put two plates in front of Mom and Pop. I looked up to see that Floyd had his eye on Susan and BJ had her eye on Floyd. I thought, Uh-oh. Alejandro had better get off the phone before I got a new sister-in-law. There were some serious hormones flying around and it was barely dusk. It was Irma's fault.

I took Susan over to one of the dozen farm tables placed around the dance floor.

"Sit with me," I said and proceeded to introduce her to the others there. "This is my dear friend Kathy Christie. We've been friends since kindergarten and neighbors for too many years to count! She lives next door."

"Next door is over a mile away," Kathy said, taking a full inventory of Susan, letting Susan know we weren't destitute.

"Hi," Susan said.

Kathy said in her profound drawl, "We are all so happy to welcome Shelby to the family."

"Thank you," Susan said. "We feel the same way about Frederick."

Kathy shot me a glance. Frederick? I could read her mind. *Is she talking about our Fred?* She dabbed the corners of her mouth with her napkin and stood to better talk to Susan. "Of course. Well, I hope you all will have the opportunity to see a bit of Charleston. How long are y'all planning to stay?"

Susan put her plate on the table, and at that moment I was glad I ordered folding chairs instead of picnic benches. I couldn't see her climbing over a picnic bench in her linen dress without compromising modesty.

"Oh, I'm afraid we're flying out early in the morning. We have an engagement for tomorrow evening."

"I see," Kathy said and arched an eyebrow over her word choice. "And where are you all staying tonight?"

"We're at Zero George. Do you know it?"

"Why, how funny! I helped Lynn decorate the place. We went to UVA together."

"Lynn?"

"Easton. She owns it. Not that y'all don't have everything you need in Chicago, but she also plans destination weddings. She's extraordinary. Really."

"I'll check her out," Susan said. "Shall we sit?"

Kathy paused for a moment, smiled that sly smile of hers, and said, "We *shall*."

Susan had met her pretentious match, and for much of the night she would be glued to Kathy's side, yakking away like they'd been friends since kindergarten. Kathy had also had two of the worst husbands in the history of marriage. One had anger issues and the other liked to shoplift. Like me, Kathy had sworn off love, preferring to garden, travel, and read.

I had to laugh to myself that one of *my* friends was going to tell Susan Kennedy Cambria a single thing. But Kathy had her finger on the pulse of Charleston. So if Susan Kennedy Cambria thought she was coming down here to strut her stuff among a bunch of isolated little lambs who knew nothing of the world, Kathy had just let her know she was mistaken. Truly, Kathy was a glamour girl next to me. For one thing, her pashminas and silk scarves always stayed in place, while I might drape a cardigan over my shoulders and struggle to keep it off the floor. She was the one who could wear lots of diamonds with jeans and look exactly right. I'd even seen her wear a boa once and it seemed perfectly appropriate. Yes, a boa.

So much for my glamorous life. The only diamond I had ever owned was on Shelby's finger now, but it didn't bother me one bit. Of course, my mother, good old Virnell, had looked at it hard and said something like *So, that's a halo, huh? Well, I hope you're happy with it now.* I had died a little when I heard her trying to tell Shelby where the bear went in the buckwheat so I jumped in and said, *Oh, it's so much more fashionable now,* as if I knew the difference. So far, if Fred and Shelby's mutual rapturous gaze was any indication, that diamond did not appear to be a bad-luck stone. And Kathy had Susan well occupied, chatting her up with everyone else at the table.

Until Floyd approached. I watched in horror as my brother led Susan to the dance floor. She didn't even seem to be reluctant. I looked around, and sure enough, Alejandro was still on his cell and BJ had a very stern face. I'd seen that exact expression on Floyd's other women and knew exactly what it meant. Start packing. The party's over. Maybe not tonight, but soon, to be sure. Oh, dear. I had to do something to keep peace, and suddenly I had an idea.

I walked over to Floyd and Susan, whose moves, just by the way, weren't earning them a slot on *Dancing with the Stars*. He was all over the place, swinging her around I don't know what and then bringing her in close, whispering in her ear. But oddly, she seemed to like it. Go figure. I tapped him on the shoulder.

"Excuse me, sweet brother."

Naturally, he stopped and said, "Yes?"

"You need to give your toast!" I said.

"A toast?"

"Your brother is quite the dancer," Susan said. Her face was flushed.

"If you say so," I said to her and turned back to Floyd. "Yes! The toast! You are supposed to welcome everyone and say how happy we are to have Shelby marry Fred!"

"Well, I promised to get my new friend here a big shot of vodka. She's not a beer drinker. Give us ten minutes and I'll take care of it."

"Come here for just a sec." I said and motioned for him to step aside from Susan for a moment. "Just two seconds," I said to her.

"What?" he said.

"BJ's got a bee in her bonnet. I don't think she's too happy with you right now."

We glanced in BJ's direction. Her expression reminded me of Mount Rushmore.

"That's so stupid," he said. "I can't live my life dealing with her insecurities. She's too moody."

"I see," I said.

"Come on," he said to Susan. "We'll be back in ten minutes."

"Sure!" I wanted to warn Susan about Floyd and his amorous ways, but I figured she was a big girl. Maybe her absence would get her husband's attention, and maybe he'd get off the phone. I watched them walk away in the direction of Floyd's trailer and thought, Boy, is she in for a jolt of culture shock or what?

I spotted Alden and worked my way through the crowd to thank him.

"Hey! Alden, thank you for tonight. The food is amazing. The tent is perfect and everything is just right."

He was sort of nodding his head in time with the music and I found myself doing the same.

"Well, you're welcome. If our performance passes muster with you and Miss Virnell, I'm a happy man."

The banjo player started playing lead, and a few minutes later the fiddler took the spotlight, followed by the bass player. They played so forcefully that people stopped dancing and stared at them as though it was a concert.

"Look at this," Alden said, "we've got our own little Woodstock going here."

"Funny. These guys are really good!"

"They sure are! The bass player is Darius Rucker's cousin."

"No kidding."

"Nope. No kidding."

Their song ended, everyone applauded, and they quickly began playing a beautiful waltz. Naturally, there was a breeze, a warm breeze laced with conspiracy and the fragrance of the rich earth that sustained us. The Spanish moss was moving in its own slow dance and the evening suddenly seemed ripe with possibilities.

"So, Diane, want to take a spin around the floor?" he said.

It seemed harmless enough, so I said, "Sure! Why not?"

I should've known I would get sucked into being emotional. How long had it been since I'd been held in a man's arms, dancing to live music, in the warm air on an early-fall night? A very long time. I closed my eyes for a moment and just let him lead. My only child was getting married. I'd longed for this moment and I'd dreaded it too. But I was happy for Fred. I really was. And for Shelby too. I wanted grandchildren badly. And I wanted my Fred to be happy and settled. But I missed him. I missed having him in my life every day. There had always been the possibility that he might return to us, and now he never would. Suddenly I understood exactly what bittersweet meant.

Shelby would be a good wife. She was really serious for a young woman her age, but maybe that was a good thing.

"What are you thinking about?" Alden said. "You're a million miles away."

"Oh, I don't know. Just musing about my boy getting married."

He held me back to have a look at my face. "Well, as you should. The time goes quickly, doesn't it?"

"Yes, and each year seems to pass with even greater speed."

He nodded and pulled me close again. "You smell good," he said.

That was all it took to throw me off. I knew I'd be awake half the night fighting thoughts of him, of being with him. I just didn't want to deal with it.

"I thought we agreed you weren't going to play with my heart," I said.

"Who's playing?" he said.

"Oh, Alden," I said, and in a moment of abandon, I let my head rest on his shoulder and thought, Oh, Irma.

"What did you say?" he said. "I thought I heard you call Irma's name."

I stood back, looked at him, and said, "She was so much more than the other white meat."

Then we got the giggles. Who besides us would've ever understood?

Minutes later I looked over to see Floyd standing with Susan and BJ by the band. Alejandro had finally joined them. He didn't seem particularly happy.

"I should go over there. Floyd's giving a toast," I said to Alden. "Want to come with me?"

He nodded, took my elbow, and we walked over. I didn't want to stand there husbandless and sentimental. I had a fleeting hope that Alden wouldn't read too much into it. Surely after all this time he understood that standing by me for a toast wasn't a proposal of my own to him. I just felt like I needed a friend.

The band stopped playing, and by the time I got there, Floyd was asking everyone to kindly pay attention. Our rowdy friends and family finally quieted down and directed their attention to him.

"I've had the great pleasure of knowing Fred since the day he was born. I'm his uncle Floyd. Most of you know I helped my sister, Diane, raise him, right here on this land that has belonged to our family since right after the American Revolution. That, folks, was a long time ago. But everything of importance to our family has happened right here. Our ancestors built this farm hundreds of years ago, only taking time off to fight in a few wars. It may seem like a humble life to some." He eyeballed Susan and Alejandro and smiled. "But to our family, it's a little bit of, well, paradise. When the peach trees blossom, you can get drunk on the air."

I heard Alejandro mutter, "That is, *if* one wants to get drunk."

Susan just arched an eyebrow and smiled. Her friend from Chicago, who arrived very late, was by her side.

Floyd continued. "Anyway, it has been one of the great pleasures of my life to have had a part of Fred's upbringing. I taught him how to catch fish, clean 'em, and cook 'em. I taught him how plant things like corn, tomatoes, and okra, which we actually love, and how to row a boat and how to swim. There are as many stories about Fred's childhood as you might imagine, but one in particular keeps coming back to me."

"Oh, no!" Fred called out. "Uncle Floyd! Not the one about the kittens!"

Everyone laughed for no reason.

"The kittens? Oh, no. No, that's not the one. I'm thinking about something else."

"Not the time I hid the ducks in the bathtub! That's a terrible story!" Fred called out again.

"You did that?" Shelby said.

Fred nodded to her.

"She had plenty of adventures herself," Susan said so loudly that I wondered how many nips she had with Floyd.

And then I had the terrible thought that Floyd had given her a few snorts from his stash of white lightning instead of regulation vodka. His firewater was 180 proof, and if abused correctly, it had the potential to bring down the workforce of Russia and Poland combined. I was sure it could lead to blindness. Lethal.

"No, no. This was a sweet memory. You see, Fred was thrifty. He never spent his money. If he earned fifty cents for doing extra chores around here, maybe he'd spend a nickel. We used to laugh and say he'd still have his First Communion money when he went to college. Anyway, one day my truck broke down. The old thing was a junker and needed everything – tires, brakes, you name it, my truck needed it. Anyone who knows us knows we don't believe in buying new cars or trucks. Fred must've been around ten. So he asked me what I was so long in the face about and I told him. He asked me how much it was going to cost to repair it. I told him I thought it was in the area of about eight hundred dollars. He agreed that it seemed like a fortune. But I needed my truck and he knew it. Later that afternoon he came to me with a contract and a ballpoint pen and offered to loan me the money at two percent interest if I paid him back within thirty days."

Everyone hooted and hollered and clapped their hands.

"I said, 'Boy? You got that kinda money in your room?' He said, 'Yes, sir.' So I said, 'I'll take the deal at one percent,' and I signed on the bottom line."

More laughing and cheering followed. Floyd continued. "What I'm telling you, Shelby, is that at a very early age, our Fred knew a good thing when he saw one. Therefore it's no surprise to us, knowing how pretty and smart you are, that he fell in love with you and intends to marry you! We are so happy for you and Fred. All the English and Stiftel family want to welcome you to our family and we all wish y'all a lifetime of finding good things together! Cheers!"

The crowd resounded with a solid "Cheers!"

I had a feeling that Floyd's toast might have sounded odd to Susan and Alejandro. There was a hint of opportunism in his phrasing. But I also knew that Floyd would not have meant it to sound that way. He was a lot of things, but he wasn't mean or even too cynical. The band resumed.

"Nicely done," I said to Floyd and kissed him on his cheek.

"Thanks," he said.

He shook hands with Alejandro and gave Susan a polite hug. BJ, who'd been standing by chugging a nearly empty bottle of André champagne clenched in her fist, was having none of Floyd hugging Susan. She moved in between them. She looked Susan up and down.

"*Really?*" BJ said, as though Susan had some nerve to be as attractive as she was.

"Really what?" Susan said, completely mystified. "This is my friend Judy from Chicago."

BJ was having none of it.

"You really think? Ha!" BJ said, and Floyd took her elbow.

"Come on, honey. Time for bed," he said.

"Don't honey me! I don't want to go to bed. I want to dance."

Thoroughly amused, Alejandro said, "Well, then, may I have the pleasure?"

"Well, why not?" BJ said, and Alejandro led her to the dance floor and held her close enough to give her the Heimlich maneuver.

"What am I missing here?" Alden said.

"Drama," I said.

"Ah, my least favorite thing," he said.

I looked around to see Susan and Floyd over by the remains of Irma doing shots with Judy. Those girls were going to hate themselves in the morning.

"This is exactly the kind of thing I feared," Susan said.

"Don't be a snob now, amorcita,*"* Alejandro said.

CHAPTER 6

moonshine and make-believe

Earlier, before the toast, we were walking down the hard-packed dirt road toward Floyd's residence when I was confronted by a large chicken directly in my path. It was staring at me. I stopped in my tracks and Floyd continued on. A few seconds passed, and as he realized I wasn't moving, he stopped and turned around.

"What's the matter?" he asked.

"That's a chicken," I said, and I knew he could sense the fear in my voice.

"Yes, ma'am, it surely is a chicken."

"What kind of a chicken——"

Before I could finish what I was going to say, he said, "Free range, I reckon."

He went on ahead and scooped the chicken up, walked ahead a few yards, and lifted the chicken over a fence, depositing her on the ground. Thank God none of my Chicago friends were here to see this.

"All right, Molly, you behave yourself." He was grinning from ear to ear. "That old girl wasn't going to hurt you."

"Oh! I wasn't afraid! I'm just not accustomed to chickens— you know, or engaging in a Mexican standoff with them." I could feel my face burning.

"Come on. You're two minutes from a cocktail. My trailer is just up the road."

"Oh! How nice!" A trailer?

I didn't think it made me a snob if I said that trailers were not for me, and not because I lived in a penthouse overlooking Lake Shore Drive. I knew enough about the weather in this part of the world to know that if you lived in a trailer, all it would take was one good hurricane to blow everything you owned to kingdom come. I was just a bricks-and-mortar kind of woman. I needed the assurance that my home was literally stable. And having a doorman was good too, that extra layer of security between you and the crazy world out there. A man like Floyd would have none of those concerns. I could just see him tying his trailer to guy wires and stakes in the ground and then holding it all in place with his formidable manly will and his bare hands if necessary. I had a quick mental image of him shirtless.

Anyway, he held the metal door open for me. I stepped

inside and hoped he didn't hear me gasp. A dog of dubious provenance who would never compete at Westminster and peculiar-looking cats were draped over the well-worn furniture. It was clear that BJ was no interior designer and neither one of them were into high-status pets.

I didn't know if I should sit or stand or look around or what. The gun cabinet filled with real guns stood on one wall, there was a framed photograph of a Harley-Davidson over the couch, and an oak and glass backlit vitrine filled with trophies. The recliner was upholstered in camo. These things set a certain tone. I was just here for a quick shot of vodka. I wasn't comfortable sitting down, making myself at home. I started getting nervous.

"Just push Moses off the sofa. He thinks it belongs to him."

"All right now, Moses," I said. "Time to move."

Moses picked up his huge head and looked at me with mournful eyes. He gave me a deep guttural bark, and when I jumped he put his head back down and resumed his nap. He was not impressed with my authority.

"Shoo, kitty!" I said to the feral-looking cats in the club chair. They sensed I didn't like them and slowly got up and hopped to the floor. I brushed away at the cushion as discreetly as I could and perched myself on the edge of the seat.

"Okay, now, we got two kinds of vodka here. Double Cross, which is my favorite. And then we got a bottle of this stuff a friend of mine makes."

"He makes it? Like moonshine?" I'll admit that *was* intriguing.

"Yeah, a lotta good old boys make liquor. You know, as a hobby."

"Like craft beer," I said, feeling pretty good at that moment about my knowledge of common trends and what went on among regular people.

"Yeah. Let's try a shot of each and you tell me which one you like better."

"Sounds like a plan," I said.

Floyd looked at me as if my approval of his plan was a slight annoyance. He poured out a measure of each vodka into two plastic cups, then turned them around in an effort to confuse me. I laughed.

"Go ahead," he said. "Knock 'em back!" He was smiling then.

"No ice?" I said.

He narrowed his eyes at me and said, "Ice dilutes the product and masks the finer aspects. When you tell me which one you prefer, I'll give you all the ice in the world."

"Of course, you're right," I said. "It's all in the nuances."

I brought the first plastic cup to my lips, smelled it, and took a healthy sip. I recognized the Double Cross right away, feeling that familiar tiny burn in the back of my throat. Yummy! We drank Tito's at home all the time, but only Double Cross in public. Alejandro felt that consuming the finest alcohol was another detail that continuously reaffirmed his reputation as a connoisseur.

I took a whiff of the second glass. It smelled sweet. Then I sipped it. It was delicious! "Floyd! This tastes like honey!"

"It sure does. I don't know how he does it, but somehow, it's infused with honey. Isn't that something?"

"I believe I could be very happy with a tad more of your colleague's honey-laced vodka," I said, as boldly as a veteran barfly, which I suppose I might have been, but only in the most civilized manner.

He filled my cup halfway and brought me a few ice cubes in another cup.

"Thank you," I said and meant it. I could feel all the stresses of the day evaporate. "So, Floyd, tell me about yourself. How did you come to—"

"Live in this beat-up trailer? Actually, I've got a spit of land on the marsh that runs through the back of our property that feeds into Shem Creek at high tide. Shem Creek feeds into the Cooper River. And if you ask me, the Cooper River is the gateway to the rest of the world."

"And?"

I held out my glass for a refill. He raised his eyebrows but said nothing and poured.

"Well, my plan has been to dredge a bit and build a house over there, but so far I've just never been able to find the time to do it."

"The marshland here is very beautiful. I would imagine if you could build a home to face east and west, the beginning and end of the day would be something rather spectacular to see."

"Yes. Yes, it would."

He looked at me, and it seemed for a moment he was surprised that I would find anything in the natural world to be aesthetically appealing. Or had we just discovered our first square foot of common ground?

I think I laughed a nervous laugh then, because I was suddenly slightly uncomfortable to be what I think they call "doing shots" with my prospective son-in-law's uncle in a trailer, away from the party given in my family's honor. It was an ill-mannered choice. I would never have done this in Chicago.

"I think that there is an awful lot to learn about the South and the way of life here. I mean, isn't it odd in this day and age to be roasting a beast?"

"Instead of what? Grilling a steak? Does this seem uncivilized to you?"

"Oh, no! No! Definitely not!" Yes, it was uncivilized to have your food stare back at you!

"It's an ancient tribal thing. People still cook whole animals to celebrate all kinds of things. Weddings, funerals, holidays, war, peace."

"So, centuries ago, countries changed hands and they roasted a goat?"

"Exactly, if you like goat meat, which I can't say I do. Around here, pork is king. Or queen. But I guess you already figured that one out."

It was then that I noticed the trophies had brass pigs atop them.

"And you won all those trophies for . . ."

"Just making good barbecue, ma'am."

"I see. Well, we had probably better be getting back to the party before Alejandro and BJ miss us. But I just have to say, this honey-flavored vodka is really a treasure. Thank you for sharing it with me."

He topped off my cup.

"Oh, that's plenty! Thanks!"

"It was a pleasure. And if the kids don't mess things up, we've got years of things to celebrate. Here's to Fred and Shelby."

"Yes, that's true. To the happy couple!"

I went to get up, but the cushions were so soft and I was sitting so deep in the chair that Floyd offered me a hand, which I took. And just like in some trashy soap opera, when he pulled me up I landed in his arms. Only this time we weren't dancing.

"Floyd," I said.

"Uh-huh?" he said.

I could feel his heart beat.

"Oh, dear," I said.

"What?"

"I think we had better go now."

"You're probably right," he said, and for the briefest second in recorded time, he nuzzled his face at the bottom of my neck.

I probably wouldn't sleep for a year. I opened my eyes to see Judy CQ through the window staring at us.

"Oh, God!" I said.

"Busted?"

"I'm afraid so," I said.

There was a knock on the door. He opened it.

"Well, hello there," Floyd said. "We were just going back to the party. I'm Floyd, Fred's uncle."

"Lovely to meet you! I am Judy Cunio-Quigley, the unexpected guest!"

"Judy! Darling!" I said, knowing that moment I inadvertently shared with Floyd would be all over Chicago by tomorrow. "What a wonderful surprise!"

"I hope I'm not interrupting anything. Hmmm? Shelby and Frederick told me I'd find you here."

Oh, she had the goods on me—or so she thought.

"Not one little bit! I thought you were fly-fishing on the great frontier or something! How did you get out of it?"

"Lauren's husband broke up with that silly twit of a girl, flew out to Montana with the most divine Piaget watch for her, and begged her forgiveness, and all is well with them. Then his plane flew me here so I could be with you and Alejandro and our precious Shelby and Frederick!"

"How wonderful! Well, we were just grabbing some vodka and ready to go back to the party." I said. "Isn't this fun?"

"Oh, yes," she said. "I'm so glad I made it here!"

"Let's go, ladies. They're gonna send a posse to find us," Floyd said, having the presence of mind to get us moving.

We left the trailer with the bottle of his friend's lovely vodka and made our way back toward the party.

"I'm going to run ahead," she said, "if you don't mind. Ladies' room!"

"We're right behind you," Floyd said.

I hoped she hadn't seen us in that very awkward embrace that lasted one second. Oh, forget it, I told myself and drained my cup.

"What are you gonna do," I said, feeling the vodka assassinate my judgment.

"What do you mean?" Floyd said.

"She's got the biggest mouth in Chicago."

"Let her talk. Call her a liar." Floyd said.

"Good idea."

At first I was horrified by my attraction to Floyd. But then I found it curious that my hormones were equal-opportunity employers. Alejandro had one kind of appeal — international playboy meets financial wizard meets the man you could never fully know. Floyd was his antithesis. Just as I was BJ's. It was true about opposites. But I would never touch Floyd. It felt incestuous at worst and undignified at best.

"Floyd?" I said as we made our way down the dirt road. Even in the dark I could see that I was covered in cat hair. Probably dog hair too.

"It's not happening, Susan."

"What do you mean? I didn't even say anything!"

"Look, Susan Kennedy Cambria from the bright lights of Chicago." He stopped and faced me. "I could take you back to my trailer and give you a night of magic and you'd be mine forever. But it ain't right. We're practically related."

"What on earth are you talking about? Have you lost your mind?" It was the weakest demonstration of indignant horror I'd ever given.

And he started to laugh. His laughter was like some Greek god shaking the heavens. He was right. I was the liar. And Judy had the goods.

"I just wanted our cake to be special!" Shelby said.

"You're special! Who cares about the cake?" Fred said.

CHAPTER 7

shelby has a word or two

Frederick and I were finished eating and it was time to cut our cake, which by the way, was pathetic, it was so blah. Three small tiers, white icing. Period. Done. No imagination whatsoever went into planning this cake. I really tried to hide my disappointment when I saw it. I mean, all they had to do was look on Etsy for three seconds and they could've bought a cute thing to put on top, like a bride and groom? Or a little guy on his knees proposing to a cute girl?

We were making our way over to the table where it was. A while ago, when Mrs. Stiftel asked me what kind of cake I liked, I laughed. I mean, was there a cake I didn't like? No. So basically, I had no idea what kind of cake was under the white icing. But I hoped it was chocolate. Who didn't like chocolate? So my head was sort of floating over — other than the cake — what a great night this had been and I was thinking about my cake-love addiction when I noticed from the corner of my eye that my mother was completely wasted. Yes, ma'am. Toasted.

And that's not all. She was practically drooling over Frederick's uncle Floyd! Gross! Did she think no one noticed? I needed to take her aside and tell her to bring it down a notch, maybe get her some coffee or something, but there were too many people between us, and Frederick was tugging on my arm, moving me along. At least my dad was off his phone. I always say that when he goes to that big investment bank in the sky he should pack his charger.

So just as we were about to cut the cake, a cow appeared out of nowhere and stuck its big damn head in the tent, scaring me to death. I screamed and Uncle Floyd yelled, "Isabella! Stop right there!"

"Love it," Mom's friend Judy said and took a picture with her phone.

Apparently, the cow was named for a former queen of Spain and every hipster female baby born in the last ten years.

It seemed to me that Isabella was going for the cake. I was terrified. All of Frederick's friends whipped out their iPhones and started laughing and taking pictures. Uncle Floyd rushed over and put his arm around the cow's neck.

"Come on, girl," he said, attempting to lead her away.

"Wow!" my mom said, marveling at Uncle Floyd's prowess. I wanted to strangle her.

We finally cut the cake and fed each other a bite. It was peach flavored. Of course it was! There were bits of peaches in the cake itself and slices in the jam filling. Oh. Great. Frederick's whole family probably expected my bridesmaids to have peach-colored gowns and for me to carry peach blossoms. They'd probably try and put peach jam in goodie bags for all our out-of-town guests! I was going to have to put a stop to it or the next thing I knew Frederick would bring home a puppy and name her Peaches!

"It's delicious!" Frederick said.

"Peach pound cake. Baked it myself," said his grandmother Virnell, who was standing by. "I've always dreamed of baking your wedding cake someday, but since you're getting married in *Chicago* . . ." She paused to deliver a dramatic sigh of disappointment. "I had to let that dream go. This was the next best thing. Yes, since you were just a little boy I had that dream." Another sigh followed.

Oh, fine, I thought.

"It's absolutely delicious!" I said because it actually was and silently said a thank-you prayer that she couldn't ruin our wedding day with another ugly cake.

"I love you," Frederick whispered to me.

"I love you too," I whispered back.

"Well, I'll let you young lovebirds have your night. Time for the old people to go to bed."

Frederick leaned down and hugged her. He whispered, "Thanks, Gram. For the cake and for everything. I love you a lot." He kissed her cheek.

She smiled and said she loved him too. I looked at her and

thought, Wow, if she had her hair done and someone did her makeup she wouldn't look so decrepit. Frederick's mother, Diane, looked very nice tonight, and it was easy to see that she had gone to a bit of trouble to get herself put together for the evening. Her dress was probably new. But his gram really looked the part of a dowdy farmer. To be fair, this was the one and only time I'd ever seen her without an apron. And his pop too. I mean, Pop was wearing clean khakis with a good-looking plaid shirt and nice loafers. Maybe it was something about his weathered skin and deep wrinkles, but there was no way you could mistake him for a doctor or a lawyer. He listed a bit from side to side like an old person when he walked. Well, duh, he *was* an old person!

But back to my overserved mother? She was never, ever, ever out of control. She looked perfectly groomed from the moment she got up until she went to bed late at night. One hundred percent. Her hair, makeup, and nails were always perfect. And every stitch of clothes she owned was couture. At one point, Daddy thought she was having an affair with Warren Edwards, because every time she came home from a visit to New York, boxes of shoes would keep arriving for weeks. My mother was a clotheshorse. I liked my mother's style, which was conservative and classic, but for me I threw in a solid dose of retro so I wouldn't look like her clone. But I have to say, I wish we wore the same size shoes.

I only point out the differences between the style of Frederick's family and mine because they are pretty stark. We probably seemed shallow to them. Even Mom's friend Judy was dripping with Chanel. Okay, we were pretty shallow, and I wasn't proud of it. But all that aside, Frederick's family gave new meaning to antifashionista. Just saying. And the only reason I knew my mother was tipsy was because she was acting way too friendly. Not that she wasn't friendly as a rule, because she was, but, well, she was laughing too loud. And sort of using Uncle Floyd and my dad to lean on. And her friend.

It was time for me to step in. Frederick's best friend from childhood, Bill Evans, had just come over to shake his hand.

"So!" Bill said. "Gonna tie the knot, are you?"

"Hey, you!" They shook hands and slapped and squeezed each other on the shoulder, sort of a man hug. "Yeah, Bill, here's why! Say hello to Shelby!"

"Hey! Nice to meet you."

Bill looked at me with approval. He seemed like a nice enough guy. In fact, all of Frederick's friends seemed very nice.

"Nice to meet you too," I said.

Frederick said, "So what are you up to?"

"I haven't seen you in a million years, man," Bill said. "Tell me about life in the big city!"

"It's pretty crazy sometimes. I'll tell you this . . ."

It was obvious Frederick wanted to catch up with his friend, which was the perfect moment for me to see about my mother.

"I'll be right back," I said to Frederick.

"Where are you going?" he said.

"To tell my mom something," I said and began working my way through all the guests.

Well, now what was I going to say to her? *Mom? WTF?*
No, I couldn't drop the F-bomb. So, *Mom? Are you okay?*
Too wimpy. Better to pull her aside and just diplomatically
get to the point. I could see from where I was that she was
listening to Dad telling a story, but her mouth was hanging open. Susan Kennedy Cambria was never caught with
her jaw hanging open like that. She was definitely bombed.
What was she thinking? And I could see the look on Uncle
Floyd's girlfriend's face. She was super pissed! Well, who
could blame her? First my mother took off with Uncle Floyd
and disappeared to who knows where for who knows how
long? And no matter why, that was a dumb idea. And before
that they were dancing like idiots. And now she's hanging on
him. This looks very bad. Very bad. I finally reached her side.

"Here's my sweetheart!" Daddy said.

"Oh, thanks, Dad." I turned to Mom and said, "Can I talk
to you for a minute?"

"Sure! Wassup, baby?"

I took her arm in mine and led her away a few feet and I
leaned in so that only she could hear me. *Wassup* indeed.

I said, "Mom? What are you doing?"

"What do you mean?"

"I mean, it's pretty obvious you're way tipsy. Like, what
are you drinking?"

"Moonshine! Isn't that wonderful?"

"What? Moonshine? What the hell, Mom!" Oh my God!
Frederick must think my family is horrible! "No! it's not wonderful! It's terrible! This is my party and you're ruining it!"

"Oh, please, Shelby! Don't be such a prude. It's not exactly moonshine, and we're just having a little fun. And watch your mouth."

"Just cool it, Mom. Okay? By the way, what have you been rolling in? The hayloft? You need a lint brush."

Then her friend Judy just sort of materialized from thin air. She was super annoyed.

"What's wrong?" I said.

"Does anyone know how to remove manure stains from linen?" she said through clenched teeth.

We looked down and sure enough, her black and tan Chanel pumps were soaked with Isabella's dark fresh poop.

"It was only a cow!" Virnell said.

"Only you would say only!" Diane said.

CHAPTER 8

party's over

You plan and plan and plan, check the details a thousand times, fret over what you wish you could have done, and poof! The whole party's over in a few hours. It was Sunday, just after church, and I was already at work in the farm stand with my mother, refilling crates of cucumbers, zucchini, and onions. I'd hardly had time to change my clothes.

"Well, the party was a big success, if you ask me. Just lovely," Virnell said. "Except for Shelby's mother." She was trimming the ends of a bushel of early beets.

"Dear Lord," I said. "The poor thing."

"I worry a little bit about what kind of a family our boy is marrying into, don't you?"

"Not really."

"And her father? Checking the soles of his shoes every five minutes? What does he think? That our whole property is a barnyard? And her friend's poor shoes too. That was a shame."

"Well, I think the visit from Isabella was Floyd's doing. And the cows and chickens aren't housebroken."

"Still, I worry that her mother is a boozer."

"Oh, Mother. She was probably just nervous. I mean, haven't you ever had alcohol sneak up on you?"

"Not since Nixon got elected."

"Were you celebrating or mourning?"

"Please! I'm so doggone old I can't remember. Push that garbage can over here, will you, please? Anyway, I'll bet you the farm she's got regrets this morning and a big head to boot."

I rolled the plastic barrel over to her. It held the remains of all sorts of things that would be mulched when it was full.

"Maybe," I said, "but she didn't strike me as the kind of person who has regrets. I'll bet she doesn't give two hoots what anyone else thinks."

"I think you're right. And you want to know what else?"

"What?"

"Alden is sweet on you." She pointed her finger at me and laughed.

"Well, I'm not sweet on him."

"Yes, you are."

"No, I'm not." Maybe I was.

"You can tell yourself whatever you want, but you're my daughter and I know every hair on your head."

"Humph." I shrugged my shoulders.

"Are they going to have a big party in Chicago?"

"Do you think Susan Kennedy Cambria would miss an opportunity to show off?"

"Well, I'm not going, because I'm not flying and your father shouldn't."

"I thought Pop did pretty well last night."

"He did just fine, but going through airports with all these nasty people and their germs? Who needs it?"

I heard the gravel crunching out back. I looked through the screen door and there were Floyd and Fred way down the road, a snapshot from the past, rolling hand trucks toward us loaded with more cartons of produce from the barn. For a brief moment, I was standing in 1998, looking down the years.

I had countless memories of Fred and Floyd together, picking peaches and other fruit and vegetables, of poring over them in the packing shed, Floyd showing Fred how to grade tomatoes and strawberries. When Fred was just a tadpole, Floyd started teaching my boy what kind of man he should become, and believe it or not, mostly by example. You never would have thought that last night, however. But when Fred was a little fellow? Every lesson Floyd taught him was always delivered with so much thought and patience. Floyd just loved kids, and I guess Fred was the son he never had. Just as his girls were the daughters I never had, except Sophie.

Floyd's first marriage was a disaster. He was all of seven-teen when he married Louisa, and within the blink of an eye she gave birth to Sophie, divorced Floyd, and moved to Seattle. So, logistically, it was nearly impossible for any of us to have had an impact on Sophie's life. I mean, as she got older she came for a few weeks in the summer, but that started to fall apart as soon as Floyd married Deb and had two more girls, Ann and Stephanie. Those girls fought like cats in a bag, to the point that Sophie came less and less. Deb died suddenly from undiagnosed lung cancer, and now Ann and Stephanie were estranged from their father. And sadly, it seems like Sophie was from another lifetime. Not one of them accepted the invitation for last night.

Last I heard, Sophie was an executive with Starbucks in their Seattle home office and we barely knew her. Ann worked for some big processed food company in New Jersey trying to figure out how to extend the shelf life of all their products, as if a year to two wasn't long enough for crack-ers to sit in a pantry. She had obviously inherited Virnell's thrifty gene. And Stephanie, who was always a free spirit, lived in a commune somewhere outside of Manchester, Ver-mont, making cheese and probably smoking enough pot to sink the QE2. Or maybe not. Anyway, they all turned out sort of just fine. At least they were financially independent. The annual exchange of birthday and Christmas cards seemed to be enough for them. Floyd had never been a needy parent. I was not needy in an excessive way. Well, to rephrase, my neediness didn't seem excessive to me. For Fred's sake, I held a lot inside. I had loved him as smartly as I knew how and he grew up and left home anyway. They were all gone. They had left us and made lives for themselves everywhere else but here. I worried what would become of us when Mom and Pop went to heaven and Floyd and I were too old to run the farm. We had talked about it plenty and decided we'd probably sell off part of the land and try to make a living by getting distribution on our jams and jellies, although I couldn't really see how that would work.

"I've got to get back up to the house soon and start your daddy's dinner," my mother said. "He's waiting on the ball games to start so that he can go crazy with the clicker, going back and forth from one station to another."

"You go on, Mom. I'll get the boys to help me."

"Okay, then I will. I have to watch him, you know. Otherwise he'll whittle in my living room and get shavings all over the place."

"Oh, come on, now."

"You have no idea! He loves that clicker because he doesn't have to get up to change the station. Men are so lazy."

We both knew it was Dad's heart condition, not laziness, that kept him in his recliner. My mother could not acknowledge the facts about certain things.

In reality, our farm operated like a tiny communist country. Floyd had no doubt been endowed with the most alpha dog macho genes ever bestowed on a Lowcountry man. But Virnell always had the last word, because Virnell still and always would control the purse until the sad day we were parted. I imagined the purse would pass on to me.

"Good morning, heathens!" I called out to Floyd and Fred.

Only my parents and I had been in the pew that morning. Everyone else had slept in.

"I'll see you up at the house," my mother said and went to the back door. "Good morning, gentlemen!" She held the door for them and gave Fred a smooch on the cheek.

"Morning, Gram!" Fred said.

"Who you calling heathens?" Floyd said good-naturedly. "Let's stack these crates over here by the wall."

"Okay," Fred said.

"You're right. I should've called my son a heathen and you a reprobate," I said. "Let's reload the string beans and the beets, okay?"

"Okay," Fred said. "Great party last night, Mom. Thanks for everything!"

"You're welcome," I said. "So, Floyd? What were you thinking getting my son's future mother-in-law all liquored up?"

"I just wanted to find out what she was really like," Floyd said.

"Oh. I see. And what did you think?" Fred said.

"What did I think? Well, to be perfectly honest, I think maybe she's a tiny bit too big for her britches," Floyd said. "But that doesn't make her a bad person."

Fred nodded, relieved. Floyd's opinion mattered to him.

"What did you think about her dad?" Fred asked Floyd.

"Her dad? Look, Fred, these people are going to be your in-laws. I don't want to go around criticizing them before the horse even leaves the barn, you know what I mean?"

"Yes, sir. But still, didn't you think it was weird that he was on his cell half the night?"

"Listen, as far as I'm concerned? He can be on his cell all night, if he thinks he has to be. But here's what I know. When BJ was just this far away," he said, holding his forefinger a hair's distance from his thumb, "from stabbing my eyes out for paying attention to Susan, he took her out on the dance floor and got me out of the doghouse."

Invisible eye roll from me.

"Let's put those muffins on the counter by the cash register," I said. "Stack them up in the basket."

"Okay. Yeah, I saw them dancing," Fred said.

"So, you know? He's probably okay. He probably has a lot of stress we don't even know about. Anyway, it's good to know he's a man's man."

Another eye roll.

"Who wants coffee?" I asked and filled my thermal cup.

"Not me. Yeah, well, he's super nice to me. He travels a lot. Which I think is hard on Mrs. Cambria."

Floyd said, "Is that what you call her?"

"Yeah," Fred said. "I asked her what she wanted me to call her and that's what she said. Mrs. Cambria."

That pretentious little witch!

"How'd you like her friend Judy?"

"I'll take a cup. Just black. That woman's not her friend," Floyd said quietly. "Mrs. Cambria, huh? That's kind of cold."

"As long as you don't call her Mom, I'm okay with it," I said, filling a cup for Floyd.

"Never in a million years," Fred said. "And even if I did call her Mom, it wouldn't mean the same thing." Fred stopped what he was doing and gave me a hug. "What are you worried about?"

"Who, me? I'm not worried one little bit!" I said and handed Floyd his cup. I thought I'd like to see one woman on this earth who didn't worry that another family might steal their child's heart, especially when the distance between them was so great and the lifestyles were so different. "So, brother dear? Everything's cool with BJ now?"

"Yeah, Lady Di. I gave her my Target card and told her to go to town on it—but I gave her a limit."

I giggled to myself and took a sip of my coffee, feeling the caffeine bringing me back to life. His Target card. I could just imagine Alejandro giving Susan or Shelby a Target card with a spending limit.

"How much?" Fred asked.

"Fred! Have you lost your mind? You don't ask your uncle things like that!" I said.

"Sorry, Uncle Floyd. But you know, I need to know these things. Like, what's the price tag for freedom from a woman's wrath?"

Floyd broke up laughing and I did too.

"Oh, my! Golly, Fred! That was funny!" Floyd said and then got serious. "Well, son, it depends on the crime you commit. I told her she could spend a hundred and fifty dollars."

"That much?" I could spend $150 before I even got to the grocery section. "You always were the last of the big-time spenders."

"Hell, it ain't her birthday, is it?" Floyd said.

"Oh, Floyd. Hey, Fred? Do they have a date for the party in Chicago?"

"Yep. The Saturday before Thanksgiving. Y'all gonna come?"

"Well, I am definitely coming!" I said.

"Me too," Floyd said. "Wouldn't miss it."

"You bringing BJ?" Fred asked.

"Maybe," Floyd said. "Maybe not."

I knew BJ would not see Chicago, at least not on Floyd's arm. BJ just didn't understand how Floyd's mind worked. All his life, Floyd never wanted any woman he could easily have unless she gave him no ultimatums. Last night she showed him some tooth over Susan, and Floyd would put up with only so much of that kind of possessiveness. Their relationship had been converted into a bomb on a short fuse. She'd be better off with someone else.

I heard a truck door slam and looked up to see Alden. I blushed, remembering dancing with him last night. As quickly as possible, I put on my mask of indifference and smiled.

"Good morning!" he said, coming through the old screen door that stood between us and the elements. "How are y'all doing this fine day?" He was grinning wide.

"G'morning!" I said. "Coffee?"

"Sure, thanks!" he said. "I just came by to meet the guys from Snyder, you know, make sure everything goes back where it should."

There was no way you couldn't love Alden. Like a brother, I reminded myself.

"That's so nice of you, Alden. Would you like a blueberry muffin? Still warm from this morning."

"Who could say no to that?" Alden said.

"I wouldn't mind a muffin," Fred said.

I reached in the basket, pulled out two, and tossed one to my son.

"Floyd? Muffin?"

He was dumping green beans and carrots into the bins from cardboard boxes.

"No, thanks. I had something earlier. Trying to watch my waist, you know."

This was another indication he was considering putting his love back on the market. I knew my brother.

I handed Alden his coffee and his muffin with a napkin. He placed it on the counter across from me and the cash register and began to peel away the plastic wrap. He took a bite and moaned.

"You do make the best muffins," he said.

"Thanks," I said.

"Let's go get another load of produce," Floyd said to Fred.

"I'm ready," Fred said and stacked up all their empty boxes, which he had broken down to recycle.

"We'll be right back," Floyd said to me and Alden. "You need anything from the house?"

"No, I'm fine. Thanks!"

My brother and son left through the back door. There was something in the air that came in with Alden.

"What's going on, Alden?"

"Funny you should ask. Well, it seems that my sister's

daughter is getting married and I need a date to the wedding. I was wondering if you'd do me the honor?"

"And be your date?" Oh, God, I thought. Last thing in the world I want is for him to think a little squeeze on the dance floor last night meant something more than what it had been.

"Yes. I thought it would be good to show up with an age-appropriate beautiful woman, and you're the only one I want to go with."

"Oh, Alden, you old flatterer. It depends on the date."

"Saturday before Thanksgiving," he said and smiled. I could see he thought we were playing cat and mouse and that I'd be his date, no problem. Why would I ever have a conflicting date?

"Actually, I have to be in Chicago that weekend."

"Oh? Visiting Shelby's parents?"

"Sort of. They're giving a party for their friends, so of course I have to be there."

"I see." He looked at me curiously. "Are you okay?"

"You know what? No, I'm really not. My only child is getting married and I haven't felt so emotional since the day he was born. I feel like I'm losing him."

"You taking anyone with you?"

"Yes, Floyd, of course. And my friend Kathy."

"Kathy Christie?"

"Yes, who else would it be?"

"Well, there are about a million Kathys in South Carolina."

"I guess you're right."

He reached across the counter and lifted my chin with his finger.

"Diane? If you need me, I'll beg off from my niece's wedding. It's not a big deal."

"You are so nice, Alden. But I think I'm actually going to be all right. Susan, Shelby's mother, gave Kathy some attitude last night and Kathy wants to have my back."

"So your back's covered?"

"Looks like it."

I could see the disappointment in his eyes, as though he and Kathy were interchangeable. At that moment I was more concerned with how I was going to get through the rest of my life without my son at my side than with Alden's imaginary romance with me.

"The men will fear you and the women will wish me dead!"
Susan said.

"Sí! It is true." Alejandro said.

CHAPTER 9

cocktails in chicago

Do I look all right?" I asked Alejandro. "Can you close the hook at the top of my zipper?" I turned my back to him.

"You look ravishing, *amorcita*," he said and closed the hook and eye.

"You don't think this dress is too tight?"

It was super stretched across my hips, so much so that if I sat it might split. I was doomed to an evening of standing in my torturous but fabulous pumps.

"That's what I like about it," he said. "What's that perfume?"

"Houbigant. Queen Victoria wore it. It's made from six hundred different flowers."

"Well, my darling, you'll be the queen of Chicago tonight."

He could be so sweet. I looked at him in his black velvet blazer over his starched white shirt and thought how lucky I was to be married to such a handsome man. When he looked at me the way he was looking at me then, I felt a little weak in the knees.

"Oh, Alejandro, you are such a treasure! You know, you have the most beautiful eyes I've ever seen." I smiled at him and thought that maybe we could get some ooh la la on the night's agenda. "You make me feel like a girl again!"

"Hush now, or I'll have to throw you on the bed and make babies with you!" He was making a joke, of course.

"You're so crazy. And I'm so nervous."

"Why? This is your millionth party! No one throws a soiree like you do."

"I hope you're right, but the caterer was late, the piano tuner was late, the flowers were droopy, the cigar roller isn't here yet! Bad signs!"

The doorman buzzed. I hurried to the call box and asked, "Yes?"

"Mr. Floyd English, Ms. Diane Stiftel, and Ms. Kathy Christie to see you, ma'am?"

"Oh, yes! Send them right up!" I said. "Alejandro! Diane and her friend and Floyd are here! They're an hour early!" Who shows up an hour early?

"Oh, my dear," he said, "don't panic. I'll make them a cocktail."

"Thank you. I'll be right along in two minutes."

"I've got this," he said and smiled that Hollywood smile of his that put everyone at ease.

I was still in our dressing room. I took a look at myself in the full-length triple mirror. My only daughter was getting married, and to my complete dismay she was marrying beneath her station in life. I hoped Diane and Floyd were going to look a little less like Mr. and Mrs. Old MacDonald. I had already heard Judy CQ's clucking from around town. *Her precious Shelby is going to marry a redneck! Yes! He's a hick from the sticks! They have an actual barn filled with cows and they have chickens! I ruined my shoes in cow manure. And they run a little fresh market on the side of the road! I swear it! And, get this! They make jam and jelly! Who knows? Maybe he can drive a tractor. Take a good look at the hottie uncle.* I would do my part to help them show well.

I had little laugh lines around my eyes. I'd just had Restylane injections and a session of Thermage on my face and neck, but I still had a bit of a wattle. Despite my dermatologist's best efforts and eight thousand dollars, there was still some waffling visible on my chin. God, I hate getting old, I thought. Well, I didn't hate getting old so much as I hated looking old. Maybe I should stop wearing lip liner. That was another thing. My lips seemed to be shrinking and fading. All the magazines this fall had touted big eyes and pale lips. But I still loved red lipstick, and anyway, who cared?

I opened my vault and took out a pair of diamond earrings and a big diamond brooch. I put them on and stood back. It was just right. I felt better. I didn't need a bracelet. It wouldn't be nice to rub the obvious in Diane's face.

"Okay," I said to no one, "it's showtime!"

I walked out to my living room and Chef Joho himself put a coupe of champagne in my hand.

"You look amazing!" he said to me. "Never more beautiful!"

"Oh, Joho! Thank you! And thank you for taking care of the food tonight!"

"For my favorite patron? This is my little gift for our Shelby and her fiancé!"

He did not mean there would be no bill. He meant lending his considerable star power to the evening by making a personal appearance was his gift. To be sure, there would be a bill and it would be staggering. He owned Everest, probably the most delicious and glamorous restaurant in Chicago.

"It's no little gift! It's an enormous thrill! We are so honored to have you here."

He gave a polite bow and returned to the kitchen. I thought, wait until Judy sees Joho here. She's going to kill herself.

I saw Alejandro on the terrace with Diane, Kathy, and Floyd. As if Floyd could sense me walking across my rug, he ran his hand through his hair and turned to face me. Lord, that man had a powerful vibe. I could hear my heartbeat in my ears.

"Hello, hello! Welcome to Chicago!" I said as serenely as I could, giving each of them double air kisses near their cheeks. "Let's get you inside so I can take your coats!"

It was very damp and chilly on the terrace. November was unpredictable. Some years you could go anywhere with just a sweater tied around your shoulders. Others might find you bundled up for a blizzard. Today's weather was ominous, a warning that a sinister winter was just around the corner.

"It's so nice to be here!" Diane said. "Your view is incredible!"

"Thank you!"

My floral designer from Ashland Addison had buried tiny white lights in all our shrubs, and they did lend a certain magic to the evening. As he always said, for a great event you have to create a bit of theater.

We all stepped into the living room, where our very special pianist had just arrived and was playing chords, testing the strength of the piano's movement. Everyone shed their coats and handed them to a member of the waitstaff. Diane and Kathy were both wearing very similar sleeveless little black dresses. Kathy wore a triple strand of pearls, which appeared to be real, and Diane had on a very large retro brooch of colored stones set to resemble a flower. It was a pretty fabulous fake. I was impressed and more than a little envious of the muscle tone of her upper arms, but I guessed that came from manual labor. I mean, it wasn't like she had a personal trainer, I'm sure.

"Ramsey! Darling! How are you?" I said to the pianist.

"I'm fine. Isn't this a wonderful night?" he said.

"Diane, do you like jazz?" Alejandro said.

"You're not Ramsey Lewis, are you?" Kathy Christie asked in a mousy little voice.

"Who else would I be?" Ramsey said and laughed.

"Oh, my goodness," Diane said. "I have an album of yours from I guess 1965? *The In Crowd!*"

Ramsey played a few bars and I thought Kathy and Diane were going to faint. Even Floyd seemed impressed.

A waiter appeared at my side.

"Let's get our guests a cocktail, shall we?" I said.

"Excellent idea," Alejandro said. "What can we get for you? Diane?"

"We've known Ramsey for years," I said. "Alejandro is a real jazz aficionado."

Everyone gave a drink order, Ramsey began to play, and soon we were toasting the children.

"Cheers!" we all said to one another. "Let's all drink to happiness!"

I watched as Floyd wandered away. He appeared to be searching for something. I followed him.

"Powder room?" I asked.

"Yes, please," he said.

"First door on the right," I said.

I went back to the others and just then Frederick and Shelby arrived with Ashley Hargrove, Shelby's best friend since childhood and also her maid of honor.

"Hello, my sweethearts! Come say hello to everyone!" I said to them.

They handed their coats to a waiter and came toward us.

"Hello, Mrs. Stiftel," Shelby said and gave her the tiniest of all hugs. "Frederick and I are so pleased you and Mr. English could come! And Ms. Christie? It's so nice to see you again."

We were not really touchy-feely people.

"Shelby, you make me feel like I was born on Noah's ark! Please. Call me Miss Kathy like a nice southern girl would do."

Okay, Kathy laughed, and I'm sure she didn't mean for what she said to sound like she had taken the liberty to correct a faux pas. But that's how it sounded. Her words landed with a thud. At least to my ears.

"She's *not* a nice southern girl," I said as evenly as I could. "She's a nice *midwestern* girl. And she's the best thing that ever happened to Frederick."

"Absolutely!" Frederick said and turned to Floyd, who had just returned. "This is what happens when there are too many hens in the henhouse." He muttered this, pretending we couldn't hear him when of course we could. Somehow his dumb joke defused the miff anyway.

Ashley said, "I'm just going to freshen up."

"Okay. Do you want me to get you a glass of champagne?" Shelby said.

"Of course!" Ashley said. "I'll be right back."

"Pretty girl," Floyd said as Ashley walked away.

I saw him eyeballing our Toulouse-Lautrec lithographs, hung as a group over the chaise lounge. Did he have an interest in art? I should show him the Renoir in Alejandro's study. Better yet, I'd like to show him the Degas in my bedroom. Naughty girl, I said to myself.

"And sweet too," I said.

"So, Susan, tell us about the wedding plans," Diane said.

"Oh, my goodness! Well, we have the ballroom at the Waldorf reserved because our guest list is already over three hundred people. And the Duke Ellington Orchestra is going to play, thanks to Ramsey, which makes me so happy I can't even tell you. Too bad Mercer's no longer with us."

"My wife never does anything halfway," Alejandro said, as though he was down to his last dollar. "Tell them about the butterflies."

Ashley reappeared and whispered something to Shelby. Shelby then whispered something to Alejandro.

"Okay, so the cocktail hour is going to take place outdoors on the rooftop bar of the hotel, which is very beautiful."

"Excuse me," Alejandro said. "It seems we have a little problem."

"Of course," I said and continued. "When Shelby and Frederick arrive and all our guests are assembled, we're going to release twenty thousand butterflies! Isn't that marvelous?"

Diane's face turned white.

"Wow," Floyd said.

Kathy said nothing.

"What's wrong?" I said.

"I don't know," Diane said. "Three hundred people? Duke Ellington's orchestra? Twenty thousand butterflies? It's just that it seems very over the top to me, but what do I know? And aren't butterflies having problems these days? Milkweed shortage?"

I stood back and looked at her and thought I might like to kill her. How dare she insult me this way in my own home?

"Well, Shelby's our only child and our friends have expectations," I said and wondered if the butterflies *were* too much. Wait! Now I'm doubting myself? Was I going to allow this bumpkin to cast me in such a light that it felt like my only daughter's wedding was going to be a crass display of conspicuous consumption?

"It just seems like a lot," she said, continuing to dig her own grave.

"Oh, well, you shouldn't worry about it anyway. When my best friend Judy CQ's daughter married that nice Indian fellow last summer at the Ritz-Carlton in Laguna Beach, they arrived at their ceremony on elephants. Of course, the wedding *was* outdoors on the grounds," I said, trying to lighten my own growing annoyance. "Over the ocean. It was absolutely magnificent!"

"Elephants," Floyd said flatly.

From the corner of my eye, I saw a flood of guests coming in, and at the same time I saw Alejandro with the toilet plunger heading for the powder room. What in the world? Had Floyd done something reprehensible to my plumbing? Then I saw the water coming from the bathroom, overflowing the hall, and heading toward my precious vegetable-dyed runner from Agra.

"Oh, no," I said.

"Listen," Diane said, "I don't mean to criticize."

That was it. I couldn't take another word from her.

"No, you listen. This is *my* wedding! Not yours! All you have to do is wear beige and keep your mouth shut."

"What kind of manners does she have?" Virnell said.

"Bad!" Diane said.

CHAPTER 10

all about beige

I was so shocked, I didn't know what to say. Was I rude? Did she really tell me to buy a beige dress and shut my mouth?

Floyd swung around to see what was so horrifying to Susan, and in the time it would take you to say *her toilet erupted like Mount Vesuvius,* he scooped up her runner from the floor.

"Where would you like me to put this, ma'am?" he said.

"Come with me," she said, and Floyd followed her down the hall.

I stood there with Fred and Shelby until they too came to their senses and went to help Susan.

"I'll call the super," Shelby said. "Get the towels from my bathroom to sop up the water."

"On it," Fred said and hurried down the hall.

I mean, it wasn't funny, of course, but I was biting the insides of my cheeks so hard I could taste blood. Sorry, it was hilarious. It couldn't happen to a bigger stinker.

Dozens of guests were arriving, and every time the elevator doors opened, another swarm would storm the foyer, discarding coats and wraps in the overloaded arms of a staffer. Trays of champagne circulated overhead and there was more caviar on little pancakes being offered than I'd ever seen in my life, not that I'd seen a lot. The food went on and on

"May I offer you a Kobe beef slider?" the handsome waiter said.

Floyd said, "Sure." And popped it in his mouth.

A moment later another waiter appeared.

"Would you care for pâté de foie gras on toast points?"

"Thank you," I said.

A moment later another waiter. "Do you want to try a lobster bite?"

And another. "Toro sashimi with a dollop of wasabi."

The food went on and on. I couldn't chew fast enough. Needless to say, we didn't eat like this in the Lowcountry. Well, maybe some people did, but we kept to a pretty traditional regional menu.

"I don't know what the hell I'm eating, but it's delicious," Floyd said.

Yet another waiter offered us something baked in puff pastry.

"Crab étouffée en croute?" he said with a smile that belonged on the big screen.

"Sure," Floyd said and took two. "Thank you."

I shook my head at him. Floyd was simply bedazzled by it all. It *was* dazzling. Dazzling, sparkling, glamorous, and about as far away from the reality of my own life as I imagined I would ever go.

I was in a daze from all the rich hors d'oeuvres, the exotic flowers that were everywhere, but most especially by all the preening in the room. It was like being in a room of beautiful parrots or toucans, each one trying to outfluff the other bird's colorful feathers, even though the female birds were almost all wearing little black dresses.

"This is some party, isn't it?" Kathy said to me and Floyd.

Kathy was impressed, and that was saying something, because she'd pretty much seen the world.

"Did you meet the Cuban guy rolling cigars in the study?" Floyd said. "If that don't beat all, I don't know what would."

"How about twenty thousand butterflies being released into the wild?" I said.

"Yes, I don't think Susan particularly cared for your thoughts on the subject," Kathy said.

"Look, I don't care how she flaunts her money," I said. "It's just that if I had it, I wouldn't spend it that way."

"How would you spend it?" Floyd asked.

"I don't know," I said. "I'd probably make Momma and Pop take a real vacation. Or maybe I'd paint the house. Update the kitchen. don't know. I'd try to do some good with it, I guess."

My dreams felt mighty small in the face of all the grandeur that surrounded us.

"Look, Diane, listen to your big brother. These are fancy people. We are not fancy people. We should try to meet them halfway. Let her have her fun with her daughter's wedding. Who cares?"

My face must have been riddled with doubt.

"You're worried about Fred, aren't you?" Kathy said.

"Of course I am! Look how happy he is."

We looked across the crowded room and there was my son, impeccably dressed and groomed, smiling and laughing, talking to another young couple, as if he owned the place.

"He seems the same to me, Diane. I think you're worried about nothing," Floyd said. "He's got a good head on his shoulders."

"Floyd, sweetheart . . ." Kathy started to say something, but I interrupted her.

"No, you should call him 'darling.' Everyone here calls each other 'darling.'"

Kathy laughed. I was right. I made air kisses and even Floyd had a chuckle.

"Floyd, *darling*," she began again, raising her eyebrows for emphasis. "Diane, as his mother, is worried that Fred's going to turn into a snotty little snob and never come home again."

"It's true he's punching above his weight here," Floyd said. "But my money's still on him."

"I'm just afraid Susan's wallet is going to swallow him whole," I said.

"Like your momma says, don't cross that bridge until you come to it," Kathy said. "Let's see what happens. If the butterflies fly, she doesn't care what you think. If they don't, well, maybe she heard you and cares how all this is making you feel. But truly, this isn't about us. It's for Shelby and Fred."

Kathy was such a good friend. I knew she was right. Time had to pass. I thought of myself at Fred's age. I remembered thinking I knew everything there was to know. Funny how the older you get, the less certain you become of almost everything except death.

The toilet situation seemed to be under control soon after the building's superintendent arrived with a serious-looking piece of equipment Floyd identified as a snake. He went in there with a fanfare that I thought was entirely unnecessary. Minutes later he came out and had a word with Alejandro. Alejandro thanked him, slipped him something that I imagined was cash, and saw him to the door.

Susan and Alejandro twisted their way through the crowd, coming toward us.

"Floyd, did you have anything to do with wrecking the john?" I said.

"Absolutely not."

"From the way Susan's been looking at you, I'd say you're going to get the credit anyway."

"What do I care?"

A superbly well-dressed and -coiffed woman I thought I recognized approached before Susan and Alejandro could reach us.

"You're Frederick's mother. Remember me? Judy! I had a

cameo at your pig picking where I ruined a pair of pumps. Stepped in Isabella's carte de visite?"

"Yes, of course. I'm Diane. Remember, Floyd, Fred's uncle?"

"Unforgettable Floyd, how are you?" she said. "Fred? Who's Fred? Do you mean Frederick?"

"Yes, I suppose so."

Floyd narrowed his eyes at her and said, "Nice to see you."

"And Kathy, my closest friend?"

"Of course! Well, here we are again, celebrating those precious kids. Again." We nodded to each other, smiling pleasantly, acknowledging one another's reason for being smack in the middle of the heady world of Chicago's elite. The noise level was growing so anything beyond chitchat was pretty much impossible. "Ramsey Lewis," she said. "Only Susan and Alejandro!"

"I've loved his music forever," Kathy said.

"Cool dude," Floyd said.

"Excuse me, did you just call Ramsey Lewis a dude?" Judy said and laughed.

"What would you call him?" Floyd said.

"How about a world-renowned virtuoso?" Judy said with an arched eyebrow.

"Oh, brother," Kathy said.

"Well, it was very nice to have seen you again," Judy said, with the phoniest smile ever stretched over her plastic surgery, before she wandered away.

"Nice," Kathy said.

"Too bad about your shoes," I said. "I don't know how I'm going to live through this,"

"Low exposure. You'll see them a couple of times a year and no more," Floyd said and sighed. "I could eat those puffy things with the crab until the cows come home."

I thought about what he said. It was true. Once the wedding was behind us there would be no reason to see them except for baptisms and birthdays and eventual graduations, and those things didn't happen so often. But the wedding was going to be a test of my mettle.

"You're probably right. I mean, I believe their love is real," I said. "I believe they make each other better people. And honestly? It seems as though they're made for each other."

"Look, Lady Di, it's not Shelby's fault her folks are rolling in it," Floyd said.

"I'm just wondering how Momma is gonna react," I said.

"Hissy fit," Kathy said.

"Yeah. The biggest one ever," I said.

"She's cracked!" Virnell said.

"Agreed!" Diane said.

"We agree on something?" Virnell said.

CHAPTER 11

lowcountry thanksgiving

It was sweater weather on Thanksgiving morning and the Slice and Dice Club was in session. My mother and I were aproned, sleeves rolled up, and at our stations in the kitchen like every other woman in the country who celebrated. I was wondering how many pounds of onions I would chop between November and December and simultaneously thinking about Fred's approaching wedding.

I diced my fifth large yellow onion, scooped all the pieces into a large bowl, tossed the skins into the compost bin, and reached into the pantry basket for five more. The peeling and chopping continued.

Ever since the engagement party in Chicago last week, Susan had been slow to return my phone calls and emails. Any conversation we had about the wedding was chilled by her growing paranoia that I was judging her. I'm sorry, but twenty thousand butterflies? She had stopped sharing details with me, and when I tried to ask Fred how it was coming along he told me that Susan wanted to surprise her guests and wedding details weren't his thing. To be honest, if Susan wanted to hire Cirque du Soleil to fly on trapezes over our heads while they juggled pomegranates, it was okay with me. But I wasn't happy to be cut out of the loop. After all, this was my only child's wedding too.

When I asked Susan for a guest list for the rehearsal party she sighed hard enough to set off tiny ripples in the Sea of Japan.

"Oh, that's right," she said as though she'd never given a thought to my role in the rehearsal dinner. "You'll need that."

"It would be helpful," I said with a laugh, a gentle reminder to her that Fred had a living, breathing mother, although I did wonder what it would cost.

I thought I was only expected to invite those people who were in the wedding party and the parents on both sides. Maybe we'd include the officiant and the organist, if they showed an interest. Susan feigned surprise that we were not intending to include the out-of-town guests as well.

"I can't see them roaming around town not knowing where to go," she said with a tone of urgency.

"How many out-of-town guests do you have?" I asked, terrified.

"Oh, not that many. Fewer than two hundred," she said. "Most of our friends live around Chicago."

I was certain she could hear me gasp in horror. She had to have known that a party of that size in megawatt Chicago would bankrupt my family.

"Good grief," I said, wondering if there was an acceptable spot in Chicago for twenty dollars a head that would pass muster with Susan and Alejandro. Probably not. No, definitely not. "I'll call you back. I need to figure this out."

"I see," she said. "If you need suggestions just let me know."

Was there a trace of snark in her voice, or stress?

"I might. Thanks."

My anxiety was mushrooming. I wasn't sleeping well. There was no way I could match her tit for tat without mortgaging the farm, and it wasn't mine to mortgage. Well, damn it all, I just didn't have resources for this. I'd never felt poor until that moment. Soon Susan Kennedy Cambria and I were going to have an awkward discussion I already dreaded.

So, on Thanksgiving morning, I ran the issue by Kathy and Floyd just to help me think it through. I called Floyd first.

"Susie Q's so full of herself it's ridiculous," he said. "She witnessed our life of luxury."

"Exactly," I said as I watched Gus the cat stroll across the kitchen counter. "Come here, cat." I picked him up with my free arm and he was draped across my arm and hip like a very furry tote bag.

"Maybe there's an Elks Club or a catering hall out there somewhere?"

"Oh, right. I can just see Susan and Alejandro mixing and mingling at a VFW. Floyd, what am I going to do?"

I walked Gus to the back door and put him outside on the back porch, shooing him away. Cat hair and food were a bad mix.

"I don't know, but I know what you're not going to do. You're not throwing a dinner for that many people. Tell her to forget it. Ain't happening."

Easy for him to say.

"What time you coming up to the house?"

"As soon as I can get a shower. The sanctity of my home has been violated by a bunch of female interlopers from Atlanta."

I knew that my brother liked nothing better than a house filled with women he could flirt with.

"Yeah, okay. I'm sure you're miserable, Romeo. I'll see you later."

I called Kathy.

"Happy Thanksgiving!" I said and told her the story.

Kathy said, "She's insane to even *think* it's okay to put that kind of burden on you. It would be like having a second wedding! Who does that?"

"MOB-zilla," I said.

"Call Alden," she said. "Ask him to duplicate the engagement party. That might have been the best barbecue in the history of barbecues."

"I can't call Alden."

"Why? What happened?"

"He wanted to take me to his niece's wedding and I declined. I just want us to be friends, you know? Besides, I don't feel that way about him," I said.

"If you say so. Methinks thou dost . . .'," Kathy said, using the Bard's line of *protest too much* that let me know she didn't believe me. "Well then, why don't you ask Floyd to cook us another pig."

"I can't see Floyd hauling a pig halfway across the country, can you?"

"Probably not," she said. "Let me give this some thought."

We hung up and I shifted my focus back to the remaining onions and the brussels sprouts. The brussels sprouts were always my job to prepare because Virnell said so.

"You have the patience to hull out the bottoms. I don't."

Who did she think she was kidding? She could hull a sprout with the best of them. I mean, who taught me to prepare them in the first place? The real reason I got the job was that her arthritis made it too painful for her to pop the sprouts from the stalk and then peel back the tiny leaves, never mind cutting away the bitter part inside the stems. It was a tedious job. I resharpened the paring knife and got back to work.

When I was just about elbow deep in the tough outer leaves, Pop came into the room, opened the refrigerator, and took out the glass pitcher of iced tea.

"Happy Thanksgiving, ladies! How's our dinner coming?"

"Coming along, baby boy," my mother said and winked at him.

There was a pitcher of freshly made iced tea in our fridge twelve months a year. He poured himself a glass and plunked a few ice cubes in it to further cool and dilute it.

"Who's playing today, Pop?" I asked.

"The Vikings. They're playing the Lions. And Dallas is going to slaughter Washington. I've got a full day ahead of me. Think I could get a sandwich?"

"We're pretty well occupied in here," my mother said. "Think you could make it yourself?"

My mother rarely turned down any request from Pop, but we were actually working at full capacity. We still had to make dressing, gravy, and pies.

"Sounds like a hectic day for sure," I said. "But, Pop, I can scramble you an egg. How's that?"

"Humph," he said, "I think I'll just eat a banana."

He took one from the fruit bowl on the table and sailed out toward the living room.

"There's an elephant in the room," Mom said.

I didn't answer her. My mother had been quietly eavesdropping on my conversations with Floyd and Kathy while she innocently peeled and chopped rutabagas. She swooped a cutting board filled with them into a pot with the blunt side of her knife, covered them with water, and added a tablespoon of salt and a smoked ham hock. She turned on the burner.

"Nobody wants my opinion anymore," she said, rinsing her hands.

Oh, brother, I thought.

"Okay, Miss Virnell," I said. "Lay it on me, sister."

She dried her hands, picked up the potato peeler, and began

earnestly scraping the skin of a yam away, beginning another pile of scraps to compost.

"Don't call me that. You're supposed to give a rehearsal party the night before the wedding. Is that right?"

"Yes. And Susan wants to invite all of her out-of-town guests in addition to the actual wedding party members. Like two hundred mouths to feed."

"Tell her no. Plain and simple."

"You don't understand, Momma. I can't just do that."

She slammed her potato peeler on the cutting board. I flinched in surprise. Virnell did not go around slamming things.

"You know, up until now, I haven't said anything. I've just been watching and keeping my thoughts to myself. But that woman's as crazy as a low-flying loon."

"Well, she certainly has no problem with being extravagant with my wallet," I said.

"Amen to that. You listen to me, Diane. You just tell her that you are dee-lighted to pay for the wedding party's dinner. And you might even ask her for ideas of where to have the dinner take place, which would give you a better sense of her expectations. But if she wants to have every Tom, Dick, and Harry attend? *She's* going to have to foot the bill for that. Good gravy! What's the matter with people? I've never heard of such a thing in my life!"

"Nobody has good sense anymore," I said.

"Maybe money grows on peach trees in Chicago, but it sure doesn't do that here! Don't you let this woman push you around."

"You're right, of course."

"I know I'm right. I'm your mother. Now, please get the dark brown sugar from the pantry. And two sticks of butter from the fridge."

"Sure." I put them on the counter next to her. "But do you understand why I might be uncomfortable to have that conversation?"

"Yes, because you're a proud woman. This woman makes you feel po'bucka and I don't like it. It's a kind of pushy bullying. Where would she be without her husband's money? And where'd she come from anyway? Buckingham Palace? I seriously doubt it." An evil little smile crept across her face and I smiled with her.

"Oh, who knows? And who cares? Maybe she grew up eating cat food in a tent."

"She probably did. Law, that woman has some high opinion of herself, doesn't she?"

"Yes, she does. I just love you, Miss Virnell. You always know how to put your finger on the crux of things, don't you?"

"Sometimes I'm better at it than others. Want to baste my bird for me? And stop calling me that!"

"Sure. What time are we going to sit down?" I opened the oven door and peered inside.

Our twenty-pound turkey laced the air with the perfume of heaven. I took the saucepan of melted butter and lemon and painted it all over the bird. I loved it that she thought of the turkey as hers and the meal as hers. It was probably a good thing psychologically for her to feel the emotional ownership of the holiday when in fact I would wind up doing

75 percent of the work. Someday, and it would come too soon, I'd be alone in the kitchen making holiday meals, and life without her was unimaginable. But who would I be cooking for?

"We can go to the table when the pies are in the oven and the bird's resting. Probably around four. Does that suit you?" Mom said.

"That suits me just fine. Gosh, there's nothing like Thanksgiving."

"It's my favorite holiday too. Be sure the table is set for eight."

"Eight? Who's coming?"

"Besides Pop and me, we've got you and Floyd, BJ, and her three girlfriends."

"Right. Which china do you want to use? The Spode?"

"Yes, yes, yes! Let's use my good Spode. I meant to ask Floyd to bring it down, but it slipped my mind every time I saw him. And by the way, you should've gone to the wedding with Alden."

I ignored that last remark.

"I'll get it," I said. "No problem."

On one wall around the top of the kitchen, where space allowed, were hung a few cabinets that reached the ceiling. That's where we kept things we used less often — the waffle iron, large vases, a chafing dish, a fondue pot, small appliances we intended to fix and never did, and the dishes we used for the holidays. They were neatly stacked in soft quilted containers that zipped to close. There were carefully placed paper towels in between each plate, soup bowl, and saucer to minimize the possibility of breakage. Unpacking them always brought back ghosts of holidays long gone, like when Fred was a little boy, saving his money all year to buy his grandmother a dessert plate for her birthday or Christmas. The pattern, called Woodland by Spode, was lovingly collected by my mother from the early nineties, one cup and saucer at a time, until she had twelve place settings, some serving bowls and platters, and, the greatest treasure of her collection, the soup tureen and its cover.

I took the stepladder and positioned it below the cabinet.

"Let me help you," she said. "Just hand them to me. Careful! One container at a time."

"Of course! You know, if you'd like, I can cut some magnolia leaves for the tureen. It would make a pretty centerpiece with some holly."

"Wonderful idea! There's no soup until we pick the bird clean, maybe Sunday night."

There was no *maybe* about it. That was how Thanksgiving always went at our house. Roasted turkey on Thanksgiving Thursday with all the trimmings, turkey tetrazzini or something like it on Friday, a break from fowl on Saturday because someone usually had an oyster roast, but on Sunday night? Here came turkey soup. Every single year for as long as I could remember.

When all the containers had been handed down and placed on the table, she began to unpack them. I refilled the containers with everyday dishes, as I did each year. I put them back in the cabinet and my mother became wistful.

"You know, Pop thought it was crazy for a woman as old

as I was to start a new collection of china when I did, but I think you should never be too old to have a little dream. These dishes just make me so happy to see them. It's like greeting old friends."

I smiled to myself then, placed the last of the quilted sacks up high, flipped the latch on the cabinet door, and climbed down. I slipped the folding stepladder into the sliver of space between the refrigerator and the counter and washed my hands. They smelled like cabbage and onions.

"When we were growing up, Floyd and I used to say our dishes were Chinese – Ding Dynasty. Do you remember that?"

"How could I forget my sassy-mouth children's opinions? These days I wait for my monthly coupon from Bed Bath & Beyond and I can buy all the white plates I want for just about the cost of a Happy Meal at McDonald's! And somehow we *still* have chipped plates."

"The chipped will always be among us," I said. "It's in the Bible."

"John chapter twelve, verse eight, *the poor will always be among you.* Don't blaspheme in my kitchen."

"Oh, heavens! Now, come on, Miss Virnell, even the Lord himself had a sense of humor."

"Not that I recall. But if you have any intention whatsoever of seeing me in heaven one day, you'd better not be blasphemous now! And don't call me that."

There were a few areas in which Miss Virnell did not play around.

"I'll be back in a few and then I'll set the table," I said, changing the subject. "The brussels sprouts are ready to go in the pot."

Of course, we had only one oven in the house, so vegetables had to be steamed or boiled or sautéed on the stove top. The dressing would be in two pink Pyrex dishes from the sixties we used for meat loaf, wrapped tightly in foil and squeezed in on either side of the turkey. Maybe someday one of those shows on HGTV would want to do a farmhouse kitchen makeover for free and I'd give them the keys to our house.

I rummaged around the junk drawer where we kept assorted things such as batteries, pens, thumbtacks, tape, and other paraphernalia and slipped the garden clippers into the pocket of my apron. Outside I had my choice of low-hanging magnolia branches to snip, and minutes later I was armed with holly and magnolia aplenty for the task.

Back inside, I took everything off the dining table and added two leaves. Then I covered it with a protective cloth and finally my mother's white damask cloth that saw the light of day only a few times each year. I spread it out and smoothed it flat with the palms of my hands. Then I went to my mother's bedroom and took two folding chairs from behind her bedroom door to give us enough seating.

"Mom? Are we using cloth napkins?" I knew the answer before I heard it. I was back in the kitchen to fill the tureen with an inch or two of water.

"I ironed them last week. They're laid out flat on Fred's bed."

Men, at least the ones in my life, didn't understand the

amount of work and planning that went into holiday productions. There were so many things that had to be done ahead of the day itself, like ironing linens and polishing the silver. Earlier in the week I'd made a double recipe of cranberry sauce and turkey stock to make gravy. Cubes of bread for the dressing were spread over cookie sheets, and turned over and over to make them evenly stale. Piecrust was made and frozen, as were biscuits and a special breakfast casserole we always had the morning after. Advance preparation made the day itself tolerable instead of a nearly impossible task.

I placed the tureen in the middle of the table and stood back. I'd cut the magnolia branches short so that they made kind of a collar around the lip of it. Then I took two longer pieces of holly and stood them in the center. They were airy and the red berries were pretty, but my thought was that we should be able to see each other across the table. I put the plates in place, folded the napkins in triangles and placed them in the center of the plates. The table looked beautiful. Each of us would discover, as we did each year when we lifted our napkins, whether or not we had the turkey, the pheasant, or the hunting dog plate. Fred always wanted the dog plate. I wondered then if he would ever want to have these dishes, then remembered that Shelby had chosen a French pattern from Limoges. Our Spode would probably not impress her. Or her mother. Oh, who cared?

My mother's flatware had belonged to her grandmother of many generations ago, having escaped the Civil War by being buried in a barrel behind the barn. Every southern family I had ever known had a story like that. It was just as likely that years ago someone bought it at an estate sale. But beside the land we farmed, her silver was still our most valuable possession, although at this point it was showing signs of wear. The edges of the spoons were worn thin from use and some of the knives were a little loose in their handles. But I loved it anyway, maybe more because of its age. Placing the forks and knives around the table always gave me a moment of pause. This was the thing about family heirlooms: humble or grand, they made the past alive again. Whether it was a spoon or a locket, a shoehorn or an old Bible, when I held these objects in my hands, I could imagine my great-great-grandparents or someone's ancestors going about their day. And I loved the thought of them setting the table for Thanksgiving, just as I was now.

Somewhere in the house there were some photographs of my grandparents on a picnic. And we had a framed photograph of them taken on the day of their wedding. Her youthful face and tiny size always surprised me. She had lived well into her nineties, and of course I had hopes that my mother would as well. It may help to watch your diet and to get plenty of exercise, but if you ask me, longevity is in the genes.

At last all the guests had assembled in the living room, cheering on the team of their choice. The table was set, the turkey was resting, and the pies were in the oven. This year we had apple and pumpkin. We'd had a bumper crop of pecans this year, and we'd sold as many pecan pies on the farm stand as we had the time to bake. Miss Virnell and I agreed that we couldn't look at another pecan for a while. So apple and pumpkin it was. And if the roasting turkey had smelled divine, it was completely eclipsed by baking apples, pumpkin, and sugar. We were going to have a feast!

I was on my way to tell Pop, Floyd, and the ladies to come to the table at last. As I reached the living room I saw my father falling to the floor. He had been holding his head.

"No!" I screamed so loudly that I scared everyone.

"Call 911!" Floyd said. "He's not breathing!"

BJ dialed 911 on her cell phone and gave the operator our address, begging them to hurry. Then she ran outside with her friends to flag down the ambulance.

My mother flew by me and dropped to the floor beside Pop. She began to shake as it dawned on her that he might be dead. Floyd had his hand, checking for a pulse.

"There's a pulse, but it's very faint," he said.

My mother leaned over my father and whispered something to him that I couldn't hear.

"Come on, Momma, let's get up now," Floyd said.

"No," she said quietly but firmly, "I'm not leaving him and he's not leaving me."

"I wish I had a normal family," Shelby said.

"Normal is pretty boring," Fred replied.

CHAPTER 12

chicago thanksgiving— shelby

My parents made a special point to say Frederick was invited to join us for Thanksgiving dinner at the Union League Club. Duh. He was my fiancé. We were almost married. What was the alternative? My mother's cooking? *We're all gonna die!* Quinoa and tofu? For real. She only liked fad food. My poor father has endured a paleo kick, an only-organic-from-within-a-fifty-mile-radius stint, a raw-only stage, raw juicing, cold-pressed juices, Mediterranean only, fish and veggies only, eating within twelve hours, and the Dalai Lama's diet. All delivered. I rest my case. How she found out what the Dalai Lama eats is anyone's guess. She probably called him up. She probably had his cell phone number. I mean, I love her to death, but . . .

"Isn't this a gorgeous buffet?" Mother said to me and asked the waiter for a small slice of white meat turkey. "No gravy. And no dressing." The waiter put it on her plate. "Thank you and Happy Thanksgiving to you!"

"Yep. It's great," I said, and I was pretty sure she didn't hear me. I let the same waiter load up my plate with turkey, a mound of dressing, and a pool of gravy.

"And Frederick, we're so, so delighted you could join us!"

"Thank you, Mrs. Cambria," he said. "Um, I'd like a drumstick and all this other stuff too. Thanks. Thanks a lot. Gravy? Oh, sure, yes. Thank you."

"I like a man who knows what he wants," Dad said. He asked for a drumstick too.

We passed down the line helping ourselves to vegetables and other side dishes, then went to our table.

One of these years I'd learn to cook a Thanksgiving meal, but this wasn't the year. With the wedding snowballing into complete lunacy thanks to my mother's nearly psychotic need to outdo all the weddings given by her friends? Let me bring you up-to-date. She was turning Frederick and me into wrecks. And she was being very prissy with Frederick's mother, which I didn't like. And this butterfly thing she was so intent on doing? It was just wrong. Butterflies were endangered, and throwing twenty thousand of them to the wind was just not going to be okay.

Also, I didn't really need or want a Vera Wang wedding dress, and she didn't need Karl Lagerfeld to whip up a custom gown for her. Last week, I told her my bridesmaids' dresses were coming from J.Crew and she hyperventilated. I had to make her to breathe in a brown paper bag while I found her Ativan. She's such a label snob. But I won that battle because the J.Crew dresses were super cute. They just happened to be a bargain. We had chosen a beautiful shade of apple green. The dresses had three different necklines and they were a short length. I didn't tell anyone that stupid lie that they could wear them again. I told them that I bought one, and the next time we got together we'd all wear them and drink champagne and watch sappy movies or something. Or maybe we'd wear them to one another's children's baptisms, if we ever stopped obsessing about work long enough to have kids at all. Or maybe we'd have a bonfire. Nearly all of my friends were getting married. Anyway, I think it was the only battle I'd won so far. On a side note, when she saw the tattoos that were going to show on two of my bridesmaids, she was going to shriek. I'd thought about steering those two, who were roommates at Northwestern, into the styles that covered their ink, and then I said to heck with that. I loved them for who they were, not for how they might fit into my mother's vision of a reenactment of Kate Middleton's wedding.

Anyway, something had to be said to stop her. She was out of control. We sat and began our meal with a toast.

Dad said, "Happy Thanksgiving, everyone! Happy Thanksgiving!"

"Mom? Can we talk about the wedding for a moment?"

"For a change?" Frederick said.

It was true. We talked about the wedding so much that

I wondered what we'd talk about when it was over. Dad laughed and pointed his finger at Frederick, indicating his agreement. I kicked Frederick under the table.

"Of course!" Mother said. "What's on your mind, sweetie?"

"Well, I looked up the butterfly source on the Internet. Do you realize you're spending forty thousand dollars on butterflies and that doesn't include shipping? And do you know that their numbers are endangered? This is just wrong."

"Susan!" Dad choked, and Frederick gave him his glass of water. Then Mom gave Dad some massive eyeball and he cowered. Sort of. "It just seems like a lot to me. Isn't that a lot to spend on something that's gone in an instant?"

"I could do doves," my mother said.

"Yes, but then they'll drop poop on all the guests," Dad said.

"I hadn't thought about that. That would be terrible," she said. "Frederick? What do you think?"

"Well, Mrs. Cambria, where I come from, we eat doves."

"Dear God," she said, thoroughly horrified. I imagined she envisioned every southern guest pulling out a shotgun and firing. I could read her like a book.

"They make a good stew," Frederick said.

Frederick's phone was flashing light and vibrating like mad.

"You can't answer it, Frederick," I said. "Strictly against club rules."

"It's my uncle Floyd. He never calls. I should take this."

"Just step out onto the terrace," Dad said, turning to show Frederick where the door was.

"Give him my—I mean, *our* best," my mother said.

I knew what she meant. She was still crushing on Uncle Floyd. God, she was so annoying.

"I'll be right back," he said.

For the few minutes Frederick was gone, my mother rattled on and on about who was doing the flowers and how many musicians from the Chicago Symphony Orchestra were playing during the ceremony. I felt my chest constricting. I couldn't swallow. Meanwhile, Dad was savoring every bite of his dinner. Clearly, he had fine-tuned the ability to put his mind elsewhere. In his head he was probably walking the beaches in Saint-Tropez staring at topless young girls from behind his Oliver Peoples sunglasses. Oh, Dad. I'm so onto you.

A few minutes later, Frederick returned. Every bit of color had drained from his face.

"Babe? What's the matter?"

"It's my grandfather. He's dead."

"'He's in a better place.' They can kiss my better place!"
Virnell said.

"They mean well," Diane said.

CHAPTER 13

burying pop

We were in a fog of grief. My mother was so stunned by Pop's sudden death, she had to go to bed. I had never seen her do that in my entire life. How could this be? She was the unflappable Virnell, reliable in a foxhole, victorious on the battlefield. Always. Any form of Collapsing Camille was not in her vocabulary. Nonetheless, the ambulance that took Pop's body away was hardly out of the driveway before my poor mother slipped off her sensible shoes and went to bed in her Thanksgiving dress with her apron still tied around her neck and waist. She did not weep or even shed one single tear.

Floyd, BJ, and her friends cleaned up our uneaten Thanksgiving meal and I covered my mother up with the quilt she kept folded on the foot of her bed.

"Sit with me a little while," she said.

"Are you okay? Can I get you anything? Water?"

"No. I'm okay for right now. I just feel, I don't know, like someone pulled the plug on me."

"That's understandable. I'm reeling myself. What a terrible shock."

"Yes. It was. Poor thing. I should've made him that sandwich."

I took her hand in mine and held it.

"No guilt-tripping allowed. You waited on him hand and foot for decades," I said. "He was a wonderful man and a wonderful father."

Suddenly I felt I was mothering my mother instead of my mother mothering me. After all, I'd just lost my father.

"And husband. He's the only man I ever loved. My goodness, we were married longer than you've been alive."

"Well, that's good to know, you know, for the sake of propriety and all that."

She smiled a little. Gus the cat padded in quietly and hopped up on the bed, curling up into a ball. She scratched him behind the ears with her free hand. We were quiet for a few minutes. I could see her mind time-traveling and I imagined she was remembering special times with him, probably when they were young. And then her brow wrinkled and I was pretty sure she was reliving his last moments.

"You know," she said, "I knew he would go before me because of his heart. I just didn't think it would be today."

"Me too." I stood up and pulled down her shades. Maybe a darkened room would help her rest. The room was cool but comfortably so. "People say when someone dies suddenly it's terrible for the survivors. And they say a long illness is easier for the family."

"What? It's easier to watch your loved one suffer and waste away? That's nonsense."

"I agree. And either way you're still going to grieve."

"Amen," she said and sighed hard, expelling her heartbreak in a long whoosh. "Suddenly I'm very tired."

"Would you like to get a little shut-eye? This is probably the last peace and quiet you'll get for a while."

"Wake me in an hour. I just need to calm myself down."

"I can ask BJ if she's got something to help you relax. Lord knows, her medicine cabinet is a pharmacy." I hoped that zinger at BJ's expense would lighten the pall that was creeping in through the walls.

"Absolutely not." She gave me a stern look. "What were you doing in her medicine cabinet?"

"I was just kidding, Mom. I couldn't care less about what she takes or doesn't take." I got up and went to the door. "I'll tickle your foot in an hour."

In fact, it was sort of remarkable that BJ was still around.

The kitchen was clean. Floyd was there alone, sitting at the table drinking a beer, surrounded by endless casserole dishes and pie plates, all wrapped like mummies in plastic wrap or encased in aluminum foil.

"The fridge is full," he said flatly.

"You okay?" I gave him a pat and a little squeeze on his shoulder.

"I guess I'm okay. How's Mom?"

"Trying to snooze. I think she's in shock."

"Yeah, that's going around. I called Fred and told him. He and Shelby are getting on a plane as soon as they can."

"Thanks for doing that. I knew he'd prefer to get that kind of news from you. How'd he take it?"

"Matter-of-factly. There'll be plenty of time to get upset."

I opened the refrigerator door and scrutinized the inside. I started pulling out unopened cans and bottles and putting them on the table.

"Well, for one thing, we don't have to chill all this beer at one time. It's not Super Bowl Sunday. And we can throw out the iced tea. It takes five minutes to make more. We don't need all these Diet Cokes to be in here either."

"Show 'em who's boss, Lady Di."

"Do we really need three bottles of ketchup? Hand me the casseroles, wise guy."

Getting all the food into the refrigerator was important because I didn't want the holiday meal to go to waste. And small task that it was, busywork was good. It was the beginning of many decisions that would have to be made rather quickly. I sliced all the meat from the turkey, wrapped it up, and put the carcass in the freezer. There was a good chance we wouldn't be making soup anytime soon. Then I consolidated condiments and stacked casseroles until the table was empty and the refrigerator was full.

"Hey, Floyd? Would you go wake up Mom? She wanted to get up now."

"Sure."

My phone rang. It was my friend Kathy. "I don't want to sound like Nosy Nellie, but I heard there was an ambulance at your house a couple of hours ago. Is everything all right?"

"No, Kathy. No, everything's not okay." I told her what happened.

"Oh, I am so sorry," she said. "What can I do?"

"I think we're okay for the moment. But thanks."

"If you need bedrooms, you know I've got six extra ones."

"Thanks. I might take you up on that."

Kathy had inherited her parents' home, a rambling but imposing old plantation with a farmhouse the same age as ours. With columns across the front, hers was much more impressive.

"It's not a problem, not even one little bit. How are you doing? And Miss Virnell?"

"It hasn't sunk in yet."

"I understand. Let me know if . . ."

But there was really nothing anyone could do besides say they were sorry for our loss. Bringing us food would've been pointless. It was Thanksgiving and every home in the country was overstocked. Besides, we had no appetite.

I made a pot of coffee. When Mom came into the kitchen I poured her a cup. Floyd followed and I poured him a mug as well. I put the creamer on the table.

"We should probably have a bit of a discussion. Do we know where Dad's will might be?"

"Yes," she said. "There's a shoebox labeled 'important

papers.' We keep things in one spot in case we have to run from a hurricane. It's on the top shelf in his chifforobe."

Our house was so old, it didn't have closets. Every bedroom had at least one armoire and a chest of drawers or it had a chifforobe with hanging space in addition to drawers, or both.

"I'll get it."

I hurried to her bedroom, found the box, and returned to the kitchen. Mom opened it and flipped through the papers.

"It's not here," she said. "I told him to leave it in the shoebox where it belonged."

"Pop didn't take direction well," Floyd said. "Maybe I'll have some pie after all."

He cut himself a wedge of pumpkin pie and put it on a plate.

"We have a lot of decisions to make," I said. "Do we know if he wanted to be cremated or buried?"

"Cremated," Mom said. "And he wanted his ashes spread here on this land in the peach grove."

"Okay, so I can tell the funeral home that," I said.

"I thought Pop wanted to be buried, not cremated, near the edges of the peach grove," Floyd said.

"When did he tell you that?" Mom said.

"Not too terribly long ago," Floyd said. "Maybe last year or the year before. He said cemetery plots were too expensive. By the way, the pie's good. Y'all want a slice?"

"No thanks. Even if he didn't say that, it's still true," Mom said. "Plots cost a small fortune. I'm pretty sure he wanted to be cremated."

"That's a pretty big decision to make without being a hundred percent sure." Floyd said.

"No pie for me, thanks," I said. "Well, without a will, we'd be winging it. I think we should make an effort to find the will."

"Fine. Let's look around, but I'm positive he wanted to be cremated," Mom said. "Of course, I would honor his wishes to go in the ground, but the last thing I need to see is my husband embalmed, lying there in a casket as dead as Kelsey's cow, while everyone mumbles about how good he looks. No thank you."

"You're certain?" Floyd asked.

"One hundred percent," Mom said.

"All right then," Floyd said.

Mom's waffling on Dad's final wishes was unsettling, but I was truly relieved that Dad wanted to be cremated. Wakes with open caskets were so horribly real and surreal at the same time. A corpse was as dead a thing as can be, and there was no confusing it with the spirit that once resided within. It was your loved one. It was not your loved one. And depending on the cause of death and how prolonged the illness was, you could be facing something rather haunting and grotesque that might be hard to forget. Or not. In any and all cases, I was not even remotely curious about dead bodies. Apparently, my mother felt the same way. Hallelujah.

The to-do list was growing. An obituary had to be written, calls had to be made. Would there be a religious service with a eulogy? Readings? Pop wasn't so religious. He was more than an Easter and Christmas kind of churchgoer, but not a regular one, unless Mom asked.

Still, so many questions had to be answered. What music

would Pop have wanted at a service, if there was to be one? Probably "Amazing Grace" and "How Great Thou Art," we decided. Who would put together a printed program? Maybe the church? Would we like to display photographs? Which ones? Did we know which prayer we'd like on his remembrance card? So many details. Something was bound to be overlooked. Someone was bound to be forgotten.

By Saturday, the obituary ran in the *Post and Courier*, Pop was cremated, and we had a plan in place. The service would take place at our church, Hibben United Methodist Church on Monday evening at six. This was more practical for friends who worked during the day and because there was to be no burial. Floyd's daughter Sophie had flown in from Seattle with someone who appeared to be her very serious other, Michael Lawrence Runey III, who stated assertively that he wouldn't let Sophie go through this funeral alone because they were so close. Ann, who arrived straight from Morristown, New Jersey, whispered to me that she had suspicions about those kinds of dramatic proclamations. I thought, Well, maybe he's just a fawner who feels the need to announce himself like a visiting dignitary. Even Stephanie came from her commune in Vermont, about which I was anxious for details, as living on a commune was the raciest thing anyone in our family had ever done. Well, to my knowledge, anyway. Of course, Fred was there, having flown in on Friday morning. Shelby was arriving later in the day.

So, as family funerals tend to become reunions, all the Thanksgiving food was warmed up and devoured, and my father was toasted long into the night. The tone was naturally

somber, but the warmth and delight we all felt at being together under one roof could not be suppressed.

"Pop would be so happy to see us all together," Mom said.
"I'm so happy all y'all came."

"All y'all?" Shelby said with a barely suppressed snicker.

Everyone ignored her, and rightfully so.

"We speak southern here," Fred said with a quiet smile,
forgiving her rudeness.

"He was a great man," my mother said, oblivious to Shelby's
remark. "Loved by so many."

"Yes, he sure was," Fred said.

"I'm sorry I never knew him," Michael Lawrence Runey III
said.

"You would've loved him. Everyone did," Sophie said.

By that time, we had pushed back from the crowded table
and we were wrapping up dessert.

"The phone rang off the hook all day," I said. "I hope the
church is big enough."

"We have enough casseroles to feed half of Mount Pleasant," Ann said.

"Now our refrigerator is jammed too," BJ said.

"And about ten bricks of meat loaf," Stephanie said. "Too
bad I don't eat red meat."

"Who brings meat loaf as a condolence?" Sophie said.
"That's super weird."

Everyone nodded, as meat loaf did seem a bit odd. Ham?
Fine. Pound cake? Fine. Meat loaf? Publix must've had a fire
sale on chopped meat.

"What? Steph! No more hamburgers? You used to be the

hamburger queen!" Ann said, teasing her little sister. "The next thing I know you'll say you can't live without quinoa and kale."

"Keen-what?" Floyd said.

Stephanie gave a sly look to everyone around the table as if quinoa and kale were the keys to living forever. "Only if it's organic," she said.

"Kale's nasty," Fred said. "Tastes metallic."

"Gimme a mess of collards any day of the week," Floyd said. "And a bottle of Texas Pete."

"Collards are good eating," I said. "Kale is tolerable if it's cooked with fatback. But I want to hear about living on a commune. What's it like?"

"It's like a kibbutz, I guess," Stephanie said. "We share the work, the living space, and whatever we earn."

"Just like we do," I said.

"Yeah. It's okay, I guess. But it's getting old. You know, what appeals to you at one age doesn't hold the same appeal as you get older."

"Good grief! You're talking like you're as old as Methuselah," Mom said.

"You're a mere twenty-three," Fred said.

"No love life, huh?" BJ said.

"Right," Stephanie said and sighed.

"So, Dad?" Ann asked. "Is BJ a mind reader?"

"Only if the mind is organic," BJ said.

"So what's your next move?" I asked Stephanie.

"I don't know. I mean, I love making goat cheese and I even love the silly goats. So I don't know. I'm just thinking about it."

"You love *goats*?" Shelby said, incredulously. And she laughed. Alone. "You're kidding, right?"

"No, not really," Stephanie answered and bit her lip, embarrassed.

If I could've read Stephanie's mind I would've said she was thinking Shelby was a materialistic little pain in the neck. I was thinking Miss Shelby had a few lessons to learn. Like, you never laugh in the face of your own family members. It's not nice.

"Awesome," Fred said to save the moment.

"Well, you can always come home," Floyd said. "But you won't find any keen-wah on the table."

By the time we got to Monday, we would be exhausted from all the attention and from just the sheer energy it took to have such a full house of people. It was especially wonderful to see Floyd with his daughters and for Fred to be with them too. Shelby had taken a real shine to Sophie, probably because she understood the relevance of Starbucks, which was a very cool brand to their generation. And I think Sophie's personality was more in line with Shelby's. I heard Sophie promise Fred and Shelby that she'd come to their wedding. Of course Ann and Stephanie said they planned to be there too.

"We need things to celebrate," Ann said and we all agreed.

With Pop gone, and my mother probably close to the trapdoor, I was soon to be the eldest. Now Floyd would be the old man. And we would be the last generation of South Carolina farmers in our family. We really should consider selling the land, after our mother went to heaven, of course. Not the house and the farm stand, but the peach groves and the other acres. Floyd had always talked about putting up a house near the creek. But maybe that piece of land was worth more than we thought because of its access to water. Neither one of us was getting any younger,.

Maybe Stephanie? I wondered if she had the farming gene. Had she not run away to Vermont to do nearly exactly what we did here? But she was already tired of it. Certainly Fred and Shelby had no intentions of living here.

Sophie? She worked for Starbucks, but what she did was so complicated I couldn't get a handle on it. I knew she traveled around the world for research and development, eating croissants in France and waffles in Belgium, but how did that impact a coffee shop business? Well, she seemed happy with her strange boyfriend and she was well dressed, so she wasn't going broke.

"I'm so proud of you," I said to her on the way to the funeral home that afternoon.

"Oh, thanks, Aunt Diane," she said.

"So, are you going to marry Michael Lawrence Runey III?"

"Probably not," she said.

"Why not?"

"Oh, Aunt Diane, he works for me."

I searched her face and then I realized what she meant.

"Then why did he come?"

"He always wanted to see Charleston. Isn't Charleston like the number-one tourist destination in the world?"

"I suppose it is!"

But what did that say about Sophie? Given the current

climate of charges of sexual misconduct, I hoped there was nothing going on between them that Sophie instigated. Not that it was any of my business, I told myself, and mentally took a vow not to ask her about it.

We met with the funeral director at the funeral home to have a moment to contemplate Pop's ashes and to have a brief private service. The plan was that they would drive us to the church in their limos. We would have the service. Afterward, there would be a reception in the library with light refreshments.

As we gathered in the viewing room to say a few prayers with Pastor Walters from church, the strangest thing happened. Ann and Stephanie threw their arms around Mom and then Floyd. Sophie hugged Mom and then me. Pretty soon everyone was hugging someone and the overdue tears began to flow. Fred and Shelby hugged each other, and for the first time since he was a little boy, Fred wept. Seeing this, Floyd went to Fred and put his arms around him.

Everyone except Shelby, BJ, and Michael Lawrence Runey III had something to say about how wonderful it was to be home and with one another, how they had nearly forgotten what it felt like to be so loved, and how much they would miss Pop. And when Mom said that they should visit more often, everyone promised they'd do a better job of staying in touch.

"Oh, I know you all have big lives, far away from here," Mom said, "but it's important to know where you still belong."

"I think what Mom means is that you are still loved and

missed by us every day that you're not here," I said, passing a box of tissues around.

"That's right," Floyd said. "The door may not be at the Ritz, but it's always open."

Somehow Pastor Walters led us through the Lord's Prayer and offered a reading from the Book of Psalms. When our private service was ended, we left the room and made our way to the waiting cars. The funeral director would deliver Pop's ashes to the church in another car and place them on a special table at the end of the center aisle in the sanctuary.

The service was lovely. My father would have been thrilled to know that so many of his customers and old friends took the time to come. The music was beautiful too. When it was all over we made our way to the library for coffee and cookies. The room was crowded and humid. Mom looked flushed.

"Do you want to sit down?" I said.

"Yes, here, take my purse," she said. "Isn't it too warm in here? Can we open a window?"

"I'll take care of it," Floyd said, and adjusted the thermostat.

I looked up into the face of Alden. He was coming over to offer his sympathies. He was with a woman. A very pretty woman who was a few years younger than I was, dressed very fashionably, with a good haircut.

"Hello, Diane," he said. "I'm so sorry about Pop. Miss Virnell? I'm so sorry for your loss."

I just stared at him. Maybe I mumbled *thank you for coming.* I can't recall.

"Thank you, Alden," Mom said. "And who's your friend?"

"Oh, sorry!" Alden said. "Of course. This is my friend Betsy Beyer. We met at my niece's wedding."

"And the rest is history!" Betsy said, smiling and then becoming serious. "I'm so sorry for your loss."

I wanted to slap her face.

They made more small talk and then walked away. I knew I was going to hear about it from Mom.

"So what?" I said to Mom.

"So you should've gone to the wedding."

"Please," I said as though I didn't care.

"You always want what you can't have, Diane. You've always been that way. You'd better do something, because Betsy Beyer's got her claws sunk in deep."

I did care. I cared a lot. In fact, as the night passed, I could not believe how seeing him with that woman was eating me alive with fury. Was this love? The next morning, as I made so many biscuits and scrambled so many eggs I couldn't count them, I was still furious. As I hugged and kissed each child of ours good-bye, I fumed deep inside. Later on, I was down at the farm stand, as usual, and Floyd came in with crates of potatoes and beets, opened them up, and started filling the bins. Dad's recliner was there in the corner, a reminder that he was gone.

"Morning!" I said. "Do you think we could get Dad's La-Z-Boy out of here? Every time I look at it I want to cry."

"I could, but our mother would probably kill us."

"Why?"

"Because it smells like him and she can sit there and be with him, sort of. I don't know, but my gut tells me it's gotta stay here for a while."

"Whatever you say," I said. "Who am I to disagree with your gut?"

"Well, I've got two other things to tell you," he said.

"Let's hear," I said.

"Number one. BJ said Betsy Beyer told her she graduated from Yale."

"Oh, la-di-damn-da."

"Well, maybe she misheard her. But I doubt it. Number two, I found Dad's will. It was in his toolbox."

"I knew something would be overlooked. I think we looked everywhere else."

"Yep."

Floyd was standing across from me leaning on the counter.

"How'd we do? Did we follow his wishes?

"We did not do so great. Get this. He did not want to be cremated."

What? I felt my temperature rise in horror.

"Oh, no! Now what?"

"Too late to fix that one. We can keep that tidbit between us. The truth would kill Mom."

"Absolutely."

Oh, my God, I thought. Oh, my God.

"Floyd, I can understand losing your reading glasses or forgetting to watch a show you wanted to watch. But a detail like this? I'm sorry."

"I agree. This is bad."

"This is very bad," I said. "We've got to keep an eye on her."

"She's losing it."

"Alejandro? Am I shallow?" Susan said.

"Amorcita? I am afraid so," Alejandro said.

CHAPTER 14

susan's chicago christmas

I just adored Christmas. Really, all of the holidays, but Christmas was so, so special. I loved unwrapping each ornament and remembering where it came from and why we bought these particular transparent hand-blown red glass orbs or those silver mercury glass balls. The beaded glass garlands from Murano and the Jay Strongwater crèche set were so spectacular they gave me chills. My Waterford crystal snowflakes were treasures, each one kept in its own suede bag inside its original box. Every year I tied fresh satin ribbons through their loops, all of them cut at different lengths, and suspended them from the arms of my dining room chandelier. Then my florist intertwined gorgeous roping of specially treated pine and juniper over the tops of my mirrors and anywhere else that seemed like a good idea. And yes, I used a florist to decorate for the holidays. What else was I to do? Roam the streets of Chicago with an ax?

But I digress. By the time the terrace was decorated, wreaths were hung, and the trees were up, even cranky Alejandro couldn't be in a bad mood, and golly, he was cranky lately. All I had to do was put on some Bing Crosby holiday music and light the Rigaud Christmas candles and my darling husband would get sentimental and maudlin. He'd make martinis and tell me about his pitifully lonely school days at Le Rosey and how Christmases spent in St. Moritz at Suvretta House, with his parents and other siblings flown in from Argentina, were the only happiness he ever knew. I'd think, Oh, brother, saved by a chalet and skiing the Swiss Alps, but I kept it to myself. It was his version of "The Little Match Girl." I'd never told him my stories about my horrific childhood, and on that odd day when he might ask me something about it, I'd keep it vague. Vague suited him. Like many powerful men, he loved to talk about himself. In fact, my past was of no interest to him. He cared more about the here and now. My job was to make sure our social life was interesting and to make our home beautiful. That was not a problem for me. But sometimes I felt like an actress.

Our co-op, high in the skies of the Windy City, was filled with the smells and sounds of the season and thousands of twinkling tiny white lights. Best of all, Shelby and Frederick were coming for dinner. They said they had something to discuss with us. And I had swatches to show them for the bespoke linens that were to be made for the wedding reception. The rental companies had some nice things, but they couldn't guarantee their condition. I had one daughter and this was her wedding. It was going to be the wedding of the century if it killed me.

The door opened at seven on the nose. Shelby and Frederick had arrived.

"Mom? Dad? We're here!"

I rushed from the kitchen to greet them. Chef Joho, who once suggested I convert my kitchen into a pantry with a small fridge, warming ovens, and a sink, had prepared a blanquette de veau for us. I'd picked it up earlier in the afternoon. All I had to do was reheat it, and voilà! A gourmet dinner would be served. I'd made a salad and sliced a baguette. And I picked up an Uncle Hansi Cake and some coconut cookies from La Fournette. We never indulged in dessert unless we had dinner guests. Although my daughter and her fiancé were family, I knew Frederick had a sweet tooth. Let's be honest, Frederick's happiness was of paramount importance.

"Hello! Hello! Oh, your cheeks are so cold! Come in and get warm," I said. "Hello, Frederick, sweetheart. Give me your coat."

"Good evening, Mrs. Cambria," he said as he unbuttoned his heavy long coat. "It's freezing all right."

"Ghastly weather," I said. "At least there's no snow."

"It's so cold today. I don't think the thermometer ever got up to twenty!" Shelby took off her hat, gloves, and coat and unwound her scarf. "Brrr! I hate winter."

I took Shelby's hands in mine and rubbed them briskly to get her circulation going.

"Well, we're going to have a lovely dinner and get you both all warmed up!" I said.

Shelby wandered into the living room and looked around. Frederick followed her.

"Wow! Mom! You've outdone yourself! Everything is so pretty!" Shelby said. "How many trees do you have this year?"

"Only four," I said.

"It makes our tree look like Charlie Brown's," Frederick said. "Your home ought to be in a magazine."

"Well, thank you! You know, I do love the holidays. Can I fix you a drink? A glass of red wine? Although I should be making hot toddies."

"I've never had one. But I'm happy with anything," Frederick said. Frederick was always game for something new.

"Where's Dad?" Shelby said.

"In his office on a conference call," I said.

"What else is new?" Shelby said, picking up a bottle of Bordeaux from the wet bar. "Can we open this one?"

"Why not? Frederick?"

"I'll do the honors," he said. "Nothing like French agricultural products."

"I'll get goblets," I said.

I took four red wine balloon glasses to Frederick and remembered that the first time he had wine in his whole life was with us, the night Shelby brought him to dinner at the club. He had surely come a long way from the peach farm. He could pull a cork like a master sommelier.

"Let's pour a glass for Alejandro. I'll take it to him. Maybe it'll entice him to hit the End button if he thinks we're enjoying this without him."

I did just that.

"Is this the '85 Pomerol I left on the wet bar?" Alejandro asked.

"Yes, it sure is."

"I'll be off in two minutes," Alejandro whispered when I handed him the glass.

Works like a charm, I thought, and smiled at him.

"Dinner's ready when you are," I said.

We went to the dining room table with our plates of food and sat in our usual places.

"This looks so yummy," Shelby said.

"I'm starving," Frederick said.

"Bon appétit!" I said and lifted my fork.

I took my first bite and the stew was absolutely delicious. The veal was so tender and moist it almost melted in my mouth.

"This is very good, Susan," Alejandro said.

"Amazing," Shelby said.

"Thank you," I said.

"What is the spice I'm tasting?" Frederick asked.

"There's a trace of nutmeg in it," I said. "Isn't it surprising? I think about nutmeg in eggnog. Or French toast. It's so unusual in a savory dish."

"Unless you go to Africa," Shelby said. "They use all sorts of spices we don't, like turmeric and ginger and a lot of paprika. Oh, and cardamom, star anise, and saffron. By the way, we would like to go on a safari for our honeymoon."

"You would?" I said. This was news to me.

"Why in the world would you want to go on a safari?" Alejandro said.

Shelby said, "Because it's exotic and we want to go someplace neither one of us has been before. We've done a ton of research. Everyone goes to Paris or the Amalfi coast."

Alejandro cleared his throat. "I don't want to burst your little millennial bubble, Shelby, but everyone does not go to Europe on their honeymoon. A lot of people go to places like the Bahamas or other islands or maybe Cancún."

"Oh, Daddy," she said. "If I'm a brat, it's your fault."

"Daddy's right, sweetie. We went to Bermuda on ours. Three nights at the Southampton Princess. Do you remember the disco, Alejandro? It was freezing in there and I was so sunburned . . ."

"But you looked so good in that hot pink maillot," Alejandro said.

"Mom! Dad! Stop it! Gross!" Shelby said.

A burst of laughter caused Frederick to spew a bit of veal, but he managed to catch it in his hand. I pretended not to see it happen. But now he had the dilemma of how to deal with it. Hide the meat in his napkin? Re-eat it? Try to be invisible and put it on the side of his plate? He chose the third option. I saw this in my peripheral vision and silently applauded his choice.

"Anyway, there is something else we need to discuss with you," Shelby said.

"What's that, sweetheart?" I said.

"Well, Frederick and I have decided to move our wedding date up to January."

I gasped and Alejandro put down his fork.

"You can't do that!" I said. "This is my wedding too!"

"Mom, no, it's not! Hear me out. I've contacted the club and cleared a date. We can have up to two hundred people and they'll take care of everything."

"Absolutely not!" I said. "Absolutely not!"

"Shelby?" Alejandro said. "Are you . . . could you be, um, in the family way?"

"Do you mean am I pregnant?" Shelby said with a laugh. "No! I am not pregnant."

"Then why do you want to ruin all my lovely plans for you?" I said. I felt like crying. I felt sick to my stomach. I felt faint.

"Because it's craziness! Mom, you are so over the top, I can't stand it! I don't want a million-dollar wedding. It just isn't working for me. And you cannot really expect Frederick's family to give a rehearsal dinner for so many people. Frederick's mother is having a breakdown."

"I wasn't spending a million dollars," I said. I was spending a lot more than that. "And tell his mother I'll take care of the rehearsal dinner."

"I don't care if it's half a million. It's still too much. It's a waste of money, Mom. Sorry, but it is. We'd rather travel with that money."

"That's not an option," I said. "I didn't give you a budget and say keep what you don't spend."

Alejandro said, "Darling, weddings are ridiculous. This is a bit like buying a Rolls-Royce with every custom upgrade under the sun, driving it around for one night, and then pushing it off a cliff. I agree with Shelby. This whole thing is out of control."

"*You* would turn on me this way? Alejandro! I cannot believe my ears!"

"Mrs. Cambria? May I say something?"

"No, you may not, Frederick. I am a little bit upset right now and I think I need to lie down. I've been going to weddings and sending extravagant gifts for the last thirty years and now I'm going to have mine. This wedding is not just about you, Shelby. You are not going to take this away from me. Excuse me."

I stood and left them all at the dining room table. I looked in my bathroom medicine cabinet, which was nicely stocked with antianxiety meds. What was the right drug to take so I wouldn't kill myself or anyone else? Xanax? Valium? Ativan? I decided Xanax would take me to a better place. I could always commit murder tomorrow.

"I am dying to call him," Diane said.

"Do it!" BJ said.

CHAPTER 15

lowcountry christmas

My mother wasn't much in the mood for Christmas, and I didn't blame her. I wasn't so happy either. After all, Pop had been gone for only a few weeks. Nonetheless, we put on a brave face, determined to get through the holiday with what joy we could muster. And I'd heard not a word from Alden. My mother continued to needle me.

"Call him," she said. "It's 2016. Women call men these days. I see it on television all the time."

"I'm not calling him," I said. I was still upset about his new flame, as though he was cheating on me. Craziness. "Hell will freeze first, then I'll call him."

"Floyd said he saw him at Lowe's," she said.

"And?"

"He seemed chipper."

"Chipper? Alden is not given to being chipper."

It was Christmas week and we were baking pies in the commercial kitchen at the farm stand to fill the special orders we started taking right after Thanksgiving. Pumpkin, pecan, sweet potato, and apple pies. They were all deep dish, with my mother's flaky crust that she twisted to the left for pumpkin and to the right for sweet potato, just to break the monotony of a pressed fork around the crimp. Of course, the top crust of the apple pies was latticework and the pecan pies had an extra braid of crust around the edge. It was those decorative touches and the extra crust that made our pies so popular. And that buttery crust (which was really half Crisco) was our justification for charging what we did. No one ever complained when the price went up each year. Our customers said over and over that they couldn't make crust like Miss Virnell's at home and how much they appreciated the generous filling.

Currently we were up to our elbows in sweet potatoes, our old KitchenAid stand mixers whirring away. And our two refurbished Garland Sentry ovens could bake a dozen pies at a time while ten pots of anything else cooked on top. But we never had ten pots going at once.

"Good thing we have our own chickens and mild weather, with all the eggs we use this time of year," I said.

"Did you add vanilla to that?" my mother said.

"You know I did," I said. "And cinnamon and brown sugar and grated orange rind."

We'd been baking together for decades and she still didn't trust me to remember how to make a sweet potato pie?

"I'm only asking because I might have added it in too."

"Oh, Mom."

"I know. I'm getting senile. I hate it."

My cell phone rang and it startled me. I pulled it out of my apron pocket. The caller ID said it was Susan Kennedy Cambria calling. I tapped the Accept button.

"Well, hello, Susan! How are you this morning?"

"How am I? I'll tell you how I am! Not happy! I am not happy!"

"Why? What's wrong?"

My mother stopped what she was doing and turned off the mixers and came over to stand next to me so she could hear.

"Your son is turning my daughter into a socialist, that's what!"

My mother gasped.

"A socialist? What do you mean a socialist?"

"I've been planning Shelby's wedding since the *day she was born*. And all through the years I've been attending one gorgeous affair after another. Now it's *my* turn! I've been planning this wedding *for months* and now they want to move it up to January!"

"January?"

"And, on top of that, they've canceled the date I had reserved at the Waldorf and booked another date without even consulting us! You have no idea how hard it is to get the Waldorf ballroom for a wedding on a Saturday night. A lot of very important people have cleared their calendars to be with us in June. All my plans are ruined!"

"Why does it mean that my son is turning Shelby into a socialist?" I really did not like her tone.

I understood why she was upset, but the socialist thing didn't make sense to me.

"Because they want a more humble affair."

What was the matter with that?

"That sounds sensible enough. What's the problem?"

"It's all because you can't afford the right kind of rehearsal dinner, Diane."

Whoa! Wait just a damn minute.

"Perhaps there's been a misunderstanding, Susan." How rude!

"Really? How's that? Seems pretty clear to me."

"Susan, it's obvious to the entire world that you have a lot more money than we do. But there are also customary norms that have to be considered."

"Really? Such as?"

"Such as, you don't invite your entire guest list to the rehearsal dinner. It's for the wedding party only. And unless you have two hundred people in the wedding party, there shouldn't be two hundred people at the rehearsal dinner."

"I told Frederick and Shelby I would pay for the whole thing, but they are determined to make this a more egalitarian weekend because of your lack of resources."

"Excuse me? For your information, I am perfectly capable of providing a very nice dinner for the people I am obliged to feed. And maybe they don't want to have a royal wedding? Have you considered that?"

"So it looks like you're going to have to come to Chicago in the dead of winter. Great."

"Have you even heard one word that I've said?"

"Thank you, Diane. Thank you very much. You've ruined my wedding."

"I'm sorry, are you and Alejandro renewing your vows?"

"Don't be ridiculous."

"Well, if you and Alejandro aren't renewing your vows, it's not your wedding."

"It most certainly is my wedding. It's my damn wedding and I am not going to sit here and let you and your son brainwash my daughter and ruin the whole thing without telling you how much I *don't* appreciate it."

"You know what, Susan? I have the feeling I'm not getting all the facts. I'm going to call my son. I'll get back to you."

"You do whatever you want. The damage is done."

"One other thing, Susan. In my world we don't speak to each other this way."

The phone went silent. Susan disconnected me.

I looked at my mother and said, "I think she hung up on me."

"Maybe it was a bad connection," she said.

"I doubt it."

"You want to tell me what happened?"

"I don't know what happened. I'm calling Fred. Apparently, they've moved the wedding to January."

"She's pregnant."

"Who knows? Maybe she is. But I just got an earful from Susan about how moving the wedding up ruins her life."

"Her mind's unstable."

"And how it's my fault."

"It is not. She's overreaching by even thinking you should go along with her plan to feed the world. And pregnant or not, Shelby's right to have a hand in her own wedding plans. Six more months of listening to Susan go on like she does would put everyone in a nuthouse."

"She thinks it's her wedding, not Shelby's. She actually said that it's our financial situation that caused Shelby and Fred to change their plans. Can you believe she said that?"

"I believe anything these days. People have no manners. It wouldn't matter who's in the White House, the people say such awful things that in my day would've been considered treasonous."

"It's true. I've got a dollar that says they changed the date because she was so overbearing and obnoxious they couldn't stand it for another minute."

"Well, I've got a couple of thoughts. One, I think Shelby has better sense than I thought, and this makes me like her more. And two? Susan with the two last names is a spoiled, superficial nobody dying to impress the world with her husband's money."

"No argument from me. Boy, she was really rude."

"After the wedding you hardly ever have to see her again."

"Of course I will. There will be babies and holidays and graduations and all sorts of reasons I'll be stuck in a room with her."

"Well, maybe. Just try to keep it to a minimum."

"I have the feeling she feels the same way."

I tapped Fred's number into my phone and got his voice mail. My first thought was that he was avoiding me. And then I realized he might be busy. It was a workday, after all. I didn't leave a message because I knew he could see that I called. And I told myself that of course he knew why I was calling. Perhaps he wanted to have that discussion away from the office. For all he knew I could be as out of my mind as Susan was.

"Let's get these pies ready to go in the oven, shall we?" Mom said.

"We shall," I said and giggled.

Strangely, I was not as insulted as I probably should have been. The truth is, I knew what she thought of us the first time I met her. She was horrified. And seeing her home in Chicago only underscored my thoughts. Our lives were worlds apart. We had almost zero in common except that our children were in love and about to be married. And it was the children I really cared about.

The day seemed to go quickly, as they always did when I was very busy. I wondered if Susan would tell her husband about her phone call to me. I wondered what he would think if she did. Was Shelby given to this kind of behavior? Not so far as I knew. Susan was not only rude, she was irrational. What sane adult speaks to another adult, a prospective in-law no less, that way?

It was just after six when Fred called.

"Hi, Mom. What's going on?"

"Well, I had a phone call from Shelby's mother this morning."

"Yeah, I was going to call you tonight anyway. So good. Um, so . . ."

"You're moving your wedding to January."

"Yeah, we are. Look, Shelby and I just want to get married. We don't want to be on the front page of the newspaper for having held the most extravagant wedding ever. Mrs. Cambria had all these crazy plans and it just got out of control."

"I see."

"Shelby was crying all the time and fighting with her mother, like, every day over one thing or another. She just couldn't stand it. I wasn't as opposed to the plans as Shelby was, but I didn't want us to be dragged into a wedding neither one of us really wanted."

"And she's not pregnant?"

"Good grief! No! She's not pregnant! Why is everyone asking that? Do we look that stupid?"

"It's a legitimate question given the circumstances."

"I guess."

"So do we have a date?"

"Saturday, the twenty-eighth."

"Okay. I just wrote that down. How's she going to get a dress that fast?"

"You don't know Shelby. She'll have a dress by this weekend. And Mom? Shelby and I want to help with the rehearsal dinner. You know, we each have a pretty big chunk of money in our savings accounts."

"I see. That's awfully nice. Well, why don't you and Shelby

choose a restaurant, figure out who's going to be in your wedding party, and then we can see what it all looks like."

"We even had a thought about having it at our apartment."

"Probably too small if you go over twenty people. But y'all decide and I'm right there with you. Look at a couple of options, Fred. And then y'all choose."

"After all, we're not exactly kids."

"That's right. You're not. I think the most important thing is that you have the wedding you want. Please tell Shelby I admire her personal restraint. It's a greatly undervalued quality in today's world."

"I will. Can I ask you something?"

"Of course."

"How terrible was her mother on the phone?"

"She has *no* personal restraint. Whatsoever. *At all.*"

"That bad?"

"Yes, it was very ugly. No filter."

"What did she say?"

"Son? They were the words of a very angry woman who feels cheated. Let's not go there. I prefer to forget it ever happened."

"And so now I have to admire your personal restraint."

"Love you, Fred. With all my heart. We will get y'all through this unscathed."

"Families are crazy, Mom. But you're the greatest. Gosh, I love you so much."

"As you should."

We laughed and said good-bye.

Later that night, after the supper dishes were all washed

and dried and my mother had gone to her room to read, I
went outside to have a look at the sky. It was a quiet night,
the air crisp and cool. I sat down on the front steps. Gus the
cat appeared from the shadows and rubbed up against me,
asking for a scratch, which I gave him.

"Come here, you furry old thing."

Gus purred and crawled onto my lap. I had a clear view
of a nearly full moon that was hanging up in the heavens,
something not quite fully formed. I thought about Fred. I
had not lost him to Shelby's family. In fact, he was a bit like
the moon, quickly becoming a fully realized man. I was so
proud of him. I loved that he supported Shelby when she
wanted to stand up to her mother. I loved that they insisted
on having control of their lives.

Susan was a real humdinger, like my father used to say.
Maybe she could manipulate everyone else in her life, but
she wasn't going to do it to my son and his fiancée. Or me. I
surely did not like the terrible things she said to me, but she
had no business having the expectations she had of me in
the first place. Still, it took her bullying for Fred and Shelby
to pull the ripcord. Her plan had backfired. And I was surprised and happy that Fred and Shelby wanted to be a part of
planning their rehearsal dinner. After all, it was their wedding, not Susan's.

And what of Alden? What was there to be done, anyway?
I was having trouble sleeping at night. Between Dad's death
and having Alden snatched away from right beneath my
nose, how was I supposed to sleep? What exactly did I want
from him? I thought again, as I had a thousand times, about

the night we were together at Fred's rehearsal party, dancing. I remembered feeling his breath on my neck. I missed him. Then I thought about Betsy Beyer. How was I supposed to compete with her? Younger. Prettier. Stylish. Gregarious. Obviously available. Yale. I hated her guts. Did that mean I was in love with Alden? Had I ever really been in love?

The screen door slammed behind me. My mother was on the porch.

"You going to bed? It's almost ten. I want to lock up," she said.

"I'll be along directly," I said. "You go on. I'll close up the house."

She ignored that and sat down next to me. Gus left me and climbed on her lap.

"Come here, Gus baby. Our Fred," she said and sighed her signature sigh. "How do you like our Fred?"

"He's got spine. He's not going to be railroaded by anyone. I like that very much."

"Miss Susan Two Last Names doesn't know who she's dealing with. He gets his courage from us."

"We are a determined tribe, aren't we?" I said.

"Yes. Some of us are more determined than others."

"What's that supposed to mean?"

"If you want something, you go and get it. If you don't want that thing, you let it go and stop brooding."

"I'm not brooding."

She stood up and Gus jumped from her lap.

"Come on, Gus. I need you to warm my bones." She patted my shoulder. "Who's going to warm yours, Diane? Who's going to warm yours?"

"Maybe I'll get a dog," I said.

"Well, you'd better decide before it's too late," she said.

She went inside and left me sitting there in the dark. For the next few minutes I contemplated my options. I had been so surprised to see Alden at Pop's funeral with a woman. I was thrown off guard by Betsy's unexpected appearance and her proprietary attitude. *The rest is history!* That's what she'd said. Really? She was too pushy for my blood. And Alden was being led around by the nose. What happened to him? Soon she'd have Alden eating out of a dog bowl. I couldn't stand by and let that happen. He was too good for her. No, she had to go.

"Was I so terrible?" Susan said.

"Yes," Judy CQ said.

CHAPTER 16

chicago fire

When Alejandro came in from work that night, I put a glass of wine in his hand and started to tell him about the unfortunate conversation I'd had to have with Diane earlier that day.

"You said what?" Alejandro said.

"I told her I was not happy about moving the wedding up to January. Because I'm not."

"And what else did you say? I know you said something terrible, because you have that twitch in your cheek you always get when you've done something regrettable."

"Oh, God. I might have said the children's rebellion was her fault because she wasn't willing or able to properly entertain our guests the night before. You know, the rehearsal dinner."

"Good grief, Susan. That's really rather low."

"Well, it's the truth," I said.

"My dear, some truths are better left unspoken. We've been down this road before when your sharp tongue gets the better of you."

"Perhaps."

"You know you must apologize to her."

"Absolutely not."

"Yes, absolutely you will. Do you want our daughter to begin her married life with an alienated in-law?"

"She's not going to be unkind to Shelby. She might resist my charms, but she's not the kind of woman who would punish a child because of something her parent did. Besides, Frederick and Shelby will be living in Chicago. It's not like his family is next door."

"Out of sight, out of mind? Please, Susan. Pick up the phone and apologize. She really had nothing to do with Shelby and Frederick changing the date. You shouldn't blame her."

"Well, then, whose fault is it?"

Alejandro's eyebrows were arched as high as they would go. He said nothing. That was the moment I saw that perhaps I had gone overboard. But I still loved the butterfly idea, even if they were endangered. They were bugs! Okay? Bugs! Phillipe, my floral designer from Ashland, and I had another idea to build an indoor garden with a bridge over a koi pond for photo ops. He was researching the cost of full-size peach trees laden with fruit to be in the background.

Or we were considering building a faux rain forest if Shelby and Frederick were considering someplace like Costa Rica for a honeymoon, which is very popular these days. We could bring in those red macaws that are so incredible. But Africa? Should we think about giraffes and other animals? Maasai dancers from the Maasai Mara? Monkeys? I had not told Alejandro about the alternatives and I couldn't bring myself to do it then. Okay, maybe it was because it was all a bit much. Maybe. Oh, what's the use, I thought, I can't be at odds with everyone.

"All right. I'll call her in the morning."

"There's a good girl. Now, what's for dinner?"

"I booked a table at the Palm."

We had a lovely dinner and turned in early that night.

"I have a conference call at six in the morning," he said, sitting on the side of the bed, setting the alarm clock.

He got under the covers and turned off the lamp.

"When *don't* you have a conference call first thing in the morning?" I said, climbing into bed.

"Well, the fund isn't performing as well as I had hoped this quarter. This Brexit business is throwing a wrench in the European markets, so I've got to move things around. Otherwise, I'm going to have a real mess on my hands."

I never understood what he meant, because finance wasn't my thing. Volunteer work was my thing, and at least I could usually work from home.

"What can I do to help?"

"Oh, I don't know. A dozen new investors would be wonderful."

"Well, I don't know a dozen, but you do have several people waiting for an opening. Remember, the problem was always that your minimum to buy in was too high. Most people don't have five million in cash lying around. They've got it all tied up."

"I'm aware. But most people don't see returns like I can produce."

"I love your gorgeous brain."

"Maybe I'll lower the minimum until this storm blows over."

"Excellent idea!"

He was quiet, and I looked over his shoulder to see that he was already asleep. How he could fall asleep just like that was another mystery. It was as though he just pressed a button and boom! He was in dreamland. Not me. I had to mentally organize my next day and reevaluate the one I'd just lived, which of course brought me back to the problem of Diane. I would call her and simply apologize. She couldn't help it that she wasn't as wealthy as we were.

"I would have told her to stuff it," Virnell said.

"She's terrible! What can you do?" Diane said.

CHAPTER 17

onions make you cry

It was December twenty-third. I still had not worked up the courage to call Alden. I'd been busy, as I always was around the holidays. I'd call him when I could think of an excuse to that wouldn't give him a chance to reject me. And I'd be nonchalant and just sort of test the temperature of his waters. He could also be on his honeymoon by now for all I knew.

My cell phone rang. It was across the room on the counter by the sink, where Mom was washing up the breakfast dishes.

"It's the queen of Chicago calling," she said, looking at the caller ID. "Probably to bow and scrape in shame."

"Well, I doubt that," I said, and took the phone from her, tapping the Accept button. "Hello?"

"Diane, it's Susan." She sighed. "I'm calling to say I'm sorry for my unforgivable bad manners. I truly regret the things I said."

I didn't say a word. I just waited for her to continue.

"Are you there?" she said.

"I'm here," I said. "I'm listening."

Did she think I was going to gush all over her? This wasn't high school.

She cleared her throat and continued.

"I think I was just so upset by the children's change of plans. Anyway, I'm sorry."

"I accept your apology, but I think you should know something."

"And what should I know?" She said this with a trace of frost.

"My son is not a child, and neither is your daughter." I said it nicely.

"I imagine you're right. It's so hard, this business of letting go."

"It is, but I raised Fred to make good decisions. If he says he wants to get married tomorrow, it's all right with me. I trust him."

"Well, that's nice. But I'm deeply disappointed. But you were right. It *is* their wedding. *Not* mine."

"Well, please let me know as their new plans come together so we can make arrangements for our side. And by the way, they are organizing their rehearsal dinner by themselves. So you and I can stop stressing over that one."

"They are? They didn't say anything about this."

The call ended on that note and I thought, You rotten stinker, you're not sorry one bit. You're disappointed you couldn't have Barnum and Bailey host the wedding and the reception. Period.

"So what did she have to say for herself?" Mom asked.

"I think she's never had to apologize for much, because she's not very good at it. And I'd bet real money that she told her husband what she said to me, looking for support. He probably told her she was wrong and to make things right."

"You think so?"

"She'd never make that phone call on her own. I suspect he has a much higher sense of right and wrong."

My mother just looked at me with a blank expression.

"What? What are you thinking, Miss Virnell?"

"I'm thinking Fred's marrying into a mess. That's what."

"What do you mean?"

"I don't know. I just have a funny feeling."

When Virnell had a funny feeling, nobody wound up laughing.

"Probably because you've been sleeping with Gus," I said and gave her a hug.

"That's what the world needs more of. Sassy-mouth daughters."

"Oh, you know I'm teasing you."

"I know, but you mark my words."

"Okay, we'll see what we see. I'm going to go on down to work and get last of the pies in the ovens."

"I'll be there soon."

I opened the farm stand for the day, and soon there were so many cars in the parking lot, we were running out of space. Mom came in and was handling the cash register so that BJ and Floyd, on board for the holiday, could help customers. I still had pies going in and out of the ovens, as I would all day until all of our orders were filled.

"This is the last batch of pecan pies," I said to Mom when I came back out front and put four pies on the counter.

"Good. The sooner this holiday ends, the happier I'll be," she said, looking at Pop's empty recliner.

"If you want, I can ask Floyd to get rid of it," I said. "It's pretty beaten up anyway."

"I'll let you know about that another time."

I knew what she was thinking, that as long as Pop's recliner stood in its familiar place, maybe he had just stepped away.

"You know, we really should put up a tree," I said. "Even just a little one."

"I just don't feel the Christmas spirit," she said.

Perhaps that would be my excuse to call Alden, to help me get a little bit of Christmas cheer in the air. He had stopped by on other holidays in the past.

Pine garland and wreaths with big red bows were hung all around the store, inside and out. Of course the wreaths were for sale, along with more garland, mistletoe balls, and red or white poinsettias. At that time of year, we had fewer vegetables to offer, so selling holiday decorations helped our bottom line, as did pies, jellies, pickles, and relishes.

"Oh! Look at this, Roberta!" one customer said to her friend.

"What is it?"

"Peach preserves. It's a perfect kitchen Santa for my neighbors!"

"You can taste it if you'd like," BJ said. "There's an open jar and some crackers on the counter. Help yourselves!"

Mom and I, and anyone else we could commandeer, would cut out red and green calico or gingham circles with pinking shears and tie them over the tops of the jars with twine, making them look like a gift. It worked. Especially when the uninitiated sampled the peach preserves. I kept a stack of paper napkins by the register for that very reason. People just loved free samples. I could put out squirrel hash and if it was free, people would eat it. That always amazed me.

Soon the last pie had been picked up and almost all our wreaths and greens were sold. It was six o'clock and the parking lot was empty.

"Time to call it a day," Floyd said. "We're closed tomorrow, right?"

"Yes," I said. "Your camo pants are tired?"

"They are. Good we're closed. I need to go get BJ something. You think she'd like a cordless drill? I have to go to Lowe's anyway. Maybe a set of wrenches?"

"Wouldn't every woman? You big jerk. I just love it that you're going shopping on Christmas Eve."

"To be honest, I didn't think she'd still be around."

"I didn't either," I said. "But she seems perfectly happy. She sure was a help today."

"Well, school's out. You want to eat, you have to help."

"No, but I mean, she seems really happy."

"Di, of course she's happy. She's living with me. She seems to have gotten over her moodiness."

"How old is she?"

"Fifty-one," he said. "At least that's what she says."

I shook my head. Had Floyd never heard of women and perimenopause?

"Fifty-one. Floyd? It's mother nature messing with her estrogen."

"Oh, yeah! Why didn't I think of that?"

"Charming as you are to live with, I'm guessing she probably got something from her doctor to squelch the blues."

"Whatever. Why don't we take the leftover wreaths and hang them on our doors?"

"Why not?"

My brother and I closed the store for the holiday and took the wreaths home with us. The nail on our front door was still there from last year. I simply put the wreath in its place and turned to Floyd.

"Mom insists she doesn't want a Christmas tree. What do you think about that?"

"I can understand it, but I don't necessarily agree," he said.

"Humph. We've been so busy, I haven't had the chance to ask you what you think about Fred and Shelby getting married next month."

"I think the sooner the better. Weddings bring out the crazy in everyone."

"That, dear brother, might be the understatement of the year."

"How are you doing, sister?"

"What do you mean?" I looked at him. Did he mean the wedding or about Pop being gone and our first Christmas without him?

"I mean, without Pretty Boy scratching at the door."

"Oh, Alden?"

"Yeah. Him. I mean, maybe we should hook you up with Match or OurTime or one of those matchmaking sites. I hear they work pretty well."

"Oh, I'm too old for all that nonsense. You know how I am."

"Yeah, I do. You're lonely. I can see it in your face. You don't want Alden, but you don't want anybody else to have him either. You know what?"

I hated pep talks.

"I think I'm about to hear," I said.

"I understand being afraid of getting involved and all that. But it's not right to be alone if it makes you lonely. There's more to life than this farm."

"You think so?" I said.

"Yeah. I think so. Anyway, I gotta get moving. I promised BJ I'd take her for a ride tonight to go see all the Christmas lights. I'll see you in the morning."

"Okay. You kids have fun."

I went inside and put a kettle on to boil water. I was feeling like a cup of tea.

"I'm going to get a sweater," Mom said. "Pork chops sound good?"

They were already cooked and resting in the cast-iron skillet. What if I didn't feel like pork chops? I'd be eating them anyway.

"Anything's fine. Thanks."

"Be right back."

She left me there staring at the kettle. I thought about what Floyd said. Did I seem a little sad? I really didn't know how I was feeling. Since when was Floyd such a genius about my feelings, or about women in general? He probably was going to buy some terrible gift for BJ. In any case, this was not going to be a great Christmas. I looked at my watch. It was nearly eight o'clock. Maybe I was just mourning my father's death. Maybe I was feeling sorry for myself. One thing was certain, having my parents in my life into middle age had given me a false sense of security about my own future.

I was almost too tired to eat. Dinner passed with little conversation. I couldn't tell you if it was delicious or not. But I thanked my mother anyway.

"Very good, Mom. Thanks. I'll get the dishes."

"Well, thank you, Diane. I've been longing for a good soak in my tub to get the funeral out of my bones. Won't seem like Christmas without him, you know?"

"It sure won't," I said.

"It's just that I can't figure out how to be in this world without him. I just can't be the same."

"I know, Momma. I know."

We were not given to weeping and wailing, but we weren't

beyond a solid hug when it was called for. So I put the plate I was scraping on the counter and took my mother in my arms. I could feel her heavy sigh and I could feel her shoulder blades through her thin sweater. She wrapped her arms around my waist and sighed again, deeply, a sigh of resignation and sadness. She seemed so tiny.

"We're going to be all right." I rubbed her back. "Remember Christmas is only one day. And everyone says the first year is the worst."

She stood back and looked at me.

"I know that. BJ's cooking Christmas dinner. God save us."

"Oh, I imagine she can cook a turkey, don't you? Now, go get your bath."

"She can always call the Butterball hotline."

"Go on now. I don't want to be in this kitchen all night."

She looked at me with her eyes all squinted as though she knew this was the night I had decided to call Alden. She nodded, as the answer must've been all over my face, and left.

"I'm going!" she called over her shoulder, and I knew she was smiling.

That woman has ESP, I said to myself.

I waited until I could hear the water running in her bathroom to get my phone. I called Alden, and after four or five rings, he answered.

"Hey, Diane! Merry Christmas!"

"Alden, it's so nice to hear your voice. Merry Christmas to you too."

There was an awkward pause. I knew right then it was a

huge mistake to have called him. I cleared my throat and spoke.

"Are you planning anything special for the holidays?"

"Miss Betsy and I are just staying at home and cooking a prime rib, but we're going on a cruise for New Year's. How about you?"

"Well, you know, with Pop just gone and all that, we're just staying close to home. Miss Virnell is really bummed out. She won't even put up a tree."

"Oh, gosh. That's terrible. Any of the kids coming?"

"No, they were all just here for the funeral. It's okay. We'll get through it. So where are you going on your cruise?"

"It's one of those cruise-to-nowhere things. Basically, we float around the Caribbean for three nights and drink champagne and eat our heads off. But I'm happy to have the break."

"Well, I hope y'all have a wonderful time. And Merry Christmas, Alden, and, um . . ."

"I know you, Diane. You don't have to say it. If I can, I'll swing around and try to cheer up Miss Virnell."

"You're the best, Alden. Thank you."

We hung up and I knew he knew exactly why I was calling. It wasn't just on my mother's behalf. Another man might not have been so understanding. Any other man might have said, *Sorry, sister, this train has left the station.* But he didn't. Why did I let him go? Because I might be a damn fool, that's why. And maybe I'm a bit of a coward too. And maybe it was seeing him hot for somebody else that made me want him to come back. I'd be a little more assertive and we could see where it might lead.

Morning came. Winter's blue light spilled across the heart pine floor of my bedroom. The sun was sneaking in under my shade that didn't quite reach the sill. Christmas Eve was here.

As soon as the roosters started crowing, I rolled over and looked at my alarm. It was just after six. Actually, the darned roosters crowed all day and night and when the mood struck, because that's what they do. But when they sang in the middle of the night, like last night, it drove me crazy. Maybe they were trying to scare the coyotes away. Or maybe Floyd left the light on in the barn again and the roosters thought it was daybreak. I'd have to check.

I got out of bed, showered, and dressed. Alden crossed my mind. I was a little bit mortified by our conversation last night. If he was taking Betsy on a cruise, he was definitely sleeping with her. Now I was deeply jealous and doubly angry with myself. My next thought was, How can he do that? Of course, in the next breath I realized I'd done everything but put a gift tag on him and stuff him into Betsy Beyer's Christmas stocking. How stupid could I have been?

I pulled out a chambray shirt and a pair of khakis from my closet and laid them across the foot of my bed. Then I thought, what if Alden came by, as he said he might? He wouldn't exactly fall to his knees at the sight of me dressed like that. I exchanged them for a fuchsia cotton blouse with black capris and twisted my hair up into a messy bun so it wouldn't look deliberate. And yes, I put on some makeup. And lipstick. I put the lipstick tube in my pants pocket so I could reapply between the time I might hear his car door close and when he might reach the door. I was ready to face him, but first I needed breakfast or something to fortify me. Why was I so nervous?

"Well, don't you look nice," Mom said, giving me the eye as I came into the kitchen. "Coffee?"

"Yes, please. Good morning! Merry Christmas Eve!"

I said this with a smile, but inside I was a little concerned. She had on her bathrobe. Like my father, she never appeared for the day in her bathrobe unless she was ill. She put a mug at my place on the table.

"I'm going to go and dress for the day," she said. "I'll try to appear to be in deep mourning." Then she winked at me and left the room.

So much for me reading something into what she was wearing. Maybe she just felt like getting a cup of coffee to have while she dressed.

She had me. My mother really did know every hair on my head. And her being in her bathrobe meant nothing.

After breakfast I went over to Floyd's trailer to see if I could do anything to help BJ put tomorrow's dinner together. Naturally, Floyd had strung lights the entire length of his portable home. And there was a fake wreath on every window but a real one on the door. Ah, Floyd. God love you, I thought.

"Come in! It's open!" she called out.

She was at her kitchen counter, weeping.

"BJ! Whatever is the matter?"

"Onions. I can't cut them up without crying my eyes out." She took a tissue from her pocket and blew her nose with vigor.

Please wash your hands, I thought and did not say.

"Girl, give me that knife. Let me show you a trick." She handed me her chef's knife. I took another onion from the vegetable basket and set it on the cutting board. "Okay, see this root end?"

"Yep."

"That thing is filled with a chemical like tear gas, the stuff that makes you cry. Ya gotta give it some respect."

"I never heard that."

"Yeah, true story. Okay, so see this other end?"

"Yeah."

"We're gonna give it a nice slice to give us a flat end." I cut a bit off the end and stood the onion up. "Now we're going to slice through the root like this." I divided the onion in two. "Now we quickly peel." I threw the peels in the compost bucket. "Now see all these little lines? We just follow them down the body and then across. Look at that!"

In less than two minutes there was a mound of perfectly chopped onion pieces on the cutting board.

"That's the best trick ever! And no tears!" BJ was impressed.

"So, what else can I do to help?"

"Not a darn thing. I was saving the onions for last because they always wipe me out. The sweet potatoes are cooked, the bird's thawed out, rutabagas are chopped, beans are snapped. I think I'm in good shape."

And Floyd loved to say she couldn't boil water? Men.

I looked at the folding card table she had set up for tomorrow. It looked pretty nice for what it was. It was covered with a deep red cloth, and a small white poinsettia wrapped in red foil stood in the center. There were votive candles in beaded holders and red goblets, and the plates had sprigs of holly with red berries painted on the rims. It wasn't anywhere near what Susan's club would be offering up to her family, but it was a display of loving sincerity.

"Your table is so pretty," I said, and meant it. I mean, it wasn't out of *Southern Living* magazine, but for BJ? This was out of *Southern Living* magazine.

"I went a little crazy over at the Pier One, but they have such pretty things. I never had any Christmas china, but Floyd said go on ahead and buy it, so I did."

Even Floyd was a soft touch when it came to Christmas. Well, for decorations, that is.

"I don't have holiday china either. Maybe I'll go over there one night this week and see what's left."

"I'll go with you. I have a coupon. I'd like to have a platter. It will all be half price."

"Okay, sounds good. So we're bringing fruitcake and sands and rum balls tomorrow. And listen, BJ, you and Floyd are so good to host Christmas dinner. I don't think ol' Virnell could take it this year, sitting at the table with a big hole where Dad used to sit. We don't even have a tree."

"That's exactly why we offered. I couldn't agree more. No tree?"

"She said she just can't get into the Christmas spirit this year. I didn't want to argue about it. I'm not feeling it so much either."

"I think none of us are, but we're trying to make the best of it."

"Is Floyd still cooking fish tonight?"

"Yes. He says he's making some new thing, like a seafood stew or something."

"Well, I'm sure it will be delicious. Maybe I'll make a lemon meringue pie."

"Gosh! I haven't had lemon meringue anything in ages!"

I heard a car door slam and I knew it was Alden. I recognized the clunk.

"I'll see you later," I said. "I think we have company."

BJ followed me to the door and looked outside. Then she turned to me and smiled.

"Hurry," she said in a whisper. "But don't make it look like you're hurrying."

Trying to be as casual as possible, I listened to the crunch of my loafers as I made my way toward the house. I was about halfway there when I looked up to see Alden lifting a fresh Christmas tree out of the back of his truck. It wasn't even six feet tall, but it was going to be all we needed to lift our mood.

"Well, hey, Alden! Aren't you wonderful?"

"Good morning! Yes, I am sort of wonderful. Sometimes, anyway." He tamped the end of the tree on the ground to shake out the branches. "I saw this sweet little tree and thought it might bring two of my favorite girls a little Christmas cheer."

"Thank you so much. You are too sweet. Let's take it inside."

"Do you know where your tree stand might be?"

"I sure do. Why don't I get it and I'll meet you inside?" I said. "The door's open."

"Okay. See you in a few minutes." He went up on the porch, opened our dirty front door like he lived there, and called my mother's name. "Miss Virnell? Hey! It's me, Alden. I brought you something!"

Maybe I'd buy the house a couple of buckets of paint for Christmas. Maybe I could cajole Floyd into helping. At least we could paint the front of the house this year.

The Christmas tree stand and boxes of lights and ornaments were in the storage room in the barn. And yes, the light had been left on. One nice thing about living on a farm with a barn was that we had sufficient room to put things away in a designated spot. But I noticed something new in the room – dozens and dozens of bottles of water, first aid supplies that could last for ages, dozens of rolls of toilet paper and paper towels, dozens of bars of bath soap, bottles and bottles of detergent for dishes, shampoo and cream rinse . . . Floyd was stockpiling again just as he had for Y2K. He really needed to stay off those Doomsday Web sites. Well, this was not the day to get excited about Floyd's paranoia. That could wait until after the New Year. I found the large plastic container of decorations and the tree stand and put them on the wagon. I locked the storage room and pulled the wagon up to the house, coming in through the kitchen door.

"I think that corner is a good one," I heard my mother say.

"I've got the stand," I said and put it on the floor.

"I know how to do this," Alden said and lifted the tree into the center of the stand. "Diane, if you'll hold it straight, I can screw it in."

"I'll go get a pitcher of water," Mom said.

As soon as she was out of the room, I said, "How did she react to the tree?"

"She was like a kid. Thrilled."

"Oh, Alden, I just love you."

"Really?" he said and looked at me strangely.

"Oh, come on, you know I do. You always do the exact right thing."

"I wish that was true," he said. "Okay, stand back and tell me if it's straight."

I stood back and was suddenly taken by the sight of Alden on our living room floor, doing something that was such a traditional holiday thing to do, and he was doing it for my mother and for me. I began feeling emotional, which I always fought like crazy because I hated being weak. But I had a vision of him putting up Christmas trees with Betsy for the rest of his life while I was over here in my old farmhouse, alone for the rest of mine.

"Is it okay?" he said. "Can I get up?"

"Oh, Alden, it's beautiful. Just beautiful." And with that, one terrible traitorous tear bubbled over the edge of my right eye and began to roll down my cheek. Then another and another.

He stood and looked at the tree, having no idea I was losing it just two feet away from him. Mom returned with a pitcher of water, took one look at me, put down the pitcher on the coffee table, turned around, and left the room again.

"I forgot something," she said.

Alden looked at her and then me and did a double take.

"Diane! What in the world? What's happened here?"

"Nothing," I said. "I'm fine."

"No, you're not fine. What's wrong?"

"I guess this is a more difficult Christmas than I thought it would be."

"Because of Pop? Of course it's hard. It's only been a few weeks."

"It's not just that," I said.

"Well then, what? What is it? Tell me. We've been friends forever."

I was quiet then, waiting for the obvious to sink into his head. It didn't, so I spoke.

"That might be the problem, Alden." I sniffed and wiped my eyes with the back of my hand. "That might be the problem."

"What do you mean? Diane, you have to tell me. I'm not psychic."

"Boy, that's for sure."

Then it hit him.

"Come here," he said. "Why didn't you ever say anything?"

He held me close and I blubbered like a teenage girl.

"You know me, Alden. All this emotional stuff terrifies me, but being terrified of it doesn't seem to make any difference. It gets to you anyway. And now I'm facing this terrible Christmas with no father, a depressed mother, my son's so far away, and you're going on a cruise to nowhere with another woman. It's just a lot for me to absorb, you know? It's a lot."

"I'll only be gone for a few days," he said, leaving me to wonder if he understood what I was trying to tell him at all.

"Oh, Alden, you don't get it, do you?"

"Get what?"

He didn't get it. There was no reason to pound the point home, which would, I could see then, lead to further humiliation for me and embarrassment for him. I stood back from him. And cleared my throat and ran my hands up the sides of my head, making sure clumps of my hair weren't hanging down all over the place.

I smiled and said, "It's okay. I'm fine. I'll be fine."

"There now. Good! Much better. Let's get those lights on this pretty little tree, huh? What do you say?"

"Sure. Let's do that."

Men.

"What if Dad says no?" Shelby said.

"He would never say no to you," Fred said.

CHAPTER 18

shelby takes a lowcountry position

I t was Christmas Eve and we were just arriving at my parents' home for a special holiday dinner.

"Mom? Dad?"

I took my bag of groceries to the kitchen and dropped it on the counter.

I knew my parents weren't going to like the plan Frederick and I had cooked up, but we were going ahead. Too bad. We'd led a self-centered life long enough. It was time to think of others. And to do something for someone else. This is just one of the many reasons I love Fred so much. He makes me a better person.

"We're in the living room, having champagne and little nibbles. Come join us!"

"Give me your coat, babe," I said to Frederick. "I'll join you in a minute."

"Okay," he said and kissed my cold cheek. "Love you."

"Love you too!"

I threw our coats and gloves and hats and scarves on the bed in my old room. I felt a chill run through me even though the room was warm. It was so cold outside I couldn't adjust right away. What a terrible winter!

On the way to the living room, I stopped to have a peek at the dining room. Mom's silver candelabra glistened like mirrors and her Belgian linens were starched to the point that you couldn't fold them or they might crack. The table was set with her Tiffany holiday china, her Lalique crystal, and her two-hundred-year-old huge sterling silver flatware. The flowers in the center of the table were drop-dead gorgeous. I didn't even know what they were. Or care. I mean, it was beautiful, but who needs all this stuff? My mom, that's who.

We were having takeout for Christmas Eve dinner. How pathetic is that? I looked in the pots. Okay, not so awful. Mom had somebody cook lobsters and take them out of their shells to serve warm over mashed potatoes. That same person, or maybe somebody else, made a fish chowder that was creamy and delicious. Being the more accomplished cook in the family, I had brought two bags of prewashed romaine lettuce to make a salad, with cherry tomatoes and a container of mini mozzarella balls in water.

"The table looks amazing!" I said to her and kissed both of her cheeks without touching her skin, so I wouldn't, God forbid, wreck her makeup. "I can't believe you did all of this by yourself!"

"Oh, please. Tina did everything. I sent her home two hours ago. I mean, it is Christmas Eve," she said. "Ashland Addison did the flowers. Aren't they sensational?"

"They're unbelievable," I said.

Daddy handed me a flute and said, "Merry Christmas, sweetheart! Cheers!"

"Try one of these," Frederick said and offered me a plate of baked cheese balls that covered up something. "There're olives inside!"

"Yummy!" I said.

We all wished each other a merry Christmas. I looked out over the skyline of Chicago and thought, Boy, is this a dream? I always remind myself that I was crazy lucky to have grown up in this life of privilege. So many people had so little. If I ever had a ton of money, I'd probably give it all away. But to be honest, I was a bit of a hypocrite, considering what I was about to ask for.

Mom said, "Let's go to the table, shall we? We can have the soup now."

"I'll help you serve," I said.

"I'll just eat the rest of these thingies," Frederick said, popping another cheese olive in his mouth. "They're amazing."

"I'll give you a box to take home. Actually, they're from Charleston! Did you ever hear of Callie's Biscuits?"

"Nuh-uh," Frederick said with his mouth full.

"You can order them online," Mom said. "Easy-peasy. Come on, Shelby. Let's feed our men."

Mom and I were alone in the kitchen. She turned up the flame under the soup and stirred it with a wooden spoon, checking the temperature with her finger. I was opening cabinets, looking for the salad bowl.

"The crystal bowl for salad is on the counter, darling. I put the oil and vinegar out for you. I'm so glad you can make salad dressing. I can never get it quite right."

On her meds, I thought.

"Happy to help," I said.

"Are you sure you don't want to get married in June as a Christmas present to me? It would make me so happy."

"Oh, Mom, let it go," I said and dropped the lettuce into the bowl from the bag.

"Okay. But you know it breaks my heart."

"Stop! You've got to *stop*! I just want to get married and live in peace, okay?"

"Okay. But you'll let me go with you to buy your dress?"

"Mom! We have an appointment with the bridal department at Saks on Wednesday the twenty-eighth. Didn't you write it down?"

"Oh, I'm sure I did."

She's losing it, I said to myself. Champagne and Ativan, jiggly combo.

I drained the mozzarella balls and rolled them on a paper towel to dry them a bit. Even I knew that salad dressing didn't stick to wet anything. Then I rinsed the cherry tomatoes and let them drain on more paper towels.

"Okay, good! Now, where's the mustard?"

She reached in the refrigerator and handed me a jar of Maille.

"Here you go, sweetie!"

Actually, I liked her better when she was like this.

"This is the best mustard in the world," I said.

I put a healthy teaspoon in the bottom of a small mixing bowl with a big pinch of salt. Then I added a bit of red wine vinegar and a slug of canola oil, whisking it all together like mad. I thinned the dressing with vinegar and thickened it with oil until I had enough for the whole salad. I added the cheese and the tomatoes, poured the salad dressing over it all, and tossed it with a large fork and spoon until it was all covered and slick. One more pinch of sea salt, one more toss, and we were ready to go. You could learn anything you wanted to know on YouTube. I took the salad to the table and came back to help Mom ladle the soup into soup plates. Then we grated a little pepper and a tiny bit of nutmeg over it.

"This smells delicious," I said.

"Doesn't it?" Mom said. "It's important to know who to call."

"Always," I said, and even though I didn't like the fact that in my entire life, she never made home-cooked meals beyond breakfast cereal with milk, I was glad that after dinner we didn't have to clean a kitchen that looked like a bomb went off in it.

We sat and Dad raised his glass. "Merry Christmas, everyone!"

"Merry Christmas!" we all said and had a spoonful.

"This is really fabulous," Frederick said. "It reminds me of the she-crab soup my uncle Floyd makes."

"I thought he was a pit master," my mom said.

"He can cook anything," Frederick said. "My mom bakes, but my uncle, well, he's sort of inspired."

"I see," my mom said, and I knew exactly what was running through her dirty mind.

"How is your family, Frederick? This is going to be a difficult holiday for them, I'm sure."

"They're pretty sad," Frederick said. "Especially my grandmother."

"Actually," I said, "I was going to ask you for a huge favor, Dad."

"Anything, princess. It's Christmas, after all."

I couldn't help thinking in that moment that he sure was filled with mirth for someone who practically spent his life with a phone at his ear, screaming in four languages.

"Well, if the plane's just sitting around, we were wondering if we could go to South Carolina and spread a little cheer and . . ." I said.

He held his hand up, indicating I shouldn't speak any further.

"Shelby, when I consider the amount of money you are saving me by getting married next month, a round trip to South Carolina is nothing at all."

"And we'd like to pick up Frederick's cousin Ann in New Jersey. It's just for an overnight. Please, Daddy?"

I saw the color drain from my mother's face. "But, but, but . . ." she said.

"But what?" my father said.

If Dad hated anything, it was being overruled.

"This is her last Christmas before she gets married!" Mom said, as if I wasn't in the room.

"There will be plenty of other Christmases," I said quietly.

"But we have a reservation at the club for Christmas Day dinner!" she said.

"So what?" my father said.

"It's prepaid!" my mother said, realizing Dad didn't care.

"So I'll lose two hundred dollars. If that was the most money I ever lost, believe me, I'd be a happy man!"

Seeing she was defeated, she rose and left the table.

"Wait just a minute, Susan," my father said.

"What?" She turned to face him.

"Do you think I might have a little more soup? Please?"

Dad smiled at Mom, letting her know the argument was over. I think that if my mother could have sent his soup plate flying across the room like a Frisbee, she would have. But she did not. She was too well mannered to throw things. Besides, she was cruising the Big Pharma River.

"Of course, darling," she said, took his bowl, and left the room.

And so Dad arranged for us to have wheels-up at ten on Christmas Day, with a short stop in Morristown to pick up Ann, and then we'd be knocking on Frederick's family's door by three. They were going to be so surprised.

"Ann is so excited," Frederick said. "She said that she realized when we were together for Pop's funeral that somehow in her mind, she just depends on things on the farm staying the same, like believing Pop would be around forever. His death really shocked her."

"I get that," I said. "Too bad I don't have any grandparents to expect to live forever."

"Yeah, it is. Well, anyway, she's psyched because she gets to see her dad and my mom and hopefully bring some joy to the day."

"I like your style," Dad said to me last night. "It's important to do things for other people, and those people, no matter how strange and peculiar they may seem to you, are going to be your family too."

"Frederick already is, Daddy."

He looked at me so sweetly, I could almost feel love coming from his eyes.

"That's so wonderful, Shelby. Give them our best, will you?"

I had promised that I would. Why did he think they were strange and peculiar? They're the normal ones, I wanted to say.

We were in the front two seats of Dad's Gulfstream G550, high above the clouds, cruising along at a cool 560 miles an hour. This G550 might be the prettiest private plane I'd ever been in. Sometimes my life was maybe like being the child of a rock star, which would have been easier to explain than what it was my father actually did for a living.

After an hour or so and the reading of a *People* magazine front to back, we touched down in Morristown and taxied to the hangar.

"Should we go get her?" I said to Fred. "She's got the tail number, but . . ."

"I think she'd like that," he said. "I mean, we're probably the only plane landing on Christmas Day, so, she's not getting lost. But what the heck?"

"Yeah, I think it's way more hospitable," I said. "And it's Christmas, after all."

We climbed off the plane and hurried over to the terminal. There was Ann all bundled up, waving at us.

"Hey! Merry Christmas, cuz!" Frederick called out to her.

"Fred! Merry Christmas! This is just the best idea you ever had!" Ann said. She was bubbling with excitement. "Shelby! Give me a hug!"

I hugged her, and between her puffy coat and mine, it was a smush collision of two comforters.

"Merry Christmas! Let's go!" I said. "No point hanging around here!"

We left the terminal and crossed the tarmac toward the plane.

"It's so cold here!" Ann said.

"Come to Chicago," Frederick said with a big grin. "It was seven degrees when we left."

"No way," Ann said, knowing it was true.

This was such a great idea! Look how happy they are! I mentally patted myself on the back.

We climbed on board and Ann sat right across the aisle from us.

"This is freaking amazing," she said, running her hand over the burled walnut paneling. "I feel like Beyoncé rolls like this. Right?"

"She probably has a fleet of planes and helicopters," I said. "And six yachts."

"And a big house in Malibu. With a pool. Hanging off a cliff. Overlooking the Pacific," Frederick said, deadpan.

I don't know why we thought that was so hilarious, but at that moment it was. Maybe we were, all of us, just ripe for something to tickle our funny bones. We started to giggle.

"Well, it's not my plane," I said. "It belongs to my dad's business."

"Don't let the IRS hear you," Ann said. "They love to audit for stuff like that. Improper use of a business asset. I know this because my boss had to pay a fine for the same thing."

"Listen, ethically it's probably a no-no, but my dad wouldn't give us the plane if it was really that terrible. I mean, I'm sure he'll repay the company what he owes for personal usage."

"I think it's weird that we are even having this conversation," Frederick said. "Anybody want a sandwich?"

"Sure," Ann said. "What kind?"

"Turkey or roast beef," Frederick said.

"I'll split a turkey with anybody . . ."

From Morristown it was an hour and fifteen minutes to Charleston. There was a car waiting for us that would take us to the farm. Tomorrow at noon, another car would take us back to the airport. Dad planned everything for us. He was so great.

"So that's what Pop's death did to me," Ann said. "It shocked me back into the real world. Look how terrific my dad's been to us all these years."

"Uncle Floyd is the undisputed greatest," Frederick said. "He made some huge sacrifices for all of us."

"So did Aunt Diane. That's exactly why I'm so glad we're doing this. We need to start doing a better job of being a family," Ann said. "I think they need us, especially now."

"This is a great beginning," Frederick said. "Sophie was

really disappointed she couldn't come. But she's spending the holiday in Bali with some friends."

"Not so bad," I said, thinking I'd like to go to Bali.

"Yeah, and Stephanie met some guy," Frederick said.

"He's a shepherd," Ann said. "No lie. A shepherd."

"I didn't know they had shepherds in Vermont," Frederick said. "Don't tell Uncle Floyd."

"No kidding," Ann said. "It's bad enough as it is with her. And he hates hippies."

I started laughing again. "I didn't know they had shepherds in the United States!"

"Seriously," Ann said. "You can't make this stuff up."

I was enjoying Ann's company more than I remembered, but then the only time I'd met her was at Pop's funeral. I mean, who's trying to charm anyone at a funeral?

We touched down in Charleston and a car was waiting for us on the tarmac. Our pilot and his copilot transferred our luggage to the trunk of the car. Soon we were on 526 East, almost in Mount Pleasant. There was no traffic.

"The driveway is just up there on the left," Fred said.

The driver made his turn and we bumped along the gravel for a minute until he came to a stop. We got out of the car, took our bags, and went into the house. No one was there except Gus, who was completely uninterested in us.

"That's a sweet little Christmas tree," I said, looking across the living room.

"At least they put up a tree," Frederick said.

"They must be at Dad's," Ann said. "Let's just leave our luggage right here."

"Funny they didn't hear us," Frederick said.

"Maybe they're playing Christmas music or something," I said. "Let's go see."

Sure enough, the closer we got to the trailer, the louder the sounds became. It wasn't music. It was BJ and Floyd, yelling at each other.

Wow! Who yells? I didn't know anyone who yelled like that. It was kind of exciting but scary at the same time.

Suddenly we saw BJ burst from the house and throw her bags in her car.

"You're as crazy as every devil in hell, Floyd! And you're stupid too! I'm never coming back this time!"

Then Uncle Floyd appeared, still not seeing the three of us standing in the driveway like garden statuary. He leaned on her car door to say something and she stomped on the gas pedal. He stumbled and nearly fell as her car lurched forward, coming toward us at full speed. We jumped aside so we wouldn't get run over.

Then she saw us, came out of her stupor, and stopped her car. She lowered her window.

"Well, Fred! What a wonderful surprise! Shelby. Ann. Ann, your dad and I have had a difference of opinion. Sorry to leave this way, but I have to go. Merry Christmas, y'all."

Then she stomped on her gas again, leaving us in a cloud of dust and flying bits of pea gravel. By this point, Floyd spotted us, and despite the drama, he was grinning from ear to ear at the sight of us and coming to greet us.

"Merry Christmas! Would y'all lookie what the cat dragged in!" He stopped and spread his arms wide.

"Daddy!" Ann said and all but flew through the air into his arms.

"Merry Christmas, baby. You sure are a sight for sore eyes."

"I love you, Daddy!"

"Best news I've heard all day!" Uncle Floyd said.

"Hey, Uncle Floyd!" Frederick said. "Merry Christmas!"

"Fred! My man! Merry Christmas! Welcome home!" They man-hugged with enthusiasm like football players do after a touchdown. "Hey, Shelby! Merry Christmas to you too!"

"Merry Christmas, Uncle Floyd," I said and gave him a polite hug.

Yep, I called him uncle. I called him uncle because I couldn't wait to be a part of their crazy family.

"So what happened to BJ?" Frederick said.

"Fred, you just can't make some people happy. She'll be back. We can't let that ruin Christmas, can we?" Uncle Floyd said. "Come on in. We were just about to eat!"

We continued walking toward the trailer.

"No, really. Y'all aren't really breaking up, are you?" Ann said.

"I doubt it. She didn't like her Santa from me," Uncle Floyd said.

"Why not? What was it?" I asked, knowing it was none of my business.

"A custom bugout bag," he said. "Now, who wouldn't want to have that?"

I had no idea what he was talking about.

"Best Christmas ever!" Shelby said.

"Mom is hot for Alden," Fred said.

CHAPTER 19

the best gift ever

Mom! Gram! Merry Christmas!"

For a split second I thought I was seeing things. It was my *Fred*! He was home! With Shelby and Ann! Oh, how wonderful!

"I can't believe you're here!" I threw my arms around him and hugged him with all my might.

My friend Kathy, who had gone to church with us and come for dinner, said, "Well, I'll be darned! We were just talking about y'all—well, before the fun began with BJ, that is."

"Hey, Miss Kathy. Merry Christmas!" Ann said. "Yeah, what the heck happened with her?"

"And to you too!" Kathy said. "BJ? Who knows?"

"You daddy needs sensitivity training," I said.

"No kidding," Ann said. "I mean, we all know that."

"We wanted to spend the day with y'all, so here we are," Fred said. "It was actually Shelby's idea."

"It was? Oh, Shelby, thank you! You're such a dear, dear girl!" I said, choking up from excitement. I hugged her tight, and then surprisingly, she hugged me back. She wasn't such a cold fish after all.

"This day just keeps getting more unbelievable," my mother said under her breath, observing the hug.

"Gram! Merry Christmas!" Fred said.

The very second he turned his attention to her, she lit up like the fake tree in the corner of the room. Just for the record, in the interest of living space, Floyd had taken wire cutters and trimmed his tree into a shape that resembled a rocket or a bomb from World War II. Then he covered it with every kind of light on the market, not necessarily removing burned-out strings. It stayed decorated from year to year, stored in giant garbage bags in the barn. Floyd was a practical man, not an interior decorator. But he had cleaned the place for Christmas. Or BJ did.

"Ah, my darling boy!" Mom said as she held his face in her two hands. "I'm so happy to see you!"

I couldn't help but notice Shelby's reaction to my mother's affection for Fred. Her face literally changed to something very sweet and tender. I loved her a little more then, for understanding how important Fred is to us.

"Dad? Is the other card table still under the bed?" Ann asked.

"Maybe," Floyd said. "Go look. We could probably use another table. And there are some folding chairs in the back of my closet."

"I'll help her," I said. I hurried to the back of the trailer to Floyd's bedroom, where big old Moses was having a nap in the middle of his bed. Ann was on her hands and knees, sliding the folding table out. "Is there another tablecloth?"

"I doubt it. That one looked new to me," she said.

"Okay, Plan B. Is there a big white flat sheet around here?" I said.

"If there is, it would be in the linen closet," Ann said.

Linen closet was a misnomer. Whatever linens Floyd owned were either on a bed, hanging from a towel rack, or in the kitchen draped over the handle on the oven door. To my surprise, there was an unopened set of king-size white sheets. BJ must've been shopping a white sale. But there were no more linens. There were flashlights, batteries, sleeping bags, blankets, and all sorts of things Floyd would need if some foreign enemy and aliens from outer space dropped a bomb on us at the same time. He was really close to going off the deep end. And what made him think that BJ would want what he bought her as a Christmas gift? I opened the package and took out the flat sheet and pushed the rest of the package back into the closet, squeezing it in between all Floyd's emergency supplies.

Ann and I took everything off the holiday table BJ had set so nicely, pushed the second card table against the first one, and draped the big white sheet over them.

"Let's push this over to the sofa so we can use the sofa as seating," I said.

"What a good idea!" Ann said.

"You can let it hang to the floor in the front," Shelby said. "The sofa side doesn't matter because you can't see it."

We stopped and stared at her.

"I've done this before," she said. "And use the holiday cloth this way."

She shook it out and over the center of both tables on the diagonal. Now you couldn't see where the tables didn't quite meet.

"Brilliant!" Ann said.

"Thanks!" Shelby said. "Our apartment is tiny. We don't have a dining room. Just a breakfast bar. So if we have friends over for dinner, this is what we do."

"Makes sense to me," Ann said.

"There are no more holiday plates," I said.

I was looking in the cabinet where Floyd kept his dishes. There was a stack of white plates. I took out three.

Shelby said, "Use the holiday plates and glasses every other place setting. We're seven, I think. Right?"

We each counted heads and came up with the same total. Then we reset the table, warmed up all the food, and put the turkey on Floyd's largest cutting board to carve.

"Damn!" he said, looking around.

"What's the matter now?" my mother said.

"BJ left without making the gravy!"

"Oh, for heaven's sake! Relax," I said. "I'll make gravy."

He was right. She had not made it. The turkey stock was in the refrigerator in a huge mason jar. I took it out, unscrewed the top, and scraped off the fat with a spoon. Then I nuked it for a few minutes, made a roux in the last clean pot he had, and slowly added the hot stock, incorporating it with a whisk. Last I poured the drippings from the roasting pan into a Pyrex measuring cup, let the fat rise to the top, removed it as well as I could, and poured the goodies into the gravy, turning it from blond to the color of a pecan shell. Beautiful.

There's nothing like a well-made gravy, I thought, and corrected the seasoning. Maybe next year someone would buy me a gravy separator.

The meal, being served buffet style from the stove, was just under way when there was a knock at the door. Floyd put down his carving knife and went to answer it. To my complete surprise, there stood Alden. He was holding a beautiful red poinsettia wrapped in gold foil.

"Well, Merry Christmas, Bubba!" Floyd said. "Come on in!"

"Thanks." He shook hands with Floyd and waved a little wave to everyone, his eyes stopping on me and then moving on to the others. "Merry Christmas, everyone! Oh! Fred! Ann! And Shelby's here too! Isn't that great? When did y'all get in?"

Fred said, "About an hour ago. Merry Christmas, Mr. Corrigan."

"Call me Alden, Fred. So how long can y'all stay? Oh! I'm interrupting your dinner!"

"Not at all," I said.

"Actually, we leave in the morning," Shelby said.

"So soon?" I said, and my heart sank.

"Yeah. Sadly, Daddy wants the plane back," Shelby said like she'd just borrowed her father's bicycle. "He's going to London or somewhere. Board meeting, I think."

"Oh, no!" my mother said. "But you just got here!"

"We're coming back, Gram," Ann said. "A lot."

Mom took Ann's hand in hers and kissed it. Then she started to cry. Right there in front of everyone on Christmas Day. Everyone was so startled that no one said a word.

"I miss him, you know? It's just not okay without him."

I felt so sorry for her then. My mother never lost her composure. Never.

Alden worked his way across the room and knelt at her side.

"I brought this for you, Miss Virnell. Please don't be so sad. Pop wouldn't want you to cry. I know he wouldn't." Before I could pull a tissue from the box on the kitchen counter, Alden produced a freshly pressed linen handkerchief from his jacket pocket and handed it to her.

"You're right, of course. Thank you, Alden."

"I just wanted to see how you were doing today. That's all," he said.

"You're such a dear, thoughtful man," Mom said and blotted her eyes.

I looked at Floyd as if to say, *Isn't he?* And Floyd looked at me as if to say, *He's a pansy suck-up, that's what.*

"How 'bout a beer?" Floyd said, giving hospitality a stab.

"Or dinner," Mother said. "We just sat down. Please join us!"

"Oh, that's so nice. No, thanks, I can't stay. Dinner's in the oven, so I have to get back or I'll burn the house down." He laughed a little and my mother smiled, looking at him like he was the crown prince of some place important.

"Come on. I'll walk you out," I said.

"Okay, thanks. Merry Christmas, y'all!"

"To you too!" Fred said.

"Have a good one!" Floyd said.

We got outside and I said, "So, how's Betsy?"

"She's a sweetheart. She sends her best to y'all."

"Well, that's so nice," I said, thinking I wished only the worst for her and reprimanding myself in the same breath. "It was very sweet of you to come by. You really didn't have to, you know. We're okay. Really, we are."

Alden gave me the strangest look, and I saw that maybe I'd said it all wrong. Lawsa, he had beautiful eyes.

"Alden, I think that came out wrong. What I meant was . . ."

"It's okay, Diane. I understand. I just thought this might be a tough day for everyone." He leaned down and kissed my cheek. "Merry Christmas."

"Oh, God," I said as he turned and walked away.

Once again, he had not understood me. He thought I was telling him not to be coming around here if he was all in love with his Betsy. Betsy Beyer the Kewpie doll. Betsy Wetsy. Please!

Floyd stuck his head out the door. "Come on! Dinner's getting cold!"

"Coming," I said.

"Didn't go right?" he said.

"Right," I said.

"It's okay, Lady Di," Floyd said and squeezed my shoulder with brotherly affection. "He's an imbecile anyway."

Not a nice thing to say.

"I don't know if that's so, but he sure is slow to process sometimes."

"Whatever. Let's eat. He'll be back."

"I doubt it," I said, because as far as I could tell Alden was totally happy with Betsy.

I went back inside and we had our Christmas dinner with all our traditional side dishes and no mention of BJ except to say her turkey was a little dry and her dressing was too. I knew it wasn't BJ's fault. The poor bird and the stuffing simply sat around too long. Every time you reheated birds or microwaved bread dishes, they died a little more. But the meal was saved by gravy. And hot biscuits.

"You hardly need teeth for this meal," Floyd said. "Everything except the bird is creamed."

He was right. We had whipped rutabagas, sweet potatoes, and beets, and creamed spinach and onions. The cranberry sauce was smooth and the biscuits literally dissolved in your mouth. No teeth required.

"This is the best Christmas dinner I've ever had," Shelby said.

"Really? Why's that?" my mother said.

"Well," Shelby said, "for one thing, it's delicious. It doesn't taste like club food at all."

"What do you mean, 'club food'?" Floyd asked.

"Food from her parents' club," Fred said.

"Your mother doesn't like to cook?" I asked, knowing the answer before she said a word.

Shelby got the giggles. "Listen, if my dad and I changed the kitchen into a sauna, it would take her a month to notice it was gone. No, my mother is not a great cook. At all. I mean, even last night on Christmas Eve, we had takeout!"

"That's funny," Floyd said.

"I don't think our kitchen's ever been dirty—like, the oven looks brand-new," Shelby continued. "This is so different. We're all here and pitching in, you know, like a real family on television."

"Babe, those people are actors," Fred said.

"You know what I mean," Shelby said. "Like *Modern Family*!"

"I'm just going to take that as a compliment," I said and smiled. And, I thought, I'll take it as a win also.

I noticed Ann putting a healthy tablespoon of my peach jam on her biscuit, then proceeding to devour it in one bite. She was telling me about her recent promotion.

"Good, huh?" I said.

"Uh, yeah. You know, Aunt Diane," Ann said, "my new job is all about making sure that our customers know we are environmentally responsible with things like palm oil and so forth. But there is an acquisitions department. There's no jam like this on our product list. It's like a live peach is in your mouth. Not too sweet. Not too tart."

"Thanks, sweetheart," I said. "You grew up eating this jam."

"Well, I don't remember it being this good. I'll bet they'd love to buy this recipe," she said.

"It's not for sale," Mom said.

"Oh, Ann, it's just the same old jam Momma's momma taught her how to make."

"Aunt Diane, it's really special."

"Well, thanks, sweetie. I'll give you a jar to take home."

"And strawberry. Give one to Shelby too!" my mother said. Shelby's stock was on the rise with my mother. And me.

All through dinner we made small talk and I kept looking at Alden's lush poinsettia on the table, sitting right next to the sweet little one BJ bought. All I could think about was Alden and Betsy sitting by a fire, feeding bits of prime rib and mashed potatoes to each other and them sipping some rare and expensive red wine, cooing at each other, and God only knows what they'd do after dinner. She'd probably show him the sexy see-through nightie she bought for their cruise and he'd probably tell her she didn't need it, that she drove him wild without any props. It was like a giant pill was sitting on the back of my tongue that refused to go down or to melt.

And poor BJ was surely not having her best Christmas either. I'd call her later.

As we cleaned up, I couldn't help but notice that Shelby and Fred were having a lot of fun just drying glasses, holding goblets up to the light and inspecting them. I was looking right into the face of love and the face of my son's future. I felt heartened then that their love was solid. They would have a good marriage.

After the dinner dishes were washed and everything was put away, we all moved over to the big house for coffee and dessert. The trailer felt overcrowded. I carried the fruitcake and Kathy had the other tins of the same things we made every single year.

Kathy said, "Miss Virnell? Can I help you cut the cake?"

"Why, yes, Kathy. That would be lovely. My legs are telling me to rest."

"I'll make us a pot of coffee," I said. "Mom, why don't you go sit with Fred and the others? I'm afraid they'll be gone before we know it. We'll be there in five minutes."

"I think I will. Thank you," Mom said and left us there.

We took out plates, cups and saucers, dessert forks, and teaspoons and lined them up on the table. I got the creamer from the refrigerator, the sugar bowl from the cupboard, and popped open the tins of rum balls and sands.

"She's so sad," I said.

"Can you blame her? First she loses her husband of sixty years on Thanksgiving Day and then she gets to think about her own mortality on Christmas. The end's not easy."

"No. It really isn't. But I have to say, she's been a trouper."

"Because that's who she really is."

"It's true."

The coffee began to drip, filling the air with its robust fragrance.

"Juan Valdez is in the house," I said. "Don't you wish coffee tasted as good as it smells?"

"Yes, I sure do," Kathy said. "So what did you think about Alden coming by?"

She sliced the fruitcake in thin pieces and put them on the plates.

"I'm glad he didn't see us moaning and groaning—well,

except for Mom's little breakdown, which I don't blame her for one bit. He's a thoughtful man."

"Two sands and two rum balls for each plate?"

"That's plenty. There's more if anyone wants it. Seems like every year we always make too much."

"Send it home with the kids."

"Excellent idea."

"Alden's still in love with you," she said. "And you've still got it going on for him, but I'm keeping my mouth shut."

She made me laugh.

"I love how you keep your mouth shut."

"It's just my opinion . . ."

"But you're keeping it to yourself?"

"Yeah, that's right."

When the coffee was finished dripping we put everything on two trays and carried them to the dining room. Floyd was seated in Pop's chair. I liked that he was assuming a leadership position, if that was what he meant by sitting there. It would make Mom feel more secure. It was interesting how one small detail, like taking your father's chair, could change a whole landscape.

"Here we go," I said, putting down the tray to rest. "Everyone, help yourself, okay?"

"I sneaked a rum ball in the kitchen, Miss Virnell. I believe they're even better than last year's."

"Well, thank you, Kathy," Mom said.

"I've never had a rum ball," Shelby said. "Or fruitcake. Isn't fruitcake supposed to be, um, disgusting?"

"That's a good one!" Floyd said.

"You tell us," I said.

She had put herself under a magnifying glass and we all waited until she took a bite.

"Go ahead," Fred said. "Eat the darn thing. It won't kill you."

She cut a bite with the side of her fork and held it up to inspect it, as if it might or might not be poison. Then she smelled it.

"Go on, child!" Mom said. "Eat it!"

She closed her eyes and put the fork in her mouth. Her eyes opened and she began to chew enthusiastically, taking another bite.

"No more calls!" Floyd said with a hearty laugh. "We have another convert!"

"It's, like, totally amazing!" she said. "Poor little cake! Why do people say such terrible things about you?"

"Because it's not my fruitcake they're eating," I said.

"Can you show me how to make it?" she said.

Alert the press! I thought. The first millennial in the short history of millennials has bowed to a baby boomer.

"And who taught you how to make it in the first place?" Mom said.

"You did, Mom," I said and turned to Shelby. "Of course. I'd be thrilled to show you. Come visit next October and we can make them together."

"This cake is from October?" Shelby said, feigning a gag.

Ann laughed and said, "It keeps like some of the stuff we make!"

"That stuff ain't food," Floyd said.

"Tell America that," Ann said. "We sell mountains of it."

"I happen to love the cookies!" Shelby said.

"It's just business," Fred said.

"You keep it wrapped in brandy-soaked cheesecloth, in the freezer," I said.

"But long expiration dates are a good idea for certain things," Floyd said. "Like what you put in your bugout bag."

"What is this bugout bag thing, Uncle Floyd?" Shelby said, calling Floyd uncle, which made Kathy shoot me a look and Mom gasp.

Here we go, I thought.

"Well, Christmas Day probably isn't the time to talk about doom and gloom, but I'll give you the gist of the theory."

"Shouldn't this wait until after the wedding, Uncle Floyd? You could scare her out of marrying me."

Fred was being pleasant and teasing his uncle, but I could see he was serious.

"Don't mind him, Shelby. When the trouble starts, he'll be glad I'm prepared."

"What trouble?" Shelby said. "What am I missing?"

Ann jumped in. "My dad thinks the end of the world is around the corner."

"He just wants to take care of his family in case something terrible happens," Mom said, defending him.

"Like what?" Shelby said. "A hurricane?"

"Yes!" Floyd said. "Hurricanes are treacherous. Rising water, high winds. They can blow you to kingdom come. But what I worry about most is the grid."

"The grid?" Shelby said.

"Power. Last time we had a big hurricane we lost power for a week. Remember Katrina? All those poor people on life support with no generator? I just want to be prepared, that's all."

"What's the matter with that?" Shelby said. "Seems like a good idea to me."

"The problem here," I said, "is not that he bought BJ a bugout bag, it's that he bought her a bugout bag for Christmas. That's the problem, dear brother. To you, a bugout bag is essential. It's not a gift. You couldn't buy her perfume?"

"Wait a minute," Floyd said. "The bag I put together for BJ is the most deluxe version there is. For example, she didn't just get a water bottle, it was a thirty-ounce Yeti for fifty-three dollars. I paid *full* price."

"That must've damn near killed you," I said.

Fred said to Shelby, "We pride ourselves on never paying full price for anything. Ever."

"Being thrifty is a virtue," Mom said.

"Anyway, to your question, Shelby, a bugout bag is like a survival kit. Let's say lightning strikes and the house burns to the ground."

"Hush! The devil will hear you!" Mom said. "He doesn't need any more ideas!"

Shelby giggled and Floyd shook his head.

He continued, "A bugout bag, if it's thoughtfully put together, can ensure your survival in almost any situation, except nuclear war, of course."

"Oh," Shelby said.

"Mine has a tent, a tarp for the ground in case it's wet,

a portable stove, a pot with a top, a frying pan, a hunting knife . . ."

"Mrs. Stiftel?" Shelby turned to me.

"Yes?"

Floyd kept going. "Protein bars, a rain poncho, convertible pants, underwear, wool hiking socks, a wool blanket, a first aid kit, all-purpose soap, toilet paper, a towel, a toothbrush, a mirror, a machete, a headlamp, and a lot of other stuff."

"A machete? A headlamp? Really? If your son gave me any of that stuff for Christmas, I think I'd run away too," Shelby said.

"You ladies would be awfully sorry if you needed it and you didn't have it," Floyd said.

"Perhaps, but that's not the point," I said and smiled.

"Aunt Diane is saying," Ann said, "that it's just not what every girl wants for Christmas."

"At all," Shelby said.

"Ever," I added for good measure.

"Women," Floyd said. "I even bought her a small generator."

"Well, brother? You can't please them all."

"Shelby? Come with me for a minute," Gram said.

I followed them to Gram's bedroom. Gram's mahogany spindle spool double bed, which she slept in with Pop for all those years, had belonged to her mother. The end tables were from Sear's, the year she and Pop married. It was probably time to change her wallpaper because it was so outdated and yellowed with age. But when I was a little girl I thought it was so pretty.

"Sit here on the side of my bed, sweetheart," she said to her. "The best Christmas gift you could've given me is bringing my grandson home to me. I just want to thank you for that."

Shelby sat down and I began pulling Mom's shades down for the night. Mom went into her chest of drawers and dug around for a minute. Finally she took out something wrapped in tissue paper and sat on the bed next to Shelby.

"Now, this belonged to my grandmother and I want you to have it for your wedding day."

Shelby unfolded the paper to find a simple but beautiful linen handkerchief edged in blue.

"Oh, it's beautiful!" Shelby said.

"Now you have something old, blue, and borrowed. You just need something new and a penny for your shoe!"

"Oh, Mrs. English! That's so sweet! Thank you!"

"Don't lose it. We'll need it in case Ann or Stephanie ever gets a man. I think it's too late for Sophie. And, oh, call me Gram."

"Gram," Shelby said. "I have a gram now. This is such a nice feeling."

"It's not too late for Sophie! It's never too late for love," I said.

"Is that a fact?" my mother said. "Hmm. You could've fooled me."

My mother always has to have the last word.

"What's all that white stuff?" Floyd said.

"The S-word," Diane said.

CHAPTER 20

diane—on the way

Back in December, in the moment when we opened our Christmas gifts from Fred and Shelby, we couldn't imagine wearing suede boots lined in shearling. Or using the cashmere scarves and lined leather gloves they sent. They were beautiful, but it was hardly ever cold enough for any of those kinds of clothes. Maybe the scarf, but gloves? We had not worn gloves in ages, except for gardening. Nonetheless, I thanked them profusely and said they would come in handy in Chicago for the wedding. *That's* why they had chosen those things for us. My son was so thoughtful, and Shelby was actually turning out to be a sweetheart.

"Floyd? Do you have a winter coat?"

"Somewhere," he said. "Seems like I used to have one anyway."

"I'll help you look," I said.

An hour of digging through closets and boxes yielded no fruit. But I did find a wedding gift with a card in a bag for Shelby and Fred from BJ and Floyd. I really needed to call her.

"Guess I'll go on L.L.Bean's Web site and see what they've got," he said.

"If they have a sale, let me know. And we probably should get something for Mom too."

Floyd had decided he was bringing the rehearsal dinner, which was to be held at Shelby and Fred's small apartment. He was packing barbecue off the bone and shredded, and shrimp and grits, in his big cooler and he was driving. And he was bringing cases of some local craft beer from Palmetto Brewery. Needless to say, he was throwing in five cases of small mason jars to use in place of wineglasses. I would've asked him to bring jars of our peach jam for all the guests to take home, but I knew it wouldn't fly with Susan. She'd see it as mutiny. However, I'd bet she wouldn't mind us giving away caviar.

"Palmetto's got one on draft now called Brassy Blonde. But I still like their amber ale."

"I like the pilsner. Maybe you should rent a big SUV, Floyd. That truck of yours has seen better days."

"Maybe," he said, considering my suggestion. "I've got points on my Mastercard. I never use them."

"Maybe now's the time," I said. "Who knows what the roads are like?"

"You're probably right. Plus, my tires aren't great."

And he was bringing a case of Double Cross vodka, a very generous wedding gift for Fred and Shelby from his friends who owned the company.

Shelby was ordering a cake, and I was to arrive in Chicago a few days early to bake corn bread, find hamburger buns, and make enough coleslaw to feed all their guests. Maybe I'd make a few dozen deviled eggs too. Everyone always loved them. Fred did, anyway, and that was reason enough.

And by the way, when they were with us on Christmas night, Shelby slept in Fred's room and Fred slept on the sofa. No monkey business in my house, thank you. I knew what went on in Chicago, but that was their business. Besides, Virnell would have pitched a fit to think that she had condoned or turned a blind eye to her grandson sleeping with his inamorata under her roof before they were married. In any case, I was still giddy over their surprise visit.

And I was delighted that Sophie and Stephanie were coming to the wedding, and of course, Ann was too. I wondered what was going on with their love lives. I'd make a point of asking them nonchalantly at some point over the wedding weekend.

So preparations were being made and we were all getting excited. Shelby had her dress and shoes. Fred had rented a tuxedo from Men's Wearhouse, which made it easy for his groomsmen to rent the same one. Even Floyd rented one, which I thought was very special.

He said, "I could buy a dark suit, I guess, but then what am I going to do with it later on?"

"I wonder if they rent tuxedoes in camo?" I said.

"They do. But very funny, Lady Di. Wait till you see me all spiffed up. Those Chicago women gonna believe James Bond is in town."

"If you say so."

He whispered in his mysterious spy voice, "Shaken, not stirred."

"Oh, brother."

I called BJ. "So, BJ, how are you?" I asked.

"Hey, Diane. I'll live, I guess."

"Well, I just found a wedding gift from you and my brother in a closet for Shelby and Fred. I will be sure to get it to them."

"I don't see Floyd dropping it off at UPS, so thanks," BJ said.

"Exactly. So what's your plan? Are you and Floyd done or is there hope?"

"No. We're all done. I just want more than he can give. It's okay. I'm moving to Atlanta February first to teach first grade at a precious school in Marietta."

"Well, you know if you ever need anything . . ." I said.

"Thanks, Diane, you're the best."

We hung up and I thought to myself, She was too nice for Floyd anyway.

I'd found a dress at Nordstrom, marked down after Christmas. It wasn't beige. It was champagne colored, with a sweetheart neck and some sparkle. I'd never owned anything quite so glamorous, because farming didn't require a black-tie wardrobe. I'd thought of using Rent the Runway, but when I found this dress, I knew I wanted to own it. I showed it to Kathy and she loved it. I asked Susan what color she was wearing.

"I haven't decided," she said.

I knew what she was saying. I could read into her reply fifty different ways, and every interpretation would be bitchy. I should wear beige. Besides, it wouldn't matter what I wore. Any choice I made would pale next to what she wore. No one would be looking at me anyway. Now that my socialist son had blown her June wedding to bits, who cared what anyone wore?

We would never be great friends. I faced this fact with a sigh of relief, because to tell the truth, the price tag of being close to Susan was no doubt too high. But surprisingly, I got a call from Alejandro.

"Alejandro? How nice to hear from you!"

"And how are you, Diane?"

"Well, I'm just fine. Getting very excited for the big day. And you? How are you doing?"

"I'm as well as can be expected given the stresses of the day."

"Oh, I know all about stress." Drought. Drought is huge stress. So is brown rot. And don't forget grasshoppers, beetles, and moths. Spring freezes were a particular nightmare of mine. "Is everything all right?"

"Oh, yes, yes, of course. I just wanted to run something by you."

"Sure!"

"Well, some time ago my company bought an interest in a small winery in Napa Valley. Their wines are quite good.

Anyway, they send me cases of every varietal when they're ready to drink. I'd like to give it to the kids for their rehearsal dinner party. What do you think?"

"I think that's very generous."

"Good! As it is, I'm stacking cases and cases in our storage unit in the basement and I can't hold much more. It would make Susan very happy to have some space for her things, and there's no point in spending money when we don't have to."

"I couldn't agree more."

"Wonderful, then I'll have it delivered to their apartment. Now, can I help you with hotel reservations?"

"Alejandro? You might be the nicest man I know. Yes. Yes, please, because I have no idea where to stay that's logistically convenient to the kids and to the wedding."

At the engagement party we had just stayed at a Marriott by the airport. It was very nice, but we spent a fortune on taxis.

"It's a pleasure to handle this for you. How many of you will there be?"

I told him who was coming and he said he would get back to me. I hit the End button.

"What's Alejandro doing calling you?" Mom said.

"Trying to be helpful, I guess."

"A big shot like him is going to make hotel reservations? A big shot like him is giving away wine? I don't know, Diane."

"You're just cynical. It's his only daughter. He just wants things to go smoothly. Who knows what Susan said to prompt his call?"

"Maybe."

The days flew by, and the next thing I knew I had a long red puffer coat from L.L.Bean across my arm, black Uggs on my feet, and I was boarding a flight to Chicago, wiping the armrest, the reclining button, and the tray at my seat with antibacterial wipes. I was sure the guy next to me thought I was germphobic, but it was flu season and I wasn't taking any chances.

I was excited and relieved we were having a wedding my nervous system could handle. Alejandro's secretary booked the entire wedding party at the Park Hyatt, where he was able to get an incredible discount. Floyd and I went online and looked at the hotel.

Floyd was suspicious. Driving me to the airport he said, "Yeah, so the room's only a hundred dollars but a cup of coffee is a billion dollars?"

I said, "I doubt it. They wouldn't set us up for sticker shock. What would be in it for them? Besides, I don't think that's Alejandro's style. I mean, I doubt it's the presidential suite, but I'm sure the rooms are fine."

As the plane climbed above the clouds, I had the thought that things were working out very nicely. What had begun as an adversarial situation had become reasonably harmonious. Susan would always be difficult. I was certain of that. But Shelby and Alejandro especially were certainly showing well. And Alejandro was sending his driver to meet me at the airport. I told him it wasn't necessary, but he insisted.

"No. I simply will not have the mother of my almost son-in-law riding around Chicago in some crazy taxi. You don't understand, Diane. You could wind up at the bottom of the lake!"

"Well, all righty then. Thank you."

What else could I say?

I was feeling pretty sad that Alden wasn't coming. I missed him. I was such a fool. Maybe Betsy would leave him. I could hope.

The flight was smooth until we began our descent, and then it was so bumpy, I was terrified as the plane lurched one way and then another. The pilot addressed us.

"Folks, don't be alarmed about the bumpy ride here. We're encountering some turbulence as we enter warmer air. We'll have you on the ground in about fourteen minutes, where the local time is three fifteen and the temperature is all the way up to eleven degrees. Please remain seated, stay buckled up, and enjoy the rest of your flight."

Easy for him to say, I thought.

But we continued to rock and roll until we landed, and as we taxied down the runway, I looked out the window. It even looked like it was freezing outside. There was no sun. Ground crew was everywhere, dressed in down jackets, with hoods pulled over knitted stocking hats. Everyone had on gloves and heavy boots. Even the ground looked frozen with remnants of a recent snowfall here and there, dirty and rock hard. If I had owned a convertible, this would not have been a top-down day. I was in a different world. One without Alden.

Alejandro's driver met me in the baggage claim area, and as soon as my bag appeared on the carousel, he grabbed it and we were on our way.

"My name is Martin, ma'am. I have been Mr. Cambria's driver for almost twenty years."

"It's nice to meet you, Martin. Thank you for coming to pick me up."

Martin was very handsome. And his manners were gorgeous.

"It is my pleasure, Mrs. Stiftel."

He opened the door for me, and soon we were in downtown Chicago at my hotel. I thanked Martin, had a brief naughty thought about him, and went to the registration desk. I went up to my room and unpacked. There was a beautiful view of the lake. It was only four o'clock and it was already getting dark. My poor son lived in this dreary place. I called him.

"Hi, sweetheart! The mothership has landed. Are you at work?"

"No, I took the rest of the week off. How was your flight?"

"A little bumpy and only twenty minutes late, which I'm told is the same thing as being on time. But fine, really. And my room has a view of the lake, which is very nice."

"How's the room itself? Are you next to the ice maker? Or next door to a room of crazy partiers?"

"Not at all. It's quiet, so far anyway. I have a gorgeous king-size bed and a bathroom fit for a queen! It's all marble and chrome, with thick towels. And there's beautiful photographic art on the walls. I even have a minibar if I want a Snickers in the middle of the night. Basically, I could live here and be very happy, except for the weather."

"That's what we all say!"

"I'll bet."

"Okay, so the plan is that I am picking you up at six, we're going to the Cambrias' club for dinner so you can see where the ceremony is going to be held, and then I'll take you back to your hotel."

"That sounds great! I'm so excited to see where my son is getting married in four days!"

"Please, Mom, I'm already a wreck. Tomorrow I thought I'd bring you over here to see the apartment and maybe you can help us figure out what we need to make the rehearsal dinner go smoothly."

"Fred, my precious heart? I don't want you to worry about a thing. I want you to enjoy this week. And your rehearsal dinner is going to be so much fun. Uncle Floyd guarantees it. I'll see you at six."

I went to the window and looked out across the gray and frozen city, wondering how my boy, a son of a peach farmer, could live in a place that was so forbidding and uninviting. In one way, it was easy for me to understand why farming didn't appeal to him. And he wanted a career that was dependable, one where it wouldn't matter if crops everywhere were infested with some biblical pestilence or severe drought. He could be an accountant anywhere and it paid well. These days kids seemed to want to test themselves someplace new, to see if they could make it on their own. But damn, it was really cold here.

In just the time it took for me to walk from the car to the door of the hotel, the stems of my pierced earrings froze and my ears began to ache from the bitter cold. But you can get used to anything, I suppose, and the cold weather didn't really seem to faze my Fred.

Day turned to evening by five and the city lights began to twinkle in the cold air. Suddenly, as I looked down North Michigan Avenue, Chicago was dazzling with powerful beauty. Maybe the population liked to see if it could withstand the awesome climate; maybe living in a city like this was a personal challenge, something that would show you what kind of grit was in your DNA. Well, bully for them. I'd take the Lowcountry humidity and mosquitoes any day over this kind of cold. At that precise moment I really but thoroughly understood why people from the North moved to the frying pan that Florida could be. They'd plain had it with winter.

We'd be home in a few days and it would be time to fertilize all the peach trees. Maybe do a little pruning. These poor people would still be dealing with subzero wind chills.

I changed into a navy knit dress Kathy made me buy and pinned a pearl brooch I'd inherited on the shoulder. I wore stockings and a pair of lowish heels and hoped there was no black ice waiting for me. I'd never seen black ice, but I'd heard terrible things about it. I'd ask Fred how to identify it. I brushed my hair and put on some lipstick and thought I didn't look too bad. In fact, I looked younger with makeup. On examination in the magnifying mirror in the bathroom, I realized that my complexion was actually fading. I needed a little color in my cheeks and on my lips. It made me look like I used to look. I wondered what would happen if I used mascara and an eyebrow pencil. That made me laugh at myself.

Since when was I so vain? How's now? Maybe I'd go to CVS and play with some Maybelline or whatever brands they carried. I'd seen that there was a salon in the hotel. Maybe I'd make an appointment for the wedding. Why not? Heck! My only child was getting married. Did I need to wear a schoolmarm's bun? I wanted to look good in the pictures. Besides, I was certain Susan was gonna put on the dog, like we say in the Lowcountry. For Fred's sake, I needed at the very least to try and be presentable.

I called the salon, left a message, explaining that this was a 911 desperado call, and went downstairs to meet Fred. He and Shelby were waiting in Fred's Jeep right in front of the hotel. A doorman opened the Jeep's back door for me and I climbed in as quickly as I could.

"Brrrr!" I said. "Hey, Fred! Hey, Shelby!"

"Hey, Mom! You made it!"

"Of course I made it!"

"Hi, Mrs. Stiftel! Welcome to the Windy City!"

"Thank you, sweetheart. But we're going to have to figure out what you're going to call me. Mrs. Stiftel is way too formal."

"You're right," Shelby said. "How about Lady Di? I love when Uncle Floyd calls you that. Plus, I love all things Princess Diana."

"Perfect!" I said.

"Lady Di!" Shelby said.

"That's me! Anyway, I'm so happy to be here. Didn't Chicago pay its heating bill?"

Shelby giggled and Fred said, "Yeah, it's pretty nippy out there."

"We'll be at the club in just a few minutes," Shelby said. "Thankfully, they have valet parking."

"I'm so glad I'm going to see your parents tonight," I said. "They must be so excited too! What a week this is going to be!"

"Oh! Gosh! My parents aren't coming tonight. My father had some kind of an emergency, who knows what, and my mother wasn't feeling so great. We're going to see them Friday at the rehearsal and then for the wedding."

"Oh, I hope everything is okay," I said.

"Daddy's just working late. This happens all the time," Shelby said. "Don't worry. They'll be fine."

I sat back and thought, Okay, I understand Alejandro working late. People do that. But unless I was in intensive care, I'd be here to welcome my new in-laws. Another reason Susan and I would never be close.

We pulled up in front of the club, a stately structure of granite and stone with the largest brass and milk glass sconces I'd ever seen. I guessed they were art deco. Overhead were enormous windows with curtains. A man dressed in an official down jacket took the car and gave Fred a ticket to retrieve it later on. We hurried inside through the enormous brass and heavy glass revolving door.

"You look pretty cute in that coat, Mom!" Fred said.

"Thanks. It's, um, not the most flattering, but it's warm. I probably should've worn the boots too, which I love, but I figured we'd just make a mad dash."

"Oh, I'm so glad you like your Uggs!" Shelby said. "I have them in pink and black. You get a lot of use out of them here."

"I'll bet you do!" I said. "Fred, we have to talk about black ice."

I said this so earnestly that their lighthearted faces instantly assumed a very serious demeanor.

"What about it?" Fred said.

"How will I recognize it? I understand it's treacherous."

Fred looked at Shelby and they both giggled.

"Well, we don't have any right now. But when snow melts and refreezes, it becomes ice, right? So if you see shiny asphalt? That might be black ice."

"To be avoided at all costs," Shelby said.

"But there's none right now," I said.

"Right," Fred said. "You're, um, safe for the moment."

"You're not too big for me to turn you over my knee, you know."

"Yeah, you can mansplain to your mom, but watch the attitude," Shelby said. "Men."

"You tell him, sweetie," I said.

We left our coats with a glamorous woman at the coat-check counter, went upstairs and immediately to our booth in the Wigwam.

"This is a lovely dining room," I said. "It feels like a club should. Cozy but still very beautiful."

The walls everywhere were gleaming oak paneling, and the vaulted ceilings were hand-plastered.

"I practically grew up here," Shelby said. "They have wonderful programming. Last year I actually heard Amanda Knox speak about her terrible ordeal in Italy."

"Amanda Knox! My goodness." I was surprised a club that

seemed as exclusive as this one would issue an invitation to someone so controversial. "What did you think of her? Do you think she was innocent?"

"I'd bet my life on it," Shelby said. "She was totally framed."

We ordered steaks and french fries, and Fred chose a bottle of red wine for us to share.

Shelby then went on to explain all the reasons Amanda Knox was innocent, which were astounding. And of course, when the Knox trial had been going on, I was usually busy in the orchard doing some hand-pollinating or pruning or working at the farm stand.

"You have to wonder how these things even happen," I said.

Shelby said, "I think it's because sometimes the police want to solve a murder, so they rush to name the bad guys and close the case. I mean, if the public thinks there's a murderer on the loose, it makes people nervous."

"And the police look bad if they can't find the bad guys right away. Hearing her was a real eye-opener," Fred said.

"I imagine so. There's nothing worse than taking an innocent person's reputation and dragging it through the mud," I said. "So, tell me how I can help you this weekend."

"Well, we have this crazy idea that we hope will be a fabulous surprise."

"Let's hear it," I said.

"We don't want our rehearsal dinner to be some stuffy night," Shelby said.

"It can't be. We're serving barbecue," I said.

"Yes, but with just a little effort we can take it to the next level," Fred said.

They laid out their plans while we ate and I literally squealed with delight.

"So, do you love it?" Fred said.

"Isn't it the best?" Shelby said.

"How did you even think of this? It's genius! I'll call Floyd. He'll help us."

When we were finished with dinner Fred said, "Would you like dessert?"

"Oh, not for me!" I said.

"Please! I have a dress to squeeze into," Shelby said.

"I can't wait to see it," I said.

"Let's go see the ballroom," Fred said.

"Let's do! Thank you both for dinner. It was delicious."

I slid out of the booth and looked back at the wall. There, right over the spot where I sat and indulged in red meat and fried potatoes, hung a life-size portrait of General Ulysses S. Grant.

"Holy Jesus, Son of God!" I said before I could catch myself. But still. "Pop must be spinning in his grave! Sometimes I forget you're marrying a Midwesterner, Fred."

Fred and Shelby laughed so hard that I began to laugh with them.

"Well, it is the Union League, after all," I said, "and he was a president of the United States."

"We're staying here on our wedding night," Fred said.

"A gift from Daddy," Shelby said.

"That is so nice!" I said.

The ballroom was gorgeous, and I knew when the tables

were all in place with flowers everywhere, my son's wedding would be amazing.

"And where's the ceremony going to be?"

"In the Wrigley Room, down the hall. Want to see?"

"Sure!"

I followed them down the hall and wondered how they were going to make this large empty room feel right for a wedding ceremony, but there was no reason to doubt that they would.

"It's just perfect, y'all," I said. "Are y'all mentally prepared for this?"

"My mother is still making me a total wreck," Shelby said. "Daddy said to just ignore her and remember that it's our day, Frederick's and mine, that is."

"Your father is a very smart man," I said.

Susan Kennedy Cambria was a head case.

I walked around the huge empty room and thought for the hundredth time, Wow, my only child's grown and getting married. Maybe someday, when Susan was finally committed to an insane asylum and Alejandro found the right woman, Shelby and Fred would open an accounting firm in Charleston. Wouldn't that be wonderful? Who was I going to dance with at my son's wedding? My brother? Oh, Lord. The thought was too depressing to explore.

The next morning, I was up at six thirty, showered and dressed by seven, and in the dining room, enjoying two poached free-range eggs, two patties of sausage, and roasted potatoes with an English muffin for sixteen dollars. Somehow, with a glass of juice, a cup of coffee, tax, and tip, the bill came to over thirty dollars. Floyd was going to have a stroke. So was Virnell. I had to find a place like Page's Okra Grill in Mount Pleasant for them.

After breakfast I went back to my room to call Floyd, turned on the news, and put it on mute. The local meteorologist was standing next to a map that showed snowflakes over Chicago. I didn't think too much of it. I mean, this part of the country got snow all the time.

Floyd answered on the first ring.

"Lady Di! How are things in the tundra?"

"Colder than my ex-husband's heart. Pack like you're going to Antarctica. No lie."

"I can already feel it. God, I hate winter weather."

"Yeah, so listen, the kids need a favor. How big is your rental car?"

"Biggest thing on four wheels. Why?"

I told him what they wanted and he thought it was a terrific idea.

"That's hilarious. Tell them Uncle Floyd has their back. Consider it done."

"Great! When are you leaving?"

"Eight o'clock tonight. The drive's a little less than fourteen hours. I'll see you for breakfast tomorrow morning. Stephanie, Ann, and Sophie all arrive tomorrow at different times. Our mother is a little nervous about the trip."

"Why?"

"She's afraid I won't stop for her to use a ladies' room or get snacks. Apparently, the last time she made a road trip was with Pop to go to New Orleans for some convention Pop wanted to attend. Anyway, he made her wait until he needed to fill up with gas, I guess."

"Well then, Floyd?"

"Yeah?"

"Just don't go all macho on her. Be sweet. She's a little old lady."

"Right. The classic iron fist in a velvet glove! Anyway, I'm outnumbered because I've got Kathy too. She's gonna help with the driving if I get tired."

"Y'all just get here in one piece, okay? Looks like we might get a little snow."

I called Fred, and he and Shelby came to pick me up. First, we went to the grocery store.

"How many people are y'all expecting tomorrow night?" I asked, putting eight lemons and limes into a plastic bag.

"Thirty tops," Fred said. "We decided to invite some friends."

"Why not?" I said.

"I'll get a cart and get soft drinks and mixers?" Shelby said.

"Good idea! And get peanuts or something for the bar. Is there a Party City nearby?"

"Sure! We can go there from here," Fred said.

Soon we had filled two baskets with everything we needed, including caraway seeds for the coleslaw.

"So, basically, we've emptied our apartment and put everything in storage in the basement. We kept our bed, TV, and enough lamps so that we're not wandering around in the dark. And we rented high-top cocktail tables, buffet tables, and some stools. We can use the breakfast bar as the bar. Self-service. But Bill . . . remember Bill Evans? He's my best man. He said he'd keep an eye on the bar, you know, ice and that kind of thing."

"Absolutely. You don't need to hire a bartender for just thirty people. What are y'all doing for flowers?"

"Ashley's arranging them. Remember Ashley Hargrove, my maid of honor?"

"Oh, of course. The pretty blonde."

"Her aunt has a wholesale flower business. She's getting tons of sunflowers to put in mason jars. And votive candles in those little glass cups."

"Great!" I said. "So I'm thinking red-and-white-check tablecloths and disposable red or navy plates, napkins, and flatware. How does that sound?"

"Everybody will love it except my mother," Shelby said. "She's such a snob."

"Not really," I said, because I felt that defending her mother seemed like the parental thing to do. "She's just used to a fancier life, that's all. There's nothing wrong with glitz and glamour either."

"Maybe. But I'm going to hear about this for a long time," Shelby said.

"I wouldn't worry about it too much. In my experience? Something always happens, and whatever I was worried about the world chewing on becomes yesterday's news in a heartbeat."

"Screw it, Shelby. Uncle Floyd probably already has Molly in the truck."

Yes. Molly the chicken was coming to Chicago to lend an air of authenticity to our Lowcountry hoedown. She would pose for selfies and be the general entertainment. And Fred had a playlist of bluegrass music on his iPhone that would last for hours, blasting through his tiny Bose speakers.

"I've even got Steve Martin's band on it," he said. "The Steep Canyon Rangers."

"Cool," I said. I secretly loved Steve Martin. Another unrequited love. Ah, well.

It started snowing around four o'clock in the morning, so by the time I woke up on Friday, there were about two inches on the ground. I made a cup of coffee and stood by my window watching it fall. Actually, it was beautiful in its quiet yet slippery, frightening way. The skies were all different shades of gray, depending where you looked, from the wispy color of Spanish moss to the deepened hues of tarnished silver. I had never seen skies like this. Chicago was hushed under a thick blanket of pure white snow that continued falling.

My message light was flashing. I had a call from the salon. They would do my hair at ten the next morning and they could cut it if I'd like. I called back, leaving another message to confirm. One less thing to stress over. Do you think Susan offered to help me with hair? Did she say, *Oh, would you like to get your hair blown out?* No. She obviously didn't really care about any of us.

Floyd, Kathy, and my mother had rolled into town around seven thirty and dropped Molly off at Fred's. Plus, the bales of hay, the beer, the mason jars, the cooler that was as big as a casket, and the vodka.

Floyd called me.

"You up? What's all this white stuff falling out of the sky?"

"A great big pain in the neck, that's what. You hungry?"

"Of course I'm hungry. We're checked in and ready to go seize the day."

"Room's okay?"

"Rooms are more than okay."

"Great! I'll meet y'all in the lobby in two minutes. Let's eat and go back to Fred's. I still have to hard-boil the eggs. I cut up all the cabbage yesterday. He's probably in a dither."

"Yeah, when I handed Molly's crate over to him he seemed a little uncertain."

"I'll bet! Be careful what you wish for! I'm on my way."

I put on my boots and coat, stuffed my hair inside a knitted cap, found my gloves, wound my long scarf around my neck twice, put my cell phone in my bag, and left the room.

"I look like I'm trekking to the South Pole!" I said and gave everyone a hug.

"It's snowing, Diane!" Mom said. "Isn't it beautiful?"

"Hey, Mom! It's beautiful, but I just hope it stops soon. It could mess up the airports and just getting around."

"Let's hope not. Hey, Diane? The hotel restaurant is upstairs," Kathy said.

"Yeah, and it's super expensive. I found us a coffee shop that's way more reasonable."

"Let's go get our coats," Floyd said.

Minutes later, when they returned to the lobby I had to laugh. I'd never seen us dressed this way.

"Floyd, hang on to Mom. I got Kathy."

Once outside, we walked arm in arm in the snow toward the Sunny Side Up & Coffee Shoppe, just a short distance from the hotel.

"Keep going! There are pancakes in our future!" I said. Then I whispered to Kathy, "How was the drive?"

"Long but good. Look, you know I love your brother, but he's got some peculiar taste in music."

"He's got peculiar taste in a lot of things."

"I love the snow!" my mother called out. "Isn't it beautiful? I believe I'd like French toast."

"Why not?" I said. "This is a special occasion."

It didn't take long for all of us to have breakfast, and the bill was only slightly higher for four of us than it had been for just me yesterday. Floyd called the bellman for the car, and by the time we walked back it was there, running and warm inside. And it was huge. The bellman had a little stool he put by the rear passenger door to help Mom climb in.

"Thank you," I said and used it too.

"I can't wait for tonight," Kathy said. "People are going to be so surprised."

"Molly looks good up on the breakfast bar, smiling so pretty," Floyd said. "She's such a pretty girl."

"She's a chicken, Floyd."

"Among her kind, she's a beauty queen," Floyd said. "Where's your sense of fun?"

"My sense of fun is just fine, thank you. The tables were getting delivered this morning," I said. "I hope the snow didn't get in the way of that."

It did not.

We spent the balance of the morning laying out the party, which was easy to do, given we only had two rooms to work with and neither one was exactly as big as a basketball court. I cooled two dozen hard-boiled eggs while the barbecue came to room temperature. Fred and Floyd broke up a bale of hay and covered the living room floor with it. Some hay went in and under Molly's crate, so in case some bodily fluid escaped, heaven forbid, it wouldn't go running down the wall. Kathy and Mom set up the buffet. I filled the egg whites with the yolk mixture and sprinkled them all with cayenne pepper. I put them in a foil deep dish with a cover.

"Think I can put these on the terrace to stay cool?" I asked Shelby.

"They'll stay cool all right!" she said with a laugh.

The coleslaw went into a giant, heavy, clear disposable plastic bowl. The corn bread was baking and smelled divine and would go into two large sweetgrass baskets Floyd brought. I cooked two large pots of grits while Mom and Floyd peeled ten pounds of shrimp.

The snow continued to fall, unabated. Shelby's phone rang. It was Susan.

"Mom! Slow down! I'm putting you on speaker!"

It was as if Susan was in the room.

"I said, the club has canceled your rehearsal. It's this ridiculous snowstorm. Judge Joiner is stuck out in Winnetka in the snow. The club's event planner, Wendy Wellin, said we shouldn't worry, that she would tell everyone where to stand during the ceremony. All we have to do is meet her fifteen minutes before the wedding."

"I don't think it's such a big deal," Fred said.

I said, "I think we've all been to enough weddings that we understand what to do."

"Diane," Susan said, "I agree. Oh, and welcome to Chicago. How was your dinner last night?"

She was letting me know that I had not called her to thank her.

"Very nice, thank you. I hope you're feeling better."

"What? Oh! Oh, I'm fine. I'm just fine. See you tonight?"

She had not been ill.

"Absolutely. We are all looking forward to it."

Snow was on the ground and, but there was a meaningful frost hanging between me and Susan.

"Shelby, dear?" Susan said. "Can you take me off speaker now so I might have a private word with you?"

Shelby rolled her eyes at Fred and said, "Of course!"

"What do you think, Mom?"

"I think we'd better make sure we get the shrimp shells out of here before the party or this place will reek to high heaven by tomorrow," Mom said.

"She's right," I said to Floyd.

"I love it when I'm right," she said.

Alejandro's wine arrived, and they stacked the cases from floor to ceiling in the bedroom. All the beer was chilling in an old tin washtub Floyd brought from home. There was a bottle opener tied to the handle with thick twine. Shelby's friend Ashley filled her mason jars with sunflowers and sword fern and placed them all around. They were just the perfect touch.

"Look what I found," she said and held up packages of disposable hand towels covered in sunflowers. "How presh is this?"

"Very presh!" Shelby said.

There were at least six inches of snow on their little terrace.

"Maybe we should turn on the television and watch the weather report?" I said.

Fred picked up the remote, looked outside, and clicked on the local news.

". . . up to eighteen inches of snow possible in the city, eighteen to twenty-four in the suburbs. Many flights are being canceled, so call your carrier before you try to go to the airport. The governor has asked that all nonessential government personnel be allowed to go home now, and people are being asked to stay off the roads. If you don't have to be on the road, don't venture out . . ."

"Holy shit," Fred muttered in disbelief. "Our wedding could be screwed."

Everyone fell silent. Then Shelby walked over to Fred and put her arms around his neck.

"Oh, no, it won't be!" Shelby said. "I don't care what happens, we're getting married tomorrow!"

We all applauded and everyone had a comment.

"I like Shelby more every day!" Mom said.

"Come hell or high water!" Floyd said.

"That's the spirit!" Kathy said.

"We'll call for dog sleds!" Ashley said, and for a moment her enthusiasm made me think she knew where to get dog sleds.

But the terrible truth was that if the weather continued this way, the airports would close. I didn't know how many people Susan and Alejandro had coming by plane, but I was guessing a snowstorm the size of what was predicted could shut down Chicago and cause a significant reduction in the number of guests. A mere two inches of snow in South Carolina called out the National Guard and shut down all the schools, bridges, and major highways for a week.

"I'll bet Susan's having a total meltdown," I said to Kathy as we lit all the votive candles.

"I'm just so glad she couldn't stick you with dinner for two hundred people."

"Me too."

By six, Fred and Shelby's apartment looked like the inside of a barn. It was so cute and festive, I dared anyone to disagree. Ann, Stephanie, and Sophie were on the last flights to land before the airport was closed for the night. Each one of them had called and was on the way to the hotel on the express train. Hundreds of flights were canceled and thousands of people were stranded. The wind began to howl. I went out on the balcony to see what was going on below us. Because the wind was so powerful—Floyd guesstimated that it was in the forty-mile-per-hour range—it seemed pointless for the sanitation department to try to clean up. I watched them plow the street, and the wind would blow the plowed snow all over the place.

"How long can this go on?" I said to Fred.

"Well, if the National Weather Service didn't know it was coming, they probably don't know when it's going."

"I'm sure you're right."

The doorbell began to ring.

"Smile!" Fred said.

"Squawk!" Molly squawked.

CHAPTER 21

party on!

Bill Evans, Fred's best man, was the first to arrive. His hair was covered in snow. He tried to brush it off in the hallway.

"You made it!" Fred said.

"You kidding me? Best man's got an important job to do!" Bill man-hugged Fred and turned to Shelby. "Hey, Shelby!"

"We're so glad you're here! Give me your coat."

"I'll take it," I said. "You go get a bath mat."

"Hey, Ms. S. Thanks!"

I hung his coat on the rolling rack we'd borrowed from the superintendent, a smart last-minute decision. Everyone who managed to get to our party would be covered in snow.

"I love what you've done with this place! What do you call it? Hayloft modern? Jesus! Is that chicken alive?"

"That's Molly," Fred said. "She wants to take a picture with you. Let's get you a beer!"

The doorbell rang again. Shelby answered it.

Susan and Alejandro had arrived. Shelby took their coats and gave them a hug.

"What in the world? Why? What have you done?" Susan said, looking all around. "Oh, my God! It's that wretched chicken again!"

Obviously pleased with himself, Floyd laughed and said, "Molly missed you so bad. I found her hiding in the back of my SUV when I got here. Hello, Alejandro. Good to see y'all again."

"Are you saying the chicken, this Molly, was a stowaway?" Alejandro said.

"Not really, but she does like a good party," Floyd said. "And I brought you some hooch from my friend back home and regulation vodka for the bar."

"Do you mean that honey-infused moonshine vodka?" Susan's eyes lit up as though a night of mischief was in the cards for her. "You are too kind."

Suddenly the queen of Chicago was no longer offended by Molly.

"My generosity is well known," Floyd said. "It's in the freezer. Can I give you a snort?"

"I'd like that very much," Susan said.

"It could be worse," Mom said, passing by with the tray

of deviled eggs. "He could've brought Isabella, our infernal cow. Would you like one?"

"Why, thank you," Susan said. "And how is the grandmother of the groom?"

Mom smiled and said, "I'm not wearing beige."

"Oh, please," I said. "What *are* you wearing?"

"Long underwear, for sure," she said, and then under her breath she said, "She's got the hots for your brother."

"You think?" I said.

Alejandro had wandered away. He wanted to check the wine.

Sophie, Stephanie, and Ann arrived together with a young man and a young woman I didn't know.

"We ran into each other on the El! Can you believe it?" Ann said.

"Yeah! We had to drag our bags through the snow!" Stephanie said.

"You did not," the young man said. "I carried it for you."

"And you are . . . ?"

"Oh, sorry! I'm Sam," Sam said and shook my hand soundly. His hand was rough. A workingman's hand.

"Sam's my boyfriend, Aunt Diane. We work together at Vermont Shepherd Mountain Cheeses. I left the commune and now I live in Putney."

"What is Vermont Shepherd?" I asked.

"We are a two-hundred-and-fifty-acre farm in Westminster, Vermont," Sam said. "We keep anywhere from three hundred to seven hundred sheep, depending on the year."

"And they make cheese. I'm the new assistant affineur," Stephanie said. "I brought a wheel. It's sooooo good!"

"Affineur," I said. "Thanks!"

"Cheese ripener," Stephanie said. "I'll tell you all about it. Where's Fred?"

She took Sam by the hand and led him into the room.

"Hang your coats in the bedroom!" I called after her.

She turned back to me with a thumbs-up.

"Ann! Hello, sweetheart! I'm so glad you got here!" I said.

"Last plane out of Newark! Boy, it's a mess out there!" she said. "Soph, give me y'all's coats."

"It sure is," Sophie said.

She and her friend began peeling away layers of clothes until they reached their sweaters and slacks.

"Ah, Sophie! It has always been too long! Thank you for making the trip!"

"Hey, Aunt Di, this is my dear friend Karen, and yes, I'm a lesbian. Okay, that's done."

"That's nice, dear." What was I supposed to say? Congratulations?

"Hi," said Karen.

"Welcome!" I said. "Come on in and make yourself at home."

Young people continued to arrive until the apartment was filled with Fred and Shelby's friends, many of whom who traveled on cross-country skis. None of Susan and Alejandro's friends showed up, except Judy CQ.

"I guess you just can't take the farm out of the boy," Judy CQ said dryly to Susan, looking around at the hay, the sunflowers, and of course, Molly. "It was so thoughtful of them to bring the chicken. What a nice touch. I feel like I'm back in South Carolina."

"Well, that was the general idea," Shelby said. "Isn't this so fun?"

"My, my," Judy said. "I'll be right back."

Judy went into the bedroom to hang up her coat and to use the bathroom. She came out a few minutes later with a bottle of wine from Alejandro's other wine that looked very expensive. She gave it to the bartender and asked him to open it. Then when he poured a glass for her, she came sailing by me and stopped to, I thought, say something nice like "Great party!"

But no, she leaned into my ear and said, "There sure are a lot of EPT tests in their bathroom closet. Good thing they're getting married tomorrow."

"Oh, come on now, Judy. Is that a nice thing to say?" And I said it as sweetly as I could. "Tell me. How did you get here?"

"Why, my driver. How else?"

I did not like that woman and I was sorry for Susan to have to deal with her.

But no one noticed her hatefulness except me. Everyone else seemed to be enjoying a barbecue sandwich or a plate of shrimp and grits or both. The music played, Molly squawked like chickens do, and she thoroughly charmed every last person. I predicted massive leftovers.

Shelby and Ashley came over with long faces.

"What's the matter, hon?" I said.

"My bridesmaids can't get here," she said. "The snow. And

the governor just declared a state of emergency. What's going to happen to my wedding?"

"It's going to be all right," I said, thinking for the first time that we might actually have a disaster on our hands. "Let's go talk to your parents and Uncle Floyd. We need a powwow."

Shelby looked as though she was going to burst into tears. We worked our way over to the terrace door where Floyd and Susan were.

"Wait here," I said. "I'll go get your dad."

I thought that he was in the bedroom, checking out his wine, but when I got there it was Kathy who was standing by the stack of cases, her jaw practically on the floor.

"What's the matter?" I said.

"I have this app called Vivino on my phone. I take a picture of a wine label and it gives me the current market value of whatever wine I'm looking at."

"Okay, so? What?"

"This wine, the Cloudy Bay, is about thirty dollars a bottle. And this Ruffino Classico Chianti is about the same. Alejandro opened those cases and started serving them. However! This freaking wine over here is worth five thousand a bottle. Did you hear me? Five thousand a bottle!" She was speaking in a guttural whisper.

"Let me see that," I said. "Susan's friend Judy took a bottle of the good stuff to Fred's best man who's helping bartend and she's drinking it?"

"Who comes in somebody's house and does that?" Kathy said. "That's some crust."

"She's not a nice woman," I said.

She shot a picture of the label on the box and she was right. That meant every case was worth sixty thousand dollars.

"See?" she said. "I mean, I know it's not right to be nosy, but you know me. I couldn't help myself."

"Your app must be broken," I said. "Did you see Alejandro?"

"Yes. He said he was stepping outside to take a phone call."

"Uh-huh. I hope he took his coat." I turned and began counting the number of cases.

"Twenty," Kathy said. "If my app is right, that's one million two hundred thousand dollars in grapes."

"That's got to be wrong. It has to be." And then I thought, What if it's not? "I'll be back."

I looked around the room and Judy CQ was gone. She must've slithered out.

I went back over to Floyd and Susan and joined the discussion.

"Here's an idea," Susan said. "You check into the club tonight and I'll bring your dress to you in the morning. And the hairdresser and the makeup artist."

"That could work," Shelby said. "I could just pack a little bag."

Ashley said, "I'll come with you!"

"You will?"

"Sure! What's a maid of honor for? Sleepover!"

"Wonderful! Frederick is not supposed to see you until the ceremony anyway. It's bad luck," Susan said.

"It's not a bad idea," I said. "Do they have any idea when the storm is supposed to stop?"

Floyd looked outside. The skies were pouring snow in great whirls. There was a foot or more on the terrace.

Floyd said, "I'm gonna go with, not yet. Dang. This is some storm."

Susan said, "Every last one of our guests from out of state has canceled, even the ones with their own planes. I'm just sick about it."

Floyd refilled her glass and said, "Listen to old Uncle Floyd, Miss Susie-Q. It doesn't matter. It's gonna be whatever it's gonna to be. I say, let's just celebrate the kids, and whoever can't make it, what can you do?"

"Come on, Shelby," Fred said. "Let's go take our picture with Molly."

"Good idea," she said and shrugged her shoulders. "Whatever it is, it is."

"I can't believe you have a chicken at your no-rehearsal rehearsal party! How cool are you?" Ashley said.

Mother Nature did not seem to care that she had thrown a giant monkey wrench in all our plans. The snow continued to fall as all the beer and the lesser wines were consumed with barbecue and cake, and it was all fine. But there was a staggering amount of snow on the ground and in the air and the wind was crazy, making it blinding.

Alejandro must've been a magician in a past life. Somehow, that very night, he found horse-drawn sleighs to take us back to our hotel.

"It was not magic! They were in a warehouse I rent to a company that supplies props to film studios that work on location here. The horses are the ones that give tours. They're accustomed to working in pairs. Believe me, if I could perform magic, I would!"

At the end of the night, when things were pretty much straightened up, we left in shifts. Mother and Kathy and I went first with Ann. My mother was thrilled to be in a horse-drawn sleigh. Susan, Shelby, Alejandro, and Ashley left in another. Then ours returned to Fred and Shelby's apartment to pick up Stephanie and Sam and Sophie and Karen. Floyd brought up the rear, and crazy as the weather was, it was an unforgettable night. We all met in the hotel bar for a nightcap.

"Well, the kids all made it, except the bridesmaids," Mom said.

"Kids are very resourceful," Kathy said. "What a night!"

"This snow is the prettiest thing I've ever seen!" Mom said. "It's like a dream!"

I cornered Floyd and told him about the wine.

"Why would he do something like that?" Floyd said.

"Maybe he doesn't know what it's worth?"

"No way. That man knows about money. Something is very wrong here. I'm going to download another wine app and I'll check it out tomorrow morning when I go feed Molly."

"This weather is unacceptable," Susan said.

"Yes, dear," Alejandro said.

CHAPTER 22

the wedding—susan

My nightgown was soaking wet. I jumped out of bed at six A.M. having suffered nightmares for hours, nightmares about being trapped in an elevator with chickens. Alejandro was still sleeping. He didn't need to share a bed with a woman in a wet nightgown. Disgusting.

I draped it over the top of my shower door and decided to weigh myself. Surely, with all that perspiring, I'd lost a few pounds. I stepped on my bathroom scale. Nothing new there. Damn it. Must've been the moonshine. I'd weighed 127 pounds for the last twenty years. I threw my cashmere caftan over my head. God, I loved cashmere, but truth? Life could be so unfair.

The Glam Squad was coming at ten. I had a lot to do before then. I put on snow boots and my long fur coat and slipped outside to the terrace with a hot cup of coffee. The city was almost perfectly still. The blizzard had passed. All that remained were flurries, and even that might have been snow blowing from the rooftops. In the distance I could hear the city's army of snowplows scraping the streets. Below my terrace I saw our super using a snowblower and his son spreading salt by hand from a bucket. It would be weeks before the snow was all gone. I knew from past experience that the city would dump tons of it in the lake and then the environmentalists would go crazy. The salt would kill the fish, which you wouldn't eat anyway, even if Thomas Keller pan-seared them for you himself. Next, they'd dump it in the stadiums and arenas and there would still be drifts everywhere high over our heads and people complaining loudly about it all. I didn't know it to be certain, but I was guessing the storm broke a lot of records.

I hoped Alejandro had arranged for the sleighs for today as well. Although, once the streets were plowed and salted, any four-wheel-drive vehicle could get us to the club safely. But last night, he was a genius. This was why I loved Alejandro so much. He could do the impossible and do it with such élan! Poof! He was like David Copperfield, never ceasing to amaze everyone.

He seemed so stressed out lately, but for once he wasn't the only one. Organizing a wedding in thirty days wasn't without its issues. And now here we were, with a greatly reduced guest list because of this horrible storm. I needed to sit down with the master list and give Wendy at the club a new head count. She would be happy, because of course I'd gone way past the limit of sending out invitations for only two hundred people. And I had to adjust the centerpieces as well, because we'd have fewer tables. With just one bridesmaid, Ashley, we needed only her bouquet and Shelby's. And the place cards had to be reworked. Wendy had them, so I needed to give her a list of which ones to keep and which ones to toss. The only good thing about this wedding was that I hadn't blown forty thousand dollars on butterflies.

I was so upset that Judy CQ came last night. Straw on the floor? Bales of hay? Disposable plates and utensils? Solo cups and beer pong? And a chicken clucking its head off? Are you kidding? She'd be all atwitter for months. How could Shelby do this to my reputation? Oh, wait. It wasn't my party. It was the kids' party. That would be how I'd defend Molly, which, if you didn't hate chickens, was pretty hilarious.

And Floyd.

Ah, Floyd, Floyd, Floyd. You make me dream of things I could never dare whisper in the light of day. Floyd was a terribly stupid name. It was an old name from *Mayberry R.F.D.* or something. A name for a very common man. But on him it took on a completely different connotation. Now when I whispered *Floyd* in my mind, I was thinking Fabio. Both of us thirty years younger, of course, sipping the sweet elixir of love, lying on the shores of Bali while whatever ocean they have washed over our tanned, firm bodies. And in those daydreams, Alejandro did not exist. I mean, I'm not the cheating kind. But those dreams were exactly that. Dreams. The days of the thrill of a new romance for me were long gone. It wasn't that Alejandro and I didn't have a romance in our lives, because we did. It was just that it was thirty-two years old, and certain things become perfunctory, if you know what I mean.

Well, old girl, I told myself, today is a very big day. Not the day I envisioned, to be sure, but still, my only daughter would be married in just a few hours. The Union League Club had a lot of rules. I mean, I understood they had an incredible art collection to protect and rare books, antiques, rugs and so on. So the theatrics I had hoped to provide got boiled down to a normal ceremony and reception. Boo.

I had to admit that I had become awfully fond of Frederick. And I was especially grateful that he wasn't running back home and trading all his beautiful suits for overalls and camouflage. His family just was who they were. I was still working on forgiving them for ruining my plans for a proper wedding in June.

I was getting chilled and wanted another cup of coffee, so I went inside. Alejandro was in the kitchen with the newspaper tucked under his arm and his reading glasses on top of his head. He was wearing his monogrammed cashmere bathrobe and leather slippers and holding a plate with four slices of buttered rye toast.

"Good morning, *amorcita*," he said. "Come sit with me. I made breakfast."

"You are too wonderful," I said and kissed his cheek. He smelled so good. "You're already up and shaved! I was trying to let you sleep in a little." I refilled my mug and followed him.

"How can a man sleep when today is the day he's giving his daughter away? I don't know why, but I'm feeling sentimental."

"Because getting married is important. Who we marry is one of the most monumental decisions we ever make."

He looked at me with the strangest expression.

"What is it?"

"Nothing. I just, um, Susan, I want you to know that I have never regretted marrying you for a single moment. Not one. I love you so much."

"Oh, darling, I feel the same way."

We went into the dining room and assumed our usual spots. I reached into the buffet and took out two Pimpernel place mats, the ones with ships, and white damask napkins. Just because our meal was only toast and coffee didn't mean it couldn't be civilized. I slipped the place mats under our dishes.

"Which section do you want?" he asked, knowing the answer.

Before I could say "Life and Style," he handed it to me without even looking up from the business pages.

"Shelby and Frederick's wedding notice will be in tomorrow's paper," I said.

"Is that a fact?"

"Remember when brides used to have their portraits made in a studio, carrying a beautiful bouquet? We have mine somewhere in what I thought was the most gorgeous gown and veil in the entire world."

"Uh-huh."

"You're not listening to me."

"I am. They don't do portraits anymore? I thought they did."

"Well, some do. But now the trend is to put on sweaters and jeans and run through a field of tall grass with your fiancé, so you look all windblown and physically fit and casual. I liked life better when things were a little more formal."

"Me too. Although last night, Molly the chicken was rather marvelous."

"Please! That bird!"

After breakfast, I called in the changes to Wendy Wellin at the club and she was delighted.

"I can't thank you enough for this, Mrs. Cambria. And don't worry about the ballroom looking cavernous. We can increase the size of the dance floor and bring in a few dozen ficus trees. This awful storm has just caused us no end of troubles."

"Mr. Cambria and I are so happy to be in your capable hands. Thank you, Wendy. Really, thank you for everything."

After the hundreds of phone calls I'd given her since Christmas, she probably hung up the phone and called me a terrible name. Ask me. Did I care?

Next, I went to my bedroom, preparing to shower and wash my hair. I took my wedding gown, I mean the dress I was wearing to Shelby's wedding, out of the closet and laid it across our bed. It was navy silk faille, Oscar de la Renta, fitted on top, full ballroom skirt. I planned to wear my triple strand of South Sea pearls with my pearl earrings surrounded by diamonds. And I had a triple-strand diamond bracelet, with round- and marquis-cut stones set to resemble flowers. I think Van Cleef made it. Oh, who cared? At the last minute I took out my diamond bow pin. Was it too much? Absolutely not, I decided. After all, this was my wedding too, no matter what anyone said.

Of course, my pumps were my old silver metallic Manolos that were well broken in. The worst thing was to have on tight shoes at a big party, and I planned to dance and dance. I put all the jewelry in satin sacks and the gown in a roomy garment bag. Then I went to Shelby's room, where her dress hung from a nail she had hammered into the top of her closet door. Her bridal gown was a delicious confection of sparkle, lace, and tulle. She was going to look like a beautiful fairy-tale princess. Too bad she wasn't marrying a prince. With all the people Alejandro knew, she probably could have. Ah, well, the die had been cast, and at this hour there was no point in not being 100 percent supportive.

There was a small stack of things on her bed to bring along. Gorgeous white silk and lace panties, a matching garter belt, sheer stockings, a blue garter, and an old handkerchief I'd never seen. Her bustier had been sewn inside her gown. And her shoes were smartly broken in so they wouldn't pinch. I put her things in the duffel bag with mine and zipped her gown and veil into the enormous garment bag from Saks.

The Glamsquad, owned by Robin Harris, arrived and did their best with my face and hair, and I had to say, the extensions they clipped into my hair added a lot of fullness that middle age had taken away. Robin swept my old and new hair up into a French twist with little wispy pieces on the sides and sprayed it to death.

"This spray is called Impenetrable. Your hair isn't moving until you tell it to."

"You know what? I think my face looks better with my hair up."

"Mrs. Cambria, at a certain point, we all do."

Reality sucks, I thought.

"Well, I think it's time to go glam up the bride. Are you ladies ready?"

"Whenever you are!" they said.

"Alejandro? I'm leaving now! I'll meet you at the club at four, all right?"

No answer.

I opened the door of his study a tiny bit, and sure enough, he was on the phone. I stepped in and tapped his shoulder to get his attention and mouthed, *I'm going now. Four o'clock! Don't be late!*

He signaled, *Okay, okay, okay, don't worry!*

I put on my long fur and grabbed my handbag. Martin was driving me to the club and Robin and her assistant were following in their own cars.

"Mrs. Cambria! Please! Let me help you with that."

With the help of our doorman, Martin slid Shelby's gown and mine through the back of our enormous SUV so that it was perfectly flat. I slipped the duffel bag in the backseat with me and climbed in. I really didn't like these gargantuan SUVs, but in this weather, it was the safest thing to drive on slippery roads. To be honest, we had kind of a car wardrobe, because Alejandro loved cars. I had my antique Jaguar convertible I'd never part with, we had the big Benz that was so nice on the road, and Alejandro had his Maserati, which was his baby, and this big clunker. I owned the Jag, but everything else was leased. Alejandro felt, and I agreed with him, that technology on cars was changing so quickly, it didn't make sense to own.

We arrived at the Union League Club and were greeted by the manager, who assured me they would have the gowns upstairs in just the blink of an eye and that they had a steamer, if anything needed a little spritz. I went immediately to Shelby's room, where she and Ashley waited.

"Hi, Mom!" Shelby said, opening the door for me. "Where's my dress?"

"It's coming right behind me."

"Good morning, Mrs. KC!" Ashley said.

"Wow, Mom, your hair looks incredible!"

"Thanks," I said, and put the duffel bag on the sofa.

The room service table was still there. I looked under the silver domes to see what they'd ordered. Remnants of chocolate chip pancakes were on one plate, and the remainder of a cheese omelet was on the other. Orange juice was still waiting to be drunk and the coffee was cold. They were sitting on their beds drinking green smoothies.

"So this is what a bride and her maid of honor have for breakfast before marching off to the gallows?" I said, trying to be funny.

"Not funny. I already threw up three times this morning," Shelby said. "I thought chocolate chip pancakes would make me feel good."

"But they didn't?"

"Obviously not," she said.

"It was pretty gross," Ashley said.

"I see. It's perfectly normal to have a nervous stomach on a day like this!"

She rolled her eyes.

"Well, sweetheart? Why don't you jump in the shower and wash your hair? The Glamsquad will be here momentarily."

"Okay," she said, and finally began moving herself, but with no enthusiasm.

I started to roll the room service cart to the hall. If she had a weak stomach, she didn't need to smell grease and coffee. Ashley's cell phone rang.

"It's my mom. She's downstairs with my dress and stuff. I'll be right back."

"Oh, good!" I said.

"If you'll hold the door, I'll roll it outside," she said.

"Happy to oblige!" I said. "Thanks!"

Good, Ashley's mother's arrival would give me a few minutes with Shelby. I went to the bathroom door and rapped on it with my knuckles. I could hear the shower running.

"Shelby? May I come in for a second?"

After a moment, the door opened. She was wrapped in a towel, and the shower was still running.

"Are you all right?"

"I think I told you I wasn't, didn't I?"

"There's no reason to be fresh with me. I'm only asking, you know, can I get you something?"

"Maybe a ginger ale and some crackers?"

The doorbell rang.

"Okay. You take your shower."

It was the bellman with our garment bags. There was a high lip on the top edge of the wardrobe, perfect to hold the neck of the hanger and suspend the gowns.

"Thank you so much," I said. "Thank you!"

He left and I called room service and ordered the ginger ale and crackers for Shelby. Then I unzipped the garment bags and shook out our clothes. I stood there looking at them for a moment, as though I was caught in a freeze-frame of time. Once I had a wedding gown that hung on a wall like this, but where was my mother's? And where was she? Useless, that's what she was. Somewhere being useless. That could've been one reason why I was so determined to give my daughter a lavish wedding. I wanted my mother to love me and she never had. I hardly ever thought about her. I wanted Shelby to feel my love. Instead, I drove her crazy. Moving the wedding date made me so angry, but it also made me feel terrible. I stood there for another few moments, wondering if daughters ever felt loved enough. Did sons?

The doorbell rang yet again. It was the Glamsquad. They came right in, saying how nice the room was, and began setting up on the desk. And it rang again: it was Ashley returning. And again: ginger ale and crackers for my bride.

At noon, I had a platter of turkey sandwiches brought up. At one o'clock, I went downstairs to have a look at the ballroom and the room where the ceremony would take place. The room where they would say their vows was lovely. There was a center aisle with eighty-four gold ballroom chairs on either side. At the end of the aisle was a low, skirted platform. On either side of the platform were two enormous sprays of white flowers, lilies, roses, peonies, and some other exotic flowers I'd never seen. Behind the platform stood a large floor mirror, so we could see the faces of the bride and groom. What a great idea!

Wendy was in the ballroom with her clipboard, giving directions to half a dozen people, where to place tables, to straighten the cloths, to fold the napkins this way, not that. Finally she set one place setting herself and stood back.

"We want them all to look just like this one. Oh, hello, Mrs. Cambria! Some days I think I should've worked on the set of *Downton Abbey*."

"There's nothing wrong with symmetry," I said. "It has a special beauty."

"Thank you! You understand!" she said.

"I do indeed," I said.

"I can already see that this will be a beautiful wedding! And I just wanted to thank you for all you've done to help us," I said, still wishing I'd been able to replicate a waterfall in Africa. Monkeys would've been so much fun.

"It really is my pleasure," she said.

By three thirty, we were almost dressed. I zipped up the back of my daughter's wedding gown.

"Turn around," I said. "Let me see."

She turned and looked at me with a very girlish giggle. "How do I look, Mom?"

My eyes welled with tears. After today, she'd be someone's

wife. I'd be that someone's mother-in-law. How did this moment get here so quickly? We were on the edge of enormous change for both of us. Ashley handed me a tissue.

"Exquisite," I said. I blotted my eyes so my mascara wouldn't run down my face. I looked at the tissue. Nothing. Not even the tiniest smear. I turned to Robin. "This mascara really is waterproof, isn't it?"

"Yes, ma'am."

"Can you leave the tube for me?"

"Of course," she said.

Juliet Elizabeth, the photographer, arrived. She was early.

"You never specified, but I thought you might like some shots of you and your daughter getting dressed, you know, maybe adjusting her veil?"

"What a wonderful idea!" I said. "How did I overlook that?"

Shelby said, "So I don't think this garter thing is going to work for me."

"It's sort of prehistoric," Ashley said. "I mean, at my friend Charlotte's wedding? She said, like, no way! I didn't blame her."

Millennials, I thought.

I attached the veil to Shelby's hair and Juliet began shooting. She was quietly taking rapid-fire pictures as though her camera were a machine gun.

"Mom, can you keep it in your pocket? In case Frederick really wants to throw the thing? Then I guess."

Click! Click!

"Are you going to throw your bouquet?" I asked, handing her the bouquet of white hydrangea and pale pink roses. I mean, was she just going to toss tradition completely out the window?

Click! Click!

"Why do I need a bouquet, anyway?" she said. "Seems like a waste of money."

"Because you can't carry a bag of groceries up the aisle," I said, thinking I was pretty funny. No one even cracked a smile. "You need something to do with your hands. They can't just hang by your side."

"I guess so," she said and finally accepted the wisdom of her elders all through the ages, practically as far back as Eve in the Garden.

It was ten minutes to four. Where was Alejandro? I called his cell. It went to voice mail. He had to be on his way by now. I called Martin. He answered right away.

"Yes, Mrs. Cambria?"

"Please tell me Alejandro is in the car with you and you're on the way here."

Juliet recorded my anxiety. *Click!*

"No, ma'am. I imagine that by now he's in the elevator on the way to your room."

I exhaled for perhaps the first time in a long while. "Thank you, Martin."

The doorbell rang.

"Shelby! Go into the bedroom and close the door."

Shelby picked up the bottom of her gown and hurried into the bedroom. Juliet took a picture of her scurrying away with Ashley behind her.

"Alejandro?"

"Yes, it is the father of the bride, here to perform his duty," he said from the other side of the door. "May I come in?"

I opened the door and let him in.

"Wait until you see your daughter. You're going to lose it."

"I am bracing myself," he said.

I straightened his bow tie. Juliet took a picture.

"You look so handsome. I'm so in love with you."

"I hope you will always feel that way," he said.

"I will. I promise."

"And you, my dear, are positively regal."

"Thank you, sweetheart." There was nothing like a million dollars of diamonds and pearls to make a girl look like a queen.

"Mom? Can I come out now?"

"Yes, come! Let your father see you!"

Alejandro's words were a brave show, but I knew he was about to melt. Ashley came through the door first and stood aside. Then Shelby walked into the room. Alejandro gasped.

"Here's my little girl all grown up," he said, raising his chin and blinking away tears.

"Hi, Daddy," she said.

He held out his arms to her and she rushed into them the same way she had since she was a toddler. Juliet went crazy, photographing them from every possible angle. He hugged her and kissed the top of her head, as he always did. For nearly the next two hours, Juliet took pictures of us. By the windows, standing, seated, one person standing, the other seated, and in every possible combination. Me pinning Alejandro's boutonniere to his lapel. Him putting my wristlet in place. On and on. This was a well-documented moment in our little family's history.

Before we knew it, it was five minutes to six. Showtime.

"Well," I said, "it's time. Let's go give you to Frederick to have and to hold."

We took the elevator down to the Wrigley Room, where Wendy waited at the door. We could hear the music, a lovely quartet from the Chicago Symphony. Floyd, Diane, and Virnell were there waiting for us as well.

"Oh, Shelby!" Diane said. "You look absolutely beautiful!"

"Thanks," she said, smiling.

"You sure do," Virnell said.

I was stealing glances at Floyd. He sure looked good in a tuxedo.

"You clean up good," he said when he caught my eye.

"Thank you, Floyd," I said as evenly as I could.

He shook hands with Alejandro and they mumbled some niceties to each other.

Wendy said, "In one minute, Mr. English is going to seat his mother in the front row on the right and come back for his sister. Then, when she's seated, he will stand to the right of our groom and his best man. Next, Mr. Cambria will seat Mrs. Cambria in the front row on the left and return here. Our beautiful maid of honor will then proceed slowly up the aisle, smiling, smiling, smiling, and take her place on the left side facing the guests. And then the big moment arrives and I think we all know what to do. Are we ready?"

"I think so," Diane said.

"I'm ready," Virnell said.

Everyone did as we were instructed. The music changed and we stood for Shelby and Alejandro. My husband looked like a movie star. He was so handsome. And my beautiful Shelby all but floated up the aisle on his arm, the light bouncing off the tiny crystal jets that were sewn in her gown, making the moment magical. She was radiant and excited. I was so proud of her. As I turned around to face Judge Joiner, I saw Floyd staring a hole through me. I smiled at him and he smiled back.

"Who gives this woman . . . ?"

"To have and to hold . . ."

"I will."

"I will."

It was over so quickly, I felt like I had missed it. I wanted them to say their vows all over again. My mind kept wandering. The recessional had begun. Shelby sailed by on Frederick's arm. Then Ashley went by on Bill's arm.

Alejandro reached over and took my hand, pulling me close to him.

"It's okay," he said, stepping out into the aisle. "Come with me. Everything is going to be all right."

"But that's my baby," I said, wanting to weep an ocean of tears. "I'm sorry. I'm just so overcome!"

I plastered a smile on my face and composed myself. I spotted Judy CQ in a gown with a feathered collar and gave her my best happy face. She applauded a little and blew me a kiss. I thought you can hide that neck, but you still have it. We went straight into the reception. There were waiters at the door with trays of champagne, white wine, and sparkling water on ice.

"Beautiful bride, beautiful ceremony," Alejandro said. "May I get you something stronger, my dear?"

"Yes, please."

Floyd appeared at my side just as Alejandro stepped away toward the bar. He produced a camouflage-covered flask from his pocket. Then he took a glass of water from a waiter's tray, drained it through his fingers into a potted palm, and covered the ice with a healthy dose from his stash.

"Cheers," he said, handing me the goblet. "Congratulations."

I took a sip. It was delicious.

"Oh, honey," I said.

"Are you talking to me?" he said.

"No, Mr. English, I'm talking to the vodka."

"Hmm," he said. "Maybe we'd better find our table."

"You're at table three," I said. "Right off the dance floor over there."

There were twenty-something tables of eight draped in white linen, placed all around the dance floor. The elevated centerpieces of pink and white peonies and roses were not only gorgeous but fragrant. I thought the club must own five hundred candelabra, because they were everywhere, burning hand-rolled ivory beeswax candles that I ordered from Perin-Mowen because they issued a softer glow. That may sound like I had overthought Shelby's wedding reception, but it's always the details that take the expected into another realm. The brass chandeliers were dimmed, but they still sparkled like mad because of their dropped crystals. Everyone looked good in the glow of beeswax. This night was like going to a ball on the inside of a beautiful jewelry box. While it was not the wedding of my dreams, I was still thrilled.

The cake stood on its own table, four tiers of vanilla cake with chocolate ganache in between the layers, and in a nod to Frederick's family, I had the pastry chef make peaches from spun sugar. I hoped they noticed.

I put my evening bag at my seat and looked around for Alejandro. He was talking to the club manager.

The Duke Ellington Orchestra had lost some members because of the weather, but oh, they were amazing anyway. Ramsey was right. Of course, we had invited Ramsey to be a guest, but he was in Montreal, performing with some famous jazz group.

I decided to go over to Diane's table to congratulate them and to say something nice. Floyd's daughters were all there with boyfriends or friends, and from a distance it seemed like everyone was finding their places and chatting away. Judy stopped me on the way there.

"What a sweet wedding," she said.

There was something so disingenuous about the way she said it that made me want to slap her. Well, I thought, I can be just as disingenuous as the best of them.

So, I said, "Why, thank you, Judy. We were almost done in by a blizzard, but I think the club did a beautiful job, don't you? What a cute little dress. Didn't I see that in an ad for Nordstrom Rack? Excuse me. I have to speak to the in-laws."

Her smile became an expression of uncertainty and I slipped away, saying hello to our friends along the way. I reached Diane and Floyd's table just as Frederick and Shelby were being introduced and having their first dance to a piece of music I didn't recognize.

"Congratulations!" I said. "We're in-laws! Aren't they a gorgeous couple?"

"Congratulations to you too!" she said. "This is just beautiful, Susan. Thank you for your incredible generosity and, well, for everything."

I looked at her for a moment. Her sincerity always startled me.

"I wish I had friends like you," I said. "By the way, that's a really pretty dress."

"Oh, thank you. I wasn't so sure. You know, we don't do this kind of thing so often. This is really a breathtakingly beautiful room. We'll never forget this night. Really, Susan."

In just that brief exchange I realized how hollow my friendships were. I swore to myself that I'd be nicer to her than I'd planned.

"Or last night either," I said. "You went to so much trouble and it was so much fun."

Floyd stepped over to us.

"What am I missing?" he said.

"Molly," I said, and Diane burst out laughing.

We stood together, watching our children dance their way into a new life together, marveling at the optimism of the night. My heart was so full of love for my daughter and her husband. The bride and the groom. Now they were both mine. I now had a son. I'd share my daughter's heart with Diane if she'd share Frederick's heart with me.

Soon I danced with Frederick while Alejandro danced

with Shelby, and then we switched partners and I danced with my husband.

"Do you know what?" I said.

"No, tell me what," he said.

"I think this might be the happiest night of my whole life."

"Don't you know you're not supposed to outshine the bride? My darling, you are so beautiful tonight."

"And every woman here wishes she was in my shoes. Do you have plans for later?" I said.

"What do you think?"

"I thought I knew him!" Susan said.

"This is catastrophic," Judy CQ said.

CHAPTER 23

jailbird blues—susan

M onday after the wedding, Shelby and Frederick were on a plane to Tanzania for a glorious four-week safari. The safari was our wedding gift to them, in addition to the small Renoir Alejandro wanted them to have for their home, a fabulous pair of binoculars with Swarovski crystal lenses, and an amazing camera with all sorts of lenses and filters. The Renoir was a painting of a little girl that my tenderhearted Alejandro bought at auction when Shelby was born. He felt it was appropriate that she have it now. So right after Christmas he had it cleaned and the frame restored. We gave it to them yesterday, when we went to their apartment to wish them a safe trip. The South Carolina contingent had just left with Molly as we arrived, missing them by just minutes. I'd call Diane Tuesday to be sure they all got home safely.

I was at my home waiting for Judy CQ to arrive. We were going to talk about flowers for the Lyric gala. I don't know why I ever agreed to cochair this massively complicated event with her. It was definitely putting a strain on our friendship. To be honest, Judy simply didn't like to work. She would tell me over and over that she was a concept person, a big-picture thinker. Then she'd give me all sorts of assignments — see if so-and-so will donate flowers or printing or buy a corporate sponsor table. But I had yet to see her pick up a phone to ask for a postage stamp. She may have thought of herself as a concept person, but she surely didn't understand the concept of cochair.

It was almost noon when the doorman rang me to say she was here and coming up in the elevator. I had brought in chicken salad and was scooping it onto the beds of butter lettuce on our plates when the doorbell rang. The files for the benefit were spread all over the dining room table, so I decided we should eat in the kitchen, where no one had ever eaten more than a cracker.

"Coming!" I called out as I reached the door.

"Hi!" she said. "I brought us a brownie to share."

"Oh, you bad girl! Come right on in!"

There was no reason to start on a bad foot, or whatever the saying is.

I took her coat and hung it in the foyer closet.

"It's still freezing outside. Snow is banked everywhere. And we're supposed to get another storm this week!"

"Please don't tell me that. I can't take another flake!"

"I know. This snow is so inconvenient."

"Amen. We're having lunch in the kitchen because the dining room has become fund-raiser central. We can work in there after we eat."

"Sounds good to me," she said.

I flipped on the news to see if we could catch the weather report. Then I quickly set the table with rattan place mats and beige napkins. I was getting silverware from the drawer when Judy screamed.

"No!"

I turned on my heels and stared at the television screen in disbelief. Alejandro was being led away from his office building in handcuffs. I quickly grabbed the remote and turned up the sound.

"After a five-year-long investigation by the SEC and the FBI, hedge fund owner Alejandro Cambria was arrested this morning for operating the largest Ponzi scheme in the history of Chicago. He was arrested on charges of securities fraud, investor adviser trust fraud, mail fraud, wire fraud, money laundering, making false filings to the SEC, perjury, and theft from several employee benefit plans. He's accused of defrauding his investors to the tune of twenty-five billion dollars. He is expected to be held without bond . . ."

"Oh, my God! This can't be! My husband is an honorable man! He would never cheat anyone out of a dime!"

The reporter went on and on about how Alejandro's hedge fund delivered higher returns than anyone else's and how that was the first red flag for the SEC.

"I don't believe it either, Susan. This has to be a horrible mistake! Sit down, sweetie. I'll get you a glass of water."

She opened my refrigerator and unscrewed the cap on a small bottle of Pellegrino, poured it in a glass, and put it in front of me.

"He had higher returns because he was *smarter* than the other guys. That's why! He told me he always hedged his bets and he followed the Standard & Poor's index. He was so thoughtful and careful!"

I drank half the glass of water in one great gulp.

"Of course he was!" Judy said.

"He isn't somebody who rolls the dice like those Wall Street guys in those giant firms! His business is so personal! He took care of the symphony's investments and the museum and the teachers union. He wouldn't cause harm to a teacher!"

"He even had my retirement money and my parents!" Judy said. " Obviously, this is a terrible mistake. Do you have somebody you can call?"

"Like who?"

"A lawyer?"

"I'll bet he already knows," I said. "I don't even know where Alejandro is! Where is the jail in Chicago?"

"Oh, I'm sure there must be more than one! With all the murders on the South Side? Let's call your lawyer right now. I'll do it for you, if you'd like."

"Thanks, Judy, but I think I have to do this."

My hands were trembling. How terrible was this? What did it mean? I got my address book from the kitchen drawer and called our lawyer.

"It's Susan Cambria calling for Michael Dean."

She put me right through.

"Susan! What has happened to Alejandro? I just got the news in my feed!"

"Michael, I don't know any more than you do! I don't know what to do!"

"I'm coming over. Don't talk to the press. Don't let anyone into your apartment. I'll be there in twenty minutes."

"All right," I said.

We hung up.

"What did he say?" Judy asked.

"He told me to not answer the door to anyone and not to speak to the press."

"That's good advice. And I was just thinking, if you have any jewelry in the house, you should probably get it out of here. The they might try to confiscate it."

"What? I didn't commit any crime!"

"Yes, but you don't know what could happen. Look what happened to poor Ruth Madoff. One day she's riding around in a chauffeured Rolls and the next day she's riding the subway. I'd hide it anyway."

"But wouldn't that be obstruction of justice?"

"You think there's going to be any justice in this? Think again, Susan. I think you're being very naïve."

My doorbell rang. Normally, the doorman called first, so it was unusual to have my doorbell ring unless it was another resident.

I looked through the peephole. It was the co-op board president, Paul Keenan.

"Don't open it!" Judy said.

"It's okay. It's my friend Paul."

I opened the door and Paul stepped inside. I closed the door behind him. He was wearing a red paisley ascot with his deep burgundy velvet blazer and gray trousers. Alligator loafers. No socks.

"Hello, Paul. How are you?"

"To be honest, Mrs. Cambria, I'm here for a very unpleasant reason."

I was *Mrs. Cambria* now, was I?

"I see. Would you like an espresso?"

"No, thank you. You've seen the news, I assume?"

"Yes. Just now. I'm sure it's a horrible misunderstanding, Paul. Come now. You've known Alejandro for almost twenty years, if my memory still serves me. He doesn't have a diabolical bone in his body!"

"Whether he's guilty or not is none of my affair at this moment. The problem is that right outside our front door is a swarm of paparazzi. Your neighbors are unable to get into the lobby without being accosted, peppered with questions, and nearly assaulted by very aggressive members of the press. I've had a dozen phone calls in the last hour. We can't have this, Mrs. Cambria."

"Well, what can I possibly do about that?"

"I don't know. But we are not the kind of building that welcomes this kind of attention."

"I see, Mr. Keenan. May I ask you something?" He nodded. "Do you believe in due process?"

"Of course I do. I am not accusing Mr. Cambria of anything. I am merely suggesting you think of something to make these vultures go away."

"Such as?"

"Perhaps you might consider taking up residence elsewhere until this storm passes."

"I see. Well, I'll consider my options."

I opened the door and stood there with my face in flames and he left. An ascot. In the morning. Indeed.

On hearing the heavy clunk of my door when it closed, Judy appeared.

"This is very bad, isn't it?" she said.

"I think my life has just been totaled, Judy. Did you hear what he said?"

"Every word. This is simply terrible."

A few minutes passed and my house phone rang. Michael was in the lobby.

"Send him up, please," I said to our doorman.

I opened the door and went back to the kitchen, where Judy was picking at her plate of chicken salad.

"Try to eat something," she said. "You're going to need your energy."

"I don't think I can swallow a crumb," I said.

"Hello?" Michael called out.

I went out to greet him.

"How are you holding up?" he said, holding my arms in between us.

"I think I'm in shock. I can't think straight. What happened to Alejandro?"

"I made some phone calls. He's been charged with securities fraud and he's being held without bail."

"Oh, no! Oh, God, Michael! Where is he?"

"He's at the Metropolitan Corrections Center."

"Oh, my God! He's in jail?"

"Yes."

"Oh, he's not going to like that at all."

"I'm sure he won't. I suspect that what will happen next is that the FBI will turn the case over to the U.S. Attorney's Office for the Northern District of Illinois and he'll be arraigned tomorrow in federal court."

"Michael! We've got to get him out of there! Alejandro can't be in a jail! He's not a criminal! Besides, he needs his blood pressure medicine and his statin!"

Judy came out from the kitchen and said, "Susan, I'm going to go and let you have some privacy. Let me know if there's a single thing I can do, okay?"

To be fair, Judy was leaving with twenty pounds of fresh wheat for the gristmill, but she had done her best to be empathetic.

"Thanks," I said. "I'll call you." *Air kisses.*

I closed the door behind her.

Michael said, "Get his medicines and anything else you think he might need. I'll take them to him."

"I can't go?"

"It's probably best for you to stay out of sight for the moment. The press will just harass you and upset you. You don't want your picture plastered all over the *Trib*."

"No, I don't. I just had a visit from our board president, who suggested I move, at least until this blows over. Maybe I should stay home."

"Hopefully, tomorrow after the arraignment, if the judge sets bail I can get him out until the trial, if there is to be one. Susan, listen, you're going to need a team of criminal lawyers who completely understand hedge funds and exactly what Alejandro does and where he went wrong. They need the actual facts, good or bad, to help build a case toward having him exonerated. This is way out of my wheelhouse. I wouldn't even know which questions to ask. I'm a real estate lawyer."

"But Michael, I don't know any criminal lawyers," I said.

"I've got a few names. This is going to be a high-profile case, so I think you want the best legal counsel there is. We should call this fellow Ed Rabin, of Rabin, Tyler and Associates." He handed me Ed Rabin's card. "Columbia Law School. Phi Beta Kappa. He's got about five hundred lawyers working for him. Some of the sharpest minds in the country."

"How do you know him?"

"We've been playing squash and racquetball together at the University Club every Saturday morning since forever. He's the guy I'd call for myself. In fact, why don't I call him and ask him to be at the arraignment. I mean, we have to ask Alejandro if he wants him. He might already have someone else in mind."

"Please do. Michael, thank you. I mean it. I don't know what I'd do if I didn't have you to call on."

"I'm glad I'm here and I'm happy to help. I'm even happier I cashed out of Alejandro's fund last year. Poor devil. Listen, I'm going to give you some advice, and I want you to listen to me carefully. For your own good and for your personal safety, and especially for the sake of Alejandro, do not talk to anyone about Alejandro's business or your life together. I don't care if Oprah calls you, tell no one anything. No exceptions."

"I understand."

"Okay, get me his meds and whatever else you think he might need and I'll go pay him a visit."

"Toothbrush? Toothpaste? Disposable razor? Deodorant? Socks and underwear?"

"I wouldn't worry about the socks and underwear. And I'd just put his toiletries in a Ziploc. They might not let him have them. I'll bring his watch home to you. Oh, and speaking of watches and jewelry, I wouldn't be surprised if they get a search warrant and comb this place for assets. So do what you have to do on that one."

"You mean, move anything I don't want to lose?"

"As your lawyer I can't advise you to break the law. But as your friend I'm saying, well?"

He put his hands up in the air.

"I understand," I said. I knew I could never do anything like that. The government wouldn't want my jewelry. That was plain ridiculous. Maybe they'd want Alejandro's watch collection.

"Certainly, the judge is going to freeze your accounts."

"Why would they freeze my accounts? I haven't done any-thing wrong."

"Do you have separate accounts?"

"Of course not. Why would we?"

"They're going to be frozen. Believe me. If you want me to, I can use your ATM card and bring you some cash."

"Michael, the most I can withdraw in one transaction is five hundred dollars. What am I supposed to do with that? Two people can hardly have dinner at the Palm for that."

"Then I'll try to go to two banks. Don't go to the Palm. Somebody will call the *Trib* or the *Sun* or CNN. Who knows? Stay home, Susan. Let's find out what we're dealing with first. Okay?"

"I wasn't planning to go out for dinner, Michael. I was merely saying that—"

"Don't even think about it. Now, let's get some things to-gether for Alejandro."

"Okay."

I took a gallon Ziploc from the box in the pantry and went to Alejandro's bathroom. I put his toothbrush and a travel-size tube of toothpaste and a disposable razor in with a sample size of some men's cologne. I found his pillbox and emptied one day's worth of pills into an aspirin bottle. I added a comb and a small size of deodorant. I couldn't think of what else he would need, so I closed the top of the bag, went back to the kitchen, and handed it to Michael.

"I feel like I'm living in a nightmare," I said. "Here. Thanks."

"This is a nightmare, Susan. But you are an exceptionally

strong woman, and I know you will handle this with the same grace you demonstrate with everything else."

I gave him my ATM card and the code.

"How could he do something so terrible, Michael? Help me understand this."

"Look, if the charges are true, and I cannot imagine that they are, I'd say he didn't intentionally set out to cheat anyone. He's not that kind of man. Maybe he just got caught up in something."

"I know he's not! Thank God Shelby isn't here to see this."

"Honeymoon? Great wedding, by the way."

"Thanks. Yes, they're in Tanzania. Safari."

I couldn't process the enormity of the charges against Alejandro yet. I couldn't understand how far-reaching all the accusations were. You never think something like this can happen to you until it does.

"You're right. She doesn't need to be dragged into the middle of this," Michael said. "Anyway, I think what happened was something like, there was a drop in the market and he probably got more people who wanted their money immediately than people who wanted to further invest. So maybe he had to take from Peter to pay Paul, so to speak. I'm guessing there was a run on his fund and he didn't have time to raise more money to cover his losses before the SEC got involved. Maybe it was just some sloppy paperwork with the SEC. Maybe there's a whistleblower in his office. I don't know. I know this, though. It's all going to come out. So brace yourself, Susan. You're going to hear a lot of things you'd rather not know. I'll be back in a couple of hours."

"Tell him I love him, will you? Tell him we're going to fight this thing together."

"Of course," he said. "I'll be back."

He looked at me with pity in his eyes. If no one else in the coming days would believe I had nothing to do with this horrible crime, Michael would. I closed the door behind him, then locked and bolted it.

How was I going to get through this?

"Currier and Ives!" Virnell said.

"I know, Mom," Diane said.

CHAPTER 24

you never know—diane

The only reason we were able to leave Chicago when we wanted to go was Floyd's rental SUV. I do believe that monster could travel the worst roads in Jakarta without causing one iota of discomfort to its passengers. We were so glad to be home. Tired but glad.

Floyd had indeed checked out the wine when he went to Fred's on Saturday morning. It was worth exactly what Kathy claimed it was worth.

"What do you think, Floyd?" I asked knowing the answer was not good. "Why would he move over a million dollars of wine to an apartment building that doesn't even have a doorman?"

"My opinion? He's scrambling. My gut says we're going to hear all about it."

"Far be it from me to doubt your gut." I said and thought, Wow. It just didn't make sense.

Fred and Shelby were off for Africa. I was very excited for them. I wondered about all the amazing sights they would see—wild animals, exotic birds, and waterfalls. Naturally, I was a little worried for their safety. But then, you didn't hear very often about lions devouring tourists. It would be terrible for business, so I reassured myself that they must have systems in place to protect visitors. And of course, I was concerned about the EPT tests in Shelby and Fred's bathroom. Maybe she'd just had a scare.

It was only eight o'clock in the morning and surprisingly chilly. The grass was glazed with sparkling frost, which was a sweet little hello from Mother Nature, nothing like the havoc she unleashed on Chicago. I was already at the farm stand working on the books, trying to figure out if we made any money last year. So far, 2016 was panning out to be about 2 percent ahead of 2015. No great shakes, but at least it wasn't a decline.

I still used ledgers and entered data by hand. Floyd seemed to think that we should have everything on computers, but I disagreed. I still had my wits about me, and doing the math by hand was a good exercise to keep me sharp. Of course I double-checked everything with a calculator. So far I had not made any huge errors. When tax time rolled around I took my books to our accountant and he told us what we owed Uncle Sam. I wrote the checks, my mother signed them, and that was it.

I was still daydreaming about the wedding. And all the snow, everywhere you looked, was more snow than I had ever imagined. The whole weekend still seemed like a beautiful dream. I had danced with my handsome son on his wedding day to the music of the Duke Ellington Orchestra, wearing a gorgeous gown of champagne silk, hair and makeup done by professionals! I never in a million years thought I would hang those words together in the same sentence. Our ride in the horse-drawn sleigh while snow twirled and danced all around us was priceless. Our mother talked about it the whole way home, while Molly *bwark*ed from her crate.

"Currier and Ives!" she said about a thousand times.

We were able to do these marvelous things only because of the resources and generosity of Susan and Alejandro. The only thing missing from the weekend was Alden. Maybe, when the pictures came back, I'd send him an eight-by-ten. I'd not looked that pretty since my high school prom. I wished I had somehow had him at my side.

Soon it was getting close to lunchtime and I was thinking about what I wanted to eat. Mom had gone up to the house to see what there was to put together. We were long on root vegetables, so my guess was vegetable soup of some sort would be simmering on the stove. I closed the books and stood up, stretching. It was time to lock up the store for an hour and a half. We used to leave the store wide open with an honor jar for customers to use in our absence. That was when we kept the cash in a tackle box, which we simply walked up to the house. But since we installed a cash register a few years ago, we decided that open-door policy wasn't such a good idea. Folks knew we closed between one and two thirty. Our telephone number was on the front door so that if someone desperately needed their parsnips that very minute we could accommodate them. We didn't have so much business that we could afford to lose any of it.

I took the spiral key chain, slipped it over my wrist, picked up my cell phone, and started walking back to the house. When I got there, no one was in the kitchen.

"Hello? Where is everybody?" I called out.

I lifted the lid on the big pot. Vegetable soup. I loved my predictable life. I checked the oven. Corn bread batter was in there, but she had forgotten to turn the oven on. I quickly set it to four hundred degrees. Poor Mom.

"We're in the living room! Come quick!" Mom yelled.

I all but ran there to find Mom and Floyd standing in front of the television.

"Lookie here," Floyd said. "Alejandro is on the way to the cooler."

"What?" I was stunned.

There was Alejandro, surrounded by FBI officers, in handcuffs, being pushed into the backseat of a car. There was no mistaking him. It was him.

"He's a dang crook," Mom said. "I knew something was wrong with that man. Decent people don't have that kind of money."

"What?" I was still stunned.

"I'm not surprised one bit," Floyd said.

"How's that?" I said.

"Remember that wine? What did I tell you?"

I said, "Never doubt your gut?"

"Yep. That sumbitch was hiding assets."

"What are you saying?" Mom said.

"That he knew he was getting busted and he was hiding assets at the last minute," Floyd said.

Mom said, "Diane, remember I told you there was something fishy about him bringing wine for the party? Who needs twenty cases of wine for thirty people? But I sure didn't guess it was worth so much money."

"You did say that, Mom. Holy hell," I said.

"This is a big-time disaster. He's finished," Floyd said. "Stick a fork in him. Done like dinner."

"Oh, Dr. Cliché rides again," I said. Done like dinner. Please.

My phone rang. It was Kathy.

"Hi!" I said.

"You watching the news?"

"Obviously. You want a bowl of soup?"

"I'll be right over," she said and disconnected.

"I'll set the table for four," I said.

"Check the corn bread in the oven," my mother said.

"Well, I guess I'll start buying the newspaper again," Floyd said. "Maybe I'll start scrapbooking or something. BJ used to do that. I think this might be the first relative we've had that's gonna do time."

"This is so terrible," I said. "You hear from her?"

"He's not blood," Mom said.

"No, but I'll bet I hear from her now," Floyd said.

"He's not blood, but he's Fred's father-in-law. Y'all, this is so awful I can't even believe it's true," I said. "I'll bet the kids don't know yet."

"Not unless they've got cell reception in the Serengeti," Floyd said. "Let's eat. This is going to be all over the news for a long time."

"In a minute," I said. "Corn bread's not done."

We watched the news for a few more minutes. I wanted the oven to have the time to heat up. It didn't matter if we switched from CNN to ABC, NBC, or CBS. Alejandro Cambria's securities fraud was the lead story on every single network.

When I felt enough time had passed, I said, "Okay. That's enough misery for now."

Just as we arrived in the kitchen, Kathy walked in through the kitchen door and said, "So, does anyone want to explain this to me? A few days ago I was doing a cha-cha with that man. Now he's going up the river? What exactly did he do? I don't understand the whole thing."

"He's gonna be a guest of the state. By invitation only!" Floyd said and chuckled. "No cha-cha-ing allowed in the Big House!" He ladled himself a big bowl of soup.

"Floyd! This is not funny! Don't you know Susan must be devastated?" I said, taking the pan of corn bread out of the oven.

I cut it in squares and dropped them all in a bread basket. Then I filled a soup bowl for my mother, Kathy, and me.

"Let's go sit down," I said. "Here, y'all, take a spoon."

We moved to the dining room and sat. I'd put place mats and paper napkins on the table with the corn bread.

"This is what happens when you ride too high on the hog," Mom said.

Floyd began singing an old Sinatra song. "'Riding high in April, shot down in May . . .'"

"Stop! Wait just a minute! We shouldn't be talking like this! As far as I know, we're the only family Susan has, besides the kids, of course. Don't y'all think we need to reach out to her?"

"Why don't we wait awhile and see if she's a crook too," Mom said. "Maybe we shouldn't get involved."

"Miss Virnell!" Kathy said. "You think Susan's done something illegal?"

"How would I know? I'm just a humble farmer," she said and shot me a told-you-so look.

"Well, we should at least tell the kids. How terrible would it be if they had to read it in the newspaper?" I said. "I mean, it's going to be humiliating enough for both of them, living with the facts of her father's crimes. That is, if he's guilty, and it doesn't look good. Does it?"

"Nope," Floyd said.

"What exactly did he do?" Kathy asked again.

"He defrauded his investors," Floyd said.

"How?" Kathy said.

Floyd said, "He blew the money his investors gave him on his lifestyle, I guess. Then the markets went to hell. People wanted their money back and he didn't have it to give them. The SEC had been watching him for, I think they said, five years."

Mom said, "That's what the man on the television said."

"Well, Mom, I know you and Floyd see some gallows humor here, or what's that word? Schadenfreude! That's it."

"Schadenfreude? That's a mighty big word for a little girl like you," Floyd said. "Did you learn that at Clemson?"

"Sure did! Especially when we kicked Carolina's butt at homecoming my sophomore year. We were knee-deep in it. We loved watching them be miserable."

"I can't believe you were ever a football fan," Floyd said. "Mom, this soup is delicious."

"It sure is," she said. "Nothing like a smoked ham hock. They're practically charmed."

"The soup is very good, Mom. Thank you for making it," I said, feeling terrible.

"What's wrong?" Mom asked.

"What's wrong? You know, sometimes I can't believe my ears," I said. "Susan and Alejandro are about to have their entire lives ripped apart and all y'all can do is make jokes."

"Aw, come on, Lady Di, we're just having a little fun," Floyd said. "What do you think we should do?"

"I don't know. But we can't stand by doing nothing," I said. "You know, on a completely unrelated topic, maybe we should make this soup to sell. What do y'all think?"

"I'll buy a quart every week!" Kathy said.

"Why not?" Mom said. "Most people don't know what to do with turnips. I know how to make 'em sing!"

"Lord knows, we've got a lot of them to do *something* with," I said.

"You're really upset, aren't you?" Floyd said.

"I feel terrible for Susan," I said. "I'm going to call her tonight."

"Well, give her my best," Floyd said.

"Me too," Kathy said.

"I wouldn't call her. How do you know the FBI isn't listening?" Mom said.

"So what if they are? As long as I don't bring up the contraband wine, I'm okay. And that's none of my business anyway. I just want her to know I'm thinking about her."

That afternoon, Mom started making the biggest batch of vegetable soup I'd ever seen, which is to say every burner in the farm stand kitchen was covered with a huge pot. I was happy she was working there, knowing I would be there and she wouldn't burn the house down. Not that she was at the point where she needed supervision.

This was the time of year that the peach orchard got its early spring pruning. Branches were tied together so they wouldn't drag the ground or snap under the weight of the fruit when it began to appear. Once that fruit was visible, we pruned them back to about a hand's width between each peach. That was so we'd get the maximum-size fruit that was very juicy, which was what we were known for. That's what Floyd and his men were doing now. At this time of year, he'd have about a dozen men working the orchard. But by summer, the number of his employees would swell to around fifty.

When the weather was chilly like it was now, we had to worry about freezing temperatures that could kill the peaches and wipe out all of our production. We used high-speed wind machines to pull warmer air from the upper atmosphere down into the orchard to raise the ground temperature. This also helped to save the crops from frost damage. Frost and freeze were perhaps our biggest worries. Sometimes I thought farming was something a person should inherit, because when I considered all the variables that had to be just right for a farmer to succeed, the odds were almost always against us. Take my advice, if buying a farm seems romantic to you, don't do it. Our family had been farming for centuries, and this generation, at least, was always a little surprised when we had a profitable year.

"How's that soup?" I called out to Mom. "Sure smells good."

"It's coming along," she said. "Maybe we should sell corn bread to go with it."

"Great idea! I'll get that together for tomorrow."

In the dead of winter, soups do well. I stepped into the kitchen to see how the production was going. On the long trestle table, she had lined up quart-size Ball jars, like a platoon of soldiers, ready to be filled.

"I still can't get over this whole thing with Alejandro," I said. "And I can't get Susan out of my mind."

"Well, now you're going to see what she's made out of."

"And now she's going to find out what kind of friends she has."

"I'm gonna guess they're all the fair-weather variety."

"I hope not, for her sake," I said, thinking Mom was probably right. I'd bet her friend Judy was already gone with the wind. "What about another kind of soup? Maybe butternut squash and ginger?"

"Listen, missy, let's get these jars filled and see what happens before we go expanding the inventory." She stopped stirring the pots, turned to me, and put her hands on her hips. "Why squash? Do we have a lot of butternut squash on our hands?"

"Tons," I said. "I'll change the blackboard in the morning."

"Yes, this soup has to rest overnight. Then we can see about the butternut tomorrow."

I took a spoon and tasted the broth. It needed salt, but I wasn't saying a word.

"Well?" she said.

"Well, what?" I said.

"How is it?"

"Very good," I said.

She tasted it.

"Needs more hocks," she said. "Not smoky enough."

She went to the freezer and lifted out a box of them. Not many people could say they had cases of ham hocks in their freezer. She tasted each pot and dropped one or two in each one.

"That should do it," she said. She raised the heat a little. "Another forty-five minutes, then they can sit overnight."

"If you want to go up to the house, I can turn the stove off and put them to bed," I said.

"Thanks. I'll get the meat loaf in the oven."

I would move them to the walk-in cooler, cover them, and let them sit on the floor. The fat would rise overnight. We'd scrape it off in the morning, divide the liquid and the vegetables evenly among the jars, and seal them the same way we sealed jam.

After supper I called Susan. My call went straight to voice mail. If she wanted to talk, she could call me back. If she didn't, I understood. But at least I had attempted to connect with her and she would know it.

"I tried to call Susan last night," I said to Mom and Floyd over breakfast.

"She's probably too embarrassed to talk to anybody," Floyd said.

"And ashamed," Mom said.

"Isn't that crazy? I'll bet you my two front teeth she had no idea what he was even up to," I said. "Yet she'll be punished for it."

"He's being arraigned this morning," Floyd said. "In *federal* court. I read it online in the *New York Times*."

"Mr. Cambria's in very deep dukey-doo," Mom said.

"Mother!" Floyd and I said together. Virnell never said dukey-*doo*, except in an extreme situation.

"Well, I hope he has a good lawyer," she said. "And a good excuse."

"I don't think a good excuse is the kind of thing that forgives securities fraud, especially to the extent he committed it," Floyd said. "Twenty-something billion—that's with a *b*, not an *m*."

"Allegedly," I said. "He's entitled to due process."

"Well, he's going to be tried in the media, because that's what they do these days," Floyd said. "It isn't right, but that's how it goes. Susan's garbage is probably being sifted through by some reporter from the *National Enquirer*."

"Good gravy," Mom said. "You're probably right."

"The meat loaf was good last night," Floyd said. "Thank you for dinner, Mom."

"It will be even better tonight," Mom said.

I thought about Susan all day long. Her life had to be so unbelievably awful right now. The betrayal and the lies and all the public humiliation! How could she even get out of bed? Of course, Alejandro was all we could talk about at supper that evening.

"What is it about leftover meat loaf?" I said.

"The flavors have to marry," Mom said,

"Well, it is better the second day," Floyd said, "like spaghetti sauce."

"*Dancing with the Stars* is on tonight," she said.

We knew it was her favorite program.

"Mom, why don't Floyd and I clean up the dishes so you can go watch it?"

"Oh, thank you. It's a blessing to have such good children," she said, looking at us, first me and then Floyd, and I knew in that moment the truth about how no matter our age, we would always be her little boy and her little girl. "I'm still tired from all those hours in the car. I'd like to get to bed early. Where's Gus?"

"Outside. He doesn't need to be in the kitchen when we eat," Floyd said. "I'll let him in."

"Go on and get your bath and don't give anything else a second thought. We'll lock up everything."

"Thanks, sweetie."

I got up and started running the water in the sink, waiting for it to get hot.

"She's getting up there," I said. "Yesterday, when I came up for lunch, she had forgotten to turn on the oven."

"Really?"

"Yeah, I'm seeing little things like that more and more. I just hate it."

We finished cleaning up the kitchen and said good night.

"The garbage is out and Gus is in," Floyd said.

"Good job," I said. "I'll see you in the morning."

Mom had fallen asleep in front of the television. I shook her gently to rouse her.

"Come on, Miss Virnell, time to call it a day," I said.

"Oh!" she said and looked around, surprised to be in the living room. "I must've drifted off."

"No worries," I said. "Let me help you up."

She took hold of my forearm and pulled against it, and when she was on her feet, she wobbled a little.

"Oh!" she said.

"It's okay. Steady there."

"I'm fine now," she said. "This getting-old business is a pain in the neck!"

"Yes, it is," I said.

"Come on, Gus. Your girlfriend needs you," she said, and smiled at me. "Did you hear from Alden yet?" She started walking toward her bedroom.

"What do you mean 'yet'?"

"Doesn't he read the news?" she called over her shoulder.

"He'll probably call tomorrow," I said and shrugged, thinking Alejandro's trouble would be a good excuse for him to call if he wanted to. "Good night!"

I was dressed for bed and just brushing my teeth when my cell phone rang. It was after ten. Who died? I thought, and my heart raced from fear that something happened to Fred or Shelby. It was Susan. I threw my toothbrush in the sink and grabbed a hand towel, wiping my face vigorously.

"Diane?" she said. "It's me, Susan Kennedy Cambria, mother-in-law of Frederick, your son. I'm just returning your call."

I could tell she was as drunk as a dog and I wouldn't blame her if she was.

"How are you, Susan?"

"You heard, I s'pose?"

"I think I know what you're talking about," I said.

"Tha' son uffa bitch's leading a double life," she mumbled.

"What do you mean?"

"I'm too bombed to 'splain it now. Call you tomorrow?"

"Sure," I said. "Anytime."

Without another word, we were disconnected. At that moment it seemed to me that the world around me was spinning in the wrong direction.

"Repent! The end is near," Susan said to her bathroom mirror.

CHAPTER 25

no forgiveness

In the time it took for the earth to make only one daily rotation, my life exploded like a Jackson Pollock into something beyond surreal.

The first blast of insult went as follows. At nine in the morning, my housekeeper had not shown up. I texted her. *Tina? Where are you?* She texted back. *Sorry for your trouble. I quit. No work for criminal. My green card too hard to get!*

Thanks, Tina, I thought. Was she kidding? We're the ones who got you that green card in the first place.

That was the nicest part of my day, the least of the unrelenting fury that followed.

Alejandro was arraigned that morning. My plan had been to go the MCC and tell him I was 100 percent on his side, that we would get through this together. Then, without any warning and against the advice of his lawyers, he pled guilty, confessing to all the charges. It was televised. He was doomed. So was I. Did anyone call me to warn me that my life was probably over? No. Did anyone have an inkling that he would plead guilty? Maybe his lawyers did, but I was one hundred thousand percent convinced that he was completely innocent. I stood there in my kitchen and heard my own death sentence delivered live on CNN.

Let me repeat that. He pled *guilty!*

I could feel bile rising in my throat, and I suddenly had the dry heaves. There would be no trial, no jury, no chance for his exoneration. It was over. He was going down. His business was finished, his assets were no longer his and his traitorous name was somewhere below scum. Where did that leave his family? In the filth and garbage of the gutter with him, that's where. I began to shake from head to toe while my stomach convulsed. I had to pull myself together, but I couldn't. My entire life as I had known it was coming to a screaming, scorching halt. I ran to my bathroom and splashed cold water on my face, over and over again. When I looked in the mirror there was nothing but horror on my face. How could he do this to me? To our daughter?

I threw myself across our bed and after a long while of sighing and sighing and wishing for the relief of a good cry that never came, it finally dawned on me that I had better make some kind of a plan.

It was a good thing Alejandro was behind bars because I would've choked him until he was dead. I mean it. I was beyond furious and beyond devastated. There were no words.

I would never get over it. So now I was going to the MCC to tell him to take himself to the bottom floor of hell as fast as he could. It really was where he belonged.

I could see the sidewalk below the terrace, and it was swarmed with press. Suddenly a drone appeared, at eye level with me, and started taking pictures. I ran inside in fear and pulled my curtains. Then I pulled the curtains in every room. Drones! My God, I thought, is there no privacy to be had anymore? What if I had not been dressed?

But getting out of my building was like a scene from a Robert De Niro movie. I wrapped my head in a scarf and put a hat on over it. Big sunglasses, Alejandro's topcoat, and snow boots. It was the best disguise I could make. I took the service elevator down to the back entrance of the building, and when I got outside, I ran for several blocks. Try running in snow boots. I was very lucky I didn't slip and fall with all the frozen snow, ice, and salt that was everywhere. I could've broken my hip and been found unconscious. Nice headline: FORMER SOCIALITE, MRS. FRAUD FOUND NEAR DEATH IN A DRIFT! Oh, God.

Finally, I hailed a cab and gave him the address where Alejandro was being detained. My pockets were stuffed with his medicine, which I should let him beg for, my ID, tissues, some cash, and a lipstick. His confession drastically changed my tune.

I entered the MCC, my ID was checked, and I was led to a visitor's booth. Here came my husband through a door wearing an ill-fitting orange jumpsuit. He sat opposite me behind bulletproof glass, which was a good thing for his sake.

I picked up the receiver of the telephone and he picked up the one on his side.

"I want to hear it from your lips. Are you really guilty?"

"Yes, I'm afraid so. I'm sorry, *amorcita,* for everything."

"Sorry? You're sorry? That's nice. You know, when I got up this morning, I thought we could fight this, that it all was a huge mistake, that we'd get it sorted out and go back to our lives. Now you're telling me that you knew what you were doing was against the law? You've got to be kidding me!"

I could feel my temper still rising when I thought I was already as angry as I could become.

"I know, Susan. Things got out of control."

"I'll say things are out of control. I think I'd rather be in there than have to go through what I'm going through out here."

"What's happened?"

"Well, for the last twenty-four hours, our building has been under siege from the media. These . . . these . . . *rodents* are driving the residents crazy! I've been asked to move out of our building until this unfortunate little misunderstanding blows over. Now that we know it's not blowing over, I imagine I will *have* to move because of some darn persnickety clause in the building's by-laws about sheltering fugitives from the law. Stop flinching, you'll make your crow's-feet worse."

I was short of breath, seething with anger. I could feel my pulse pounding in my ears.

"I knew that you'd be forced to leave. The only good thing is that they have to pay fair market value for the shares, according to the by-laws, that is. But the money may not go to you."

"What do you mean?" I said.

"The federal government is going to work very hard to find and seize all of my assets. They will want to sell everything I own to make reparations to the people whose money I lost."

I was going to be homeless? Wait a minute. What?

"So, them paying fair market value benefits *you*, not *me*? There you go! Always putting yourself first! How can you sit there as cool as a cucumber when what you've done is throw me in the streets? What's the matter with you?"

"I'm sorry."

"Let me ask you something. Would you rent an apartment to me? No! No one will! And what am I supposed to do for money?"

"Believe me, darling, I am mortified and ashamed beyond anything you can imagine. Do you think I planned to blow up our lives?"

"Well, you certainly did a fine job, and I'm not your darling anymore. My life is blown to smithereens! How deep will they go? I mean, can they take my assets as well?"

"It depends. If there's jewelry or a painting or something I bought you that they decide was paid for with ill-gotten gains? Yes. I'm sorry."

"I'm sure you're as sorry as can be. 'Sorry' is such a tiny word. It's way too small to cover what you've done." I just stared at him. I was in a state of disbelief. "Tell me, how did you get caught?"

"My secretary called the FBI."

"Why would Nadia do that? She adores you!"

"Oh, Susan. You're going to hear everything, because it's all going to come out. I'd rather you heard it from me. The truth is, she does adore me. I've been involved with her for years. It got out of control. She wanted me to divorce you. I refused. She called the FBI. That's the truth."

"*WHAT?*"

"I'm sorry."

Holy hell! I had become that wife who was the last to know. Why was I surprised? If one billion dollars wasn't enough for him, why would one woman satisfy him?

"Alejandro, you've been lying to me for years. Why would I believe a word you say now?"

I felt like a complete fool. I was numb with shock.

Now he had tears coming down his face.

"Save your crying for the judge," I said.

"True. I don't blame you if you don't believe me. God, on one hand I'm so relieved this is over. It has been excruciating to live with so many lies. On the other hand, I wish I was dead." He said this in a dramatic whisper that didn't make me feel one iota of sympathy. I was beyond furious. I was a woman betrayed and scorned, filled with the fury of hell.

"I wish you were dead too. I really do. Do you realize that you have destroyed *my* life as well as yours? What about our daughter? This is going to break her heart! She idolized you! And now you drag our name through the mud like this? Do you know *how many* people's lives you ruined? And these were our *friends*, Alejandro! People who trusted you! Old people! Shame on you, Alejandro! You son of a bitch. Do you understand how deeply you are despised? Do you understand that you are lower than Judas?"

"I know. Do you think I think of anything else? I am racked with regret and guilt! Consumed by it!"

"Let me tell you something. My pathetic mother is sitting in a penitentiary somewhere in the middle of Tennessee for blowing my abusive father's brains out. *Now* I understand why she did it."

"So that's what happened to her. I just assumed she was dead."

"Yes. The bastard deserved it too."

"God, I never knew."

"May I point out that you never asked? You might recall that because you're so self-absorbed, we've literally spent *years* talking about you. I don't like to be reminded of it or her. And especially him."

"I understand."

"And *I* understand from the news, because that's where I learn about my family now, that you might be sentenced to serve up to one hundred years. Is that right?"

"Yes," he said. "Maybe more."

I paused for a moment and then let him have it.

"I want a divorce."

"You're not going to stand by me, *amorcita*?"

"And I am not your *amorcita*. Fuck you, Alejandro. What would you like me to do? Spend the rest of my life waiting for you to get paroled? And, *amorcita*, I'm taking my name back. Get your whore Nadia to stand by you."

"It's you I love, Susan. You know that."

"Right. Wait until your daughter hears about this, Alejandro. You've placed such a shameful burden on her she'll never escape. To think that I loved you. I never even suspected for even one tiny moment that you were capable of something so devastating and heinous."

"Where will you go?" he said.

"Don't worry about me, Alejandro. I'm sure there's a cave somewhere for us. Oh, I gave your Crestor and blood pressure medication to the guard. And when you're served with divorce papers, sign them."

I hung up the receiver, got up to leave, and saw he was still talking. I picked the receiver up again.

"What?" I said. "What is there left to say?"

"I love you, Susan. Take up tennis. You can use my racket. I know you've always wanted to play."

"Have you lost your damn mind?" Tennis? I hung up again and left, never looking back, not even once.

Somehow I got back into my building easily through the service entrance as it was getting dark. When I was I my apartment, I called the doorman.

"Frank, just say yes or no. Are there members of the press still hanging around?"

"They seem to have gone home for the day," he said. "But I'm sure they'll be back in the morning. Bright and early."

That wasn't exactly a yes-or-no answer. Who is *he* to complain about the press? He wasn't a resident! I should've told him to enjoy his fifteen minutes of fame.

"Thanks, Frank."

It was just four thirty, but already dark. I could zip out and get a manicure and a pedicure, both of which I needed very badly. And I needed a distraction, to feel normal again. I ditched my disguise and put on a cashmere turtleneck and a pair of pants. I ordered an Uber, threw on my regular coat and scarf, and took the elevator down to the lobby. Thankfully, I didn't run into a soul I knew.

"I'll be back later," I said to Frank as he opened the door of my Uber for me.

I was back sooner than later, because here's what happened when I got to Joy Art Nails.

"Hi!" I said as I walked in. "I need a manicure and a pedicure, please."

A young girl from Taiwan, one I'd never seen before, said, "You, please! Pick a color!" Newly single, I thought I'd try a red, something bold to show I wasn't in mourning. Why not?

Then Francine, the owner or manager, I was never quite sure which, who also barely spoke English, came over and whispered to me. "You have to go now."

"Why? You're not that busy."

I looked around. All the girls gawked at me. The patrons who had been staring quickly resumed reading or doing something on their iPhones. One snapped a picture of me.

"Sorry, we can't do your nails anymore. Sorry, your husband is no good for business."

"Francine! I'm not a crook!"

She took my arm and gently but forcibly led me to the door.

"You make the other clients very nervous. You should go now and not come back. Sorry."

I was in shock again, standing on the sidewalk. She closed the door in my face. Well, so much for Joy Art Nails. Maybe I should call the Department of Immigration and suggest they look into Francine's business.

I called another Uber, which arrived minutes later. I'd find another nail salon. They were a dime a dozen. I'd go to one on the other side of town. Big deal. Who cared? I did. I was embarrassed. Thanks, Alejandro.

I went home and called Judy. She didn't take my call. Well, maybe she was legitimately busy. She'd call back. When six o'clock became eight o'clock and she hadn't returned my call, I texted her.

Judy, please call me. I pushed Send. *Whoosh!* Off it went.

Bing! Her reply was swift and cruel.

My lawyer says I shouldn't be talking to you unless I want to be a part of the FBI's investigation, which I do not. About the gala: Leave your paperwork with your doorman, I'll pick it up. How are you and Alejandro planning to pay us back? I mean my parents too, Susan. You defrauded ninety-year-old people. Nice.

I wanted to answer her and say *Well, you've always been a bitch anyway and I didn't do it, Alejandro did,* but I did not. But her response told me a few things I didn't want to hear. The FBI was coming. I was a social persona non grata. And I was guilty of Alejandro's crimes.

I was going to do something I had not done in years. Emotional eating, pizza. I called Pizza Castle and ordered a pie with pepperoni, onions, and mushrooms. They said it would be forty-five minutes for a delivery. I said that was fine. The fellow taking the order sort of gasped when I gave him my name and address. I thought, Oh, great, he recognizes my name, and popped the cork on a bottle of champagne left over from one party or another. It was the only thing chilled, and I thought the carbonation would pair nicely with the tomato sauce of the pizza.

I took a deep sip right from the bottle and turned on the news. There was Alejandro, being led away by federal marshals. Again. There must've been nothing else to talk about on the news, because my husband's face was plastered on every network. He'd worn his navy suit to his arraignment. He was still a handsome devil, no matter what. Michael had come by this morning to pick it up and take it to him. But he had done something so terrible, the disgrace of it would follow us to the grave and beyond into eternity. This lying son of a bitch that I'd been faithful to for all these years just deliberately ruined my life and the lives of everybody I knew.

"You think you're so smart! You're a monster!" I screamed so loud he could probably hear me at the MCC. Then I got a pad of paper and a pencil, sank into a chair at the kitchen table and cried. I took several big gulps of the bubbly and began to make a list of things to do.

Number one, divorce lawyer. Yep. I needed a divorce lawyer. I'd ask Michael to recommend someone. It would not be a complicated divorce. There would be no division of property and assets because there'd be nothing to divide! I just wanted to be sure no one could sue me for what Alejandro had done.

"Asshole!"

I screamed and took another few gulps and then wept some more. My life was *ruined!* I wouldn't be welcome *anywhere!* For the rest of my life! I was a pariah! Filth! Scum! *This* is what you did to your loyal and faithful wife? And your beautiful, innocent daughter who literally adores you?

"You're a monster!" I screamed and took another gulp. I was sobbing then. How could he do this to us?

Okay, get a grip on yourself and think! I wiped my eyes with the back of my hand.

Number two, legal protection. I needed someone to defend me against some kind of agents of the federal government trying to take my jewelry and our artwork and my silver. I made a note to ask Alejandro's lawyers for their advice. Maybe we could reach some kind of a settlement with the government, leaving me with enough to eke out some kind of meager living.

Number three, apartment. I was going to need a new place to live. Someplace that was discreet, for sure. I made a note to find a broker and to have a civil discussion with our board president, Mr. Keenan, about how this might play itself out and to try to put together a time frame.

I had some stocks and bonds, enough jewelry to choke a camel, and who knows what else was around here that was worth confiscation? I decided to take a walk around the house and see what I might identify as things we had owned before we got married. There wasn't much. All of my china and silver was bought after we were married. And how would I know if the things we bought to set up housekeeping were bought with dirty money? When did Alejandro's life of crime and deception begin? Ten years ago? Twenty years ago? To make that determination was going to require someone like a financial forensic accountant, if such a person even existed. So far as I could tell, the only things I really owned were my old car and my engagement ring. That wouldn't get me far.

I continued swigging champagne. Diane had called me last night. Diane! I had roughly three hundred people's names, e-mails, cell phone numbers, and home addresses in my address book, and Diane was the only person in the entire world who called. She might be the only thing close to a genuine friend I had. I needed to call her back and tell her what was really going on. And then I started to cry and have a conversation with the thin air.

Damn you, Alejandro! Damn you to hell! What have you done to us? And you were screwing Nadia all this time? You liar! You damn liar! You make me sick with your lies! Where am I supposed to go to get a job? There isn't a company in this entire United States of America that would trust me with a rubber band! I'm going to finish my life in poverty because of your damn endless greed? Don't you know how regular people hate rich people? They *love* to see us fail! And the farther we fall, the better! I got thrown out of my *nail salon* this afternoon! *A nail salon!* If Francine did that to me, what would happen everywhere else. Damn it, Alejandro!

The house phone rang. I picked up.

"Pizza delivery," Frank said.

"Send him up," I said.

I went to my purse and took out some money. My doorbell rang. I wiped my eyes, and I imagine I smeared mascara from one side of my face to the other.

"Coming!" I called out, carrying the champagne and a fistful of cash to the door.

I opened the door, took the box, handed him thirty dollars, and he snapped a picture of my face with his phone. Then he ran to the elevator, where his friend was holding the door.

"What kind of person are you? Shame on you!" I slammed the door and thought to myself, Oh, go to hell.

"I feel terrible for her," Diane said.

"Me too, but I'd be surprised if she didn't know SOMETHING!"
Virnell said.

CHAPTER 26

diane is awesome

We were having breakfast and I was thinking about Susan. She had been too tipsy to talk last night. I couldn't blame her for that. If I had a husband who disgraced me the way Alejandro did her, I'd probably tie one on too! Even Mom and Floyd agreed.

"You know, she might be getting her comeuppance now, but I still feel sorry for her," Mom said. "Would you pass the pepper, please?"

I picked up the pepper mill and placed it by her fork.

"Thanks," she said and gave it a few grinds over her eggs.

"She's not really a bad person, once you get past the pretension," Floyd said. "She was just doing what smart women do."

"And what might that be?" I asked.

"She acted like that because she was an extension of Alejandro. Every man has a fantasy of the perfect wife. She was trying to be his fantasy. You know what I mean?"

"That's ridiculous," I said. "Another biscuit?" I offered the bread basket to him and he took two.

"Thanks," he said. "Pass the jelly, please?"

I put the cut-glass jar of jelly in front of him. Using a crystal jelly jar was my nod to gentrified living. I had a thing against putting commercial containers on the table. No ketchup bottle, no cartons of juice or commercial jars of jelly, even if the jelly was jelly we made.

"No, it isn't ridiculous to try and be your husband's fantasy," Mom said. "Think about it."

"And I'll bet you a dollar that she's about to become a very different person," Floyd said.

"We'll see," I said. "I'll bet her mind is going in a million different directions at once."

"The poor thing," Mom said. "Well, we've still got soup to put up in jars waiting for us."

"And corn bread to bake," I said. "Floyd, if we've got eggs, send them up to the store, will you?"

"You bet. And I've got trees to prune," Floyd said.

"I'll call Susan tonight," I said.

Mom and I did the dishes and Floyd went outside to meet his crew. When everything was put away, we walked down to the farm stand together and opened up.

"The days are getting longer and the air is getting warmer," Mom said. "I love to see the first signs of spring."

"Me too. And I love when our daffodils peek through the dirt. I remember planting them with Fred when he was about twelve. I think we put in thirty-six bulbs."

I took the pots of soup out of the cooler, putting one on the table and the rest of them on the unlit stove. With a large spoon I began scraping away the congealed fat on top.

"We must have a thousand daffodils now," Mom said. "But if you divide them every year, that's what happens. They multiply like rabbits!"

Mom took the pot when I was finished, and using a ladle, she filled each jar halfway with only broth until there was no more to dispense. Then, using a small cup, she divided the vegetables, filling the jars to the bottom of their necks. I took a spoon and sampled the soup.

"Ham hocks did the trick," I said. "If it's this good cold, I can't wait to taste it when it's hot."

"What did I tell you? Sing, my little turnips! Sing!"

We both laughed then.

"Well, I've missed dividing my bulbs a couple of years, but not many. We should grow daffodils to sell too. They seem to love the dirt here."

"And zinnias too. When I was a girl, this yard was covered in them."

"It was?"

"Yep. I planted them with my mother. Every color too. Fuchsia, purple, scarlet, and all kinds of color combinations that were so exciting to me."

"Well, when the daffodils start coming in, let's put some zinnias in too. Why not?"

The remainder of the day went like that. I baked a mountain of corn bread, cooled it, and wrapped big pieces of it in plastic wrap. Then I labeled them, weighed them, and priced them. And Mom sealed the jars of soup in boiling water, cooled, and labeled them.

I took the fat pink stick of chalk and went outside to change the blackboard. I erased STOP THE CAR! YOU NEED PIE! and wrote, STOP THE CAR! YOU NEED SOUP! I added, AND CORN BREAD! in parentheses. Late that afternoon, when people were on their way home from work, we did a steady business selling quarts of soup, corn bread, and small boxes of Carolina White Rice. Everyone loved to serve rice with vegetable soup, which technically was no longer vegetarian with the addition of the hocks.

"What kinds of pies do you have?" a customer asked Mom.

"Frozen," she said. "Pecan, apple, and strawberry rhubarb."

"I'll take apple, thanks!"

"Be right back," Mom said, heading for the freezer.

I was ringing up her sale when my cell phone buzzed. I looked at it. It was Alden calling.

"Mom? Finish up for me, okay? I have to take this call."

"Yes, ma'am," she said, and I moved aside. "Did you ring up the pie?"

"No, ma'am. Add it in."

I walked outside into the cool afternoon air.

"Hello?" I said and pulled my sweater around me.

"Hey, Diane, it's me, Alden. You got a minute?"

"Sure! What's new?"

"Um, Alejandro Cambria is in the slammer? What the hell?"

"I know, but who knew? Turns out he had his hand deep in the cookie jar. I don't think he's ever getting out of jail."

"And I thought he was such a nice guy," Alden said. "When he wasn't on the phone, that is."

"I think he was a nice guy who did a very bad thing. You know, hate the sin, not the sinner."

"How's Susan holding up? She's got to be completely destroyed."

"I'm pretty sure she's devastated. I'm supposed to talk to her tonight. I'll let you know. Right now, I feel pretty sorry for her."

"You don't think she knew what he was doing?"

"Not the first clue. I don't think she had even an inkling."

"How can you be so sure about that? I mean, if we were married, you'd know what I was doing all the time, wouldn't you?"

I got stuck on the *if we were married* part of his question.

"If we were married? Um, I'd trust you, probably the same way Susan trusted her husband. She's pretty wrapped up in all kinds of volunteer and board work. And to be honest, I don't think she really understands securities. The night of our party, the one you so perfectly engineered and executed, I asked her what he did for a living. She explained it in such a simplified way that either she thought we were a bunch of bumpkins that wouldn't get it or she didn't really understand it herself."

I figured there was no harm in a little flattery.

"Really. Wow. Well, I'm no financial wizard either, but from what I've been reading online, hedge funds have more tentacles than a science fiction monster. I think it's a world people would never understand unless they lived in it."

"I'm sure you're right."

There was silence then. I didn't want to ask about Betsy. And whatever his reason was, he wasn't asking about me.

I said, "You should come by. Mom and I just made awesome soup and corn bread."

"Really?" he said. "Did you say awesome?"

"I think I did," I said.

"Let me see if I can shake loose over here. How's seven?"

"Seven's just perfect. See you then."

I was just thinking that if he came by the store, I'd give him a jar or two to take home. And he thought I invited him for dinner. Talk about fate: This was divine intervention if ever there was.

"Uh, Mom?"

"Yes?" She looked at me and I knew she knew something was up. "Spit it out."

"Alden's coming for dinner tonight," I said.

"Really? Too bad I'll miss him. Your brother's taking me to the Citadel Mall tonight."

"Since when do you go shopping at night at the Citadel Mall?"

"Since I want to be out of the house when he comes so that nature can take its course. Now, please go home and wash your hair. And for heaven's sake, put on some makeup and perfume."

"I don't have any perfume," I said.

She looked at me though slits of eyes and her mouth was stretched wide and taut in exasperation.

"That's pitiful," she said.

"I don't need it," I said and then remembered I had some samples the ladies who did my hair and makeup in Chicago gave me.

"Well, for heaven's sake, try to be alluring, if you know what I mean."

"He's coming for a bowl of soup, Miss Virnell. Not a rendezvous with Julia Roberts."

"A little more allure and a little less soup wouldn't kill you," she said. "And don't call me Miss Virnell."

There was no ruining my good mood. We closed the store at six but I went back to the house at five. I took a shower, washed my hair, and blew it out as carefully as I could. I had let the girl in Chicago reshape it so it looked a lot more like the year 2017 than 2000. Even I could make it actually look like something. I could hear Floyd in the other room arguing with Mom.

"I hate the Citadel Mall," he said.

"Your sister has a date tonight with Alden," she said.

"She does?" He said this with too much amazement in his voice for my blood.

"I can hear you! 'She' is the cat's mother!"

"I'll take you to the Cracker Barrel for dinner," Floyd said.

"And I'll take you to Barnes & Noble to look around. But please don't make me go to the mall."

"Go warm up the truck," she said and stuck her head in my room. "Get your business done by nine thirty. I doubt if I can keep him out any longer than that."

"Mom!" I pretended to be grossed out, but the truth was, she was hilarious.

I set the dining room table for Alden and me, wishing I had flowers for the center or candles, but that might have been too much. Candles and flowers might have made him nervous. Or made me nervous. In any case, I had made a decision to let go of my inhibitions and worries over relationships. If I couldn't trust Alden to treat me the right way, there wasn't a man on the planet I could trust.

I made a pot of rice and put the soup on the stove to warm up. I wrapped the corn bread in aluminum foil and put it in the oven on low heat. I looked around to see if we had any booze in the house and I couldn't find a drop, except for the cheap sherry my mother liked to sip on occasion when she said her bones were cold. That stuff was so terrible. It was too late to run to a liquor store. I could have raided Floyd's liquor cabinet, but I thought better of that too. So I did what southerners do when all else fails. I made a pot of sweet tea.

It was six fifteen. I hoped Susan would still be sober, so I called her. She answered right away.

"Hey!" I said. "How are you?"

"Well, for someone whose life was completely shattered, I'm doing okay, I guess."

"You want to talk? I'm happy to listen. I've got plans at seven, but until then, I'm all yours."

"You are too nice, Diane. In fact, you might be the nicest person in my life right now."

"Oh, Susan, tell me what's the worst part of all of this, for you to handle, I mean."

"That's a good question." I heard her sigh so hard, it broke my heart a little. "I think the worst part is the sweeping betrayal and the lies on top of lies."

"Yeah, when I find out someone's lied to me I have a hard time ever believing them again."

"Exactly. And Alejandro became the consummate liar. We're getting divorced."

"Oh, no! Oh, Susan, I am so sorry."

"Don't be sorry. He is likely to get a hundred years or more, but he's also been sleeping with his secretary for years. She's the one who turned him in."

"Oh, dear. What's the matter with some men? How stupid. I am so sorry."

"You know, in the last forty-eight hours I've been relieved of my duties as cochair of the Lyric gala, which raises money for our opera company. After twenty years of sitting on their board, I'm supposed to understand that my name was removed from all the printed materials associated with the event and the institution. If that's not bad enough, I've been asked to resign from the symphony board and the board of the Art Institute."

"Oh, how terrible. Aren't people just awful?"

"My best friend asked me not to call her anymore."

"Floyd didn't like her. I wasn't crazy about her either."

"And I'm being thrown out of my co-op! I'm going to be homeless!"

"How can they do that? Don't you own it?"

"Yes, but I've been informed by Ed Rabin, Alejandro's lawyer, that any minute, the federal government will be taking all of Alejandro's assets to pay back the people he robbed. That includes this co-op."

"Can't you or his lawyers do something about it?" I said, thinking why should she suffer for what he did? She didn't do anything. At least I *assumed* she hadn't broken any laws. "They can't just throw you out into the streets. They just can't."

"Diane? Let me just tell you how bad this is . . ."

She told me a story about how her manicurist asked her to leave her salon, saying that she made other customers nervous, and believe it or not, we laughed and laughed.

"That's just about the worst thing I've ever heard!" I said. "Hey, do you think the kids know?"

"There's actually no cell reception where they are. I could reach them through the tour company, but I keep thinking I don't want to ruin their honeymoon. They'll find out everything soon enough."

"That's true. Gosh, I know I'd do anything to protect Fred from heartbreak. I know you must feel the same way."

"I sure do. When someone tells you they've had a bad day, tell them about me. I didn't do anything except love and honor my husband for thirty years, and look what happened. I just hope this doesn't cause the kids to lose their jobs too."

"I had not even thought about that. Let's say a little prayer for them."

She was quiet then, and that's when I realized she probably didn't pray.

"I haven't been in a church since I was a little girl," she said.

"Well," I said, extremely careful not to sound like I was proselytizing, "prayer is a funny thing. I figure it can't hurt and it might do some good. Right?"

"Maybe," she said. "Oh, Diane, thanks for listening to me."

"Anytime," I said and meant it. "I'll call you tomorrow. By the way, Mom and Floyd send their best. And my friend Kathy too."

"God." I could hear her voice catch. "That is so nice. Please tell them I said thanks."

"I surely will," I said and pressed the End button.

I heard Alden's car door close and I looked at my phone. It was seven on the nose. I went to the front door and here he came bounding up the front steps with flowers in one hand and a bottle of wine in the other. It was as if he knew this was not going to be any old night around Virnell's table.

"Hey, gorgeous!" he said.

"Hey, yourself," I said with an irrepressible grin. "Come on in!"

"I brought you something. Actually, I brought the wine for us. The flowers are for you."

"Alden! You are so sweet! I think this is the first time you've ever brought me flowers."

"It is," he said. "It's also the first time you've asked me to come over for dinner."

"No, that can't be," I said. "But we've known each other for years!"

He followed me to the kitchen. The evening was off to an excellent start.

"It's sad but true. Anyway, I stopped at Whole Foods because they have the best flowers and a nice selection of wine. This is a pretty decent Barolo."

"That they do. I love red wine," I said and handed him a corkscrew. "Will you? I'll get some glasses."

I put two wineglasses on the kitchen table and took a vase from the cabinet to arrange the flowers.

"Happy to," he said, slicing away the foil on the neck of the bottle. "So how was your day?"

"Great, actually," I said, thinking, If all my days ended in a kitchen with you, it wouldn't be the worst thing in the world. "Mom and I cornered the market on the soup and corn bread we're having tonight."

"The *awesome* soup, you mean," he said.

"Ha-ha! Well, you'll be the judge."

"Where is she, anyway?"

"Floyd took her out to eat," I said. "They'll be back by nine thirty."

Why in the world did I have to tell him that?

Alden arched an eyebrow, poured a glass for us, and handed me mine.

"A toast?" he said.

"Sure! What are we toasting?" I said and raised my glass.

"Slowing down time," he said, adding, "Cheers!"

"Cheers," I said, taking a sip. "This is delicious. Thank you. Why, I'm almost afraid to ask, do we want to slow down time?"

He took my glass of wine from me and put it down on the table next to his.

"Because . . ."

I could see that look in his eyes. He wasn't kidding either. He pulled me into his arms.

"Wait a minute! Wait a minute!" I said.

"Nope, I'm kissing you right now. It's easier to ask for forgiveness than permission."

"No! Wait! What about Betsy?"

"She's my cousin," he said.

"What?" I said. His cousin?

"My mother's side. Her first cousin's son's ex-wife or something."

"So, that would make her your ex-cousin-in-law. No blood."

"No, wait. I know there's blood. Maybe I explained it wrong. Now, where were we?"

Twenty rather intense minutes later I said, "What about dinner?"

I knew then there was a high probability of my pants hitting the floor. And if I'd known he could kiss like that, I would've been at this a long time ago.

"Right," he said. "The awesome soup."

"This is some awesome kissing," I said. "How come I didn't know you could kiss like this?"

"Me either. I'm inspired. God, you smell good. What are you wearing? I'll buy you a gallon of it."

"Free sample," I said.

And then we started to laugh.

"Diane? You are so funny and you don't even know it."

We went back to the very pleasant business of examining each other's lips.

"We've got to stop this or I don't know what will happen!"

"Yes you do."

"But, Alden, we can't do this here."

"Why not?"

"I don't know! It's our first date, isn't it?"

"The first real one, I think," he said. Then we stopped. "Okay, I understand. If Floyd walked in and caught us . . . well, you know, *caught us,* we'd be very embarrassed."

"Virnell would take a switch to our behinds!" I said, laughing at the thought of that.

"I guess it's time to eat, right?"

"Okay," I said and stood back a bit. "Do you swear Betsy's your cousin?"

"On my honor as a Boy Scout of America," he said.

"Then why did you let me think there was something going on between the two of you?" I took the corn bread out of the oven. It was steaming hot.

"To see if you'd get jealous. Sure took you long enough."

"I should've gone to your niece's wedding," I said and filled our bowls with soup.

"You should've invited me to Fred's!"

"I thought you were, you know, all involved with Betsy! You know that."

"Whatever. So tell me all about Chicago and the wedding and what the hell happened to Alejandro and Susan."

I put the flowers on the table and we began to eat. I told him all about the snowstorm, Molly our chicken's debut as a party animal, the wedding, and all that happened to Susan and Alejandro.

"He's going to be in jail for the rest of his life."

"Rightfully so," he said.

"Agreed. She's the one I'm worried about. She could crack, I'm not kidding. What she's going through shouldn't happen to anyone."

"Sounds like it. Hey, Diane?"

"Yeah?"

"Soup's awesome."

"Okay, I'm searching my soul and I think I need a GPS,"
Susan said.

CHAPTER 27

susan's reflection

Y ou have to eat something," Michael Dean said to me, putting the bags of groceries on the kitchen counter in Shelby and Frederick's apartment.

"I have no appetite," I said. "The kids are coming home today."

"Do they know?"

"No. And thank God they've been gone for a month. At least Alejandro's off the front page of the papers. I told them to call me the minute they landed."

"Do you want me to be here to help explain the situation to them?"

"No. It's probably best if I do this on my own," I said. "But thank you. You've done so much."

Michael and his wife, Patty, were my lifeline to the outside world. And Michael was giving me five hundred dollars a week, swearing to me that he'd get it back when I settled with the court, promising me that no judge in the world would leave me completely destitute.

"I understand that it's better if you explain it to them without an audience, but you still have to eat. You're already too thin, Susan."

"You can't be too thin or too rich. Ask Alejandro. By the way, have you seen him?"

"Yes, he signed the divorce papers yesterday."

"I can't imagine he was surprised to be served," I said.

"Not at all. In fact, he understands and *wants* you to distance yourself from him so you can have a life."

"Well, having a life after Alejandro is proving to be almost impossible. He really left me in the middle of a minefield."

"He sure did. But listen, there was a day when he sent so much business my way, I owe him forever. Taking care of you until we get everything settled is my pleasure. I want you to know that. Patty and I love you, and we'd be helping you even if you didn't want us to."

At least I still had two friends in Chicago.

"You and Patty are all I have, you know."

He shook his head and said, "Call me if you need anything, okay? We'll be home all weekend. And don't answer the door unless you know who it is. Use the peephole!"

"Don't worry! I will."

I closed the door behind him and bolted it. He'd installed a peephole for me to protect me from the ruthless opportunists.

Case in point: The pizza delivery guy sold that lovely picture of my mascara-smeared face, with me swinging a bottle of champagne, to the *Chicago Tribune*. My drunk ass was on the front page three days later. People can be so cold.

I was staying at Shelby and Frederick's apartment, sleeping on their pullout sofa. Federal marshals showed up two days after Alejandro's arraignment and took possession of our apartment, evicting me. Ed Rabin told me they were coming and to prepare myself. Michael was there with me. I had to answer questions and open our vault. There was no point in their taking a crowbar to a thirty-thousand-dollar custom Traum safe.

I was horrified to see one of the marshals throw my three fur coats over his arm.

"Please! My fur coats are twenty years old. It's zero degrees outside. They're not worth anything to anyone except me."

"Sorry, ma'am," he said. "The court order says to confiscate all luxury items. If they decide they have no value, they'll be returned."

Yeah, right, I thought. Bastard! Your fat little girlfriend will be squeezing herself into one before dark.

So far, no one from the press knew I was staying at my daughter's, and as each day went by, they were less interested. Still, my life had become madness. When I got the phone call from Ed that I was going to be evicted, I had packed some clothes for ten days, but nothing that would draw attention to me, and left. All my jewelry was left at home in the vault except for my wristwatch, my engagement ring, and an amethyst ring I'd had since college. But the day I went to the co-op, I left those things at Shelby's. Even though I had a legal opinion from Ed and Michael that those items were mine, I didn't feel like getting hassled.

My emotions were all over the place. One minute I was in tears, missing Alejandro and the love we used to share. Then I'd remember Nadia and my temperature would soar until I broke a sweat. A minute later I wanted to kill him for the mess he'd made, the pain he'd caused so many people, the disgrace he'd brought to our family, including the loss of everything we owned. I needed a shrink desperately, but since I no longer had medical insurance, it was out of the question. At least I had Michael and Patty, but their empathy was rooted in obligation. Diane was the only real friend I had, and if she really knew me, she probably wouldn't like me either.

My phone vibrated and rang, flashing a light as well. I really needed Frederick to adjust my settings. It was Shelby.

"We landed!"

"Wonderful! I'm at your apartment with food. I can't wait to see you both. Was it incredible?"

"Yes! We took a million pictures. We'll see you very soon."

The last few weeks had given me a lot of time for introspection, something I usually liked to avoid. But now there was no choice except to examine my conscience and figure out how I might resurrect myself and how my new life might look. For one thing, I had to stop being such a bitch. I knew my soul was a little bit black with tarnish. I had quietly but absolutely flaunted my wealth at every opportunity and written people off if they served no purpose in my stratospheric climb. I didn't know it at the time, but the only place I was climbing was into my own grave. Just like Alejandro ran out of time to refund his funds, I was on a similar downhill slide. How was I ever going to leave a legacy that my daughter could be proud of?

I could write a tell-all and travel around talking about the importance of truth and integrity, but who would believe I knew anything about truth and integrity? And the idea of writing made my head hurt. One thing was certain. If I wanted a judge to make a generous settlement on my behalf, I had better watch myself. That was why I'd left all my jewelry behind. And our art collection. And my silver and anything of value, really. Even my furs—although they were pretty old, I wasn't taking any chances. I never dreamed they'd take those old coats.

But was I only trying to behave out of fear of further punishment, or did I have any real interest in atonement? Well, the concept of atonement and rehabilitation of character was interesting, but I didn't want to live under a bridge in a cardboard box either. And while we're being so darned refreshingly honest, it had dawned on me that talking to Diane made me behave differently. She was so good, I mean, really and truly good, that I was sort of wondering what it would be like to see the world through her eyes. But how would I accomplish that? Pay her a visit and milk the cow?

I was confused. And I was still a bitch, unaware of how cynical I'd become through the years.

I'd spent the last thirty years trying to stay on top of a heap of superficial social nitwits, and for what? To have our names

carved into a wall in a lobby? Even if our names weren't going to be chiseled out because of Alejandro's crimes, they
would be chiseled out eventually to make room for new do-
nors a few generations from now. There was only so much
wall space to be had. What was the point? Recognition, or, as
Andrew Carnegie said, doing good.

What was I going to do with the rest of my life? So far one
door had closed but the other had yet to open. I had a lot of
thinking to do. I could not live out my days on my daughter
and son-in-law's sofa in their one-bedroom apartment in an
emerging millennial neighborhood. I know, I needed to get
over the emerging part. I was probably lucky that I wasn't
in jail with Alejandro, so I should be grateful to have a roof
over my head. Maybe that was one thing I could learn to
do—count my blessings.

Speaking of blessings, I found it so interesting that Diane
referenced prayer as a way to deal with crisis. Maybe I'd try
talking to God and see if that helped. It couldn't hurt, as she
pointed out.

I'd had a meeting with Paul, or I should say, Mr. Keenan,
our co-op board president, the day after I got tossed out of my
home on my ear. I wanted to tell him he could find me at my
daughter's and to give him my cell phone number. He had
taken some time to wrestle with my reduced circumstances,
meaning he probably combed every nasty thing said about
my husband in print and on the Internet, and decided Alejandro had done me dirty as well. He was sympathetic.

"I was thinking about you when you called," he said. On
that afternoon, his velvet jacket was gray paisley and his

ascot was lavender. Please. "This has to be a *terrible* ordeal for you!"

"It's unbelievable," I said. "I'm living a nightmare all day, every day."

"And you obviously had no idea what he was doing, did you?"

"Not one hint of anything. He should've been a poker player," I said.

"The scoundrel," he said. "I'm so sorry. Is it true you're getting divorced?"

He wasn't sorry.

"Yes. I mean, what's the point of staying married?" I said. I said nothing about Nadia because I knew he was only engaging in this chitchat to have something to discuss over cocktails.

"Quite," he said. "So the plan is?"

"The federal marshals have the keys. You'll have to ask them."

Speaking of keys, I was completely lost in my thoughts and almost didn't hear the key turning in Shelby's door, but I came out of my fog and rushed to open it.

"Shelby?" I asked before I turned the bolt, being mindful of my safety.

"It's me! Open the door!" she said.

I unbolted it and swung it open wide.

"Look at my girl! You're absolutely radiant!" I hugged her with all my might. "Frederick! Sweetheart! Welcome home!"

"Thanks, Mrs. Cambria!"

"You should probably call me something else from now on. Get yourselves inside. We need to talk."

She looked at my suitcases stacked against the far wall.

"You're staying here? I mean that's fine, but why?"

"I got evicted from our apartment," I said as calmly as I could.

"Why? Holy hell, Mom! What happened?"

"Take your coats off and sit. I've got a story to tell you you're not going to like."

"Uh-oh," she said and sat on the sofa. "Is Daddy in trouble with the IRS?"

"Worse. Our apartment was seized by the United States federal marshal, along with everything else we own. Past tense. Owned."

Frederick's jaw was quite agape, and Shelby's was as well. She sank deeper into the sofa cushions.

"Where's Dad? But I think I already know the answer."

"Dad's in jail. Securities fraud and a dozen other charges. He's probably going to be there for the rest of his life. And we're getting divorced." Might as well get it all on the table, I thought.

"*What?* You're divorcing my father because he's in jail?"

"No. I'm divorcing your father because he's been having an affair with Nadia for years."

"*What? I don't believe you.*"

"That doesn't mean it's not true. In fact, Nadia is the one who turned him in to the FBI."

"That nasty bitch!" Shelby said and started to cry.

"You can say that again," I said. "Don't cry, sweetheart."

"I'm sorry," she said. "It's just a shock. A really giant one."

I handed her a tissue. If I still knew anything, it was the location of the tissue box.

"Listen, think what you missed. Dad on the front page of the paper in handcuffs. Plastered all over the network news doing the perp walk—they tell me that's what it's called. I've been stalked by reporters. I've had drones outside my windows taking pictures."

"Drones! Oh, God! Mom! That's, like, super scary!"

"I've been asked to resign from every board I was on. Our membership at the Union League Club has been revoked."

"Wow, and I really liked that place," Frederick said.

"Me too. I have no health insurance. I can't even get a manicure. No one will rent to me—so far I've tried at least ten buildings. I had nowhere to go, so I came here. I'm sorry to intrude like this. I'll find a place. I'm sure there's some kind soul out there who will rent to me."

"Mrs. Cambria, uh, should I call you Ms. Kennedy now?"

"For heaven's sake, Frederick, call me Susan. It's fine."

"Well, I was just going to say you're welcome to stay with us forever, if you'd like. I mean, we're family. We can get a two-bedroom, maybe? We're both due for a raise. And it's okay to call me Fred."

Diane raised a fine young man. I ignored the part about calling him by a nickname.

"You're very sweet, and that's an extremely generous offer, but let's see what happens when you return to work. I hope you both still have a job. Your father really did a number on the family name."

"We shouldn't lose our jobs for something Dad did, or could we?" Shelby said.

"I don't know. His criminal behavior surely wrecked my life. I guess we just have to wait and see."

"Damn," Frederick said.

"Well said," I said.

"Mom, I can't believe you've had to go through all this alone while we were gallivanting all over Africa! Why didn't you call us? We would've come home right away."

"Because I feared that your gallivanting days would be over soon enough and I wanted you to enjoy your honeymoon. I was thrilled to spare you the god-awful embarrassment of the horrible spectacle he made."

"I can't believe you just downloaded this whole story just as we walked in the door."

"I know. I'm sorry, but as soon as you turned on the television you would've known. It's still in the news every day."

"I'll bet," Frederick said.

"Well, we have news too," Shelby said and looked at me with a huge smile. "We're having a baby and you're going to be a grandmother!"

"What? Oh my God! You're sure?" They bobbed their heads with pure unmitigated glee. "How absolutely wonderful! Oh! I am so thrilled!"

I threw my arms around Frederick and then Shelby, and then the tears came. I cried and they cried and then we cried some more.

"This is wonderful! Heaven knows, we were in dire need of some good news!"

"We think so too!"

"And when are we expecting this little miracle to arrive?"

"End of June," Shelby said.

I thought for a moment and realized we had an engagement baby coming.

"Oh, who cares?" I said. "Let people talk. They're gonna talk anyway."

"I'm so excited, Mom."

"So am I, sweetheart. So am I. Have you told Diane?"

"Nope, you're the first person to know," Frederick said.

There was a little bit of extra joy in that for me, knowing they told me first, but why was I competitive with anyone? They could not have possibly known the depths to which my spirit had sunk or how badly I needed something, anything, to make me feel better. And on an odd note, the first person I wanted to celebrate the news with was Diane, so maybe I wasn't really competitive at all. In fact, I could see Diane and me somewhere down the road, watching our adorable little grandchild running around a yard, discovering the world.

"It's as plain to see as the nose on my face!" Virnell said.

"It's also awkward, don't you think?" Diane said.

"Love will never be denied," Virnell said.

CHAPTER 28

diane on the farm

The first thing I did when we got the news was to dig my crochet hook out and find a pattern I liked. I wanted the baby to be able to say, my grandmother Diane made this blanket for me. I was busy making little squares and throwing them in a box. My yarn was white, pearl gray, and apple green. If she delivered a boy, I'd give it a pale blue border, pink for a girl. I was secretly hoping for a girl because I never had one.

The first thing Virnell did was take a pile of Pop's shirts and cut them up into triangles to make a quilt, so the baby could say, my great-grandmother Virnell made this quilt for me from my great-grandfather's shirts. Her pattern was a tiny patchwork.

"I hope she gives us a boy. Pop had a whole lot more blue shirts than pink!"

"I don't think she will even care, as long as the baby's healthy."

"Well, I figure if it's a girl I'll cut out some pink teddy bears and quilt them over the patchworks."

"Miss Virnell? That's a piece of genius," I said.

"I've still got it, missy," she said and tapped the side of her head. "And don't call me that."

We were beside ourselves with happiness. A baby! I was so proud of Shelby's and Fred's courage. Fred called.

"What are you going to say about this if people count the months on their fingers?" I asked.

"Mom, that's your generation. Not mine."

"Oh," I said, feeling every one of my years.

"If anyone says anything mean or nasty to me, I'll tell them to mind their own business."

"Just say that they won't be getting an invitation to the baby shower. But you're right, who would say such a thing these days?"

Mom was all cozy in Pop's recliner watching television in the living room. Kathy and I were in the kitchen, sharing a bottle of wine. She'd brought over a pan of lasagna. We had salad and garlic bread to go with it, and it was delicious. Even Floyd approved.

"It was just Stouffer's," she whispered to me when everyone was gone.

"Really? Well, it was very good," I said. "And we didn't have to cook!"

"That might be the best part. What's the latest dirt from Chicago?" she said.

"Well, Shelby is getting very excited about the baby."

"Of course! So am I!"

"Me too. They're going to pay us a visit next month. They're coming out to get Fred's baby crib."

"Wonderful! Floyd was awfully good to rent that apartment for Susan. How's she doing?"

"Oh, I think Susan's doing pretty well, considering the utter hell she's been through."

"Isn't that the truth? I can't imagine the turmoil she had to endure. Bless her heart."

I smiled then, knowing Kathy meant, *Well, now Susan with the no-longer double last name is seeing how the 99 percent live.*

"They've become very good friends, haven't they?" She wiggled her eyebrows.

"Kathy Christie! What are you implying? I'll bet you every last nickel to my name that hell will freeze before Susan ever gets herself involved with a man for the rest of her life."

"I know I wouldn't! I had two husbands and that was God's gracious plenty. One was worse than the other."

"Yeah, if you ever get involved with a man again, I get to hold a vetting process."

"Good idea," she said.

"Anyway, she sent me some pictures of her little studio. She put in a Murphy bed and furniture she bought online. Lord knows, the apartment's only three hundred square feet."

"Murphy beds scare me to death! Three hundred square feet? That's not big enough for a palmetto bug! Although she's so skinny, she doesn't take up much room."

"She says a tiny spot suits her just fine. And she even laughed and said it's a lot more spacious than Alejandro's cell. At least it's in Shelby and Fred's building. I think the plan is for Susan to watch the baby while Shelby and Fred work."

"Are you jealous?"

"A little. But maybe I'll get him for a stretch in the summer."

"How are their jobs going?"

"Well, I think Shelby's position is less stable than Fred's. Their boss told them they wouldn't be fired because of her father's notoriety, but he implied that they'd probably have a hard time getting promoted."

"That just doesn't seem fair."

"Kathy, life's not fair."

Where was Alden? Well, Alden, who was firmly established in my life as *with privileges,* had an event to cater that night. He was so wonderful. Why had I waited so long? He made me feel alive again. I mean, really young and alive. Amazing.

It was the week after Easter. Asparagus, some lettuces, and strawberries were ripe for harvest. Floyd's crews were beginning to increase in numbers, as they always did this time of year. By May, when the peaches began to come in, he'd put a hundred or so people to work, picking peaches, grading them, and packing them up to ship.

We grew strawberries, Sweet Charlies, mostly for ourselves and for jelly and jam to sell in the store. They were getting better each year, mainly because we figured out how to improve the drainage and how to stop the birds from eating them. The berries were coming in so plump and sweet that we were talking about doubling the crop in the fall. We all agreed that it was important to diversify. Floyd planted them in an annual hill planting system, but last fall he began experimenting with a gutter system, because the harvest was much less backbreaking. Unlike our strawberry plants, which lasted five or six years, some of our asparagus rhizomes were nearly forty years old. We grew other things for the store—tomatoes, peppers, pole beans, field peas, collards, chard, cucumbers, corn, onions, and, of course, sweet potatoes. I couldn't wait for the day when I could lift my grandchild high in the air to pick his or her first peach with a fat little dimpled hand. I wanted to see that child dribble peach juice down his or her little chin and fall in love with this land so hard that she or he never wanted to leave. That was what I wanted.

For the next few weeks, we counted the days until Shelby and Fred's arrival. It turned out that Susan was coming too.

"Is that okay?" Fred said.

"Of course, it's fine! You and Shelby will have to sleep in the extra bedroom at Uncle Floyd's and I can put Susan in your old room or she can stay with Kathy. I'm sure Kathy wouldn't mind a bit."

"We'll just stay with Uncle Floyd, if it's okay with him."

"Of course it's okay! Gosh! I cannot wait to lay my eyes on you!"

Meanwhile, Floyd pulled the crib out of storage and cleaned it up. It needed a new mattress, but other than that, it was in good shape. He cleaned and oiled the movement that raised and lowered the side. Then he washed and dried every inch of it and gave it a fresh coat of paint. It looked brand-new.

"Floyd, thank you for this. I think they're going to love it," I said.

"Wait until they see what I've done with the chickens," he said. "It's a surprise."

"Susan sure likes nothing better than a surprising chicken," I said, wondering what in the world had he come up with now?

I was running my hand over the headboard and remembering hearing Fred's cries in the middle of the night. I would rush into his room and scoop him up in my arms so he didn't wake up the whole house. Then I'd rock him and sing him lullabies in whispers until he fell asleep again. Shelby and Fred had those sweet moments in their future and so many others. The first time you see your child is unlike any other first of your life. And then there's the wonder of a sleeping child. You watch them, marveling at their perfection, wondering if they look like you, if they will be like you. Shelby would soon know that as the mother she could soothe her baby better than anyone. Fred and Shelby would come to the realization that the love they shared brought another human into the world. These were not givens. These were things that had to happen to you for you to understand them. Fred and Shelby were on the threshold of one of life's most profoundly moving experiences. A baby was just what we all needed to send a signal to everyone we knew and to ourselves that life does indeed go on.

"I can't wait for the baby to come," Floyd said.

"I'm feeling really sentimental too."

"You want some butter beans for supper?" he said.

"I always want butter beans," I said.

Cucumbers, sweet corn, butter beans, and the first peaches of the season were coming in. We had cherry tomatoes and Early Girl hybrid tomatoes that were new for Floyd this year. The real jewels, Better Boys and Big Beef, wouldn't be in for a few more weeks. To this day, there was no meal you could put on the table in the dead of summer that was more satisfying than a platter of tomato and Vidalia onion sandwiches. Later in the summer we would get a crop of Viva Italia and Mama Leone plum tomatoes and, of course, San Marzano to put up in jars. That would be fun to do with Shelby, if she wanted to learn how it was done.

Fred, Shelby, and Susan finally arrived on May 13 and came right to the store, knowing exactly where we'd be on a busy Saturday. It was late in the afternoon when they pulled up right in front. Our hellos were effervescent and buoyant, all of us so happy to see one another. Gus, of course, immediately walked in and around Susan's legs. I shooed him away.

"Go kill some mice, you silly old cat! Shoo! Sorry, Susan! Hello! Welcome!"

"I'm so happy to see you again!" Susan said and gave me an affectionate hug, the kind I didn't know she was capable of giving.

"We finally made it!" Shelby said, arms outstretched.

"Oh! Look at you, darling girl!" I hugged her. "You're just in full bloom like a beautiful flower!"

"Thanks!" she said. "I feel great—for a whale, that is."

"Hey, Mom!" Fred said and gave me a hug. "Gram!"

Shelby was clearly in her eighth month and her round belly was so adorable.

Mom couldn't get out from behind the cash register fast enough. Fred picked her up and swung her around like he always did, and she ordered him to put her down like she always did.

"Gram!" Shelby said.

"Dear girl," Mom said.

We all laughed and hugged some more. I was so happy then, just to see them, to know that they were here safe and sound. I was especially glad that Susan had come.

"I love the sign outside," she said. "'Stop the car! You need peaches!'"

"Let me tell you something, when folks find out our peaches are in? They stop the car," I said.

I closed the store around six and I went up to the house to see if everyone was settled. Mom had left earlier to take a nap. Since Pop died, she'd started taking naps every afternoon.

Susan was on the front porch reading a book.

"I set the table for dinner. I hope that's all right," she said.

"All right? It's much appreciated! So how was your afternoon?" I said.

"I've been sitting right here, rocking away, reading my book and enjoying this beautiful day. Miss Virnell is inside. She said she's catching forty winks."

Susan was practically glowing and her hair was goofed up in the back. Something was up.

"She likes her catnaps," I said.

I looked out behind me, taking in the view that Susan had. Clay pots of colorful gerbera daisies and impatiens were on the front steps. White oleanders stood in the yard along with our huge magnolia tree, which was filled with flowers so big and perfect, they seemed impossible. Pink bougain-villea climbed all over the fence, and the smells of our mock orange tree floated across the porch with every breeze. Sum-mer was here and it was gorgeous.

"It's the simple things, isn't it?" I said.

"Yes. I'm starting to appreciate them more and more," she said. "Can I help you get dinner on the table?"

"Why don't you sit right there and I'll get us some tea?"

"Oh, that would be so nice."

"Have you seen Floyd?"

"Yes, he came by to say hello."

He said more than hello, I'd guess.

"Good, well. Well, don't move."

Of course I intended to serve her iced tea infused with peach syrup, just as I had the first time we met. And even though we were going to eat supper shortly, I thought I'd slice a little pound cake too. I put a few strawberries on the plate as well. The color was so pretty.

When I came back out to the porch with the tray, she jumped in surprise. "Oh, Diane! I didn't mean for you to go to so much trouble!"

"It's no trouble at all. It's just how we do things around here and always have."

"It's so civilized," she said. "Thank you."

"I just thought it would be nice for us to share a moment before everyone gathers to eat."

I poured tea and handed her the glass. I filled a glass for myself and took a seat in the rocker next to hers.

"This is Miss Virnell's pound cake. Have a pinch," I said.

"That's so southern to say 'have a pinch,'" she said, pinching a piece of cake and popping it in her mouth. "I love it. This cake is a sin."

"There was a time when many southern wives had a pound cake in their kitchens in case someone dropped by for a visit."

"It must have been so nice to grow up here," she said. "It's so pretty it makes you forget about the outside world. I've never had a garden."

"Gardening is a great meditation. It was nice growing up here. I'll have to take you out to the old plantation, Magnolia Gardens."

"Oh! I've never seen a plantation."

"Magnolia is a gem. There are so many astonishing flowers in bloom, they call it a romantic garden or an extravagant liar because it was designed to make us forget our humdrum life."

"What an idea! I'd love to visit. And I'd love to have a humdrum life."

"I'll bet. Wonderful. Maybe we can grab a few hours on Monday. That's our slowest day."

"Great. This has been some six months, hasn't it?"

"I'll say it has. How are you doing? Are you okay?"

"I'm getting used to my new life, and in an odd way, the whole disaster has been a real learning experience."

"How's that?"

"You think if you marry the right guy that you never have to worry about anything."

"Finding the right guy isn't so easy," she said. "You've got Alden. He's an angel."

"Yes, but I made him interview for the job for ages."

"You know, when you're married to a powerful man, there are all these ridiculous expectations placed on you. My whole life revolved around what I thought Alejandro wanted me to do or to be. I never gave much thought to what I might like to do. Or who I'd like to become."

"Do you feel different now?"

"Well, for the first time I can hear myself talking. I've been pretty much a jerk for so many decades, I don't know if I can dig myself out entirely. I'm just glad all those people are out of my life. They can go think what they want to think."

"They're probably going to anyway," I said.

"Agreed. Anyway, it was a shallow life filled with phony people. It had to be the best this and the most expensive that. Ridiculous. Now I feel like every day is a new day, but as long as I'm in Chicago, it's hard to reinvent myself."

I didn't know how to respond to that, so I said, "We're going to be grandmothers. What do you think?"

"Now, that's important! I am so excited I could come out of my skin," she said. "But the first person that calls me granny gets a black eye."

"Agreed. I can't wait to see who this baby is! What do you want to be called?"

"I don't know. What do you want to be called?"

"I don't know either. Probably time to give it some thought," I said.

"I was three weeks early when I delivered Shelby," she said.

We looked up to see Floyd approaching with Fred and Shelby. Floyd had a ceramic dish with something in it and Fred carried a handbasket of vegetables. Shelby was waddling.

"Y'all ready for some supper?" Floyd said. "I'm gonna put this pork loin and this corn on the grill."

It was almost dusk, my favorite time of day. The heat of the day was past and darkness had not yet found us. During the summer months there was an evening light that stayed with us long after the sun set, sometimes until almost nine o'clock.

"Let's see what you've got in there, Fred," I said.

There was corn, tomatoes, a handful of basil, and some eggs. Oh, and a bottle of vodka.

"What are the eggs for?" I said.

"Cocktails!" Floyd said.

"Eggs for cocktails? Are they hard-boiled?" I asked.

"Yep," Fred said, grinning.

"Why are you grinning like that?" Susan said. "What am I missing?"

"You'll see," he said. "Can I make you a big old vodka on the rocks?"

Susan looked at her wristwatch.

"Well, it is close to seven o'clock," she said. "So yes, please."

"Y'all stay right here on the porch, ladies. Shelby? You too," Fred said. "The men have dinner handled."

"Y'all have seen enough action for one day," Floyd said.

They went inside and slammed the door behind themselves.

A few seconds later I heard my mother's voice yelling, *"I imagine it was time to get up anyway!"*

All of us giggled.

"I can't teach Floyd anything he doesn't want to learn," I said.

"Alejandro was the same way. Do you want to hear something crazy?"

"Sure," I said. "We specialize in crazy around here."

"Frederick says southerners *pride* themselves on crazy family members," Shelby said.

"Ahem!" Susan said.

"Sorry, Mom, you were going to tell us something."

"I went to see your father the afternoon after he was arraigned and he apologized for being such a crook and womanizer and for ruining my life. And he told me to take up tennis. Tennis! He told me I could use his racket. Wasn't that nice?"

"How weird!" Shelby said.

"He was under a lot of stress," I said.

"The case that held his racket was jammed with hundred-dollar bills."

"What? What did you do?" Diane said.

"I told the federal marshals if they wanted to play tennis, they shouldn't miss the racket in the hall closet. I said, it's probably worth a lot of money."

"Oh, that's hilarious!" Diane said.

"And there was one more attempt on Alejandro's part to hide money, at least one more that I know of. Nadia could have a trunk of cash for all I know. Remember all that wine he had delivered for the rehearsal party?"

I had wondered what she did about that. So had Floyd. But we had never said a word.

"Yes," I said.

"I found out it was worth over a million dollars," Susan said.

"Mom! Whoa! Are you kidding? That's totally crazy!"

"Actually, Floyd was the one who tipped me off. He called me and said, 'Look, don't think there's not going to be some furious auditing that goes on in the aftermath of this.' I had my lawyer verify its worth and then we notified the FBI. I had no idea."

I said, "You have to believe he was just trying to leave you with some resources. I mean, it was against the law, but he probably wasn't thinking straight at that point."

"I wondered where it went. I thought maybe you moved it to the storage rooms downstairs," Shelby said. "We didn't even taste it!"

"You can't drink alcohol anyway, little lady," Susan said.

"True," Shelby said. "Still."

"At some point someone would have found out the cases were not accounted for. Anyway, the point is, you think you know someone and you don't," Susan said. "Your brother is the greatest."

"He's pretty special all right," I said and thought, Floyd! You old rascal, you! You do care about Susan. I was staying out of that one.

The door opened and it was Floyd, with Susan's cocktail and three eggs in a bowl with the saltshaker and a knife.

"Thanks, Floyd," Susan said, taking a demure sip, which was surprising. "Ah! It's the jet fuel from your friend!"

"Special occasion," he said, peeling away the shell on one of the eggs. Then he held it in a napkin in his hand, poised to slice it in half with his knife. "Y'all ready?"

"Fire away!" I said.

He sliced it in half and stood back, showing it to all of us. The yolk was bloodred.

"Is it blood?" Susan asked.

"Nope! Ha! How do you like that!" he said.

"What in the world did you do? Dye it?" Susan said.

"Cool!" Shelby said. "But eggs make me gag right now."

"Understood," Floyd said. "Who wants to try it?"

I looked at Susan. "Should we be the guinea pigs?"

"Why not? I think it's weirdly sort of beautiful."

We each took a half, sprinkled a little salt over it, and took a bite. The flavor had a hint of something—was it cayenne?

"Delicious!" I said. "Okay, how'd you do it?"

"I was watching *Chef's Table* on Netflix and they had this guy on, Dan Barber. He owns a restaurant in New York called Blue Hill at Stone Barns."

"I've met him," Susan said.

"Hey, no big-timing the natives," Floyd said.

"You tell her, Uncle Floyd!" Shelby said.

"Well, I have," Susan said.

Shelby rolled her eyes.

"Anyway, he's all involved with engineering seeds for flavor instead of simply longevity or disease resistance. Super interesting fellow. So, he was working with a man who makes chicken feed, and they figured out that if you feed a chicken high-carotenoid peppers, it turns their yolks red. Pretty cool, huh?"

"You should sell them to Alden when he's doing deviled eggs for a catering gig," I said.

"That's not a bad idea," he said. "Anyway, I share his farming philosophy on a lot of issues. He helped develop a new squash called honeynut. Very flavorful. I just ordered some seeds from him for some other things."

"Do you grow that squash?" Susan asked.

"No, but we're going to!" he said. "I'm gonna throw this pork loin on the fire."

"He's awesome," Shelby said, watching Floyd go down the stairs.

"He sure is," Susan said.

"I heard that!" Floyd said. He looked at us up on the porch and smiled at Susan. "You're right. I am."

Mom came out to the porch.

"Please don't give him a fat head," I said. "I have to live with him."

"He already has one," Mom said.

"We could not have anticipated this," Floyd said.

"I can't stand this!" Virnell said.

"Yes, we can. We are a strong family," Diane said.

CHAPTER 29

OMG!

june 14, 2017

Floyd, Mom, and I had just finished lunch and we were going back to the store. We stopped to look at the sky. We had just been saying to each other how wonderful it had been to have Fred and Shelby for a few days, and if anyone had ever needed a change of scenery, it was Susan.

"She's coming around, isn't she?" I said.

"Well, Lady Di, she sure had her sails trimmed, didn't she?"

"She sure did," I said. "Smells like rain."

"Yeah. Look at those clouds. We need it."

It was June and hurricane season had officially begun. But so far all we had had were occasional and short-lived late-afternoon thunder boomers. The peach trees needed extra watering to help them plump up to harvest. Everything else did as well. We had our own well for irrigation, but it was good for only so long. We needed rain. It was overcast and gloomy and a storm was brewing all around. I was standing on the porch with Floyd, feeling the wind picking up. The temperature was dropping quickly.

"I'm gonna put Isabella and her friends in the barn. You'd better be sure Gus is inside."

"Right."

Still, we stood there, watching. It was a fast-moving storm, with steel-colored, low-hanging clouds blanketing the Low-country as far as we could see in every direction. The rumbling was so loud, we could barely hear each other. Fat raindrops began to fall; there were loud cracks of lightning, one after another. Floyd all but jumped off the porch and began running toward the barn.

"Go inside the house, Mom. Right now," I said.

Frightened by the proximity of the lightning, she hurried back in the house. I turned the rocking chairs on the porch over and took down the wind chime. Then I moved the pots on the steps into the foundation bushes so they wouldn't blow away. Suddenly there was a gust of wind that had to be over fifty miles per hour. The rain hurt, it was pelting me so hard.

I looked up over beyond the barn where the peach grove stood and I saw something I'd only ever read about. The cloud that stretched the length of the grove and beyond was opened on the bottom in the middle, as though it had been slit from by an unseen machete. It dropped a bomb of rain filled with lightning bolts on the orchard. I was holding on to the rail of the front steps with all the strength I had in me because the wind threatened to take me to Oz. Crouching for safety, I was completely transfixed. The cloud continued dumping what I can only describe as a rain bomb on the grove for just a few minutes more and then it was gone. A few minutes later the entire storm had moved through. I was soaked to my skin and shaking in fear.

I turned to see Alden getting out of his car.

"Oh, God! Diane! Are you okay?"

I couldn't even answer. He put his arms around me. I was still shaking.

"Let's get you inside," he said. "I was on my way here and I saw the microburst. It seemed to be right over your farm. I came as fast as I could. That wind had to be a hundred miles per hour!"

We went up the steps and inside. There was no electricity.

"I'm okay," I finally said. "Please. Go find Floyd. He was running down the road to the barn to put up the cows. I just want to know he's okay."

"Sure," he said. "I'll be right back."

I was in the hall, dripping, a puddle of water at my feet, not yet fully comprehending what had just happened. As

Alden said, it was a microburst. I had never seen one and I hoped I never would again. I hurried to put on dry clothes and combed my wet hair into a ponytail.

"Mom!" I yelled, pulling on barn boots. "Where are you?"

"Coming! Coming! We lost power." She took a look at me and said, "You didn't have the sense to get out of the rain?"

"Apparently not," I said. "I'm going down to the orchard to see what happened. I've got a bad feeling in the pit of my stomach."

I jumped in my SUV and gunned it, driving down the road at a pace that was surely unsafe. Inside of a minute, my worst fear was realized. The peach orchard had been leveled to the ground. There stood Floyd next to Alden. Alden's arm was flung around Floyd's shoulder. It looked like an actual bomb had been detonated. Over five hundred peach trees, fully loaded with semiripened fruit, were lying in splinters, flung in every direction. Hail the size of baseballs was strewn everywhere. The packing sheds, never considered an architectural prize by anyone, were flattened. The storm had not impacted the barn or the strawberry fields. Only the peaches.

"Oh, no!" I said. "This is a complete disaster."

"Come on," Alden said. "Let's all go get drunk."

Alden had never been drunk in his life. I didn't know that I had either. But Floyd? He kept a box of Goody's Powder in his house at all times.

"Excellent idea," Floyd said. "But first, we have to notify our insurance company."

"I'll call them," I said. "The power's out."

"Okay. Then I have to call my foreman to get over here right away, take some pictures, and assess the damage to see if we can salvage anything. Then we can crawl in the bag."

"This is unbelievable," I said.

We'd had crop insurance through the USDA for as long as I could remember. I didn't know what our deductible was. I had the paperwork in my files. Then I recalled that I had just renewed our policy a few months ago. We were covered.

"I can't believe you're so calm," Alden said.

Floyd looked at him and shook his head.

"Alden, my man, when you're a farmer, you learn to take the good with the bad. This would be the bad. And believe me, I'm anything but calm."

"Want to stay for supper?" I said to Alden.

"Sure. Why don't I go get us some steaks? Seems like we need a solid meal to fortify ourselves."

"I haven't had steak in a while. That sounds great. Get a box of red wine too."

Alden looked from Floyd to me to see if Floyd was kidding.

"He's not a connoisseur," I said. "He drinks beer and vodka."

"Not at the same time," Floyd said. "I'm gonna go shower up while there's still light. I'll see you at the house in a bit."

"Okay," I said.

"Let me see what I can find. I'll be back soon."

I gave Alden a ride back to the house, where his car stood with the door left open. "Would you like me to come with you to tell Miss Virnell?"

"No, but thanks. She's going to be upset, and she wouldn't want to show it in front of you."

He looked a little hurt, but then he said, "Of course. I understand. I'll be back in an hour or less."

"You're a sweetheart," I said. "Thanks." I gave him a kiss on his cheek and watched him get in his car and drive away.

I went inside. "Mom?"

She was in the kitchen, washing and drying lettuce.

"How bad is the damage? I can tell from the look on your face that it's very bad."

"Devastating. The packing sheds are beyond salvage and the peach orchard was obliterated."

"Oh, no! Merciful Lord!"

"But we have insurance and some of the fruit might be salvageable if we work quickly."

"Oh, no. I can't believe it. Gone?"

"Every last tree is lying on the ground, some of them are split down the middle."

"I planted some of those trees with your father and now they're gone, just like he's gone."

She began to cry, and I felt terrible for being so blunt. But she didn't like the news sugarcoated any more than I did.

"Floyd and I planted a lot of them too, Mom. Listen, nobody got hurt. We're fine."

"I know, I know."

"We've been through drought, infestations, hurricane damage—you name it. Most of the trees were almost twenty years old and ready to be replaced anyway."

"Now what?"

"We're simply going to do what we always do. Clean it up.

Pull ourselves up by our bootstraps and figure it out. Come on now."

She blew her nose in a tissue. She always had one in the pocket of her apron.

"You're right. Of course, you're right. I was feeling weepy before you got here. Is Alden staying for dinner?"

"Yes. He just left to buy steaks for us," I said.

"Well then, for heaven's sake, Diane, go do something about your hair. I'll set the table."

"I just love you, Miss Virnell," I said.

"Don't call me . . ."

"Sorry."

Dinner was delicious, but there wasn't a lot of enthusiasm for it around the table. Alden and Floyd cooked the steaks and the potatoes on the grill. They were outside together, discussing the various attributes of various dry rubs and marinades while killing a lot of beers. Mom and I lit candles, drank a little wine and talked about replanting the grove.

"You know, maybe we should think about planting cling-stones. Keep the freestones for the store. Then we can give the clingstones to a packer to sort and pack. Maybe sell to Kroger's. Then we don't have to rebuild the packing sheds," Mom said.

I thought about it for a moment and said, "Maybe. I say we bread the waters with all the chains and see who takes the bait."

"We need more hands around here," she said.

"We sure do," I said.

The kitchen door opened and the smell of the steaks and potatoes Floyd carried was mouthwatering.

"Okay, ladies. Here they are!" Floyd said.

In the next few minutes we lit more candles, fixed our plates, and took a seat at the table.

"This is so perfect. Alden, thank you so much," Mom said.

"It's a great end to a terrible day," I said.

"Maybe we should go into the toothpick business," Floyd said.

"Oh, Floyd," Mom said.

Just as I was about to put the first forkful in my mouth, my cell phone rang. Usually I never take calls during a meal, but something told me to answer it. I'd left it in my bedroom, so I rushed to get it.

"Excuse me," I said. "I'll be right back."

"Hello, is this the grandmother of a perfect baby boy?" It was Fred.

The baby was born! I had a rush of adrenaline from the back of my head the whole way down my spine.

"Oh! Oh! How's Shelby? How much did the baby weigh? Where are you?

"At the hospital. Shelby's fine. The baby's fine. I cut the cord and nearly passed out on the floor. I'm a father! I can't believe it!"

"Oh, sweetheart! Congratulations! I'm just overwhelmed with joy for y'all and for us too! Is Susan with y'all?"

"Yeah, she's in there with Shelby. They're both bawling like babies and the baby is sleeping."

"Send a picture. You want to talk to Gram and tell her yourself?"

"Sure," he said.

I went back to the dining room and handed my phone to her.

"We're eating," she said, whispering.

"I think you want this news," I said.

"Hello? What? Oh! Oh! Oh, how wonderful!" She paused for a moment. "What's that? Yes, your uncle Floyd is right here. Hang on." She passed the phone to him. "I'm a great-grandmother now."

"Is that baby here?" Floyd said, knowing perfectly well that he was. "What's that? Oh! Well, Fred, that's quite an honor. Of course I'll teach him to fish . . ."

In a minute or so the call ended. Floyd teared up and had to wipe his eyes with his napkin.

"Guess what?" he said.

"I couldn't tell you," Mom said.

"They're naming him Floyd," Floyd said. "After me and after Pop. It was Susan's idea."

"Good gravy," Mom said.

"A trailer? I love it!" Susan said.

CHAPTER 30

road trip

The very next day after he was born, we brought young Floyd home to Frederick and Shelby's apartment and laid him in Frederick's crib. His eyes were open and you could see him literally coming into the world, becoming more conscious, with each passing minute. He was absolutely precious. Precious and beautiful and perfect.

"When I had you," I said, "I stayed in the hospital for five days."

Shelby said, "Now they practically kick you out the door. But it's probably safer to get out of there, especially with all the germs. MRSA and all that."

Little Floyd mewled, that sweet cry that all newborns have.

"You're one hundred percent right," I said.

"Are you hungry *again*?" Shelby said to Floyd.

She had a new voice, the sweet one stored somewhere in us, the one that waits for a child to love. It was marvelous to hear.

She picked him up, took him to the rocking chair, and nursed him as though she'd been nursing babies for years. In my generation, nursing was considered déclassé. Now it seemed like child abuse if you didn't nurse.

"He sure wants to eat a lot," Shelby said.

"I guess that's normal," Frederick said and then turned to me. "Is that normal?"

"It's normal," I said.

There had been no baby shower because we had no one to invite. Thanks, Alejandro. But the girls in Shelby's office had a sheet cake and a joint gift from all of them on a pretty June day before she went on maternity leave. They gave her a car seat. Privately? I thought it was a dull gift. But as a practical matter? She had to have one.

"It was a bona fide pity party," she said. "But I thought it was sweet anyway."

"When I brought you home from the hospital, I sat in the backseat and held you in my arms. You're probably lucky you're alive," I said.

"Today you'd be charged with child endangerment!" Shelby said.

"Whatever," I said.

Last week when Shelby was just beginning labor, or so she thought, her doorbell rang. Michael and Patty had come by to see Shelby and they rolled in a beautiful carriage that converted to a stroller. I happened to be there folding laundry, which, to my complete surprise, I kind of liked doing but I'd never admit it.

"Well, hi!" I said, opening the door. "What a wonderful surprise! We actually didn't buy a carriage yet! Come in!"

"This is so perfect! Thank you so much!" Shelby said, hugging them and then inspecting the attachments. "Mom, I might be in labor."

"Oh my!" Patty said.

"How far apart are your contractions?" I said.

"I had a few this morning. And one just now when I stood up. It's calm now."

"I think you've got a while yet," I said, thinking she probably was having Braxton-Hicks contractions. "Would you like a cup of coffee?"

"Oh, no," Patty said. "But thanks."

Shelby said, "Well, I really love the carriage slash stroller!"

"We can't stay long," Michael said. "Anyway, they told us this was the latest thing from Sweden."

"Denmark," Patty said. "Doesn't matter. The Scandinavian countries make the coolest baby products. But I saw a video of all these mothers in Sweden or Denmark walking their babies to a coffee shop, and they leave their babies outside while they go get their coffee."

"*What?*" Shelby said. "Don't they have kidnappers there?"

"Apparently not!" Patty said. "Isn't that completely insane?"

"Totally," I said. "Have you seen Alejandro?"

"No," Michael said, "but the judge is handing down his sentence next Tuesday. I'll be there for that."

"Maybe I'll join you," I said. "After all, we were married for thirty years." I wanted to see Alejandro get his.

"There will be a number of his former clients there. It could get ugly."

"He could not have decimated their lives any more than he did mine," I said.

"Yes. That's true. But they view themselves as victims, not you."

"Well, they're wrong," I said.

"Of course they're wrong. But in their minds, there was a period of time when you knowingly or unknowingly benefited from their loss."

"Thanks, Dad," Shelby said.

"So I'm guilty by association," I said. "That's so unfair. Am I going to see a settlement from the judge anytime soon?"

"You should. I think the judge wants to talk to you in chambers after she renders her decision. I'll call Ed this afternoon to confirm. He'll know if you're on the docket."

"Okay, thanks."

A week before Shelby went into labor, I went to Target with my son-in-law's credit card and filled a cart with all sorts of onesies, swaddles, and other things I—I mean, Shelby—would need for the baby, like diapers, wipes that came with a warmer, baby soap, shampoo, a baby bathtub, sheets, and super soft towels. Shelby picked out everything online, but her feet were too swollen to shop, she said. I didn't mind because I could improve her choices. There were so many things to buy, it boggled my mind. I found the chest of drawers with a changing table on top that she wanted. It was too big to carry.

Shelby also wanted a rocking chair and a bookcase. Maybe they delivered? But I could take home a diaper pail and a night-light and a hamper and a mobile that played "Rock-a-Bye Baby" as little pale pastel bears circled overhead.

I pushed my overfilled cart up to the customer service desk.

"Can I help you?"

"Do you deliver?"

"For thirty-five dollars you can have the whole store."

"Okay, thanks."

I'd never be able to fit any of the furniture in my old Jaguar, which I was considering selling. It would be nice to have the cash. I was waiting, though, to hear the judge's decision.

I was in the process of checking out and swiped the credit card down the side of the reader. I signed Frederick's name and rolled the cart out to my car. Barely squeezing everything in, I found myself smiling and humming a little song I used to sing to Shelby when she was a baby. So far I loved doing grandmotherly things. Target was going to deliver everything else within an hour.

In the days leading up to Floyd's birth, and again the day after he was born, I was back at Target. It seemed like Target was just going to be a part of my life for the foreseeable future. This trip I filled my cart with groceries and cleaning supplies. I paid the bill and loaded my car.

As I was backing out of my parking space, my cell phone rang, so I pulled back in to answer it. It was Diane.

"How's the baby?" she said.

"Delicious! I can't wait for you to meet him!"

"Well, I'm afraid that won't be for a while," she said. "We've got a disaster on our hands."

"What's wrong?"

"It's called a microburst . . ."

I was just flabbergasted as I listened.

When she was finished with the terrible story I said, "Oh, my God! How awful! You must've been terrified! What can I do to help?"

"I don't know. Probably not much. We're filing a claim with our insurance company and waiting to hear from the claims adjuster. It's a mess. I think the sooner we clean it all up, the better we're going to feel. And we don't have any electricity."

"Awful. Do the kids know yet?"

"No, they've got enough to deal with, just bringing a baby home and all that. I thought I'd trust you to tell them when the time is right."

"I will. Please give your mom and Floyd my best," I said. "Is Floyd excited to have a baby named for him?"

"Susan, I think it's the thing that's holding him together, if you want to know the truth. I've never seen him so upset. He's not a yeller or a screamer. He smolders. And it's very emotional for Mom too. She and Pop planted that grove together."

"I'm so sorry," I said.

I wanted to say, *Tell him the reason I suggested naming the baby Floyd was so that I could say* I love you, Floyd, *and no one would think a thing about it.* But for the time being, I was keeping that to myself.

We hung up and I thought about the loss of their beautiful peach grove all the way home. It was so sad. Later, I put dinner together while Shelby rocked Floyd to sleep.

"Mom, I still can't believe I'm rocking my very own child in the coolest rocker ever! Thank you so much for pulling a nursery together."

"I loved every minute of it."

Actually, I really had enjoyed it.

The coolest rocking chair ever was a midcentury-looking upholstered piece made by a Japanese company that was under three hundred dollars. In fact, the whole nursery bill for furniture and accoutrements was under a thousand dollars. I could recall dinners with Alejandro for a lot more than that, and in that moment, I saw how greedy he had been. But I had not complained about it, had I? I had sat there eating foie gras and drinking Cristal and never questioned Alejandro's endless quest to be King of the Hill. Lord, my conscience needs a lot of help, I thought, and then wondered if that had been an unconscious prayer, a plea? Or was it just an observation?

I was learning to cook from recipes I found online with videos. It wasn't impossible. Over dinner of chicken, salad, and boiled potatoes, mashed with butter and salt that I actually prepared, I explained to Shelby and Frederick what happened to the farm. Shelby was trying to breastfeed, and that had almost all of her focus.

"I think I need nipple guards," she said. "This is pretty uncomfortable."

"Can you wait until morning?" I said. "I'll make another Target run."

"Sure," she said, wincing in pain.

The good folks at Target would see me after dinner.

But I could almost hear the wheels turning in Frederick's head.

"This is a real problem," he said. "It's going to take a lot to fix it."

"Yes, it will," I said, agreeing. "And no electricity."

"It's not just a loss of resources, it's a huge loss of income. I mean, even if they planted new trees tomorrow, they won't bear fruit for three years. I need to call the girls. Guaranteed Uncle Floyd didn't tell anyone."

"He strikes me as stoic," I said.

"That's the understatement of the night," he said. "Thanks for dinner."

"Good grief, it is the least I could do," I said.

While I washed the dishes, which was another newish thing for me that I sort of enjoyed but would never admit, I heard Frederick talking to Sophie first, then Stephanie and Ann.

"I've got good news and bad news," he said to each of them, telling them about the arrival of the baby and then the ruination of the farm.

From what I could make of the side of the conversations I heard, they were all quite shocked and very upset for Floyd and Diane and their gram. But how in the world could they help?

It was to be the first of many conversations between Frederick and his cousins as they tried to hatch out a plan.

Our plight was decided for us. Frederick went back to

work the following Monday and discovered he had a new boss whose first order of business was to fire him. This fellow did not come out and say that it was because of Alejandro, but it was implied. Then, on Tuesday, the judge sentenced Alejandro to 130 years in jail. He was to be transferred to a medium-security federal prison in North Carolina. There was cheering in the courtroom, and my ex-husband was led away in handcuffs with his head lowered like the bum he was. It was very likely the last time I would ever see him. Then the judge agreed to see me in chambers, and I went there with Ed Rabin and Michael.

"I have agreed," she said, "to repay Mr. Dean from your husband's remaining assets. But there will be no more money for you. I'm sorry."

"What am I supposed to live on?" I said, shocked.

"Figure it out, Mrs. Cambria. Like everybody else in the world."

She stood and left through the door behind her desk.

"Wow," Ed said, "that was cold."

"I'll say," Michael said.

"It wasn't fair and it wasn't nice," I said and thought, Oh, God, what am I going to do?

When I came home from court I stopped by Shelby's to see little Floyd, and to my surprise, Frederick was sitting on the sofa with Shelby and the baby.

"How would you feel about a road trip? And maybe a reinvention of our lives?"

"I think I'd be so happy I wouldn't know what to do," I said. "The judge cut me out completely. I am officially dead broke."

"It's okay," Frederick said. "I got fired."

"And I quit," Shelby said.

"I say, let's load up a U-Haul and get out of Dodge," Frederick said.

We ordered a pizza with a side salad for dinner, but this time I'd be in another room when it was delivered to Frederick, just in case. It was so good, I wondered why I didn't have it more often.

"Shelby, would you like me to hold the baby so you can eat?"

"Yes, please. Maybe you could see if he needs a new diaper?"

"Sure," I said. "Come to Mimi."

"Mimi!" Shelby said. "I love it!"

"Anything but Granny, okay?"

I took the baby from her and held him close. I could feel his little heart beating. I took him into the bedroom and laid him down on his changing table to have a good look at him. He opened his eyes and looked at me. And I looked deeply into his. I knew him. Don't ask me how, but I knew this baby and he knew me. In that moment, we connected, and I knew nothing would ever make me change the overwhelming love I felt for him. This was real love, deep and sacred. I looked up to see Shelby at the door, taking a picture of us with her phone.

"He's so wonderful, isn't he?"

"He sure is," I said.

I never mentioned the fact that her father would never know little Floyd. There was no reason to let his horrible sins dilute this moment or any moment thereafter.

Later that night, I decided I would sell my engagement

ring to further sever any ties with Alejandro. The pink diamond center stone was six carats, with half-moons on either side, each of those weighing two carats. Alejandro always said the stones were flawless, just like me. Now I'd know for sure. I wondered if Nadia had one. Flawless or not, ten carats might bring enough money to keep me afloat for a long time. I wanted to go to New York to do it. I'd known a jeweler on Forty-seventh Street years ago, a diamond specialist. I had his number somewhere. I'd find it and call him in the morning. Shelby decided to sell the Renoir, probably for the same reasons.

"I don't need a Renoir," she said.

"That's entirely up to you," Frederick said. "That's your painting."

"Let's take it to Christie's," I said. "Years ago, I knew someone there in the Impressionist department."

"Let's do it. Should we call for an appointment?" Shelby said.

"I'll be happy to do that," I said, taking the reins.

Since our worlds had blown up, I had become closer to Shelby and Frederick. Whatever tension there had been between us before the wedding seemed to have disappeared. Or maybe, and this was just a maybe, I wasn't as manic. (I still thought the butterflies would have been a good idea.) I didn't know why and never would, but I felt completely welcome when I went through their door, just as they were when they came through mine. Somehow all this turmoil had an end result that took us to a saner and happier place. No doubt little Floyd was a large driving factor too.

Since our apartments were on a month-to-month lease, it was easy to leave. There wasn't a single reason we could think of to stay in Chicago, and there was every reason to go to South Carolina. I sold my Jaguar and Frederick rented a Ryder truck. I would ride with Shelby in their SUV and I'd buy some other kind of vehicle when we got there.

I called Floyd.

"Hey, it's me. Susan. How are you? I heard all about the storm."

"Yeah, it was terrible. We've got a mess."

"Y'all got power?"

"Not yet. All of Charleston's in the dark. The National Guard's everywhere. It's a good thing I stockpiled all the provisions I did because I've been selling all kinds of things — eggs, paper towels, Band-Aids and water to neighbors through the farm stand. Flashlight batteries are on special."

I laughed at that. "Really? Wow. That's wonderful."

"Grocery stores are closed. No lights. No refrigeration. We're selling everything we've got. I've got our refrigerators running on a generator with fuel I keep for the tractor."

"This is serious," I said.

"Sure is. The word is we're supposed to get power back soon. Even Lowe's is closed."

No doubt an occasion for him to wear black, I thought.

"Well, don't pay July's rent," I said.

"Why not?" he said.

"Because I just got an engraved invitation on a silver platter to come help you clean it up."

"Shelby, Fred, and little Floyd coming too?"

"Yep. The judge cut me off, Frederick got fired, and Shelby quit. They think I should come with them. What do you think?"

"That's sort of like the hand of God, that's what I think."

"Come on, gorgeous, don't torture me. Do you think I can stay somewhere on the farm?"

"What color trailer do you want me to rent?" he said. "When the lights come on, I'll get you one."

"Something with a little charm, if you can manage it," I said. "But it's only temporary."

"Has to be rented, because I'm fixin' to get plans together for that house on Shem Creek I've been talking about building since forever. Maybe you'd like to help me design it? I'm gonna have to start building soon."

"I'd like nothing better," I said. "Are you thinking about gardens too?"

"You mean flower gardens? Why not?"

"I've always wanted to grow flowers," I said.

"Is that a fact? Is your divorce from that sumbitch final?"

"It sure is."

"Good. Be sure to get gas in Columbia. Nobody's pumping here."

"Okay."

It was hard to hide my excitement from Shelby and Frederick, but I think they all knew how Floyd and I felt about each other. Neither one of us could help it. We knew in the moment we met that somehow we would wind up together. Maybe there was hope for my heart yet.

We arrived in New Jersey and checked into a Courtyard Marriott right outside of New York City. Shelby would stay at the hotel with little Floyd, who behaved like an angel the whole trip, sleeping and eating, sleeping and eating. Frederick and I would Uber into the city with the painting and my diamond.

"Good luck!" she said when we left her.

"I'll call you when we're done," I said.

"Call me if you need anything," Frederick said.

The painting was wrapped in bubble wrap and covered with brown paper. It was small, so it was easy to carry.

Our Uber driver got us through the tunnel and into the city in less than forty minutes and dropped us off at Christie's right on time.

"Uber is genius," Frederick said. "I wish I'd thought of it."

"We all wish we'd thought of it," I said.

If we had, I wouldn't be selling my diamond, I thought, and you wouldn't be selling your Renoir.

We went right to the information desk and asked them to call Claude Paquin to let him know we had arrived.

"Claude is an old friend. I'm surprised he's still here, but I'm glad he is."

A few minutes later, Claude appeared. "Susan! How wonderful to see you! You haven't changed a bit! Still as beautiful as ever!"

Air kiss to the right. Air kiss to the left.

"Claude! Darling! Say hello to my son-in-law, Frederick."

"It's nice to meet you, sir," Frederick said.

"Well, well. It's nice to meet you too," Claude said. "A son-in-law! Shelby grew up and got married. Where does the time go?"

"And I recently became a grandmother to a darling little boy," I said.

"My goodness. Let's get you into my office where we can have a bit of privacy," he said.

We followed him to the elevators that took us to the higher floors, where the executive offices were located. We followed him down the hall until we reached a door that said NINETEENTH-CENTURY EUROPEAN PAINTINGS, CLAUDE PAQUIN, HEAD OF DEPARTMENT.

Once inside, we passed his secretary and went into his inner office, where he closed the door.

"Do you care for coffee?" he said.

"No, thank you," I said.

"I'm fine, thanks," Frederick said.

"Well then, shall we see what you've brought us?"

I said, "Yes. Frederick, let's unwrap the painting."

Frederick unwrapped the small painting of a little girl and placed it on the easel. She was indoors, in perhaps a living room, dressed in a pretty dress with a large square white collar. Her long red hair cascaded down her back in ringlets, and her little dog, some kind of terrier, I'd always thought, sat at her feet. It was very charming and innocent.

"Oh, this is a honey!" Claude said.

"We've always loved it," I said. "I imagine you know about—"

"Yes, I was so sorry to hear it. How stressful this must have been for you."

"A nightmare. But it's in the past. We are divorced and I'm moving ahead with my life."

"Good," said Claude. "That's the only thing there is to do."

"Mr. Paquin?" Frederick said. "May I ask you for an approximate range?"

"Of course! Just recently a woman in West Virginia accidently bought a Renoir at a garage sale for seven dollars. She sold it at auction for a hundred thousand dollars. But his masterpiece *Bal du Moulin de la Galette* sold for seventy-eight million. So the range is a broad one." Claude turned a black light on the painting and took out his loupe, peering at the canvas from top to bottom. "This canvas is larger than the West Virginia discovery, it's in excellent condition, and the frame is in perfect shape—I'd venture a guess of one hundred fifty thousand to two. Maybe slightly more."

"I think we paid fifty for it," I said. "Should've bought more."

"Everyone says that," Claude said.

"Holy smoke," Frederick said.

"We have an auction in September of French Impressionism and Dutch Masters. This will fit very nicely in the sale. Do you want to leave it with me?"

"I think so. Frederick, what do you think?"

"I think definitely, as long as it's covered by—"

"Insurance?" Claude said. "Of course! Let's begin the arduous process of filling out a mountain of thoroughly detestable paperwork."

An hour later we were outside in Rockefeller Center.

"Let's stroll around a bit," I said, "we have time and it's just a few blocks to Corey's. It's such a nice day."

We passed one of my old haunts after another. Funny, I thought Cartier would pull at my heartstrings, but suddenly it felt like quicksand. The desire to constantly acquire beautiful things and the temptation to possess them at any cost, like the gorgeous jewelry Alejandro bought me, led him to a life of crime and unthinkable disgrace for the rest of us. No, I wanted to get as far away from that life as I could.

Before I knew it, we were in the lobby of 50 West Forty-Seventh Street, having our pictures taken, my handbag sent through a detector, and sent up to where to the offices of Corey Friedman Fine Jewels are.

"There are no buttons to press in this elevator," Frederick said.

"It's preprogrammed so we don't get lost. This isn't the kind of building that wants you to just wander around."

"Talk about security. Wow."

"Wow is right," I said. "This way."

We were buzzed in and Corey greeted me with open arms.

"Come in. Oh, you poor girl! What you must've been through. I'm so sorry."

"Thanks, Corey. Say hello to my son-in-law, Frederick."

They shook hands.

"Can I get you some coffee? Pellegrino? A sandwich? Did you eat?"

We walked into his office, which had a view of midtown

Manhattan that was heart-stopping. We sat in the two beautiful white leather chairs facing his desk.

"Wow," Frederick said, looking out over the city.

"Yeah, it's something, isn't it?" Corey said. "I pinch myself
every day."

"Corey? Actually, I'd love a pastrami on rye if someone will
share it with me. Where I'm headed, they've never heard of
real New York deli food."

"Elyse? Sweetheart?" he called out to his beautiful daughter. "Order us a hot pastrami on rye and a hot corned beef on
rye too. And extra pickles."

"Now I'm starving," Frederick said.

Corey said, "Don't worry. Two sandwiches will feed six
people."

"Well, let's show you my ring," I said. I reached into my
bag for the little satin sack that held my diamond and brought
it out. I opened it and put it on the black suede presentation
board in front of us.

He picked it up.

"This is a very special stone, you know," he said. "I'm just
going to steam it so I can get a better look."

"Sure," I said.

Corey stepped out of the office. Frederick was doing his
e-mails or texting or something.

"Guess what?" he said.

"What? Is Shelby okay?"

"Oh, this is from Stephanie. Granola Girl and her boyfriend, Sam the shepherd . . ."

"As in Sam Shepard? The playwright?"

"Oh! I never thought about that! Funny! Well, they quit their jobs and they're coming home. They want to keep sheep, spin yarn, and make sheep's milk cheese."

"You're kidding!"

"Not a bit. Here you can read this for yourself."

The text message read, *Why should I do what I'm doing to make somebody else rich when my own family needs me more?*

"I told her that Shelby and I reached the same conclusion."

"Frederick! This is wonderful news!"

"It sure is! You know, I'd been wondering how Uncle Floyd and Mom were going to continue. They're not exactly young, you know?"

"True," I said.

"Not long ago, I couldn't see myself living anyplace except Chicago. And now I can't see us anywhere else except home in the Lowcountry working together to restore what we had. This is much more important than working for some accounting firm that doesn't give a damn about you."

"It sure is, Frederick. You're a good man. I'm so proud of you."

"Thanks," he said. "Do you think you could call me Fred?"

"Never," I said.

Corey returned and sat behind his desk.

"I can't believe I'm going to do this, but I'm going to offer you four hundred and eighty thousand dollars for your ring."

"Make it five fifty on the nose and you've got a deal," I said.

"You're killing me," he said.

"Corey, look up Sotheby's London. They just sold one not as nice as mine for six."

"Your mother-in-law is unbelievable," he said, and we shook hands. "Elyse! Where's that lunch? Spending money gives me such an appetite." He reached into a drawer and pulled out his checkbook. "I'd send you the check, but then I'm taking a chance you'll walk. Best to close the deal."

I winked at Frederick and he laughed. I took Corey's check and put it in my wallet.

I didn't know it then, but by the time we crossed the South Carolina state line, Floyd's daughter Ann, his older daughter Sophie, and her partner had pulled up stakes and were headed to the Lowcountry too. We were rolling down I-95 South. I was in the backseat, cooing with little Floyd, falling more in love with him every minute. Every time he opened his eyes and looked at me, I nearly swooned.

We stopped every two hours for Shelby to nurse her beautiful infant son and give him a change. We'd pull into a parking lot, Frederick would get gas and snacks, we'd chat a bit, and then we'd be off again.

"Mom?" I looked up to see Shelby looking at me in her rearview mirror.

"You want me to drive now?" I said.

"No, no. I'm fine. I was just thinking you look so happy."

"Because I am! Tell me how life gets any better than this? There is a house filled with people who can't wait to see us." *Floyd.* "Those people love us in spite of everything." *Floyd.* "They want to help us. We want to help them. And best of all, we have little Floyd." *And big Floyd.* "I love this little boy so much, sometimes I feel like my heart will explode. I can see the future and I like it." I hoped Floyd was getting some rest.

"Me too, Mom. Me too."

At one point we left I-95 and got on Highway 17. As we passed through a place called Jacksonboro, we began to cross short bridges. These bridges took us over the curves of a river with water so blue it almost hurt my eyes to look at it. There were little docks with boats tied to the moorings and enormous white birds I would learn were ibises and egrets. I would never tire of this place. I wanted to be a part of it because life here was good and it had purpose. Poor Alejandro. He was so clever until his reach exceeded his grasp. I wonder whether if I'd known what he was doing, I could've stopped him. So many lives were in ruins. In this strange but wonderful turn of events, mine was not. I was being given a second chance. I knew that. I was going to prove myself worthy.

epilogue

The lights went back on and power was completely re-stored as soon as they arrived and Shelby lifted baby Floyd into our arms. Really. They literally did.

It was the spring of 2018. To our astonishment and absolute delight, the Renoir sold last fall for $240,000. Shelby and Fred used part of the money to buy computers for everyone and build a Web site, and then Sophie put our whole business online, including a page that offered pies, muffins, and jelly to ship.

www.MissVirnellsFarmStand.com

She also set up an 800 number, and we proudly accepted Visa and Mastercard. The younger generation had taken over, or so we let them think. At first we had a bit of a chaotic situation. Everybody was trying to do everybody else's job, no one seemingly taking responsibility for the quality of their performance. Floyd and I had a sidebar chat.

"We need an organizational chart," he said.

"Agreed. If they want to help one another, that's fine. But we don't need three people to keep the Web site going or all of them in the kitchen at once."

That's how my mother, Miss Virnell, came to be named the chairwoman emerita. Floyd and I became co-presidents.

Sophie and Ann were the co-vice presidents overseeing mar-
keting and sales, Stephanie was the vice president of development, setting up artisanal cheese production and asking
for goats. Shelby and Fred were the co-treasurers, although
Mom still signed the checks and would until she decided
she didn't feel like doing it anymore. Susan was in charge
of all flowers and herbs, from planting to design and decor,
which she financed herself. Sophie's partner, Karen, didn't
care about a title. She just wanted to work in the store. In
fact, none of them seemed to care about titles, but at least
they had accepted our division of labor. Mom and I were
thrilled to have the help. Sam was tending his growing flock
of sheep. And Alden asked Floyd if it was okay with him if
he asked me to marry him! He sure did. But you know Floyd.

He said, "You probably ought to ask her first, you know, to
see if there's any interest."

Alden said he was unsure of how to respond. Had Floyd
missed the fact that every time Alden and I had a date, I
came home when the sun came up? Yes, probably, since
when I came home I'd see Susan or Floyd sneaking back to
their trailers like teenagers. When was Floyd going to make
an honest woman out of her? Just yesterday I went down
to Susan's trailer to give her some tomatoes and she wasn't
there. So I knocked on Floyd's door and it was locked. Walking back, I heard people (them) moaning and the rhythmic
squeak of his box spring. It went on and on and on for so long
I thought, Oh dear Lord! Please don't kill her. In fact, every
time we turned around Susan and Floyd were MIA and his

door was locked. Please. Those two. But I must say I think their antics contributed to her becoming more agreeable.

My birthday was this past February, and Alden gave me a diamond the night of Valentine's Day. We went to Grill 225 to have a romantic dinner. We ordered chocolate nitro-tinis, martinis that came with a warning attached to them. He stood up. I thought he was going to the men's room, but then he dropped to one knee.

"Alden!"

I had no idea he had bought a ring, but he pulled it out of his shirt pocket.

"So will you be my forever valentine?" he asked.

"Of course I will!"

Everyone in the restaurant started clapping, and our waiter brought over two glasses of champagne on the house. Then Alden kissed me, and sugah? That man could kiss. He sent chills up and down my spine, just like that old song said.

Not that it mattered, but my new diamond was twice the size of the one I gave Fred to give Shelby.

"Very pretty," Mom said when I showed it to her the next day. "When's the big date?"

"There's no date for now," I said. "I'm happy as is."

"That's trampy. You're sending the wrong message to the young people."

"Oh, please!" I said, knowing the so-called young people couldn't care less.

With the money from the USDA insurance policy, we replanted four hundred clingstone and two hundred freestone peach trees, one hundred more than we'd lost. Two hundred of them would bear fruit this summer because of a new growing technique Susan, believe it or not, found on the Internet that involved building a greenhouse over them and aggressively pruning. Apparently, she had a thing for research.

We had a morning meeting every day at seven thirty, something instituted by Floyd, to be sure the day was organized and got off to a good productive start. The young people complained about the hour, except Shelby, who was always up early with little Floyd. I just called it breakfast, since I had the joy of cooking for eleven people every day, but they all did their part in the cleanup. Susan buttered toast, saying it was her specialty.

"Technically, this breakfast is a tax deduction," Fred said.

"Really? Do you think the business can renovate this kitchen too, since we meet here three times a day?" I said.

"There's nothing wrong with my kitchen," Mom said.

"Face it, Miss Virnell. It could belong to the Waltons," I said.

"Don't call me that," she said.

I gave a kiss on her cheek.

"I found another article about how they grow peaches in Japan," Susan said. "They put brown paper bags over each peach and they ripen on the branches into a solid peach-colored round fruit, no red splotches. Rounded bottoms. Like it's a perfect peach! They probably charge more for those. I mean, I would."

"Too labor intensive," Floyd said.

"I'm aware," Susan said. "But it might be interesting to try it on one tree, just for the fun of it."

"I love your curious mind," Floyd said.

"I love yours," she said.

"Good gravy," Mom said.

Susan smiled in such an angelic way that it was astonishing to me. She was still a bitch, make no mistake about it. But now she seemed to watch her mouth a little better.

We were back in business and stronger than ever.

Sophie had smartly maintained her connections with Starbucks, and they wanted us to bake peach muffins for their southeastern stores. That was 2,233 stores in ten states that wanted our muffins? Really?

I said, "Why don't we start with the hundred or so stores in South Carolina and see how it goes?"

Floyd said, "We don't have that kind of capacity to produce, wrap, and ship. Anybody do the math?"

"I did," Fred said. "You can't spend more than a dollar on ingredients or ship less than a dozen at a time if you want to make any money."

"I think we can manage with six ovens," I said, "if we can ship frozen. If we can, we need two standing freezers. At least."

"I think shipping frozen is fine," Sophie said.

"I'll go to Lowe's," Floyd said.

Lowe's was to Floyd what Bergdorf Goodman used to be to Susan.

"I'm just waiting to hear back from my old company," Ann said. She had flown back to New Jersey with Virnell's biscuits and a dozen jars of jam to see if she could sell the recipe to the condiment division. It would have its own label—Miss

Virnell's Heavenly Peach Jam. Or strawberry. Naming it after her was the only way she could get Virnell to disclose her much-guarded recipe. She said the folks at her old company found it to be a charming idea.

Susan's flower business was really coming together. She had planted hundreds of daffodil bulbs last fall and hundreds of tulips in the earliest weeks of spring, in beds Floyd dug for her. Zinnias were everywhere, dressing up the landscape with a profusion of color. Next, she would plant roses. She started putting together hanging boxes for windows and fences.

When Floyd saw what she was spending on window boxes, he said, "I can make those."

"I didn't want to bother you," she said.

Believe me, they loved nothing better than bothering each other. All they did was coo like doves, or so it seemed, except when she was giving him hell, which Momma and I loved. Nobody had ever called Floyd on his nonsense or Susan on hers until Susan migrated here.

"What do I do, Lady Di? She won't make a commitment to me," Floyd told me when no one else was around.

"Well, for heaven's sake, Floyd, she's been traumatized her whole life by one terrible thing after another. Starting with—"

"Her momma and daddy getting drunk every night and screaming and then him whaling on her and her momma? I'd have shot the sumbitch too."

"Build your house the exact way she wants it. She'll commit."

"Probably good advice. She's not going to live in that trailer forever, even though hers has bumpout sides, granite countertops, and a king-size bed."

"You're too generous."

So Floyd built the hanging boxes for windows and fences and she filled them and sold them as soon as she put them out front. But he also broke ground on the Shem Creek house, and once that happened, he and Susan became completely inseparable. Outside of the store, she arranged buckets and buckets of blooms and changed the blackboard to say, STOP THE CAR! YOU NEED FLOWERS! It seemed that everybody wanted flowers with vegetables or their pie or their muffins in the morning.

Susan and I, more like sisters than friends given the amount of bickering between us, were the happiest watching little Floyd. He was crawling everywhere faster than a speeding train. Now he had two little bottom teeth and wanted nothing more than to stand up and run. He was the best part of our lives, reducing all of us to sentimental mush.

Shelby and Fred said they'd like to carve out a little piece of land for themselves down near the creek too. Mom had no objection, and neither did anyone else, but everybody wanted the same thing for themselves. There were too many trailers for everyone's blood. Sophie and Karen wanted to build a house that would be on the small side. Stephanie and Sam wanted to build a tiny house, a concept that was beyond me. Ann was happy to take Fred's old room when Fred and Shelby moved out and maybe build something later. Or not.

"It might be nice to have a condo for all of us at the beach," she said the last time we talked about it.

I'd always dreamed about having one.

It was late afternoon and Susan and I were sitting on the porch, drinking sweet tea. The days were getting longer and warmer, but we still needed a sweater or something after four in the afternoon. We had just left the farm stand. Karen offered to close up for the day.

"Fred and Shelby are so happy," Susan said.

"Did you call him Fred?"

"Yes, honey, I did." Then she laughed. "What a year this has been. I've forgiven Alejandro, but I'm going to be angry with him forever. To think I loved him once! What a fool I was!"

She was looking out over the yard, remembering.

"Every woman worth her salt has been a fool at least once. Yes, ma'am, it's been some year," I said. "Terrible. But wonderful too."

"Yes, but you know what? The bad parts brought us to the good parts. I wouldn't change a thing. I've never been so happy in my whole life."

I reached over and patted the back of her hand. "Me too. And me either," I said.

"It's so improbable that I should be here, and yet there's nowhere else I'd rather be. What is it about this place?"

"That's funny. Look, I don't know if it's the smell of the earth or the night skies with all the stars or what, but I think it's a bit like making a cake. You wouldn't eat butter or flour or vanilla by themselves, but when you combine them with eggs and milk, they become something else. That something else is the magic of the Lowcountry, Susan. What did that crazy cocktail napkin say? Nobody ever retires and moves up north."

"You're right," she said. "Let's go start supper."

"I'll be with you in a few minutes," I said.

I needed a moment to reflect. Susan hadn't said *dinner;* she'd said *supper,* like we did. She didn't even say *you guys* anymore. She hadn't come around to *y'all* quite yet, but she would say *all of you.* Someone once said to me that you become like your environment, and I think that's true. Susan had changed dramatically in the short months she'd been with us. But I also knew you couldn't really fix a person's unhappiness until you healed the hole in their soul caused by some terrible incident. The microburst storm and her mother's and husband's crimes were a subject of conversation anytime we felt the need to vent. As was her abuse.

Yesterday she told me a little more. "My mother was a drunk and as crazy as could be. My grandmother was the one who saved me. When things got too violent at home, she'd take me to her house."

"Thank heavens you had her."

"I thank God every day. It's a new thing I'm doing. Thanking God, that is. So far it's a one-way conversation."

"That's good," I said. I had smiled at that.

Her violent childhood and Alejandro's crimes had left deep scars on her in the areas of religion and trust. And the Can You Top This Club was back in Chicago and out of her life. But at least she was no longer pretending to be something she wasn't.

The loss of Pop and the terrible storm left scar tissue on

the rest of us. We all knew that this life would not last forever. Pop's sudden death showed us we had better love when we feel it and while we can. The storm had reminded us how fragile the world could be. What we were doing was taking part in something larger than ourselves. Being a good and a whole family. Treating one another with love and respect and tending to the needs of our family as a whole.

I didn't know what waited for me in the years to come. How long would I have Alden? Would Fred and Shelby give us more children? Would the others? Would Miss Virnell leave us soon? There was a picture in my mind's eye of her reunited with Pop that I pushed away every time it came into view. But the truth of all these things would not be revealed until it was time for them to be revealed. That what farming taught you—everything in its own good time. But meanwhile, our tribe had been restored and there was room in our enormous hearts for everyone. I knew that we were going to take good care of one another, better than before with each passing day, and that was enough for me.

acknowledgments

A lot happened during the writing of *By Invitation Only*. Our daughter and son-in-law brought Theodore Anthony into the world. We are beside ourselves with pure unmitigated joy every single day. I have roughly a thousand pictures of him on my phone and we FaceTime every few hours. Yes, even though I took an oath I wouldn't be one of those babbling grannies pushing pictures of my remarkable grandchild on anyone who will listen, I have become exactly that person. Sorry. Not sorry. And we are completely thrilled that our son William married Maddie. What a wedding! What a gorgeous bride! And of course, what a handsome groom! It was these two weddings (Victoria's in 2015) and the birth of Ted that planted the seed for this novel, although there's not one detail in these pages that isn't fiction. Last year we were wondering how being a grandparent might change us. This year I know. Being a grandparent is the absolutely coolest thing that ever happened to us, right next to being a mother-in-law.

Now to the business at hand. Using a real person's name for a character has been a great way to raise money for worthy causes. And in *By Invitation Only*, many generous souls come to life in these pages as my characters. I have met some of these folks only ever so briefly, so I can assure you that I would be astonished if the behavior, language, proclivities, and personalities of the characters bear any resemblance to the actual people. From a lunch in 2016 for the Friends of the Shelter in Basking Ridge, New Jersey, I'd like to thank the following: Shelby Cambria, Fred Stiftel, Judy Cunio-Quigley, Alden Corrigan, Diane English, Kathy Christie, and Susan Kennedy. Every one of you plays an important role in this story, and I feel certain Dawn Kettling, who organizes this spectacular event, wouldn't mind me saying how important it is to support efforts to end domestic violence, how important your support is, and how grateful we all are to have it. So thank you.

Special thanks to Ashley Hargrove and Virnell Bruce for their support of Literacy for Life in Williamsburg, Virginia, a mighty worthy cause. Thirty-two million people in this country are considered illiterate. If you don't have the ability to read and write in English, it's extremely difficult to lead a successful life. I applaud the excellent efforts of Literacy for Life and Ashley and Virnell for their meaningful support.

Abby's Friends of Daniel's Island, South Carolina, which works to end juvenile diabetes, is grateful for the support of the Runey family and in particular, Michael Lawrence Runey III.

Thank you, Betsy Beyer, for your support of Van Vleck House and Gardens in Montclair, New Jersey, another fine nonprofit that's dear to my family.

Special thanks to Irene Hamburger of Blue Hill at Stone Barns for the inside skinny of Chef Dan Barber's ingenious egg yolk coloring. And special thanks to Sally Metzler, Ph.D., of the Union League Club of Chicago for verifying that it is a portrait of General Ulysses S. Grant which is installed there. And big thanks to Bill Lasche of Bill Lasche Ltd., Interior Design, for identifying the Chicago spots where the elite meet.

I hope Wendy Wellin, Robin Harris, Lynn Easton, Juliet Elizabeth, Ramsey Lewis, Chef Joho, Warren Edwards, Ed Rabin, Jackie Tyler, Claude Paquin and Corey and Elyse Friedman will be tickled to pieces to find themselves in this crazy story. I enjoyed thinking of y'all as I wrote your names over and over!

Special thanks to George Zur, my computer web master, for keeping the web site alive.

To Ann Del Mastro, Stephanie Dunn, and my cousin, Charles

Comar Blanchard, all the Franks love you for too many reasons to enumerate!

I'd like to thank my wonderful editor at William Morrow, Carrie Feron, for her marvelous friendship, her endless wisdom, and her fabulous sense of humor. Your ideas and excellent editorial input always make my work better. I couldn't do this without you. I am blowing you bazillions of smooches from my office window in Montclair.

And to Suzanne Gluck, Michelle Feehan, Andrea Blatt, Hillary Zaitz Michael, Matilda Forbes Watson, Tracy Fisher, and the whole amazing team of Jedis at WME, I am loving y'all to pieces and looking forward to many more years together!

To the entire William Morrow and Avon team: Brian Murray, Liate Stehlik, Lynn Grady, Kelly Rudolph, Julie Paulauski, Kathryn Gordon, Kate Hudkins, Katherine Turro, Carolyn Coons, Lisa Sharkey, Frank Albanese, Virginia Stanley, Andrea Rosen, Josh Marwell, Andy Le Count, Carla Parker, Donna Waikus, Michael Morris, Gabe Barillas, Mumtaz Mustafa, Elise Lyons, and last but most certainly not ever least, Brian Grogan: thank you one and all for the miracles you perform and for your amazing, generous support. You all still make me want to dance.

Special thanks to Marah Stets and Carey Jones for their help with recipes and cocktails.

To Debbie Zammit, okay, so how long have we known each other? No one needs to know! Our years together in this endeavor have now surpassed our years together on Seventh Avenue. What a spectacular friend you are! We finish each other's sentences, reading each other's minds—what's left of them anyway. As the years try to snatch our mental acuity and recall, we need to stick together. Thank you over and over for well, everything.

To booksellers across the land, and I mean every single one of you, I thank you from the bottom of my heart, especially Aaron

Howard and Melinda Marquez of Barnes & Noble and Vicky Crafton of Litchfield Books. To my family, Peter, William and Victoria, I love y'all with all I've got. Victoria, you are the most beautiful, wonderful daughter and I am so proud of you and I'm just crazy about our Carmine, which he knows. I love everything about y'all. William? You are so smart and so funny, but then a good sense of humor might have been essential to your survival in this house. And proof of your intelligence is to be found in the simple fact that you brought Maddie into the fold. We are so very excited. I'm so proud of all of you. Every woman should have my good fortune with their husband and children. Peter Frank? You are still the man of my dreams, honey. Thirty-five years and they never had a fight.

It's a little incredible to realize it's only thirty-five years, especially when it feels like I've loved you forever.

Finally, to my readers to whom I owe the greatest debt of all, I am sending you the most sincere and profound thanks for reading my stories, for sending along so many nice emails, for yakking it up with me on Facebook and for coming out to book signings. You are why I try to write a book each year. I hope *By Invitation Only* will entertain you and give you something new to think about. There's a lot of magic down here in the Lowcountry. Please come see us and get some for yourself! I love you all and thank you once again.